Praise for the Davis Way Crime Caper Series

DOUBLE WHAMMY (#1)

"Funny & wonderful & human. It gets the Stephanie Plum seal of approval!"

– Janet Evanovich

"If Scout Finch and Carl Hiaasen had a baby, it would be Davis (Way.) *Double Whammy* is filled with humor and fresh, endearing characters. It's that rarest of books: a beautifully written page-turner. It's a winner!"

– Michael Lee West,
Author of *Gone With a Handsomer Man*

"Archer navigates a satisfyingly complex plot and injects plenty of humor as she goes. This madcap debut is a winning hand for fans of Janet Evanovich and Deborah Coonts."

– *Library Journal*

"Fast-paced, snarky action set in a compelling, southern glitz-and-glamour locale. A loveable, hapless heroine Jane Jameson would be proud to know. Utterly un-put-down-able."

– Molly Harper,
Author of the Award-Winning Nice Girls Series

DOUBLE DIP (#2)

"A smart, snappy writer who hits your funny bone!"

– Janet Evanovich

"Archer's bright and silly humor makes this a pleasure to read. Fans of Janet Evanovich's Stephanie Plum will absolutely adore Davis Way and her many mishaps."

– *RT Book Reviews*

"Snappy, wise cracking, and fast-paced."

– Mary Marks,
New York Journal of Books

"Slot tournament season at the Bellissimo Resort and Casino in Biloxi, Miss., provides the backdrop for Archer's enjoyable sequel to *Double Whammy*...Credible characters and plenty of Gulf Coast local color help make this a winner."

– *Publishers Weekly*

"Hilarious, action-packed, with a touch of home-sweet-home and a ton of glitz and glam. I'm booking my next vacation at the Bellissimo!"

– Susan M. Boyer,
USA Today Bestselling Author of the Liz Talbot Mystery Series

"A roller-coaster of a read. Gretchen Archer has given us enough red herrings to fill the buffet table at the Bellissimo Resort and Casino. The protagonist is smart and sassy with a wise- cracking sense of humor...if you like betting on a winning mystery, then you should be reading *Double Dip*!"

– Cheryl Green,
MyShelf Reviews

"Take a gamble and read *Double Dip*! Five stars out of five."

– Lynn Farris,
National Mystery Review Examiner at Examiner.com

"Davis and her associates, in particular Fantasy and No Hair, are back in this sophomore drama by Ms. Archer that does not disappoint in delivering delightfully charming and amusing adventures from the halls of the Bellissimo."

– Dru Ann Love,
Dru's Book Musings

DOUBLE WHAMMY

The Davis Way Crime Caper Series
by Gretchen Archer

DOUBLE WHAMMY (#1)

DOUBLE DIP (#2)

DOUBLE STRIKE (#3)

DOUBLE MINT (#4)

A DAVIS WAY CRIME CAPER

Gretchen Archer

HENERY PRESS

DOUBLE WHAMMY
A Davis Way Crime Caper
Part of the Henery Press Mystery Collection

First Edition
Trade paperback edition | May 2013

Henery Press
www.henerypress.com

Cover art by Fayette Terlouw
Author photograph by Garrett Nudd

This is a work of fiction. Any references to historical events, real people, or real locales are used fictitiously. Other names, characters, places, and incidents are the product of the author's imagination, and any resemblance to actual events or locales or persons, living or dead, is entirely coincidental.

ISBN-13: 978-1-938383-36-6

Printed in the United States of America

For my husband, who's running this show.

ACKNOWLEDGMENTS

Thank you Deke Castleman, Stephany Evans, and Kendel Lynn.

ONE

A little unemployment goes a long, long way, and after more than a year of it, applying for every available position in L.A. (Lower Alabama), I took a right and tried Mississippi. At the end of the road I found Biloxi, where instead of applying for fifty different jobs, I applied for the *same* job, fifty different times.

My final interview, like the dozen before it, began with a polished executive-type, Natalie Middleton. From there, the others had gone in several directions. There'd been a marksmanship test with long-range pop-ups (I aced it), an ink-blob and dot-to-dot psychiatric profiles (not sure about those), and an extensive photo shoot with costume changes and wigs. No telling what this one would bring.

"You'll be meeting with Richard Sanders," Natalie said, "our president and CEO. The final decision is his, and it will go quickly."

I applied for this job six weeks ago. It is two hundred miles from where I live. Most of the interviews have been all-day ordeals. This had already not gone quickly.

Richard Sanders' office had museum qualities: everything was quiet, valuable, and illuminated. Natalie directed me to a leather chair I was afraid to sit in. "He'll be right in."

Right in, for the record, was almost an hour later.

I'd just helped myself to a fifth red-hot cinnamon candy from a crystal bowl on Mr. Sanders' desk when a hidden door on the right side of the room slid open and a man stepped through, then froze, staring at me as if I was sitting there naked. Eating his candy. Little red squares of cellophane floated through the air as I jumped out of my skin.

Finally, he crossed the room with a guarded smile, hand outstretched.

"Richard Sanders."

I skipped around the candy. "Davith Wathe."

He took his place behind the desk and reached for the folder in front of him. I could see the right angles of a stack of photographs. Of me. The dress-up interview.

I sat up straighter, looking for somewhere to lose the candy. I gave him the once-over while he pored over the photographs, discreetly working the candy at top speed, the roof of my mouth on fire.

The quickest way to describe Richard Sanders was rockstar-turned-executive: early forties, six-two, close to two hundred, strikingly fit, blond, and either perpetually tan or just back from the Bahamas, since it was the dead of winter and he had a late-July glow about him.

He looked up. Baby blues. "Davis?"

The cinnamon disk burned going down. "Family name."

"Davis Way," he tried it on. "And you're from Pine--?"

"Apple." The hot candy brick was stuck sideways in my throat.

"Two words?"

"Ach." I discreetly pounded my chest Tarzan-style. "Garkle."

"Are you okay?" he asked.

I was anything but.

He pushed a button on his phone. Two seconds later Natalie snuck up from behind, gently patted me on the back, then landed one between my shoulder blades that almost knocked me into next week. She poured me a glass of water.

I chugged it, putting out the fire.

Richard Sanders slid the candy dish out of my reach.

As soon as it appeared I would live, Natalie said, "Well then," smiled, and disappeared, leaving us alone again.

"Why don't we start over, Davis?"

"That'd be great."

"Just where is Pine Apple, Alabama?"

"South of Montgomery."

Other than the red hots, the real-live Monet on the wall, and the million-dollar Oriental rug under my feet, I was in very familiar job-interview territory. I had applied for everything with a heartbeat, and the resulting interviews had all had common elements. First, my name threw people off. In my thirty-two years it had been pointed out to me thirty-two thousand times that Davis Way sounds more like a place than a hundred ten-pound female. After that, potential employers like to suggest that I've written down my hometown incorrectly. My resume clearly states my credentials, including two college degrees: one of in Criminal Justice and the other in Computer and Information Science. As such, would I really forget where I live?

Next, trust me, he will bring up my size, because I'm considered underheight in general, but especially so for the line of work I'm in. (I'm five-foot-two.) (And a half.)

He threw me for a loop when he asked, "How large is the police force in Pine Apple, Davis?"

"There are two of us." There *were* two of us. Surely he'd read that far.

"Is there a lot of crime in Pine Apple, Alabama?" He leaned his chair back, elbows to armrests, his hands meeting mid-chest. He rolled a thin platinum wedding band round and round his left ring finger.

"The usual," I said. "Domestic, vehicular, theft. We double as fire, too."

"So you've had EMT training?"

"Yes."

"And you write computer programming?"

"I'm not sure I'd go *that* far," I said. "Pine Apple's a small country town, Mr. Sanders, not exactly a hotbed of criminal activity. I had a lot of time on my hands, so I tinkered with the computer."

"It says here you rewrote the program for incident reporting statewide."

I hadn't put that on my resume. What else did it say there? "Not so much, Mr. Sanders. I only eliminated the inefficiencies of the old program, and it went viral."

"Why do you want to leave Pine Apple, Davis?"

Oh, boy.

"You know what?" He looked at his watch. "Let's save that for later."

Yes. Let's.

He started up with the wedding band again. "I'm going to say something that could be construed as politically incorrect." He made direct eye contact. "With your permission, of course."

"Sure."

"I have a thirteen-year-old son," he tapped his chin with two fingers, "who has at least five inches on you and probably fifty or sixty pounds."

"Is he my competition?"

Richard Sanders unexpectedly laughed. "Not hardly. Maybe if we were looking for someone to play Xbox."

"For all I know, Mr. Sanders, you *are* looking for someone to play Xbox." I surrendered. "I've been interviewing for six weeks, and I still don't know exactly what this job is."

"I don't either," he said.

Could we get someone in here who does?

After losing my old job I'd made it my new job to get out of bed by ten and drink hot chocolate until early afternoon in my new office, a corner booth at the coffee shop on Banana Street, directly across the street from the police station. Just in case. I'd been doing that for a year when one morning, a few days before Thanksgiving, I sat down to see a section of the weekly Pine Apple Gazette in front of me, folded into a perfect quarter, a one-line ad circled. Like a personal invitation. I drove to Biloxi, Mississippi the next morning, and began the long application process for the unspecified security position at the Bellissimo Resort and Casino.

Six weeks, sixteen interviews, and I had yet to be asked the first question that came close to anything secure.

The last two interviews had been with two mammoth men: a shiny bald one who looked like Mr. Clean, and another one with the largest, brightest teeth I'd ever seen in my life. Natalie Middleton introduced them to me as if I hadn't already seen them following me around; I'd spotted one, the other, or both giants every time I'd been here. They'd jumped on elevators with me, the bald one had been at the shooting range, and the one with the teeth had actually followed me home once. I played along. Nice to meet you, large total strangers.

Those interviews had started out pleasantly enough, if being alone in a witness-interrogation room for hours on end with men the size of economy cars is one's idea of pleasant, but as the clock ticked, the mood worsened. (Mine.) I got the distinct feeling that neither of these guys wanted me to have this job. They tried to trip me up at every turn.

The one with the teeth wore exceptionally nice man clothes. Always tip-to-toe monochromatic: all black, all gray, all navy. The one with no hair wore strange ties. So far I'd seen Tabasco hot sauce, Forrest Gump, and the Tasmanian Devil tied around his neck. Neither big man was unattractive, but menacing, because there was just so much of them.

The two giants had drilled me on subjects far from security. My waitressing skills, or rather my lack thereof, had been heavily discussed. How did I feel about gambling? (I felt like you shouldn't do it with other people's money.) Would I care to explain that? (No, thank you.) How did I feel about hundreds of pounds of dirty linens? (Opposed.) How about scrubbing shower stalls? (Again, opposed.) Did I know or had I ever known or had I ever seen photographs of someone named Bianca? (No. Isn't that a breath mint?) How many times had I been married? (None of your business.) Could I type? (How many fingers are we talking about?) Had I always been a redhead? (I'm not one of those pale, freckled, flaming-carroty redheads with pastel eyes and no eyelashes. I tan easily, my hair is a coppery-caramel color, and my eyes are the same color, but darker.) Had I ever been convicted of or committed a felony? (Which one? Convicted or committed?) Either. Both. (There's a big difference.) Let's hear it. (I would like to use a Lifeline.) Did I have culinary skills? (Could I cook Pop Tarts? Yes. Do I know what to do with a dead chicken? No.) Had I ever held a customer-service position? (Not specifically. More no than yes. Okay, no.) The hairless one asked me if I could operate an industrial vacuum cleaner. I didn't know such an animal existed.

Now here I was at my final interview, with the top of the food chain, and any second now, I expected him to ask how much experience I had hula dancing or performing tree surgery, because he didn't know what he was interviewing me for any more than I knew what I was applying for.

"It's a new position, Davis, and a highly classified one. If I knew exactly what you'd be doing on a day-to-day basis," Mr. Sanders said, "I'd tell you."

Finally, some bottom line.

"You'll be working undercover throughout the casino and hotel, and if you want to know more than that," he said, "you'll have to agree to the terms."

"Are you offering me the job, Mr. Sanders?"

"Do you *want* the job, Davis?"

I'm not so sure I *wanted* it. I'm very sure I *needed* it. "The terms," I said, "what are they?"

"In a word? Discretion." He steepled his fingers, then used them as a pointer. "Your job is to be discreet."

"And?"

"Use discretion," he said.

Use discretion while I'm being discreet. Got it.

"Don't talk to anyone on or off this property about your job," he said. "And don't reveal your identity under any circumstances."

"When do I start?"

"How soon can you start?"

"I'm good to go, Mr. Sanders. You say when."

"Today's as good a time as any." His hand went for the phone. "You can start right now."

My eyebrows shot up. I didn't mean this minute. I was thinking Monday. Or the Monday after that.

"Do you need time to think about it?" His hand hovered over the phone. "Because the iron is hot now."

Wait a minute. No one had said a word about *ironing*.

"Davis? Do you need a little time?"

Yes. "No."

"Good," he smiled. "Welcome to the Bellissimo."

And with that, I was well on my way to prison.

TWO

Natalie Middleton's office was adjacent to, and just as nice as, Mr. Sanders'. She had the Junior Suite. His smelled like cinnamon; hers smelled like roses.

Natalie was within a year, one way or the other, of my age. She was, as the first line of defense to the president of a place like this would be, Cover Girl pretty, and always impeccably dressed. Today she was wearing a dark suit, a creamy silk shirt peeked out from under the jacket, and a pair of spike-heeled black pumps at the end of her long bare legs. She wore very little makeup, and much of her medium-long medium-brown hair escaped a silver clasp at the nape of her neck. Designer eyeglasses completed her Sexy Librarian look.

"First, Davis, I want you to know that your new job was my idea."

So she would know how the industrial vacuum cleaner came into play.

"Therefore it's of utmost importance to me that you're successful."

She leaned heavily on the words "utmost," "me," and "successful."

"Whatever you need, come to me first. When you have information, bring it here. If you have questions," she said, "fire away. Night or day, day or night."

"Start at the beginning," I said, although I should've been more specific. I meant the beginning of my new job requirements and she started with the very first flash of light that shone on the dark mass of what would be Mother Earth.

She gave me the corporate orientation speech: state gaming laws, barge permits, net revenues, three movies filmed here, Hurricane Katrina, Cher. She told me about herself: single, graduate degree in marketing, Mr. Sanders' personal assistant for seven years. She told me who I could speak to: Mr. Sanders, herself, Jeremy Coven (the bald one) and Paul Bergman (the one with the big teeth). Then she talked about the resident royals: Mr. Sanders (very complimentary), Mrs. Sanders (not so much), their son Thomas (typical teenager), and in all of that, the word *vacuum* didn't come up.

"She's a Casimiro."

"Who is?" I asked.

"Mr. Sander's wife."

"What's a Casimiro?"

She paused. "Really? You don't know?"

I shrugged.

"Her family owns half the Las Vegas Strip."

"Whoa."

"Right. Avoid her at all costs," Natalie advised. "It won't be hard. When Mrs. Sanders is here, you won't be."

"Why is that?"

Natalie leaned back in her seat, pulled off her designer frames and dropped them in the middle of her desk. "She's hardly ever here, Davis," she dodged the question. "It won't be that big a deal."

Either I wasn't asking the right questions, or she was deliberately passing out wrong answers. I wanted some go here, go there. Shoot this, shoot that. "Natalie?" I asked. "What is my job other than avoiding Mrs. Sanders?"

"You're our new super-secret weapon." She stood. "Come with me."

I hopped up.

"Leave your things," she said, "we're not going far."

I dropped my purse in the chair, then followed her across the room at a clip. Natalie, if the fancy machine on her credenza and the empty cups and saucers on every corner of her desk were any indication, consumed large amounts of high-test coffee; the girl was jacked up on caffeine. We were headed straight for a wall when she stopped so fast I all but ran into her.

"Get dressed." She pushed and a seamlessly hidden door swung in. "Then we'll talk more."

The door closed quietly behind me of its own accord, and I was alone in a lounge of sorts, but a lounge as large as my bedroom at Pine Apple Luxury Living Condos. How convenient. It was library quiet and smelled like a rose garden. The room was barely lit and there were no windows, so it took a second for my eyes to adjust. When they did, I was met by more of the red/gold décor that was the theme throughout the Bellissimo. A plush red sofa was against the wall to my left, with a mammoth gilded mirror above it. Two gold wingback chairs were separated by an oblong side table on ornate pedestal legs opposite the sofa, with a wide aisle of thick gold carpet between. A stained-glass Tiffany lamp on the table emitted a dome-shaped glow, the only direct light in the room. This is exactly where you'd want to be if you were having a migraine. Or an affair.

A wide arched doorway between the two seating areas led to a traditional ladies powder-your-nose room where I found a change of clothes, a wig, contact lenses, and really cute boots.

Fifteen minutes later, fourteen of them poking myself in the eye, I stared at a stranger in the mirror. The stranger had thick, dark, shoulder-length hair and Martian green eyes. The jeans were pencil, designer, and a perfect fit. They were paired with a Christian Dior vanilla-colored cashmere pullover that floated. I could only have been identified by the tomato-red Tory Burch peep-toes I had on, which were mine. (Technically, they were my sister's. I'd accidentally borrowed them.)

"I guessed you at a six," Natalie said when I'd worked up enough nerve to leave the red and gold retreat, a boot in each hand.

"Six and a half," I apologized.

"Now we know."

"I can try to get into them," I offered, because they were gorgeous and I could take a little pain in exchange for the mid-calf chocolate-brown leather.

"I'm a six." She gave me a wink. "I'll find something to do with them. Take a seat," she waved, "and relax a little."

I hadn't moved my head; I'd never worn anyone else's hair on it. I had plenty of my own and it was pressing against my scalp like socks stuffed into a hat that was already too small.

"You look great."

I looked like someone else, which was, I suppose, the point.

She passed me a fat stack of paper, as thick as the Montgomery Yellow Pages. "Sign here, here, and here."

I signed there, there, and there.

She whisked the phone book away and replaced it with a gorgeous brown-leather Marc Jacobs messenger. "Your room keys are in here, a little cash to get you going, a new cell phone, and ID."

I had no idea what I'd just signed, but the wardrobe and accessories for my new job were great.

"You're already checked into your room and everything you'll need for the next few days is there."

And still, I sat on the edge of the chair.

"Right." Natalie clapped her hands together. "As our in-house investigator, Davis, your first assignment is to play video poker."

In-house what? I thought this was a security job. And how might one go about investigating video games? Or for that matter, securing them?

"Double Whammy Deuces Wild. Progressives." She stood and walked around her desk. "Double Whammy Deuces Wild," she said again. "Got that? Go right through the middle of the casino, then take a left. You can't miss them." She waited to speak again until she was sure she had my undivided attention. "Play it, learn it, come back and tell me how it's won."

Is that all?

"Good luck, Davis."

I swallowed hard.

"I hope you win!"

THREE

Bellissimo guest room 20027 was, like the rest of this place, Five Star. It was a showroom of luxuries and amenities, including a full ocean view, Jumbotron flat screen, and great big bed with at least a foot of air between it and the thick gold carpet. The linens on the bed were stark white, with gold pillow accents everywhere and a giant red duvet folded across the foot. Five Star and Fancy.

Natalie Middleton, I could see, had gone to a lot of trouble on my behalf. The armoire contained at least five days' worth of clothes, all my size, ranging in style from a pair of J Brand jeans to a bright blue-silk cocktail dress with a swooping jeweled neckline that I was tempted to put on right then. In the drawers I found Ralph Lauren silk pajamas, an extra-large Bellissimo T-shirt, two Calvin Klein bras, a demi and a push-up, both 32C, perfect, a rainbow of Hanky Pankys, and three additional cashmere sweaters. It would seem that Bellissimo In-House Investigators dressed to kill, and that might be the saving grace of this "security" job. Well, the expensive clothes and the gorgeous hotel room. Well, the expensive clothes, the gorgeous hotel room, and the paycheck. But in-house investigator? Police officer-to-investigator is the same as executive chef-to-fry cook.

All this time, I'd been applying for a security position, not an investigator position. You can't spend ten minutes in law enforcement, even in a place as small as Pine Apple, much less the years I had in blues, without hating the words *private investigator*. An in-house is nothing but a private who stays put. Their cousins are mall cops and third-shift parking lot attendants. Investigative services are a thing of the past, back when you couldn't find people in two seconds flat through social networking. Facebook and Twitter are good for two things: hooking up with people you never got to sleep with in college, and skip tracing. It takes one Follow and two Tweets to locate a skip. Ditto insurance fraud with current electronics: Hack into the boyfriend's cell phone and browse the photo album. He's taken fourteen pictures of Miss Bad Back snowboarding. Busted.

These days, PIs do absolutely nothing but take photos of cheating spouses. Adulterers are generally smart enough to keep it off the World Wide Web, and it still takes hard evidence to get your fair share in divorce court, especially when the stakes are high. (I know all this first-hand.) I seriously doubted the Bellissimo hiring me had anything to do with cheating spouses; they didn't take me on so I could run around the casino taking Polaroids of adulterous clients, when they had better surveillance than NASA.

I dumped out the contents of the Marc Jacobs bag onto the king-sized bed. I found a cell phone and a wallet with Mr. Jacobs' name all over it. It would seem that I was now Marci Dunlow from San Antonio, Texas—my Photoshopped likeness on the driver's license was a dead ringer for my new look—and Marci had a thousand dollars in cash so fresh off the press I had trouble separating the bills to count them. Marci was tempted to shimmy into the blue dress, take her thousand dollars, and head for the hills.

I opened my own purse, a beat-up Louis Vuitton knockoff, and dug for the noisy bulky mass that hid the key to my black Volkswagen Beetle. First things first, I checked the room with my handy-dandy radio-frequency detector. As Seen On TV. I found two signals: one emitting from the smoke alarm in the dead center of the ceiling (clever – who'd look there?) and one from Marci's cell phone on the bed.

What did they think they were going to hear in my hotel room?

Thankfully, there were no cameras—I'd have hit the road—and there were no bugs in the bathroom, which is always a good thing. It was spacious, decorated like the bedroom in a sort of antique French Riviera, with a recessed makeup table that would serve me well as a desk, so I deemed it headquarters. I sat on the wide edge of the bathtub with the two cell phones, my own and Marci's. Marci had a nice phone: a 4G, with Wi-Fi, Bluetooth, GPS (immediately disabled), a quad-core processor, a 20MP camera, and a high-resolution backlit TFT display. I popped off the side panel, no larger than a splinter, and found 64GB of memory and a 2GB SD card. I popped off the back of my own phone, and sure enough, found a new memory chip that Natalie had slipped in. ("Leave your things. I need to plant a bug.")

Time to go shopping.

And for the record, I didn't particularly trust them either.

* * *

No doubt someone was busy installing a tracking device in my car that I'd parked in the seven-level garage adjacent to the main building. I didn't want to interrupt, so I decided to grab a cab.

The glitzy street entrance of the Bellissimo was packed with people—working, coming, going—and even more cars. The lane closest to the six double doors was specified for drop-off traffic, the next two for valet parking, an unspecified lane in the middle, a lane lined with black limousines, and a lane of taxis. I could easily have gotten a ride there. But another more discreet entrance on the east side of the main building had caught my eye. Several times I'd seen the same dirty white taxi tucked a half a block away from the doors, almost hidden behind thick landscaping, and I took off in that direction, heading east through the lobby. I thought I'd reached a dead end when I noticed gold lettering on dark-glass double doors to my right: VIP.

I took a deep breath and pushed through. This would be where the rich people checked in and out. Several heads turned my way. I gave them a nervous smile, crossed the quiet room, and stepped outside, where I was met by a blast of winter. January only looks like June on the Mississippi coastline. The difference is the icy, wet wind whipping off the Gulf, and this entrance to the Bellissimo was two feet from it.

Three limo drivers perked up. Spotting the taxi I was looking for, I waved them off.

I woke the driver, a black man who was probably in his sixties, with a knuckle on the window. He seemed none too happy to see me.

"Unavailable," an old man said without looking at me. "Off duty."

"Really?" I wasn't climbing the hill to the other thirty-five cabs. I'd turn into a block of ice before I could get there. I dug out one of the hundred-dollar bills and slapped it against the glass. That got me a huge sound of disgust from the old man, then the door locks clicked open. I hopped in the back.

"Could you turn on the heat, please?" It was ten degrees colder inside the cab than out. He pushed a button on the dash, then the cab filled with burning dirt.

"Do you want to go somewhere or not?"

I batted at the cloud of singed dust with both hands. Maybe not.

He drove me to a super sell-all store several miles down a busy road. Every time I looked up, I caught the old guy staring at me in the rear-view mirror instead of watching the road. I unearthed the seat belt and buckled up. I don't think anyone had been in this cab in the past decade, and I certainly didn't intend to get in it again if I managed to get out of it this time with life and limb. The only thing in the car that wasn't retro, including the driver, was a custom-installed satellite radio/scanner, lighting up the dash like New Year's Eve.

I knew we'd arrived because he slammed to a stop so fast I added neck brace to my shopping list.

"I need you to wait on me."

"Then you'd better hurry," he said.

I purchased a pre-pumped cell phone, had someone at the customer-service desk break into it with a chainsaw and power it up, then made my way to the deserted automotive department, where I dialed my parents' phone number as slowly as humanly possible.

My mother could answer a telephone in the most hostile manner imaginable. She'd say "hello" but it came out "WHAT?"

I steeled myself. And there it was.

"Mother, it's me."

A giant pause. "Well, Davis, so good of you to call. Make it quick; I'm in no mood to talk. In fact, talk to your sister."

See?

"Hey, Sweetie," my sister Meredith (note the non-talking-point name) said, and thankfully her voice wasn't dripping hostility like Mother's. But then she ruined it with her next cheery line. "We miss you!"

Meredith—my rock, my shield, my salvation from Mother, and my only sibling—had her own sugary way of sticking it to me. Her "we miss you" was Mer-Code for where the hell are you, Davis? And where have you been? And when will you be back?

"Davis?" Meredith asked. "What's going on?"

I fingered the packages of windshield-wiper blades that hung on hooks in front of me, getting them all swinging and bouncing off one another.

"I've taken a job in Biloxi."

I heard the back door squeak on Mer's end. "Davis! You have not!"

"I have."

"Why *there*?" Meredith demanded.

"You're the one who told me to get out of town."

"That's *not* what I said. And even if, there are a million towns, Davis. Why that one? How can anything good come of following him down there? You *know* if it was *anyone* but Daddy, you'd have restraining orders on you that would put you on a different *planet* from Eddie. You can't go sit in his lap! You'll be in jail by the end of the week!"

Yes, Eddie. My rat ex-ex-husband, Eddie Crawford, formerly of Pine Apple, has been scratching his raging gambling itch in Biloxi for years. And, yes, I married him twice. And yes, it'll be a nightmare if Eddie and I cross paths, because I had a $150,000 bone to pick with him, and he wanted me locked up in a loony bin.

I'd taken the second divorce pretty hard, if burning down his double-wide bachelor pad (he started it, I just didn't put it out), taking cheap shots at him with my service revolver (grazing his girlfriend Danielle's fat ass once), and giving him salmonella poisoning constituted taking it hard. And that was just in the months leading up to the divorce. As a result of the misbehaving, I lost my job, then got nailed in divorce court, which irritated me even more, often at three in the morning when it was just me and my laptop. Eddie found himself badly burned by identity theft, had a credit report that would prevent him from borrowing a wooden nickel for the rest of his miserable life, and one night I was so mad, I plastered him all over the National Sex Offender List. Eddie had the nerve to take me back to court, where Pine Apple's one and only judge—a friend of our families—said that what I'd done to him was no worse than what he'd done to me, and he told us to stay far, far away from each other. For as long as we both shall live. Taking a job in the city where I knew he was holed up wasn't exactly staying far, far away. I was well aware, but it didn't keep me from trying to talk my sister into it.

"This isn't Pine Apple, Mer. Fifty thousand people live here and another blue gazillion pop in and out of the casinos every day. It's not like I'm going to run into him on the street corner. Besides," I scratched the itchy wig, "even if I do, he won't know it's me."

"He'd know you a mile into a dark cave, Davis, because you'd be the one shooting at him."

"You know Daddy took my gun, Meredith. I'm not going to shoot anyone."

I could see my sister on the back porch, shivering in the January chill, a mirror of my mother thirty years ago, looking out over the seven acres that made up the family homestead.

"I've taken the job, Mer. And I'm not getting anywhere near Eddie because I don't want to lose it before I even get paid. You're the very one who insists I need to get my fresh start on."

"You're not going to get your fresh start on in the same city Eddie's in, Davis, and you know it. Job or no job."

Speaking of my new job, I needed to wind this up. A blue-vested boy who'd been hanging on my every word and peeking at me from between containers of transmission fluid and pine tree air fresheners had worked up the nerve to approach me directly. Not to mention I had a new purse full of my new employer's new money, and should probably get back to my new job. "Just cross your fingers for me, smooth things over with Mother, and don't tell Daddy anything. Let me handle that."

"Be careful, Davis."

"Oh, Meredith," I said, "you worry too much."

"Wait! Don't hang up! First of all, I want my shoes back."

Shoot.

"And second of all, where is it you're working? What is it you'll be doing?"

"I'm not sure."

"You're not *sure*? Which part? Where or what?"

I heard the squeak of the back door. Meredith either went back into the kitchen or she was standing there with the door open to aggravate Mother by letting out all the heat. Wait. That would be me.

"When you figure it out," my sister said, "let us know."

"I will."

"Love you."

"You, too." I made kissy noises.

* * *

On the ride back to the hotel, Bad Attitude at the wheel, I stared out at the gray afternoon, wondering how the highlights—some might say lowlights—of the past decade of my life had escaped an organization as seemingly shrewd as the Bellissimo. True, there was no hard documentation of my end-of-marriage misdeeds, but only because my father hadn't arrested me for them, and I knew how to get on and off a computer without anyone knowing. But truer than that was that our divorce played itself out on the sidewalks of Pine Apple, in the produce section of the grocery store, at the Gas and Go on Banana Street, and everywhere else Eddie and I happened upon each other. Every resident of Wilcox County, Alabama, knew every detail. How had the Bellissimo missed it?

I had a leg out the door, ready to be away from the surly cab driver, when I glanced up and caught him watching me again in the rear-view mirror.

"Surely you don't expect a tip."

He continued to stare. I reached up to pat my head; maybe the wig was on fire.

"I'm going to give you some advice," he said. "First time and last time."

He pivoted slowly to face me directly. He had the eyes of a thousand-year-old and they gave me the willies. I pressed myself into the backseat.

He spoke slowly, enunciating every word. "Get in your car and go back where you came from."

Probably shouldn't have slammed the car door that hard, but I didn't want any advice from a total stranger. I had enough to last a lifetime from people who knew me.

FOUR

Twenty minutes later, with one last look in the mirror, I agreed with Marci Dunlow's reflection: my own mother wouldn't recognize me.

I made my way from my Five Star hotel room to the casino floor (about four miles), which, let me tell you, is a noisy, bright, and busy destination. Seven of my five senses went on overload. Other than the perfume of it all—liquor, cigarettes, desperation—it reminded me of Chuck E. Cheese's. Chuck E. Cheese's for grownups. There were flashing machines as far as the eye could see. Row after row after row. I was going to need a treasure map to find the Whammy one I was supposed to play.

Shoulders back, wig held high, I made my way through the middle of the casino. I had three cell phones riding inside leather on my right hip; their weight and placement reminded me, as my sister had earlier on the phone, of my pistol-packing days. Meredith had grown up at Mother's knee, learning how to sift stuff. I cut my teeth on my father's lap, learning how to keep a gun oiled. And it was a good thing that the bag was full of AT&T and not Smith & Wesson, because one of them went off. I stopped short and dug through the collection for the alarming one. "Davis Way."

"No, you're not."

Natalie Middleton.

"Take a right. The Double Whammys are on your right."

I glanced up at the three thousand camera orbs dotting the ceiling.

"Good luck." She hung up.

Sure enough, a rotating neon sign announced that my wandering days were over: Double Whammy Deuces Wild. Beneath that, a scrolling number was whizzing through the mid-seven thousands. That's it? They had me in witness protection over seven thousand dollars? They'd spent that on the wardrobe and cell phone.

Nine gambling machines sat under the scrolling number. Four lined one side, four backed against them facing the opposite way, and one end was capped with a Double Whammy machine. Two elderly women were poking the display screens on my right.

I skipped the third seat, and parked myself in the fourth.

Now what?

The women cut their eyes my way. One half-smiled, then they both went back to their poking. I had the distinct feeling I'd invaded their territory.

Digging one of the crispy hundred dollar bills out from the cell-phone collection, I inserted it into a protruding slit that practically begged for it. It had a blinking backlit graphic depiction of George Washington, strategically placed so you couldn't miss it. The machine gobbled up the money so quickly, I jerked my hand back.

A counter rolled up credits. It would seem I had one hundred. The touchscreen offered lots of options, and the shelf below it contained buttons with the same offerings. I could Deal; I could Bet Max; I could Double; I could Whammy (what?); I could Hold; I could Cash Out; I could Jump Off a Bridge. The bridge sounded best to me, but I pushed Bet Max instead, because it was the one blinking.

Oversized video likenesses of playing cards turned over in five spots on the screen, each with a pleasant plinking noise. I stared at the screen a little more. An entirely new set of options were offered as the machine began singing an impatient song.

"You got a whole fleet!"

I turned to my right. One of the elderly women was speaking to me. She repeated the odd phrase.

"Excuse me?"

"You got sailboats, honey."

"Fours," the other lady, the one who'd half-smiled, explained. "Fours look like sailboats. You got four fours. That's a whole fleet."

Oh dear. I looked from them to the screen, then back to them. "What do I do now?" My new hair swung back and forth with my head. All the fours, or the sailboats as it were, had a word flashing across their hulls: HOLD.

"Take the money and run," the first woman said.

"Shouldn't I try to get *five* fours?" Clearly, the machine had malfunctioned, because it was also advising me to hold the red two, occupying the middle slip between all the boats. And it didn't match.

The two women exchanged a look. The one closest to me leaned in, "Honey, there aren't five fours in a deck of cards."

And this isn't a deck of cards!

"And besides, you *have* five fours," the other said. "Your deuce is wild!"

Were these women speaking a different language?

"You could Whammy," the first one said, "but I wouldn't do—"

Too late. I pushed the big red blinking Whammy button before she had the warning out, if for no other reason than to shut up the edgy machine. And oh, Lord, if it didn't put larger cards in front of me, but only two. Where'd my boats go?

"Pick," one of the women said. "You have to pick a card."

Easy enough. I tapped the one on the left. It flipped over and revealed a four of the suit that looks like a paw print. Clubs, I believe. And they said this machine didn't have any more fours.

Both of the women sucked in a breath. Before I could ask if I'd done something wrong or try to scoot the new four in with the absent old fours, of its own free will, the machine turned over the other card: a three of hearts.

"Well, I'll be dipped," one of the ladies said.

"Holy Moses," the other said.

"Double Whammy," they said in unison, shaking their heads.

"Did I win?" I asked. The machine was screaming.

"Sixteen hundred dollars, honey. And on your first spin," one said.

"I've never seen anyone whammy on a four," from the other.

Damn. I could get used to this.

And I did.

* * *

On my second afternoon of gainful employment, I woke the same grouchy cab driver by slapping a different hundred-dollar bill against the window, one I'd earned. Sorta. I wasn't really clear as to whose money the gambling winnings were, so I thought it best not to wire any of it to my bank in Alabama, but spending a little on necessities, cabs and such, seemed permissible. I had the surly driver— as happy to see me today as he'd been yesterday— take me to the closest electronics superstore, about forty minutes away with him at the wheel, because he stopped at all traffic lights and waited for them to turn red.

"You know," I started, "it's dangerous to stop at yellow lights. You're going to get hit."

He threw it in park. Right in the middle of the intersection. "Do you want to drive?"

This was my last clandestine mission; I'd had enough of this guy.

He parked as far away from the door as he could and pulled a black knit cap over his face.

I sat there a second. "Would you mind dropping me at the door?" It was cold!

He lifted the cap to reveal one bloodshot eye. "You got legs. Use 'em."

I'd been in the casino since nine that morning, ending my gambling shift after eight straight hours, when four lovely ladies lined up in a row: queen, queen, queen, queen! I whammied, my ten beating the machine's eight, and my new friends, the sisters Maxine and Mary who, it turned out, were locals, retired school teachers, and came to the casino every day except Sunday (the Lord's Day), celebrated with me. They called four queens a hen party, which I thought was funny. The game was entertaining, the elderly women great company, the drinks kept coming. When I remembered, with a jolt, that I was supposed to be working, I calmed myself with the certainty that if someone here wanted me to stop, they'd let me know.

As jobs go, I may have hit the jackpot.

Inside the store, I purchased the world's smallest laptop computer. I would have happily used the laptop delivered to my room while I was downstairs lining up snowmen (eights) and cowboys (kings), instead of taking it for granted I could spend the gambling winnings that were technically not mine, but I didn't want Natalie, or anyone else, tracking my cyber steps. I needed my own juice for my bathroom office.

Not soon enough, we were back at the Bellissimo.

"Are you the only cab driver on this side of the building?"

"Who wants to know?"

"Never mind."

Thankfully, he had no advice for me today.

The computer, only slightly larger than a hardback book, easy to hide, cost a little more than two hundred dollars and couldn't do much, which was fine; I wasn't trying to hack into government databases or write a dissertation in the bathroom. The scrambling software I downloaded onto it cost quite a bit more.

Back in my room, sans itchy wig, it took ten minutes at my bathroom desk to learn the game the sisters and I were playing reached a positive expectation point for the players when the jackpot climbed past seven thousand eight hundred dollars, which it was closing in on. It was simple math calculated after a quick computer search yielded a complicated website that called itself Winner Winner Chicken Dinner Video Poker Calculator. I plugged in the numbers it asked for, which took donning the wig again for a midnight trip downstairs to memorize the machine's payout schedule. The chicken calculator came back at me with this advice: Play the game after the big number goes past seven thousand eight hundred. At which point, so said the chicken, the player's chances of winning the big pot by being dealt a royal flush—a ten, jack, queen, king, and ace of the same suit—were optimal.

This would be the hot iron Mr. Sanders mentioned.

* * *

Feeling froggy on the third morning of my new lease on life, I took my time getting ready for work, which is to say I flipped the pillow to the cold side and slept until ten. When my toes finally found the thick carpet, I emptied a bottle of aromatherapy goo into the lap pool this place called a bathtub, and stayed in so long I had to take a shower to recover from taking a bath. Thirty minutes later, I was prancing in front of the mirror admiring my trés chic outfit, and anxious to join my new friends Maxine and Mary at the poker game.

Five hours into my workday, I was stuffing my winnings into Calvin Klein's miraculous push-up bra because Marc Jacobs' equally miraculous messenger bag was full.

Six hours after that, I was back in my room, standing at the same window-wall, this time counting the stars. I climbed into bed with a goofy grin on my face, which might have been from the three cocktails I had for dinner, but I didn't think so. My warm glow was a result of having landed the World's Greatest Job.

The next day, I quit.

FIVE

Morning Four of the World's Greatest Job began peacefully enough.

"How do you *know* all this?" I asked the sisters. I'd just taken my seat, and before I could even prime the video poker machine with cold, hard cash, Mary and Maxine began telling me what I'd missed so far. Their shift started at eight o'clock sharp; my shift started after I talked myself into the wig.

"We taught school for forty years, Marci. We see everything," Maxine said.

Marci? Oh.

"We can spot troublemakers from a mile away," Mary added. "We know a prankster when we see one."

From Maxine and Mary's sixty-hour-a-week perches, they watched the comings and goings in the casino, and were very well-versed in all things Bellissimo.

"So this guy is having an affair with *two* women, and they're both here today?" I asked.

"I think it's going to be a cat fight before the day's over," Mary said.

"He's the pit boss," Maxine said of the two-timer. "And both the girlfriends are blackjack dealers."

"And get this, Marci." Mary leaned in. "He's *married.*"

"Nooooo!" I threw my condemnation in there, too.

So the guy was a *three*-timer. That couldn't be good for the pit he was boss of. I took a pause to watch the sisters, who expertly played the games in front of them, all the while keeping tabs on the dramas unfolding at the blackjack tables and beyond. It wasn't necessarily the video poker that brought the sisters here every day; it was the soap opera of it. All My Addictions.

We played until noon with the sisters giving me the dirt on almost everyone who passed by: their fellow regulars, the barely-dressed girls handing out cocktails, and the purple-jacket people who made up the casino-floor security team.

"Those security people are just here for show," Maxine said. "They're about good for nothing unless your machine jams up. Not a one of 'em could catch a cold."

Not necessarily welcome news.

"Now, that bartender?" Mary tipped her head. "He clocks in then sleeps till noon. He gets between those whiskey bottles and acts like he's doing paperwork, but he's sawing logs."

I nodded along. "Why doesn't the other bartender say something?"

"Because when the one is sleeping, the other one isn't ringing up drinks," Maxine explained. "He's getting out of the way of the cameras and stashing the cash."

"And that one there?" Maxine gave a nod to a passing waitress carrying a tray loaded with liquor at nine in the morning. "She's pregnant again, but doesn't want anyone to know just yet."

"She had a little girl last October," Mary said. "Seven pounds, eleven ounces."

Maxine leaned in. "Named her Devon. Isn't that cute? Dev-on?"

I hit two straights in a row, whammying the second time. After several false starts, I finally got it out. "Ladies," I cleared my throat, "how do you win *that*?" I pointed to the dazzling marquee above our heads.

"The jackpot?" Mary asked. "You don't."

"We don't, anyway," Maxine added. "It will hit tonight about midnight."

"Really?" I asked. "How do you know?"

"Because it's time."

The three of us looked up. $7,883.60. $7,883.97. $7,884.22. The Chicken and the Sisters were in agreement.

"And we've watched them do it," Mary said.

"Watched who do what?"

The sisters communicated silently, debating. Maxine gave Mary the go-ahead nod, then Mary motioned me into the sister circle. We huddled. They wore the whispers of the beauties they'd been back in the day, and they wore bright red lipstick that tried to sneak away from their thin lips.

"There's a man who works here who has teeth so white they'll blind you," Mary said. "He's a big ole guy, Dapper Dan type, and he has great big white teeth."

I believe I've met him.

"He comes by late," she said, "when there's not a living soul in sight, and I don't know what he does, but the game flashes."

"It *what*?" I asked.

"It just bleeps." Maxine clapped her hands. "He waltzes by, doesn't even really slow down, but when he's ten feet gone," she said, "the whole game goes black for a second, then it pulls right back up. It's real quick."

"And you've seen this?" I asked.

"Four times," Maxine said.

Mary held up four crooked fingers.

I nodded. Go on.

"The big guy leaves, then about twenty minutes later," Mary said, "a really good looking young man comes and wins it."

"Every time?" I asked. "Same two guys every single time?"

"About every three weeks," Mary said, "like clockwork. We leave in the evening and the total is seven-thousand eight-hundred and some change. We come back the next morning and its reset back down to five thousand."

"We just can't stay up that late," Maxine said.

"Does the good-looking young man work here, too?" I asked.

"No," Maxine said. "He's from Alabama."

They said it on the same beat: "His name is Eddie."

* * *

Natalie Middleton was nowhere to be found, so I quit my new job in writing on a sheet of paper I tore off her monogrammed notepad. I told her I'd wait in my room until I heard from her. I left it taped to her coffee machine.

She asked me to play the game (check), learn it (check, check), and figure out who was winning it (check, check, check). That's where I quit. I couldn't turn Eddie Crawford in. If I pointed one finger at Eddie Crawford, he'd point all ten of his at me. (Or would that be eight?) It wouldn't *get* ugly; it would come out of the gate ugly. They wouldn't hold Eddie ten minutes after he started spilling my secrets; they'd be slapping the cuffs on *me*. And my father had no jurisdiction in Mississippi. At the very least, I'd be out on the street. Finding a new job after I'd been fired from my last one had taken more than a year. Finding a new job after being fired from *two* would take, what? Ten? Thirty?

This couldn't be happening.

It's not that I didn't want my sister to be right (which I didn't) about this town not being big enough to hold both me and rotten, rotten, snake-in-the-grass Eddie Crawford. And it wasn't that I was so thoroughly exhausted with Eddie Crawford tripping me up at every single turn. (For two decades.) (Which I was.) It wasn't even the combination of the two. The problem was, and the reason I was out of there: this smelled like a trap. I only knew one thing about my new job: these people wanted me to figure out the whammy-whammy game, and that could only mean something fishy was going on with it. If the fishy odor was coming from my ex-ex-husband Eddie, I had a way bigger problem on my hands. Taking him down won't be the end of *him*. It'll be the end of *me*.

Why would someone want to end *me*?

There wasn't even a remote possibility that Eddie Crawford set this up. Eddie Crawford couldn't set up breakfast. That meant it was either a nightmare of a coincidence (I don't even *believe* in coincidence) or someone here was playing me.

Best, all things considered, to never know.

So much for my new start on life. I could find another job playing dress up and casino games (luxury accommodations included), that passed out cash and was on the beach.

In about a million years.

* * *

After some liquid courage from the Five Star mini bar, I decided Natalie wasn't going to call and the best thing to do was leave. She'd figure it out. During this decision-making process, though, I accidentally took a little nap. I napped through the night, and I'd have probably napped until noon if bells and alarms hadn't started blaring like demented electronic roosters. The sirens were coming at me from all directions: the phones in my purse, the bathroom, the desk, and beside the bed.

Dammit.

I batted for the closest one.

"Davis, be in my office in an hour."

I protested vehemently, but only after Natalie hung up. It was then that I remembered the previous day's events and the fact that I'd quit my new job.

I reached up and gently examined my head to see if it might have railroad spikes embedded in it. I tried to recall the events of the previous evening, and the only thing that stood out was the mini bar. I looked around without moving my head and managed to locate the fridge.

Yep. Wide open and empty.

I lobbed one limb at a time off the bed and didn't get anywhere near upright when I attempted to stand. It was all I could do to walk across the floor because it was a landmine of teeny bottles. I drank three gallons of water straight from the tap, then washed down a Migraine Unlimited with a fourth.

Natalie Middleton's office always smelled like there were a dozen roses in it, but today wasn't my day, so it almost knocked me down. She dropped her sexy glasses in the middle of her desk, sat back, crossed her arms, and waited for me to sit.

I glanced at Mr. Sanders' closed door.

"He's in Dubai."

Do what?

"How are you this morning, Davis?"

I gave her the blankest of blank looks. "Did you not get my note?"

"I did." She waved it. "Did you not get a copy of the employment agreement you signed?"

The telephone book.

"You agreed to work here for a minimum of ninety days or reimburse us the cost of hiring you. So your choices are to write me a check or fulfill your commitment." She crushed my resignation letter into a gumdrop-sized ball. "Up to you, Davis."

Oh, dear.

"It's a simple breach of contract," she explained, "just as lying on your application, withholding pertinent information, or misrepresenting yourself during any of your interviews would be breach of contract."

Oh, double dear.

"How much money are we talking about?"

"Oh, I don't know," Natalie pushed the resignation gumdrop around. "Somewhere in the small-car range."

"It cost a small car to hire me?"

"Your background checks took an unusual amount of resources, Davis."

I see.

"I asked you to play the game, learn it, and tell me how it's won," she said. "You walked off the job just before the jackpot hit."

Did she stare at the casino cameras all day long?

"If you think someone's stealing the jackpot," I suggested, "can't you just arrest him?"

"Him?"

"Or her! Or it!"

"No, Davis." Natalie sat back. "We can't just arrest *him* for winning. I want to know *how* he wins it. That was your assignment."

"Can't you ask the man with the big teeth?" I was trying to come up with Teeth's name. I grabbed for my phone and pulled up the contact list. "Jeremy?"

"Jeremy?"

"Is he the bald-headed one?" I asked.

"Yes."

"Then the other one," I said. "The one with the really white teeth."

"Paul," Natalie supplied.

"Right." Amundo.

"Why would I ask Paul?"

Something in the tone of her voice let me know we'd changed lanes. I had no idea why, nor did I want to know. "I thought I saw him," I said.

Natalie's fingers tapped out a tune on her desk. "He works here, Davis. You'll see both Paul and Jeremy often." She rose, poured two cups of coffee, then returned.

I thanked her, then burned my mouth.

"I'll give you the chance to make this right in a few weeks, Davis. The jackpot will climb back up, then you can try again." She picked up the paper ball that was my resignation, then let it drop on her desk. "And I'm going to ignore this." She leaned in, taking me into her confidence. She spoke slowly. "I don't know if you saw a *ghost*, or if someone offended you, or if you simply don't like the food here."

"Oh, I love the food."

"Good to know, Davis." She rolled her eyes a little bit. "Good." She sat back and crossed her arms again. "You're welcome to go if you want to." She gave the door a nod, "but you've made a ninety-day commitment, and I'll need a check from you before you leave."

I was brokity-broke-broke-broke. And then some.

"I went to bat for you, Davis."

I saw a little mean streak in her who I hadn't met before.

"And I don't want to talk to Mr. Sanders and have him ask me how it's going with you, then have to tell him *this*." She tapped the resignation ball.

I slinked around in the chair.

She passed me a teal-blue canvas duffel with caramel leather trim. "Take the weekend, Davis, and be back here Monday morning at eight. Your assignment won't be in the casino."

I couldn't think of a thing to say, but opened my mouth and spoke anyway. Mostly vowels.

"That'll be all, Davis."

* * *

Welcome to Pine Apple, Alabama. Population 447.

We thought of ourselves as larger, counting all the populace and some of the livestock just past the city limits signs as city-dwellers too, but the fact remains: Pine Apple is too small for me to sneak home and my mother not know. There are twenty miles of AL-10 to cover between I-65 (civilization) and Pine Apple (back, back woods), and I promise you, my mother's phone rang every other mile marker. "Davis just zipped by here, Caroline."

At every family gathering a story is referenced. Somehow, someway, at some point, someone sneaks it in. My mother, a maverick of her day, went to college. She swapped her mortarboard for a white veil and married my father the afternoon of the same day she graduated. Here's where the bottom dropped out for Caroline Annette Davis Way: She immediately became pregnant with me.

The obstetrician asked her if she wanted to hold her baby. "No," she said. "Give her to her father."

Daddy and I have been inseparable ever since. I worship the ground he walks on, meanwhile my hair stands on end at the very thought of Mother.

One lazy Alabama afternoon when my sister Meredith was pregnant with her daughter, Riley, I sat at one end of the porch swing with Meredith, propped on pillows and stretched across, resting her swollen feet in my lap. We were drinking the kind of lemonade that's nine parts sugar and one part lemon, swatting flies and praying for her labor to begin. Meredith was tracing beach-ball circles on her distorted abdomen. "What if we're like you and Mother, Davis? What if the baby and I just don't *like* each other?"

* * *

I drove straight to the police station.

"There's my girl!"

I collapsed into my safe place without speaking. My safe place wrapped his arms around me.

"Where the heck have you been, Sweet Pea?"

"Daddy," I took the perp seat beside his desk, "I got a job." I think.

"It's a good thing, too, because your landlord's threatening to evict you."

"Mother's so full of hot air," I said, dropping my purse to the concrete floor.

"Oh, now," my father said.

"If she evicts me, she'll have to move all my stuff back home."

"She claims she's going to have the Goodwill pick it up."

"Isn't the property in your name too, Daddy? Can't you control your own wife?"

"I'm much better at controlling her than I am you."

"Oh, Daddy." I took a swat at him. "Hey, has anyone been nosing around about me?"

"Let me get us a cup of coffee," he said, "then we'll talk."

It made the back of my knees cave in to see my father aging. When I was ten, there wasn't anything he couldn't do. I walked to the station after school every day. "I can't run this place without you, Deputy." My part-time job responsibilities included making yards of paper-clip necklaces, Wanted Dead or Alive posters, and snack duty—graham crackers and milk or Fritos and Dr. Pepper. One day, something catching his eye, he turned to me, "I'll be right back, Punkin. Stay put." He'd spotted elusive Old Man Brinkley slinking out of the hardware store. Daddy hollered for him; Old Man Brinkley made a run for it; my father took chase, running up and over a parked car in a single leap, as if it he'd jumped a fire hydrant.

When I was seven years old, I watched him cut down, chop, and stack the logs of a giant sugar gum tree in our backyard, single-handedly, in one day. Mer and I were shoulder-to-shoulder at the kitchen window from sunup till sundown, Daddy throwing us waves and winks and giving us the signal that yes, now, bring him a glass of iced tea, as the tree that had shaded our childhood surrendered to our father. "Watch this, girls!" he hollered. He stood back, the sun beating down on his slick chest, and blew with the same force it takes to blow out candles on a birthday cake. The tree went down with a scream and a crash that shook the floor under our feet. "Daddy's so strong," Meredith panted. "The strongest," I agreed.

Once he snuck into our room in the dead of night, crouched between us, and whispered, "Come on, girls, it's Sissy's time." We watched our father, the man who blew down trees and leapt cars, deliver a litter of pups with such tenderness and care that it made the momentous event more about him than the warm new puppies. Neither I, nor Meredith, nor Sissy, could take our eyes off him. He held three of those pups in his one hand.

My daddy could snap his fingers and we would come running. He chastened us when he needed to with a cut of his eyes, and it felt like a sword slicing through. And this man, who I truly believe hung the moon in the sky, now rose from his chair with an unconscious groan and took his seat again, placing a hot cup of coffee in front of me with a deep sigh.

"Oh, these old bones," he said.

"I love you, Daddy."

He smiled, and the gullies around his eyes deepened. "So what have you gotten yourself into, young lady?"

I squirmed, wondering what I could and what I should say. "It's security work."

"That much I gathered."

"With one of the casinos in Mississippi."

"In Biloxi," he said.

Meredith ratted me out.

"Don't blame your sister."

Daddy read my mind.

"Blame Blanche."

Someone needed to go down for this. Might as well be Blanche, one of Pine Apple's two bank tellers.

"She called several weeks ago because your debit card was being swiped in Biloxi, and since then, by my count, you've been there seven more times." He crossed his arms and leaned back. "I'm relieved to hear you say this is about a job, and not about Eddie." He smiled. "Congratulations."

World's Greatest Father.

"Now, what can I do to help, Davis?"

Universe's Greatest Father.

* * *

On Sunday, I went through my apartment dumping out everything—closets, drawers, and cabinets—and attempted to put it back in a more orderly fashion. I didn't intend to give up my apartment just yet, but should Mother make good on her threat to give away my worldly possessions just because my rent was a few dozen months in arrears, I could have Meredith intervene. It would be easier for my sister if she didn't have to decide what to do with the baton collection left over from my high school fire-twirling days. Anything that in any way reminded me of my marriage went into black lawn-and-garden bags.

It was time.

Throwing away stack after stack of four-year-old magazines, restraining orders (so unnecessary), and eviction notices (from my own mother) gives one time to think. In the light of the sober day, it occurred to me that Natalie Middleton hadn't asked me to tell her *who* won the Double Whammy game at all; she wanted to know *how* it was won. I had eighty-something work days to figure out *how* the game was won and avoid Eddie the Ass while I was at it. The farther I went down the I-screwed-up road, the hotter my face felt. Natalie Middleton must think I'm half crazy. I blamed it on the clock: gambling round the clock, liquor round the clock, and clocks in general, because time heals all divorces, and I was tired of waiting on it.

The clock struck three when I hoisted the last garbage bag from my old life in the big blue dumpster, and with it, I mentally wiped my new-job slate clean. I'd show Natalie Middleton I could be trusted to stay on my rocker, I was grateful to her for giving me a second chance, and I couldn't wait to check back into my hotel room. The Bellissimo was a big place and Eddie Crawford didn't know Marci Dunlow. He wouldn't know it was me if I walked up and slapped him. I turned to see Daddy's patrol car winding down the long drive.

We sat at the kitchen table, a football game on television providing background music.

"I wish I had something to offer you, Daddy, but tap water's it."

"I'm fine."

"There's no reason for me to fill this place up with groceries." I gestured wide. "I'm leaving for Biloxi in a couple of hours."

"About that," my father said, then landed a case file between us.

It turns out that Richard Sanders, President and CEO of the Bellissimo Resort and Casino, began his career at the age of sixteen as a part-time bellman at Glitz, a 4,500-room hotel and casino on the Las Vegas Strip. He remained employed at the Glitz through college, then UNLV's graduate program. A few years down the road, he was the casino manager, and engaged to marry the owner's youngest, Bianca Casimiro. Fifteen additional years brought us to today. The Sanders had one child, Thomas, the Xbox gamer who was twice my size. The move to Biloxi happened seven years ago, the same month I was trotting down the aisle for the second time, when the Casimiros, already the owners of eight resorts in Las Vegas proper and two in New Jersey, acquired additional properties in Indiana, Louisiana, and Mississippi, in cash deals.

"Who has billions in cash sitting around?" I asked.

"Casinos."

Right.

"This," my father pushed a photograph my way, "is the guy who had lunch at Mel's."

"Teeth."

Daddy rotated the picture and took another look. "He does have a mouthful."

"If he mentioned my name at Mel's, you know he got an earful. They don't serve anything but cholesterol, heartburn, and the We Hate Davis special."

Mel, of Mel's Diner, a run-down greasy spoon and permanent resident on the health department's disaster list, is my former father-in-law. My former mother-in-law, Bea, runs the cash register and her mouth.

My father shrugged. "You're probably right, but you never know. This fella," another mug shot slid my way, "is the one Meredith met."

"No Hair."

Meredith is the owner/operator of a curiosity shop a block east of the police station, on the first floor of the three-story antebellum my father grew up in. The main parlor and the receiving room across the hall are where she sells toys, doodads, antique toys, and antique doodads. The former library is also the current library, where you can thumb through rare and collectible books, mostly mysteries, packed in the old floor-to-ceiling wall shelves and displayed in antique curio cabinets. (People come from everywhere for those dusty old books—go figure—but never stay. Which is how she met Riley's father, who didn't stay either.) The library (where Riley was conceived, not something Meredith broadcasts) leads to the old sitting room that she keeps stuffed with racks and trunks of crazy vintage clothing, and she converted the kitchen to accommodate an old-fashioned soda-fountain lunch counter, with huge glass jars full of candy you can't find anywhere, like licorice jujubes, bubble-gum cigars, and Razzles. She serves homemade vegetable beef soup and grilled-cheese sandwiches that she prepares with three slices of buttered Texas toast and about a pound of Velveeta each. It's a heart attack on a plate, and my father eats one every single day. You need a crane to pick it up and a nap immediately after.

Meredith changes the storefront window every week, pulling the front curtains closed on Friday afternoons. Three counties turn out on Monday to see what she's done. One week she might have a Big Band theme going, an upright piano front and center with horns of all shapes and sizes suspended above and around it, Tommy Dorsey piping through the store and onto the sidewalk. The next week it could be a Mary Poppins window with parasols, stuffed penguins, and mannequins decked out in full regalia just like Julie Andrews and Dick Van Dyke. The funniest is when my four-year-old niece Riley is part of the storefront, dressed up as a fuzzy little chicken for a hoedown-themed display or as a baby-girl Elvis for a King of Rock and Roll window.

Not only do Mother and Daddy *both* like Meredith, she has an endless supply of energy and imagination. The woman is crafty, clever, and six inches taller than me. It's a wonder we speak.

"He told her he was just passing through," my father said.

"Sure he was. To where?"

Daddy drummed his fingers on the table. Everyone knew Pine Apple didn't lead to anywhere else.

"What did she tell him about me?"

"She didn't. He didn't ask. He poked around, had a chocolate malted, bought three books, a handful of old neckties, then left."

I wasn't surprised about the ties, but I wondered what he could possibly want with three crackly books. The huge man with dark beady eyes and without a hair on his head didn't strike me as the curl-up-by-the-fire-and-read-a-musty-book type.

"And this last guy," my father pushed an index card my way, then tapped it. "George Morgan?" Tap, tap. "Nothing, Sweet Pea. I couldn't pull up a current residence, a full Social, or even a library card. I couldn't find where he's ever purchased a piece of property, borrowed a dime, been in the Big House or the military. All I could find was a vehicle registration and license, and you gave me those. Who is this guy?"

"He's my driver."

"Your driver's living in his car."

"I suspected as much."

"How is he in play, Punkin?"

I thought about it a second. "I think he's been on the Job."

"Is that so. And?"

I shrugged. "Makes you wonder." Which, it didn't. We both knew why a law enforcer might disappear, and it wasn't pretty.

"Watch your back, Davis."

"Always, Daddy."

I watched from the window until his taillights disappeared. The sun would set all too soon—I hate winter—and I had three hours of road to cover.

I'd savored the surprise of what great getup Natalie had in store for me until now, glancing at the duffel bag expectantly several times. The dress-up aspect of my new job was the best part—it made me feel safe and I loved the clothes. I unzipped the bag slowly, tooth by tooth, like opening a present. Natalie Middleton had missed her calling; she should have been a personal shopper instead of a personal assistant.

Inside the duffel I found an envelope with my name handwritten across the front. There was a short page of blah-blah, go here, go there, blah-blah, a car key on a round silver ring, and a tarnished metal key on a green plastic key fob, number thirty-four and Econo-Lodge stamped in flaking gold ink. Under the envelope were a maid's uniform, flesh-colored support hose, a dark brown pony-tail wig, and thick-soled white industrial shoes. Size six and a half.

SIX

The EconoLodge sucked. The housekeeping job sucked harder. Two weeks into both, I was sleep deprived, my hands were raw and blistered, my back broken, my feet blown up to small pillows, and I didn't have a clue who was stealing money from guest-room safes. More than that, I barely cared.

The good news was I'd all but forgotten the bad taste my first Bellissimo assignment had left me with, and the drudgery of this new assignment only had a bad odor. My ninety-day commitment was down to the high-sixties.

A heap of junk that Nattie insisted was a rental car was parked outside room thirty-four at the EconoLodge the first night. "Housekeeping personnel don't drive brand-new shiny cars, Davis. Drive the rental back and forth to work."

That pile of scrap metal reeked, died twice at red lights, and the radio only hissed. I decided quickly that my first commute in it would also be my last. I'd rather take the bus. I'd rather hitchhike. I'd rather crawl. I parked it in the employee parking garage, which, as it turned out, was in a totally different zip code than the Bellissimo. As I switched off the ignition the damn thing backfired, the amplified bomb blast bouncing off the concrete walls, taking ten good years off my life. I left that rattletrap there for good. I left the keys in it, very tempted to leave it running. I could walk to work and back in thirty minutes. It wouldn't kill me.

Eight hours later I was so near death, that walking to the EconoLodge would have been the last straw. At the end of my first day with Guest Services, I felt like I'd pulled a log truck uphill by the bit between my teeth all day. I'd been screamed at in rapid-fire Spanish often and at length. I'd been forced to hover over an endless succession of toilets. I'd inhaled toxic chemicals all day. I'd manhandled mountains of suspicious bed sheets. I'd picked up a thousand gooey bars of soap, and, possibly the worst, I shattered a mirror into a million shiny slivers.

As I stood in line to punch out, everyone else jabbering cheerily as if they'd spent the day poolside, the very effort of inhaling and exhaling was about all I could manage. Walking to the hellhole EconoLodge was no longer an option. The thought of meeting up with the clunker I'd said goodbye and good riddance to almost brought me to tears, and then I remembered my friendly cabbie.

I couldn't very well whistle through VIP in my maid getup and hail myself a taxi, so I left through the employee-service entrance and circled around the property on foot, which was about six miles cross country; I could have walked to the EconoLodge just as easily. George was right where I left him, and he was asleep. I found a nice big magnolia tree to hide behind and lobbed cherry LifeSavers, one at a time, onto the hood of the dirty white car.

The LifeSavers came from a guest room I'd all but licked clean, at the bottom of a basket of goodies the room's last occupant had walked off and left, along with a rancid water glass full of drowned cigarette butts on a non-smoking floor. The rule seemed to be if the guest was still a guest, leave everything as close to where you found it as possible. If the guest had checked out, anything they left was fair game. This was explained to me in pantomime.

I eyed the basket.

Finder's keepers—the only, single, solitary perk of this job.

There were only two LifeSavers left when George finally stirred, craned in my direction, and beckoned me with no energy and no recognition.

I ducked my head and made a run for the backseat.

He let out a huge sigh. He didn't turn when he said, "You make a better redhead."

I froze. I stared at the back of his head until he turned around and acknowledged me. We locked eyes. "Shut up, George, and drive."

He cranked her up. "Where to?"

"The EconoLodge."

I swear I heard him snicker.

We pulled into the parking lot, and he drove straight to my Volkswagen. I knew I was right about him; he'd been on one side or the other of the law. Otherwise, he'd have had no idea what I drove. Or what color hair was under the wigs.

"What time do you want me to pick you up in the morning?"

See?

I huffed. "Six forty-five." I passed him a plastic bag full of loose change I'd collected off nightstands and dressers. He shook the bag, then looked at me.

"What? I can't pay you a hundred dollars every time you take me three blocks!" I got out, slammed the door, and braced myself for my next chore—surviving the EconoLodge a second night.

* * *

"It couldn't be *that* bad," Natalie said. "There's very little turnover in housekeeping."

"That's because they're raking in the dough on that job. The housekeepers are filling up ten bags a day each with loot from the rooms."

At the end of my second week, Natalie and I were having a sit-down at the casino next door, the Gold Mine, hidden amongst gigantic slot machines.

"Why are we here?" I'd asked.

"I love their coffee," she'd replied.

"The job is nasty, Natalie," I told her. "People are just *gross*. And they steal everything that isn't nailed down. Today? Today I had a room that had a *lamp* missing. I cleaned the same room yesterday and the lamp was there."

"What about the safes?"

Each guest room has a ten-inch recessed wall safe inside the closet. It was there to tease the guests: *Go to the casino and get a pile of money to put in me*. When the guests check in the little vault is wide open, the instructions loud and clear: leave this thing as you found it. If they have any reason to use the safe, they program their own top-secret four-digit code that allows access to whatever valuables they place in the safe, and if they happen to check out without opening it, the housekeeper has to stand there and try four-digit number combinations until they guess the correct one.

Just kidding.

Ninety-nine percent of the time the wall safes, like the two sheets of Bellissimo stationery in the desk, aren't touched. Here's an interesting fact: the Gideon organization doesn't place a free Bible in casino hotel rooms. Does that make any sense? You'd think they'd put *two* in every room.

"Everyone seems to follow procedure," I told her. "If we get to an unoccupied room where the guest left it locked, we call the supervisor. She brings the master key and opens it."

"Have you run across that?"

"Once," I told her.

"What was inside?"

"French fries."

Natalie's head jerked. "What?"

"Congealed French fries. I swear." I flashed her the Scout's Honor salute. Or maybe it was the Witches' Honor. "They were swimming in so much ketchup I thought someone had locked up a body part, like a kidney or a big nose."

"What did you do?"

"I had to pick up the nasty things, then scrub out the safe."

Nattie recoiled.

"See? I told you."

* * *

The room safes were being broken into randomly; the common denominator eluded me other than baby powder, because traces of it were found all four times. All I really knew was that I hated cleaning hotel rooms and that the thief was wearing Pampers.

I had *Jeopardy!* turned low on the television to muffle the noise of my neighbors, who'd had screaming sex twice already, once during the news and then again during *Wheel of Fortune*, with the four incident files and a take-out pizza spread out on the EconoLodge's version of a bedspread: it was made of plastic, didn't provide a single blanket element other than covering the cardboard sheets, and it smelled like feet.

I'd studied these files for two weeks now, and still a pattern hadn't emerged. Truth be told, I only glanced at the stack the first week, unable to hold anything as heavy as a sheet of paper after my grueling day shifts, but began digging through them in earnest over the weekend. Two things dawned on me while staring at the stain patterns on the thirty-seven EconoLodge ceiling tiles: one, the Bellissimo had higher sanitation standards than the EconoLodge, and two, the reward for catching the thief would be a different assignment, something that didn't involve removing gooey things from the bottom of hotel garbage cans during the day or having pervy neighbors at night.

The security footage was the same. I ran all four clips a dozen times on my teeny computer, backed them up, and watched them a dozen more. A dark-haired man, the same man each time (who knew the camera angles, because I couldn't get a full shot of his face), stood outside a guest room chatting it up with the housekeeping floor supervisor. She used her pass key to give him entrance to an occupied room where he went on to relieve the room safe of its pesky contents. Only, as it turned out all four times, he wasn't the occupant.

The timeline was erratic, the first theft occurring in August of last year on the twenty-eighth floor, the second in November on sixteen, and the last two during the same week in December, the first on the twentieth floor and the follow-up break-in on floor thirteen.

The victims claimed losses that totaled forty-nine thousand in cash, with the third incident on the twentieth floor including jewelry, bringing the grand total up to almost sixty-thousand dollars the guy had walked off with.

For the late-summer heist, he was decked out in golf attire, lugging a bag of clubs. For the second, he wore tennis whites, a racquet tucked under one arm, hands full of Bellissimo Café take-out. The third—this was cute—he wore a spa robe and slippers. For his final act, only two days after his lucrative spa adventure, he seemed to have run out of energy. He was dressed in nondescript street clothes: khaki pants, a V-neck sweater over a button down, and leather loafers.

How did he know there was anything in the safes worth stealing and how, once in the room, was he getting into them?

* * *

It was noon on a bright sunny Monday, my third on the housekeeping assignment, and I knew it was his room the second I entered it. You don't marry someone twice and not know a bed they've slept in.

Sixteen hundred and twenty guest rooms, more than five hundred people issued the same black, tan, and white uniform I was sporting, and somehow I was the lucky one who knuckled the door ("Housekeeping!"), card-swiped the lock, strategically blocked the door with my cleaning cart, and entered my ex-ex-husband Eddie's hotel room. I fell against my cart, sending a hundred tiny shampoo bottles flying off the other side.

"Okay? Okay?" Santiago, my coworker, cleaning the even-numbered rooms to my odd, raced across the hall to lasso the shampoos. "Okay?"

"I'm fine, Santiago," I panted. I squeezed my eyes shut, pinched the bridge of my nose, and tried to concentrate on standing upright.

"Bad stinks?"

That would work, so I nodded.

"You me do?"

I shook my head. "I'm fine, Santiago. I'm going to close this door so no one walking by gets a whiff of this." I waved my hand in front of my face.

Santiago gave me his I-have-no-idea-what-you-said smile and asked again, "You me do?" this time, pointing to me, then himself. He drew his toilet-brush sword. He tilted his head back, sniffing the air.

"No, Santiago, but thanks." I closed the door to an urgent string of speedy Spanish. An interpreter would have come in handy just then, because what Santiago was trying to tell me was that we weren't allowed behind closed doors in a guest room. We used two card keys: one to enter and clean the room, the other to exit and let all interested parties—our boss, the front desk, and, as it turns out, Natalie Middleton, should she want to know—that the room was ready. If the door closed between the two swipes, warning bells sounded all over the building: Someone on the housekeeping staff was locked up in a guest room. Hello, lawsuit.

Santiago was on the other side of the door hollering about piñatas, enchiladas, and conquistadors. The housekeeping supervisor was thumping down the hall, slinging Spanish curses right and left. Natalie Middleton was in action, sending an emissary to both save me and read me the riot act.

I was behind closed doors, so I didn't know.

I fingered Eddie's hanging shirts and poked around in his shaving kit. No surprises. I grabbed my clipboard and flipped through, wondering how I'd missed this. We're issued our marching orders at the beginning of every shift. If almost always gives us the surname of the guest in the room and if not, it gives clues. VIPs are highlighted with a pale green stripe, which most of this floor was, and Casino Marketing guests are listed as just that. No name, just Casino Marketing Guest. You don't know a thing about the room's occupant other than they were there on the casino's dime. So Eddie Crawford was a Casino Marketing guest. Which is exactly when it hit me. Buried deep in the incident files, behind the reports, profiles, photographs, claim forms, and interview transcripts, were the single-sheet housekeeping assignment charts for the day of each robbery. All four room-safe thefts had occurred in Casino Marketing guest rooms.

An urgent pounding on the door scared the very life out of me. It was most certainly Eddie.

I dropped my clipboard, clapped my hand over my mouth to muffle my screams, and wondered, wildly pacing a small circle, what to do. My eyes were drawn to the Gulf of Mexico, out the window and nineteen floors down. Suicide? This early in the morning?

He knocked again.

I jumped a mile and screamed into my hand.

"Everything okay in there?"

It wasn't Eddie.

I stretched to the peephole, and saw a perfect set of glow-in-the-dark choppers. Their owner could have chewed through the door. Accompanying the teeth, a great big man dressed in head-to-toe white. He looked like Dr. Death.

Shit. Shit. Double shit.

SEVEN

“Is this it?” George shook a can of mixed nuts.

“It can’t be Christmas every day.” In the two weeks that George had been shuttling me back and forth to and from the lovely EconoLodge, I’d loaded him down with things I found in the guest rooms: food, candy, wine, soft drinks, bottled water, flowers, T-shirts, coffee mugs, four hundred little jars of condiments, visors, golf balls, hand lotion, and enough cell phone chargers to open his own kiosk at the mall. The first few days I simply left the loot in the car. The day he almost got us killed because he was craning into the rear-view mirror to see what I’d be leaving instead of watching the road was the day I began handing the boodle to him when I got in. For reasons I might never know, old George loved the flowers the best, although he’d be driving the governor’s limo before he’d let on. The most I ever got out of him was a grunt. The three times I’d climbed in and passed him flowers, though, he’d been speechless, which is to say he didn’t grunt. So old George did have a soft spot.

He shook the can again. “Peanuts?”

“I only cleaned two guest rooms, George. And unfortunately for you, I didn’t find a pot of gold in either.” I rubbed my temples. I needed a drink.

“You spent all day cleaning two rooms?” He waited until there wasn’t a car within five miles of us in either direction before pulling out onto Beach Boulevard. “Must have been some big rooms.”

I didn’t have the energy.

“And is that the new maid’s get-up?”

I didn't owe George a wardrobe explanation.

"You don't strike me as the kind who'd take the time to be good at that sort of thing."

Was George baiting me?

"I probably would have let you go two weeks ago."

I shot up in the seat, my energy miraculously returned. "I didn't get *fired*, George. I'll have you know I stared at a computer screen all day."

George made a noise he was so good at, I think he invented it. It said, *uh-huh, sure you did,* in just one guttural syllable.

I came *this* close to bailing out of a moving vehicle, because breaking a leg or two would have been the best part of my day.

Three blocks later he asked, "What'd you find?"

"I'm not speaking to you again, George. Ever, ever."

"Fine."

"Nothing," I caved. "Nothing."

We were at a red light. He twisted in his seat. "Did you have a bad day?"

I started bawling.

Teeth had yanked me out of Eddie Crawford's hotel room by the ear, then pulled me kicking and screaming into a stairwell where he ripped me a new one. I thought he was going to bite my head off. I'd been on the receiving end of many protocol and procedure lectures before (the circumventing of), but never across from those kind of teeth. He gave no indication that I had been in the wrong room, or that there was any connection between me and that particular room, he gave me down the road in general about being in *any* room alone with the door locked. "Were you *looking* for something?" When he'd had his say, his parting words were, "Go see Natalie."

I wasn't about to tell Teeth or Natalie it was the collection of my ex-ex-husband's personal effects that had prompted the breaking of all those cardinal rules (which I knew absolutely nothing about beforehand), so bracing myself for another lashing, avoiding both the guest and employee elevators (something they had bothered to make me aware of), I hoofed it to the Executive Offices. I poked my head in Natalie's door.

"Davis," she smiled. "Come on in. The coast is clear." She was refilling Mr. Sanders' cinnamon candy bowl from a ten-pound bag of the offensive stuff, the sight of which made me a little dizzy. Natalie was crisp, cool, calm, and didn't appear to be the least bit upset with me. She offered me a cup of coffee; she didn't offer me a cinnamon candy. "Now, Davis," Natalie smiled. "What can I do for you?"

I scratched at the wig a little. I thought *she* had asked to see *me* for round two of Chew Davis Out. "I need a computer," I said, "and a desk."

"Okay," she said. "Why don't you step in the back and change out of your uniform."

Gladly. If she'd suggested I step in the back and change out of my *life*, I'd have taken her up on that too.

After fitting me with street clothes, Natalie set me up in an empty cubicle in the print shop, located several miles under the basement of this gargantuan place. "Keep your head down," she said. "You won't run into anyone because the print-shop employees only work graveyard. But if for some reason you do, keep quiet."

Aye, aye, Captain.

"And don't ever do that again."

She said it to my back as I was making my escape. I barely turned, one foot already out the door. "Sorry." Hand in the cookie jar. "I won't."

"Is there anything else, Davis?" She tapped a pen. "Anything we need to talk about?" Her expression was as blank as a Bellissimo bed sheet.

I fell against the doorjamb for support, because with her words, a ghost had snuck up from behind and knocked my knees. Then laughed. "Not that I know of, Natalie."

I got out of there as fast as I could.

* * *

Not many people go into police work for the money. The ones who do aren't protecting and serving the public, they're protecting and serving the dark side. The most I'd ever earned in my life was peanuts, and I hadn't saved a one of them because at the time, I had a nest egg. Today, at age early-thirties, I had no nest egg, I had no roof over my head, and I'd never work directly in law enforcement again. I could get a job as a computer programmer, but I'd probably blow my brains out by the third day.

This job had shocked me stupid three times now. The whammy-whammy game had slapped me so hard I actually quit. The severe tongue-lashings, both directly and not so directly, I'd received today set me back and gave me more to chew. But both of these events and their bright red Eddie flags paled in comparison to the shock I received when I checked my bank balance.

The Bellissimo was paying me a brain surgeon astronaut's wages.

In all the interviews, the subject of salary never came up. Not once. I never asked; they never offered. I emailed Natalie my banking information after opening a local account, and she replied that my paycheck would be directly deposited every Friday, and instead of wondering how much it would be, I consulted a calendar, counting the number of Fridays in ninety days. (My interest was more on Visa's behalf than my own. And I owed my sister a little. My grandmother, too. My father had paid for my car, something my mother didn't know.)

It took every dime I had to divorce that rat-bastard Eddie Crawford, immediately followed by extreme unemployment. My finances had gone from sad to tragic until I began squirreling away Bellissimo paychecks. Things were looking up in my financial department; Visa and I were both very happy about it. My ninety-day commitment was nearing the four-week mark, but they were paying me so much I caught myself thinking if I could stick it out six months, I could be debt free both inside and outside of my family. If

I could hold out an additional six months, I'd have the makings of a savings account.

I looked at myself in the reflection of the elevator doors on my way to the print shop, and gave myself this advice: "Make this work, Davis."

* * *

I was certain the same Casino Marketing person booked the four guest-victims, but ten minutes after I settled in to solve this caper, I hit a wall. Four different casino hosts were assigned to the four injured parties.

If it wasn't a casino-host culprit, who was it?

I had no choice but to hack into the mainframe, which, let me assure you, raises your blood pressure through the roof. Years ago, out of boredom, I wrote a program that would shut a system completely down the millisecond it was compromised. The only reason I hadn't tried to sell it to Microsoft or the iPod people was because I hadn't had time to develop Part Two, a sprinkler-system device in the monitor that blasted the hacker with tear gas. Hack *that*, buddy. (The real reason I hadn't pursued it was is because if it did fly, my hacking hobby would be over.)

Boom. Gotcha. I was in.

I examined the four guest portfolios from their inceptions. After three hours and a headache, I found nothing but typos. No one had altered anything.

It had been a long, long day. I'd been traumatized, terrified, told off, and I'd struck out. Tears were in order.

George waited patiently until I stopped leaking. "What were you looking for?"

We were stuck at a railroad crossing while an endless succession of gang-graffitied railcars rolled by, so I let my head fall back and closed my eyes. "I'm looking into this casino host business, how it works."

"Nothing to it."

"How's that, George?" My head snapped up. "What? Are you a casino expert now? I haven't seen you in there yucking it up with the casino hosts."

"Don't mean I don't know about it." He turned and made the rare eye contact again, but I didn't cry this time.

"I'm listening." I crossed my arms.

"It's a sweet gig."

"In what way?"

"It's the easiest job in the building."

"That couldn't be true," I said. "It looks to me like they take care of the whims and fancies of a thousand people each." Clicking on the client-list link of a casino host's profile, a Rhode Island roster ensues. Page after page, thousands of guests, are assigned to each of the fourteen hosts.

"They have people to do all of their grunt work," he said. "They spend their time in the restaurants and out on the golf course."

Thirty minutes later, ignoring my next-door neighbors' headboard trying to beat its way into my room again, nose to computer screen, I had my mark: Miss Heidi Dupree, Executive Assistant to the casino hosts. She was one of eight executive assistants, but hers were the only administrative initials on the portfolios, a zillion computer screens back, for the four rooms that had been pilfered. I recognized her from her employee profile, too; I'd seen her stepping into a guest room carrying a bucket of flowers.

* * *

The next day, I cleaned seventeen guest rooms. Three were barely touched, only one corner of the bed turned back, and a single pillow had a head dent. I'd learned quickly that not all the guests were there for the glorious guest rooms, extra glorious to me now that I knew EconoLodge squalor. A good portion of Bellissimo guests checked in, threw their bags inside the door and hit the casino, never to return.

I'd had one room for three consecutive days, nineteen thirty-seven, whose occupant had yet to get near the bathroom sink, tub, shower, or, for all I could tell, their suitcase. Down the hall, I had adjoining rooms that made up for that one; the occupants and the preschool they brought with them had moved in. Stuffed animals, gummy worms, hills and mountains of discarded clothing, bowl after bowl of liquefied ice cream, tubs used as toy storage, and half-full juice boxes everywhere. In another room, it had rained shiny black condom wrappers, and in yet another guest room, the ravenous occupants had ordered one of everything on the room service menu, taking a single bite out of each dish, leaving all the uneaten food and enough tableware to set a table for ten for me to deal with. The room safes today, like almost every day, hadn't been touched. The best part? Eddie Crawford had checked out of his room. A guy named Millard Martin had checked in it. I had no beef with Millard.

My coworkers didn't take lunch breaks so much as they took extended smoke breaks. As the clock inched toward noon, and I said job-well-done to myself about guest room nineteen-thirteen, Santiago, my work buddy, exiting nineteen-fourteen and in the throes of severe nicotine withdrawal, asked, "We lunch?"

"Sure." I couldn't see him through the king-sized bed roll of laundry I was hefting. I tipped it into my bin. The muffled music of broken glass filled the space between us. It sounded like I'd dropped a chandelier.

"Oh!" Santiago's eyes were saucers.

We both cut our eyes up and down the hall, and seeing no one, I shrugged. Santiago shrugged. Whatever I'd just rolled up in the dirty sheets was now Coast Laundry Services' problem.

I had the small break room behind our supply room all to myself; everyone else had made their way to the employee smoking patio on the sixth floor.

I dialed the Casino Host's office extension. "Heidi Dupree, please." I studied my ravaged cuticles and listened for the door. I remembered that I forgot to look under beds all morning. No telling what I'd missed.

"Casino Marketing," a soft voice said. "This is Heidi."

She didn't sound like a safe cracker.

"Hello," I said. "I'm in housekeeping and one of the guests is complaining they didn't get a fruit basket."

"Who is this?"

"Housekeeping."

"We order the amenities," she said, soft voice gone. "Room service fills the orders. Call them." And she hung up on me.

* * *

"I need a hardware store, George." I dropped the day's treasures over the seat: two paperback books, a three-pack of disposable razors, and four Snickers bars, one smashed flat.

"No, you don't."

I reached over the seat, took the loot back, lowered the window, and tossed it to the traffic.

(No, I didn't).

"What makes you think you know what I need and what I don't?" I demanded.

"I just do. Because you can't get in those safes with a tool."

My jaw unhinged. How in the *world* did George know what I was doing?

"Those are S700 Protectaguards," he went on, "and you can't hack in. You've got to use the code or the electronic pass key. That's the only way. Whoever you're looking for has the code or the passkey."

"I'll tell you what, George. You take me to a hardware store and we'll talk about it some other time." This guy could get on my last nerve. More than that, he was just about to scare me.

"It's your money."

Soon enough he was backing into the loneliest parking space Center City Hardware offered.

"George," I whined, "come on. It's raining. It's raining *ice*. Let me off at the door."

He ripped into one of the candy bars. "If you're going to waste your time and mine, you can waste some of it walking."

I could reach up and smack the back of his head so easily.

"And don't get a jackhammer," he said through chocolate. "If you're going to get something, get a multi-tool, like a Gerber."

Gibberish. "What?"

He swallowed and caught my eye in the mirror. "You think you're going to break into the safe, right?"

I blinked.

"Don't think they're going to let you lug a power tool into a hotel room. Get a multi-tool, like a Swiss Army knife, that you can slip in your pocket. But it won't work. All you're going to do is tear the thing up."

I had one angry foot out in the rain, and I quickly pulled it back in. "How do you know that, George? How do you know *any* of this?"

He shrugged one shoulder.

I got out, slammed the door as hard as I could, and ran through the biting rain.

* * *

Twenty minutes later, we pulled up to the entrance of the Silver Moon Resort and Casino, a shrunken Bellissimo, and the only other show in town that bragged on their website about the foolproof S700 Protectaguards. A bellman craned his neck our way. George waved him off, because *he* didn't need any help with *his* bags. "Are you going to get out or are you going to sit in my car all night?"

My new goal in life was to slam the car door so hard that it fell off. Of course, if I were successful, it would probably land on me.

The bed begged me to get in, the thick white comforter screaming, "I'm soft! And I smell good!" and I complied, for two dreamless hours I don't remember a second of. The rest of the time I tried to break into the S700 Protectaguard safe with no luck whatsoever. None of the ninety-three tools that jutted out from the eight-pound thing I'd purchased at the hardware store, including the two-tine fork, fazed the safe. The only thing I managed to do was scratch the hell out of it and ruin most of the appendages on the tool.

"So?" George asked the next morning.

"I'm late, George. Get going."

The next night, I dialed the hotel operator after an hour-long blistering shower. "My safe won't open." She transferred me to the security office.

"Have you forgotten your code?" a man asked.

"No," I lied. "It just won't open. It's stuck."

"What's in it? You might have jammed the door."

At which point my mind began racing. The safe was empty. I had a little more than forty dollars in cash, which wouldn't impress them much.

"We'll be there in ten minutes," he said.

I looked across the room to my purse. My wedding rings were somewhere in the bottom keeping company with lint, year-old peppermints, and loose change.

EIGHT

There's a framed photograph of my first birthday celebration at my parents' house, on the shelf of a bookcase in the upstairs hallway, right outside of Meredith's old room. In it, I'm barely balanced on roly-poly legs in the middle of the dining room table at ground zero of a cake and frosting explosion. It looked like fun, and I wish I could climb on a table and eat birthday cake with both hands again, although I wouldn't smear it in my hair this time. On one side of me are my parents, my father beaming, my mother glazed over. On the other side is my mother's childhood friend, Bea Crawford, her eighteen-month old son Eddie in her lap. So I never actually met Eddie, he just always was. Eventually he became, out of small-town boredom, my boyfriend, and I was sort of dating him when it was announced I was pregnant (again, out of small-town boredom) at the ripe old age of sixteen. It was my mother, the keeper of the inventory of feminine hygiene products, who broke the news to our family at breakfast one morning, and none too gently. I was as stunned and slack-jawed as my father and sister were. In retort, I threw up everywhere, providing my mother with the proof she sought.

"See?" my mother demanded.

No one wanted to see.

"I knew it," she spat.

My mother was thrilled at this new development—her being the goose to my gander—insisting all our lives that her four years of higher education were a complete waste of time and money (cutting her eyes at me) and Meredith and I might as well skip it and go straight to the real deal: dirty diapers, pot roasts, and ironing boards.

Mother wasted no time telling Eddie's parents, turning their breakfast into a celebration. His dad probably wrestled him into a bear hug and gave him noogies. "Way to go, son!" Mel and Bea Crawford were beside themselves with glee, because we were as close to royalty as it got in Pine Apple. They envisioned a future of no parking tickets, the end of those annoying restaurant report card failures, and they probably thought sharing a grandchild with the Chief of Police/Mayor of Pine Apple would make them exempt from federal taxes, too.

Why, after all these years and heartache for everyone involved, I still lugged around my wedding rings was anyone's guess. They weren't worth hocking should I need the cash, the combined weight of the diamond chips maybe totaling an eighth of a carat. They had no history; it's not like they were Crawford Estate jewels retrieved from a vault hidden behind an oily portrait of great granddaddy. They weren't even pretty; they had been on clearance at Sears, the rock of the Westside Mall in Montgomery.

There were two reasons I kept them handy: they reminded me of what could happen if you lived a big, fat lie, and they were proof that no matter how hard you tried, some points weren't worth making. There was a distant third reason; I secretly longed for the opportunity to give them back to Eddie in a fashion that would require subsequent surgical removal from his person. With long, pointy tongs. And no anesthesia.

They sounded like two pennies going into the safe as the knock came on the door.

"Security," I heard.

I closed the safe door, pressed in the code I'd assigned the night before, pushed the star button to lock it, tied my robe tighter, and let the crew in.

Same drill as the Bellissimo: to get into the room safe of an occupied guest room, it took one housekeeping supervisor pass-card swipe, one security pass-card swipe, and two other employee witnesses, one from housekeeping, the other from security. Everyone, including me, had to sign on the dotted line before and after.

They all peered at the pathetic wedding rings. They all turned to me.

Really?

I smiled.

* * *

I had Natalie Middleton's blessing to stay at the Silver Moon as long as I was working. So I could justify the two glorious nights, but I couldn't justify a third on Bellissimo's dime because I now knew there was no entering the safe without an authorized break-in crew, two passkeys, the code, an act of Congress, or a bulldozer. Did I give George the satisfaction of hearing those words pass these lips? No, I did not. But I didn't have to; I'm sure he figured it out when I pushed through the doors the next morning with all my earthly belongings in tow. It was Thursday. I'd been on this assignment for two and a half weeks, and I suppose I was headed back to the EconoLodge after my shift today. The Silver Moon rooms were three-hundred dollars a night and I didn't have that kind of extra loot lying around. The best I could hope for was that the porn stars next door had moved on.

The shift started, like every other shift, with Maria, our supervisor, complaining Spanish-style about the shoddy job we'd all done the day before. It was a total waste of time, the purpose of which was to give Maria's pets time to drag into work. The second they staggered through the door Maria announced, "Dat all. Geet to de work." I sat through the ten-minute pep talk every morning wondering how Maria managed to maintain her perfect manicure. Her fingernails were blood red, out to there, and her index fingers had geometrical designs in white. At the end of today's lecture, I gave Maria a big hug when she passed me a clipboard full of room assignments. She pulled away from me and looked at me as if I'd lost my mind. I pulled away from her with a passkey to every room on the floor.

At eleven that morning, six guest rooms spicked and spanned, Santiago knuckled the door frame of the room I was cleaning, lucky number seven, and in his heavy accent called, "Anna? Anna?"

I rose to my knees. I'd been between the queen-sized beds spot cleaning red wine off the carpet. At least I hoped it was red wine. "Do you need me, Santiago?"

He blabbered in his native tongue. I didn't catch a word of it. Then Miss Heidi Dupree's lovely frame stepped into the open doorway beside Santiago's. In her arms she held a basket. I could see the top half of two dark bottles of wine pointed in opposite directions.

"I need in a guest room," she said. "And this guy can't hear a word I'm saying."

"He hears you." I stood, smoothing my uniform. "He doesn't speak fluent English."

"Then he shouldn't work here." She shifted the weight of the basket to her hip. "I'm in a hurry. Come open this door for me."

Protocol was crystal clear: never let anyone in a guest room for any reason, that's the supervisor's call. I'm sure, though, somewhere in small print, it says that temporary residents of the Econo-Lodge wearing hot, itchy wigs were exempt.

"Which room?" I asked.

She took off.

I followed.

"Here you go." I used the passkey I'd stolen from Maria to open the door of room nineteen-twenty-two. She and her basket breezed by me, then spun.

"I've got it from here."

I smiled and stepped back an inch.

"Really." Miss Dupree was becoming impatient with me. "I'll only be a minute." Then the bitch slammed the door in my face.

I sprang into action, using Maria's key again, to slip into the room directly across the hall where I could watch from the peephole. I wish I had knocked first.

"Nelson?" A wild-haired woman sat straight up in the bed, saw me, and screamed out a lung. "*Who are you*?" The part of her I could see was completely naked. She grabbed for the covers. "Get *out*! Get *out* of my room!" She flailed an arm at the door, showing me the way.

"Oh!" I screamed. "Pardon! Pardon!" I used my best Tex-Mex accent. "Excuse! Excuse!"

Heidi Dupree and I spilled into the hallway on the same click of the second hand, and she looked at me as if I were crazy, which, at the moment, I was. I fell against the wall to catch my breath and Heidi Dupree took off in a hurry, but only after throwing me a parting glare. She had one hand balled into a fist, like she was holding something. As soon as she turned the corner to the elevator, I took off after her, my orthopedic shoes falling like bricks on the carpet. I slowed and waited until the elevator doors opened, then closed, peeked around the corner and saw a wad of wet tissue, still grooved from her grip, in the ashtray between the elevator doors that I'd just cleaned and stamped a perfect script "B" for Bellissimo into not an hour earlier. I really didn't like this girl.

I ran back down the hall and stopped outside of naked wild-haired woman's room. If she was on the phone tattling on me, I'd probably be able to hear her muffled outrage, and if that were the case, I planned on hiding. I couldn't hear a thing over my accelerated heartbeat from all the running; hopefully naked woman had gone back to sleep. I counted to twenty, then pulled a new set of latex cleaning gloves from my pocket, tugged them on, and used Maria's key again to enter the room Heidi Dupree had done her business in.

The gift basket containing the wine was on a table in front of the Gulf-view window. A card was tented in front of the basket.

Congratulations! Present this for a Couple's Massage at four o'clock this afternoon at the Bellissimo spa as our honored guests.

It was signed Mark Fredrickson, a name I recognized from the Casino Host roster. I walked to the closet. Pulling the doors open, I was greeted by the unmistakable tang of hair spray.

* * *

From the housekeeping break room, which I had all to myself, I called Natalie. "I need a quiet place, a computer, and street clothes."

"For how long?"

"At least a few hours."

"Give me ten," she said.

Hours? This thing would be said and done in ten hours.

"And I'll need computer clearance again for restricted files, Natalie." I could almost *hear* her raising one perfect eyebrow.

"Which ones?" she asked. "Internal or client?"

"Both."

I tracked down Maria, fifteen tissues to my face, blowing my nose with gusto.

She put all ten of her red fingernails straight out, hands splayed. "Stay over," she warned me. She eyed me, up and down. "I take guess. You feel no good?" She blinked a hundred times.

I coughed for her.

"Aye, aye, aye." She shooed me away.

Natalie set me up in an unoccupied guest room on the fourth floor, which was—I hate to complain—not as spiffy as the rest of the place. The higher up you go in this building, the better the facilities, all the way to the top floor, which was rumored to be one massive breathtaking suite fit for Elvis. Hotel floors four, five, and six were the junket floors, where busload after busload of retirees were temporarily housed. Don't get me wrong, these rooms beat the Econo-Lodge's rooms to death. And I was happy, happy, happy to be in one without a cleaning cart.

A chocolate brown Nike warm-up suit in a clingy knit blend, strappy tank in the trim color, a bright teal, and Airs with a bright teal stripe were on one of the beds. Dropping my ponytail wig to the floor, I got out of my housekeeping uniform and into my tennis star outfit as quickly as I possibly could, shaking my hair out, loving Natalie.

A laptop computer was on the desk. I fired it up. I would watch my steps while romping through Bellissimo's cyber world, just in case someone was following me. I didn't really need to know hot, hot, hot Richard Sander's exact age, or see his Las Vegas wife's photo. There is a time and place for everything. This wasn't it.

The registered guest in room nineteen twenty-two was Robert Edding, and I supposed his wife Gracie was with him, because the hair-sprayed closet had several womens' blouses hanging in it. The Eddings were from Corpus Christi, Texas, and the computer told me that they'd visited four times the previous year, staying three nights each time. I pulled up Robert Edding's play history. He was a slot player, and his casino activity rated him a five, meaning, after a ton of calculating on the casino's part, he could be counted on to leave five thousand dollars here, more or less, each visit. In the big picture, that made him a decent, steady player. Put him in the company of a hundred thousand others who came four times a year and dropped five thou each and you've got yourself a nice bottom line. And fives were the least of it; the Eddings were small potatoes here.

However, Robert Edding found himself at the right place at the right time this morning. His electronic portfolio showed him charging two buffet breakfasts plus a six-dollar tip to his room at nine thirty-eight, and at ten fifteen, hitting a slot jackpot of $22,500 on machine 238007. Woo-hoo! Way to go, Robert!

And that's how Miss Dupree knew there'd be something in the safe. And she knew when they'd be out of the room, too, because she'd booked the spa herself.

Two questions remained: who was her partner and how was he getting into the safe? A third question loomed. If I ordered a room-service lunch, would Natalie have a cow?

* * *

I held my fake Louis Vuitton hobo wide open over the bed, flipped it, and set the vast collection free. I gave it a good shake to dislodge the stuck-on stuff and twice as much fell out. Goodness gracious. I waved through the toxic cloud and vowed to clean out my purse more than once a year. I needed the three cell phones, my three pounds of keys, and should probably keep the seventeen or so paperclips, but as far as I could see, everything else could go. I found a ten-dollar bill in the mix, freed a penlight from my keychain, and pushed the rest of it into a small mound for later.

Downstairs, hugging the walls, with my head down, I ducked into the gift shop, the twenty-four hour variety that sold beef jerky, contact lens solution, and K-Y His-and-Hers. I stood in line to purchase an ounce and a half of hairspray for five dollars, and a miniature plastic container of baby powder for the outrageous price of four dollars. There wasn't a baby butt out there that needed to smell *that* fresh; save your money and just put the kid in the tub. I thought of my sister Meredith, after Riley was born, telling me that until I had a child of my own, my nuggets of parenting wisdom weren't welcome.

Back in my room on the fourth floor, the first thing I did was remove a pillowcase from one of the bed pillows. And you know what? Not the same thread count as the higher floors. I pulled open the closet doors. The florescent interior light came on automatically. Guess what? These were half the size of the upstairs closets.

Next I stepped into the bathroom and pulled a handful of tissues from the box on the vanity. I passed them under a slow stream of water, then swiped back and forth across the keypad of the wall safe. I blew the keypad dry, then gave it two good squirts of hairspray, put the pillowcase over my head, and plopped down on the floor to wait. I hummed to pass the time. After two stanzas of *We Wish You a Merry Christmas*, I stood, felt around, and found the edges of the safe. I stabbed in the general direction of the keypad quickly, four times, before I could seriously orient myself to the ten-digit keypad, and even so, I'm pretty sure I pushed one, three, seven, and nine. I yanked the pillowcase off my head, dug the flashlight out of my pocket, and pointed it directly on the keypad.

Nothing.

I angled the beam. More nothing.

I squeezed a perfect circle-dot pattern of the baby powder into the palm of my hand, then blew it onto the keypad like fairy dust. While it clung, sort of, I still couldn't see anything noteworthy, even with the flashlight. I stepped in, pulled the doors closed to eliminate the overhead light, and tried the flashlight again.

Bingo.

In the ambient darkness, the thin illumination revealed three smudges in the light powder film: numbers four, five, and six. Wait a sec. I'd pushed four buttons.

The World Wide Web told me that there were twenty four possible combinations of four different digits, but because I like to make things as hard on myself as humanly possible, I'd pushed one of the numbers twice, which bumped the possible combinations up to thirty six. Even so, a ten-year old could sit down with a pen and paper and come up with the thirty six possibilities in a flash. Me being far past ten, it took almost fifteen minutes. And another twelve minutes testing them. I hit pay dirt about halfway down the list: five, six, four, five sprung the safe open. On my sixth go-around, I popped it in less than four minutes, probably because I skipped the pillowcase part and just squeezed my eyes shut until I could see dancing dots. By now it was almost three o'clock and I was choking on hair spray and baby powder.

Show time.

With a weary sigh, I dug through my cell-phone collection for the Mac Daddy. It was time to do what I'd managed to avoid for a month: Make direct contact with No Hair and Teeth.

* * *

The grainy overhead-perspective surveillance video of the previous four room thefts had masked how young Heidi's partner in crime was. When I finally got a good look at him, he appeared to be late 20s, early 30s, and my best guess was that Heidi was both splitting the take and spending quality naked time with the guy. They would miss each other when they went to prison for ten to twenty.

It was four-fifteen. We'd taken our places as Robert and Gracie Edding checked into the spa.

I was in the closet, mostly in the dark, wedged into the opposite corner from the safe behind two hanging Bellissimo robes and Mrs. Edding's blouses. The top of my head just cleared the hanging bar. I watched the live feed coming from the hall on a three-inch handheld. My breath was coming at a slow, steady pace, with adrenaline pumping through me that was more about never seeing the EconoLodge again than anything else. I'd been in tight positions many times through the years, with opponents far more armed and dangerous than this guy. Speaking of armed, I was packing again. Pepper spray and handcuffs, but, hey, you gotta start somewhere.

The teeny camera feeding me video was tucked between potted hydrangeas on a flower cart driven by—this is hilarious—No Hair. Teeth was waiting downstairs outside of Heidi Dupree's office so he could give her the good news. We met at Natalie's place a half hour ago, and the two men flipped a coin for the jobs. No Hair, sporting a tie with a sleeping Garfield the Cat on it, lost.

"Two out of three," he said.

"No way, man. We don't have time for that." Teeth took his win and ran with it.

Natalie drummed her fingers on her desk impatiently. "It doesn't matter. Get going, one of you."

"I can't get in a *closet*," No Hair, a.k.a. Jeremy Coven, said it to Teeth, a.k.a. Paul Bergman, as if he'd suggested he ride a tricycle through the casino. "Are you out of your mind?"

I'd only seen these guys in I'd-like-to-rip-your-head-off mode, and it was nice to know they were, indeed, humans, as opposed to straight-up killing machines. They were each the size, shape, and weight of refrigerators, and having spent half of the afternoon inside a closet, I agreed: No way No Hair could hide in the closet, even the ones upstairs that would hold a twin-size bed. Not that Teeth could.

"Clearly—" They turned to me like *who are you again*? "Neither one of you is going in the closet. I'll do the closet. You wait outside the room in the hall."

No Hair said, "No offense, little lady, but you couldn't take down a bunny rabbit."

"You'll be right behind her, man," Teeth said.

"I can do my job, thank you," I assured them.

"What am I supposed to do in the hall?" No Hair demanded. "You think the guy will blow me a kiss then go load up the cash?"

He had a point. These two could clear a church of nuns; a thief would most certainly tuck and run.

Natalie reached for her phone. "This is Natalie Middleton from Mr. Sanders' office. I need a room service uniform in size..." she looked up at No Hair. He let his meaty cheeks fill with air, then let it out slowly. If I'd been wearing a hat, I'd have been chasing it.

"Fifty-two." We barely heard him.

"What?" Teeth asked on a laugh. "Fifty-*what*?"

"Shut up."

"Well, what about housekeeping?" Nattie asked. "Do you have a fifty-two in a housekeeping uniform?" We all waited. "Send it up," she said. No Hair threw his hands in the air. Natalie dialed another number. "I need a horticulture cart," she said. "I don't care. Whatever you have. And right now."

So No Hair, in a forest green jumpsuit, was pushing a cart full of pretty potted flowers when our mark strolled down the hall in one of his previous disguises, the spa robe and slippers. On the tiny screen it looked like he was running, so No Hair must have had the cart on the move, going about his blossom business in the opposite direction. And just in case I was in the closet doing my nails and eating bon-bons, No Hair's voice boomed through my earpiece, "Coming your way."

"Right," I said, just as I was attacked by serious vertigo. No Hair must have swung the cart around, and sure enough, there was our mark's backside.

"I forgot my inhaler," he pleaded to the second-shift supervisor, who I hadn't had the pleasure of meeting and who, incidentally, spoke perfect English. "And my wife has our room key," he added.

"I need some identification, Mr. Edding."

He showed off his spa wear. "I don't have any! It's in the spa locker." He looked down the long hall. "Do I need to go get it?" Right about then, he sucked in a huge gulp of air. "I need in," he squeaked, pointing at the door.

"Okay, hold on, hold on. Let me make a call."

I measured him against the door and got a feel for how much space he would take up in the closet, choosing the spot and angle he'd most likely work from based on his size. No Hair and I continued to eavesdrop as the housekeeping supervisor called the spa. She asked if there were a Mr. Edding checked in. "And what's his room number?" She said thank you and snapped the phone closed. She whipped out her passkey and granted him entry. "Have a nice day, Mr. Edding. Hope you get to feeling better."

I drew a huge breath when I heard, and felt up and down my spine, the door to the room close. I switched the handheld off and dropped it into the pocket of a robe.

His padded footsteps grew closer, then the closet doors burst open. He didn't pat around behind the robes for anyone hiding. First hurdle jumped. Almost immediately he pulled the doors closed behind him, plunging us into total darkness. He clicked a flashlight on; I could see the glow. The whole time he made a quick and quiet clucking noise with his tongue.

It took the guy four hours to get the safe open; you'd think he'd never done this before. I listened to my heart beating in time to his clucking and talked myself out of screaming and running for what felt like forever, but turned out to be only a hair more than three minutes.

When he finally got it open, I took my shot straight to the back of his knees with a quick kick, both shocking the holy stew out of him and sending him flying out of the doors and down to his knees. The bright lights popped on, and I let him get half of his bearings before I knocked his legs out from beneath him. He went down in an angry, fighting pile.

"Come on!" I screamed into my piece, and heard my own echo.

No Hair was right beside me. He planted a foot in the guy's back, surely rearranging his vertebrae, and sending his curses and cries straight into the carpet. No Hair bent to calf rope the guy, and as he did, a tearing noise ripped through the air. The seams of No Hair's flower-boy jumpsuit gave completely away, and it fell off him in shreds, like a monster green banana being peeled.

The worst of the entire assignment, EconoLodge included, was finding out that No Hair actually had a lot of hair.

* * *

Heidi Dupree and her brother, Mike, via separate service elevators, were thrown in an interrogation room together ten minutes later. Teeth and I watched through a two-way; I was still panting. Heidi Dupree took one look at her brother, then went for the garbage can, sticking her whole head in it—a nearly foolproof admission of guilt.

"Where's Jeremy?" Teeth asked me.

"Putting some clothes on." Thank goodness. Speaking of clothes, Teeth was dressed, top to bottom, in a dark camel color, including accessories: belt, tie, socks and shoes. As much as I hated to admit it, it was a snappy look.

No one else at the Bellissimo had a clue as to what had gone down, and the Edding's room had already been put back together; they would never know what almost happened. We still had the red tape to deal with, but overall it was a quick and quiet takedown.

All of a sudden, though, it was anything but quiet. The Dupree siblings were trying to kill each other.

"I'd better get in there," Teeth said.

"Wait a sec," I held up a finger. "Wait and see what they say to each other."

"Why? We've already got them."

I turned to Teeth. "Do you really think they could have pulled this off alone?" I asked. "Look at them."

Heidi had launched herself onto her brother's back, beating him about the head, and he was riding her around the room trying to sling her off. The metal table was on its side, four metal chairs were on everything but their legs, and, gross, the garbage can was upside down. The soundtrack was deafening, the language atrocious.

Teeth pushed an intercom button. "You two settle down."

The Duprees froze and both looked up as if God had fussed at them, then went right back at it.

"Neither of them is the mastermind," I told Teeth. "There's no way they pulled this off themselves."

He looked at me a long minute. He had huge pores. "We've done this job for years without you." He hiked his pants up. "We've got our guys." With a nod in the Dupree's direction, he said, "I'm getting in there. You can sit this one out."

Almost immediately, Richard Sanders stepped in and replaced Teeth. He took a look at the Duprees. "Those two are going to kill each other!" As Mr. Sanders spoke, the room filled with the spicy scent of cinnamon. I fanned my face a little.

We both recoiled as Teeth accidentally took one on the chin that was meant for the brother, at which point, he'd had enough, and the family feud ended as Teeth promised them both they'd be leaving on stretchers if either of them moved another muscle or opened their mouths without permission. He could have put it this way: "Either of you move and I'll bite you." That'd have done it.

Mr. Sanders turned to me. "Great job, Davis."

I said thanks, and then gave all the credit away.

"That's very gracious of you, but I've worked with these guys for years, and they couldn't have done it without you."

I was too tired to explain to Mr. Sanders that it wasn't that I was particularly good at this so much as I was, at times, particularly lucky. And luck, as everyone here knows, eventually runs out.

"How do you screen potential employees for this type thing?" I asked the boss.

"There's no way to." He shifted his weight. "You see, Davis, the thing is, I have a small percentage of honest employees, and I have an equally small percentage of dishonest employees."

"And the rest?"

"Are just like these two." He tapped a knuckle on the glass that separated us from the siblings. "They're the middle ground," he said. "They could go either way. And if a situation like this isn't handled with discretion," he paused, "and becomes a hot topic in the employee cafeteria, five hundred in the iffy group would figure out a way to do it bigger and better."

His words hung in the cinnamon air, and it felt like there was something he wasn't saying. I looked up.

"You're my discretion, Davis."

He put so much emphasis on the words that a goose walked over my grave. This man was putting too much faith in me, because I wasn't exactly an expert in discretion. I had no idea what to say, and decided to let the moment pass without blubbering. When I'm tired, I say too much. So I summoned the most serious look of acknowledgement I could, then turned to watch the rest of the show.

Heidi and Mike Dupree were spilling their guts, confessing everything from stealing Double Bubble from the corner store to peeking at Christmas gifts, repeatedly incriminating each other for both the ancient and current crimes. Heidi was sobbing, her brother was staring at the wall, his chest rising and falling rapidly, and again, I felt certain that these two weren't alone in this.

Out of the corner of my eye, I watched Mr. Sanders sneak a peek at his watch.

"I've got this from here, Mr. Sanders."

"Are you sure?" he asked.

"Positive."

"I could use some sleep."

"Go ahead. I'll stay with them until they're booked."

He stuck his hands in his pockets and began backing toward the door. "If you're sure."

"I'm sure." I tried to smile. Not sure how it came out.

He gave me a smile and a wave, then I collapsed into a chair.

The sun rose and ushered in Friday before No Hair and Teeth finished up with the Duprees and called Metro to come get them, and not once in all that time did Teeth begin to ask if there'd been anyone else involved. He didn't even hint at it.

I tied up the loose ends with Natalie ("Davis! You need some coffee!"), then fell into the backseat of George's cab. I hadn't slept in more than thirty hours. He'd actually shown some concern for me, so I jumped all over that.

"Where to?"

My head was back, my eyes were closed, and I pointed in the direction of the EconoLodge.

"Staying there?"

I pointed to Alabama.

Three blocks later, he stopped for a red light. "What in the world is the matter with you?"

"I was up all night."

"Well, you look like something the cat dragged in."

"Thanks a lot, George."

"You don't need to be driving to Alabama."

And here, I took my shot. "I can make it today, George, but I really need your help on Monday."

"I wasn't volunteering to drive you to Alabama."

I used my last drops of energy to roll my eyes. "I need your help on Monday, George, not right this minute."

I asked him to drive me all over Biloxi looking for apartments.

"Why?" he asked.

"Why?" We were staring at the EconoLodge. "*Why*, George?"

He hemmed. He hawed. He threw in the towel.

"I'll meet you at the regular place on Monday?"

He waved me off, which was George's whatever, anything to shut you up, just get out of my car.

"See you then?" I had a weary leg out the door, the teeniest bit energized by knowing I'd never be back at the EconoLodge again. "About noon?"

He waved again.

I dragged myself the rest of the way out of the car, and was pointed toward my own car when George cracked his window.

"Good job."

I barely heard him. "*What?*"

"I said good bust."

I stood there, staring straight ahead, feeling George's eyes on my back. There was almost no way for him to know what had happened. No way at all. No police chatter, no Bellissimo Security breach, he'd have to have been a fly on the wall.

"By the way," George said, "their mother's a blackjack dealer."

I spun. "*What?*"

"Different last name. Kempler. Lorraine Kempler."

He had his hand on the gear shift, about to drive off.

"Wait! Wait! George!" Somehow my legs managed to close the space between us. I took a peek at his radio scanner. (Off. But probably warm.)

He stared straight ahead.

"What the hell is going on, George?"

Finally, he turned his head. There were the eyes, the thousand-year old eyes, the eyes that had seen Evil.

From the EconoLodge parking lot, George's taillights long gone, I located the Bat phone and chose the first big guy on the list, hoping it was Teeth. I pushed Go.

"What?"

It sounded like Teeth. "A blackjack dealer named Lorraine Kempler needs to be picked up on the room-safe thefts. She's the mother of the two we just turned over to Metro."

"Who told you that?"

I hung up. Jerk.

NINE

After an equally glorious and nightmarish weekend—which is to say after time spent with one's immediate family—I saw my twin. They say everyone has a twin, but I always thought it meant someone on the other side of the world. Like Iowa. I found mine in Biloxi, practically my own backyard. She was me, plus a billion dollars.

Natalie put me on the road after the Duprees were behind bars with the only clue to my next assignment being nose into a marriage. (Marriage, my specialty. I couldn't wait.)

"And let's look at Wednesday morning, okay, Davis?"

"Sure."

"Take a long weekend. You deserve it."

I hadn't had any decent sleep in so long, I'd've agreed to take off until May.

"Also, Davis," Nattie pushed a set of keys and a brochure across her desk, "I want you in the executive apartments for your next assignment. I'm sure you're tired of living out of a suitcase."

Dammit. I loved the Bellissimo.

She caught my look. "Don't worry," she laughed. "I can assure you that you'll be back in the hotel soon enough. For now though," she said, "we'll do the apartment. I'll have it set up for you by Tuesday afternoon, and I'll see you on Wednesday."

"See you then, Natalie."

But at the strike of noon on Monday, not Wednesday, I parked the Bug in the parking garage for casino patrons, then hiked the mile to George. I had zero intention of spending my nonworking hours under Bellissimo surveillance if I could help it, and now that I had my own paycheck, I came back early to find my own apartment.

I was weaving in and out of the landscaping, taking the exterior shortcut to the VIP entrance when my twin exited the building through the gold doors.

I was fifty feet away, between Southern oaks wearing thick capes of Spanish moss, about to step onto the sidewalk, when I heard someone say *Mrs. Sanders.*

My head snapped up and my feet quit working.

This was Bianca Casimiro Sanders? I caught my breath, my mouth hung wide open, my heart stopped beating, and I couldn't have looked away if the trees I stood between had burst into infernos. I almost passed out. There was no doubt in my mind we'd been poured from the same mold. We were double whammies. She was me on my forty-sixth interview for this job: the blonde wig, the green contacts. I remembered Natalie taking all those pictures. I remembered Mr. Sanders looking at them when he interviewed me. They *knew* we looked alike!

I didn't sit down so much as fall down on the hard cold ground. I'm pretty sure I still hadn't taken a breath.

The thing about her husband, Richard Sanders, is that he was so perfectly accidental, as if no part of what made him tick was an effort. His wife Bianca Casimiro Sanders, the woman in front of me, was the opposite. Her jaw, a perfect replica of mine, was set in stone. Her entourage, a black-suited human cocoon, gave her two feet all the way around and looked straight ahead or at the ground, not at her.

And get this: to compensate for her stature, which was within a whisper of my own, she was wearing what had to be eight-inch heels. Stilettos peeked out from under the pelts of several hundred small animals sacrificed, I bet, just for her. Her blonde twist-up do was pulled back so severely it made *my* temples hurt.

The ocean quieted, the air stood still, and traffic at the VIP entrance, creature and otherwise, came to a dead standstill as her team escorted her to a black stretch limo. A Louis Vuitton trunk was carefully loaded into the back, accompanied by several matching bags.

Mrs. Sanders was on the move, and so, apparently, was my driver.

Of all things, George, who I would swear hadn't gone anywhere the entire month of January except when I begged him to, took off after the limo. All kinds of questions raced through my mind. Was George some sort of covert tail on the boss's wife? Was *she* the reason he parked three blocks away from everything? Another huge question: How in hell was I supposed to go apartment hunting without my driver? I can barely navigate the four roads in Pine Apple after having trod them my entire life. If left on my own here, I'd wind up in Texas by the end of the day.

I was having trouble processing it all, so I stayed on the cold hard ground watching the entourage pull out, including my ride, waiting for my heart rate to return to normal, all the while contemplating the largest curiosity of them all: was I a stunt double (whammy!) for the boss's wife?

"Davis."

I screamed.

Natalie's voice was cool. "I thought we said Wednesday."

I stammered a few syllables that came out, "Ya, ya, daaa."

"Get your things," she said. "Come with me."

* * *

"Do whatever you want, Davis."

Natalie wasn't very happy with me.

"But don't ask for a housing allowance."

She poured herself a cup of coffee. She didn't offer me one.

"It's not that I don't appreciate the executive-apartment offer, Natalie," I lied, "it's that, you know," I stumbled around, "the ocean and all. I'd like to be closer in." And have a little privacy, I didn't say.

"It's February, Davis. Not exactly ocean weather, and we call it the Gulf. Not the 'ocean.'"

We had a little stare off, the stiff-smile variety.

"If I were you," she said, "I'd think carefully before signing a lease."

Funny she hadn't had any advice for me when she'd given me three seconds to sign the encyclopedia she called an employment agreement. "I'll keep that in mind, Natalie. Thanks."

"Do that." She drummed her fingers on her desk with one hand and reached for her coffee with the other. "As long as you're here," she said, "you might as well get to work." She pulled a file from somewhere behind her desk, opened it, and a photograph of a man appeared. "The husband, Hank, is a slot tech."

She seemed rattled, jumpy, not her usual perky self, and that was in addition to being irritated at me. I think she hadn't wanted me to know just yet that I was a dead ringer for the boss's wife.

"What's a slot tech?"

"Technician. He repairs and maintains slot machines."

"And the wife?" I asked.

"She's a casino host. Beth Dunn. She was here first. He came onboard five or six months later. They were married a year after that. And now we're six years down the road."

"What's the problem?"

Nattie reached up and pushed hair out of her eyes. "Her clients win too much money."

"How much?"

"A better way to put it might be that an unusually high percentage of her clients don't ever lose."

"Gotcha," I said. "What else do you already know?"

"Well, just like with the room safes, we looked into it. We assigned surveillance to the Dunns, but that's tricky. When we shadow one of our own, they figure it out or the guy next to them does, which gives them time to stop whatever they're doing and cover their tracks on anything they've already done. We wasted a hundred security hours on the Dunns and came up with nothing. So we put our internal auditors to work on it, and they came back agreeing that a high percentage of her clients had unusually profitable play, but nothing jumped out at them." Natalie shrugged. "So let's get you in there, Davis. Let's see what you can dig up."

This could go one of several ways. I sure hoped it didn't go the slot technician way. I could barely change a light bulb.

Reading my mind, Nattie said, "Our plan was to register you as one of Beth's players, but with Heidi Dupree's exit, there's a seat to fill at her elbow."

I nodded along with it all, catching every tenth word: auditors, technicians, elbows.

"I'll get the paperwork run through HR," she said, "and you be here at seven-thirty *Wednesday* morning." She shot me a look. I crawled under the chair.

"Any ideas about where you're going to set up camp?" she asked.

"I'll get a newspaper and figure something out." I tucked the two files into my gigantic tote bag and stood.

"Let me know where you'll be and I'll have some things delivered."

The most promising thing I'd heard all morning. "Oh, hey, Natalie." I turned at the door.

She looked up.

"What's the deal with Mrs. Sanders?"

One of her eyebrows rose. "What do you mean?"

"What do you mean, what do I mean? Isn't it obvious?"

The other eyebrow rose. "I'll see you Wednesday morning, Davis."

I stumbled out mentally checking box four (times this job has sent me reeling) and calculating my debt against my paycheck (still the largest reel).

I couldn't quit just yet.

* * *

I had to have somewhere to sleep. And now I knew I looked just like the boss's wife, I needed something furnished, because I had no intention of sticking around long enough to find out why. There were exactly three classified ads for furnished rentals: one had to be the EconoLodge, the word kitchenette was in there, another must have been a penthouse with twelve bedrooms and four butlers, and there was one in the middle, a one-bedroom terrace condo, Gulf view, available for a six-month sublease at a reasonable price. Perfect.

Pushing my laptop aside, waving the waitress and her carafe of blistered coffee away, I flipped open my cell phone and dialed the number.

After three rings, a female answered. "Grand Palace Casino. Mr. Cole's office."

Of course, it would be a casino. This city was Little Vegas. "I'm calling about the condo," I said.

Turns out, Bradley Cole was the lead of three in-house attorneys at Grand Palace.

"Wow," I was duly impressed. "Very cool."

"It's really pretty dry stuff, Miss Way," the secretary explained. "About once a week, someone walks in, pulls a banana peel out of their pocket, then hits us with a slip and fall lawsuit. Otherwise, it's just contracts."

"Who would ever put a banana peel in their *pocket*?" I asked.

"We're in the middle of one right now," she said, "in which a patron claims he was poisoned by the landscaping."

"How so?"

"He ate a bunch of trumpet lilies out front and they made him sick."

"Well, duh."

Like the Bellissimo, the Grand Palace's parent company was in Las Vegas, and Mr. Cole, according to Chatty Cathy, was there, negotiating something or another, and the lease on the condo was a one-shot deal for six months only. Exactly what I was looking for.

The casino was easy enough to find (curses on you, George), because it was on the same strip as the Bellissimo, only several miles east and tucked back off the road. A nice place, the Palace: low-key, very little neon, no more than seven or eight stories high, but on almost as much property as the Bellissimo. Three hundred and eighty guest rooms to the Bellissimo's sixteen hundred. I'd call it a boutique gambling resort. It had an itty-bitty casino floor that catered to high-rolling table players, lots of dimly lit private gaming venues off that, and according to their website, not to mention the lobby that looked like a Pro Shop, had some major golf going on.

I followed Bradley Cole's secretary's assistant to the condo, so I didn't get lost. Her job must have been to safety-sample every morsel of food the kitchens prepared and log it for future food-poisoning claims—"It couldn't have made you sick. I ate three pounds of it and I was fine" —because she was one extra-large girl, about the size and shape of Teeth. If she hadn't had relatively small teeth, I'd swear they were siblings.

She eyed me. "You don't take up much space, do you?"

I showed her *my* teeth.

"I got a leg bigger than you."

One step into the quiet condo and I said, "I'll take it."

After writing a check for the first and last month's rent, I tore it off and passed it over, and with it, I added six months to my ninety days.

"Your name is Davis *Way*?" she looked up. "Like a *place*?"

I flashed my teeth again.

"And there's actually a city called Pine *Apple*?"

I should get married again, and quickly. Or at least change my address.

TEN

I married Eddie the first time because I was pregnant.

My mother, who was driving my life anyway, had the whole thing done in less than two weeks. The times I opened my mouth to protest, I either lost my nerve or my breakfast. I sloshed to the police station one day in monsoon rains to confess all to my daddy (who couldn't even look at me), but the note on the door—even his handwriting looked heartbroken—said he was out on a deer-in-the-Wilson's-kitchen-again call. The thought of which made me lose my lunch.

The problems with the program were too numerous to list. There aren't sixteen-year-olds anywhere, under any circumstances, who have any business being married, and Eddie and I topped that list, mostly because it wasn't his baby. I, of course, knew it. He, genius that he was, suspected it—and here's how stupid he is—because we'd never had sex. He was too busy enjoying all the attention to admit that all we'd done in his dumb truck was drink Bud Light and listen to Nine Inch Nails. And let's not forget that I really didn't *like* Eddie, on any level. I was only hanging out with him so that no one would suspect who I was really hanging out with.

I married Eddie at sixteen out of fear. I married him ten years later out of guilt, boredom, and pheromones. Double Whammy.

Luckily, the first time around, I had an almost clear-thinking brand-new adult in whom I could confide, whom I trusted, and who had a vested interest. The vested-interest part was because it was his baby.

Jason Wells, recent college graduate and the most exciting thing that ever happened at Pine Apple High School, taught me way more than History.

"You still haven't had sex with him?" Mr. Wells took a sick day ten days into my marriage and picked me up behind Mel and Bea Crawford's double-wide, my terrifying new home. "Isn't your plan to make him think it's his baby?"

"I can't have *sex* with him!" I cried. I sobbed. I wept. "He's a *freak*! I don't think I could have sex with him if someone held a *gun* to my head!" I was shrieking. "And I thought he *was* going to shoot me the other day because I used his stupid hair brush. And then I got *sick*!

"You're just nauseated because it's the first trimester, Davis."

"You're damn right I'm nauseated!"

With Mr. Wells' help, I ran away. ("Please stop calling me Mr. Wells, Davis.")

I didn't have to be emancipated from my parents, because that had effectively happened when my mother signed off on the marriage license. I didn't have to get a divorce; a mail-order annulment was all that was necessary, considering the marriage hadn't been consummated. I didn't have to scrape up the money to move into the Methodist Maternity Home in Birmingham, because Mr. Wells handled that. And I didn't have to meet the sweet couple from Tennessee who adopted the seven-pound six-ounce baby girl I delivered, but I wanted to. I wanted to see the people who would raise my child.

I cried. They cried. We all cried.

I was allowed an hour alone with the tiny creature who tore out of me, and I told her everything I knew. The other fifty-five minutes, I sang to her, wiping my tears off her tiny face.

Mr. Wells deposited five hundred dollars in a checking account for me. I was seventeen years old, five days postpartum, standing on the steps of the maternity home, hugging my very pregnant housemates goodbye. To my name I had a General Education Diploma, two sweatshirts, one pair of extremely tight jeans, the five hundred dollars, and a bunch of literature on birth control. As I started down the concrete steps, crying *again*, my daddy pulled up in his patrol car.

Finally, I found my voice. “How did you know, Daddy?”

“I got a very nice letter, Punkin.”

“From the nurses here?”

“No.”

“Why didn’t you call?”

He swallowed hard before he spoke. “You have to live with your decision for the rest of your life, Sweet Pea.” My daddy’s chin quivered. “I couldn’t interfere.”

“What about Mother?” I asked.

Daddy stared at the road ahead.

“We’re not going home, are we?”

Instead of answering, he took a right. Pine Apple, it would seem, would have been a wrong.

“Daddy,” I said, “tell me something about home. Anything.”

“The new teacher at the high school left.” He cut his eyes at me. “Transferred. I never heard where.”

We said goodbye at 1720 2nd Avenue South, where I got a degree in Criminal Justice from the University of Alabama in Birmingham. Dorm life was a shock, because no one there was pregnant. Thinking things had cooled off in Pine Apple, I made my way home, hoping to go straight to work with my daddy, but all I managed to do was stoke a sleeping fire. This town wasn’t big enough for me, my mother, and Bea Crawford. Within three weeks, I was back in Birmingham, back in school, and working toward a second degree in Computer and Information Science. Two more years passed, and I dropped my bags inside the door of the police station.

“I’m back, Daddy, and I’m not leaving. This is my home, too. Mother and the Crawfords are going to have to learn to live with it.”

Daddy was propped up against several huge boxes. “Can you help me set up this computer?”

* * *

I believe, deep down, my mother loves me. I do think she'd turn the garden hose on me if I were on fire, and just as far down, I love her. I wish my mother nothing but good health, prosperity, and happiness. But for whatever reasons—stretch marks, maybe?—she has always refused to cut me even the smallest amount of slack, and I didn't/wouldn't/can't stop pushing her buttons. (All my life: "Mother's going to *kill* you, Davis!" Me: "She'll get over it.") On the flip side, Mother and Meredith are like two peas in a pod. When Mother looks at me she sees a pitchfork and dancing flames, and when she looks at Mer, wings and a halo.

It was the way things were, until I moved back home and went to work for my father, at which point, they got worse. And worse. And worse. I was young; I was busy; I mostly avoided her. After my second divorce, though, there was no dodging her utter disapproval, and the situation became unbearable for everyone. When the war between us reached an ear-splitting crescendo, Meredith cornered me and, as our Granny Dee says, read me from the Good Book.

"You're killing Mother and Daddy, Davis."

"*What?* Meredith. You're so dramatic."

"No, Davis, listen to me."

She'd tracked me down—not hard to do in Pine Apple—at the coffee shop where I parked myself during the day so I could keep an eye on Daddy, on a Tuesday morning several months after I'd relinquished my badge. My niece Riley was having her way with a six-pack of mini powdered donuts and a tall glass of milk. After one donut, she looked like she'd been whitewashed.

"Our parents no longer speak to each other, Davis."

I sucked in some oxygen. I did feel a stab of guilt at the pitiful state of our parents' marriage, which wasn't marriagey at all; it was hostile-roommate standoff. The big gridlock was ME, of course—Daddy's "failure to allow me to suffer repercussions for any of my actions" and Mother's "lack of human compassion for her own child."

(Guess whose side I was on.) (Poor Meredith was on both sides.)

"Sunday," I said, "he asked her to pass the butter beans. They're making progress."

"What he said was, 'Caroline, do any of the rest of us get butter beans or are they all yours?' and then two seconds later, 'Powder Puff, Creamsickle, Apple Dumplin', Froot Loop, would you please pour Daddy two drops of tea?'" Meredith drummed her fingers on the cracked Formica that separated us. "That's not progress."

I dove under the cracked Formica.

(No, I didn't.)

"Davis," Meredith's voice softened and she reached out and hooked pinkie fingers with me. "Honey. I love you. Mother and Daddy love you."

"I wub you, Dabis."

Tears sprang to my eyes when my little niece threw her two-cent's worth in.

"But you've got to move on," Meredith said. "You are a wall between Mother and Daddy that they can't see over anymore."

Meredith passed me a wad of napkins and waited for me to stop blubbering.

"I love it here." Meredith spoke softly. "I'm a small-town girl. I love raising Riley here, and I've never wanted anything but this. You, however, have got to get out if you're ever going to be happy. I'm not suggesting you run away to the North Pole, Davie, maybe just Montgomery. Get a life," she said. "Get out from underneath Mother and Daddy, and let them *breathe*."

Riley panted like a puppy, her little chest rising and falling.

"Be brave, Davis. Do the brave thing. Get out of here, and maybe you'll find a job that's a better fit. You could, maybe, start paying a few of your bills. It'll make you feel better to not have all that hanging over your head. Maybe you'll meet someone, which, if nothing else, will keep you from marrying Eddie again."

"Eddie!" Riley banged a donut on the table. "Eddie's a ass-ho!"

"Davis!" Meredith was furious.

"*I* didn't say it!"

It took two weeks for Meredith's pep talk to sink in so far I was ready to jump off Pine Apple's only bridge, a bridge I'd burned a hundred times already, and the only thing that stopped me was a well-timed job interview. In Biloxi. At the Bellissimo. And here I was. Mother and Daddy were *breathing,* and according to Meredith, *heavily.* (Gross.) I had a job that was a better fit. I did, for the first time in a long time, feel like I had a life. I liked being busy; I loved the thought of being debt free. Meredith was right about everything, even the meeting-someone thing. I hadn't met anyone, but I was actually entertaining the idea. For the first time in a long, long time.

I was on the right road. Finally.

I think.

* * *

The knock on the door was a Bellissimo bellman, not the pizza I'd ordered, although the pizza guy stepped off the elevator a minute later. I tipped the bellman, paid and tipped the pizza guy, and tore into both the pizza and the bags Natalie had sent. Both were somewhat of a disappointment: the pizza had green olives, not the black I'd ordered, and another hot itchy wig popped out of the first bag from Natalie.

Beneath the mousy-blonde wig (about the color of dead grass) was a laptop. The first thing I did was grab another slice of pizza and pick off the green olives. The second thing I did was fire up both computers, inserting a blank disk into Bellissimo's. After that, I typed this command: xcopy32 c:<*.*/s/e/r/v/k/f/c/h. (Try it. You could download the Pentagon's files with that simple command at the set-up screen, but don't. It's a federal offense.) One more slice, and I'd copied the hard drive.

I loaded it onto my own computer, in the privacy of Bradley Cole's condo with no Bellissimo eyes and no Bellissimo ears, logged onto the Internet, and with my IP address scrambled, went to the

Death Master File for Clark County, Nevada. My driver George was completely off the grid, had eyes and ears everywhere, and now he was chasing the boss's wife. He wouldn't be the first person to be operating under the cover of dearly departed.

There were seven dead George Morgans listed, none of them my George. I needed someone born in the 1940s, or thereabouts, and these dead guys were way off in both directions. It was almost a relief. Sometimes I'm a total conspiracy theorist, and I was glad this wasn't one of them, because I wanted and needed George to be one of the good guys.

I stood, stretched, and admired my new apartment. I eyed the wine rack. I opened and poured myself a glass of wine, holding it aloft. "Thank you, Cole Bradley, half a continent away." I took a sip. "I mean Bradley Cole."

Sometimes I amaze myself.

I ran back to the computer, my fingers flying across the keyboard. It wasn't George Morgan; it was Morgan George. Not only had my personal driver been dead for many years, so had his son, Morgan George, Jr. They both died within months of Richard and Bianca Casimiro Sanders moving from Las Vegas, Nevada to Biloxi, Mississippi. I web-searched Morgan George, Sr. and there he was—one of Las Vegas' finest. It was my George, alright.

I sank into Bradley Cole's sofa with another glass of wine, a blank stare, and a sick heart. The simple fact was that this wasn't a simple job. I'd been trying to convince myself I could handle it, and what I was netting from the job far outweighed the risks, but the scales were steadily tipping the other way. I peeked around the corner of possibilities, squinted, hated what I saw, so I dug through Bradley Cole's desk (eight million printer, PC, and phone cords, eight hundred loose keys) for a calculator. If I could keep my head down and fulfill my ninety-day obligation, I could pay off my sister and grandmother, plus make a decent impression on the past-due people at Visa. There was the six-month lease I'd just signed, with a *lawyer*, no less, but he'd never find me, because I'd be in Bora Bora braiding tourists' hair.

More wine. A pretty substantial panic attack that included some wallowing, some "Dammit, karma!", and the bottom of the wine bottle, which led to a tropical daydream in which Bradley Cole actually did find me in Bora Bora. And we lived happily ever after. Eventually, though, I found the bottom line: if I don't stick this out, the end result will be personal bankruptcy, moving back in with my parents (who will immediately divorce), starting a cat collection, and gaining a hundred pounds.

This job was my shot, and I had to take it.

There was a big picture and I probably should set about seeing it. These little assignments—hanging out in the casino, rubbing toothpaste off mirrors, figuring out how a married couple paid for his-and-hers Range Rovers—weren't the real deal. They had me here for something else altogether, and the only things I knew so far were that it involved the whammy game, my ex-ex-husband, Bianca Sanders, and a cab driver from Las Vegas.

ELEVEN

"You're late." It was my new coworker and trainer in Casino Marketing, a girl named Heather McDonald, a tall, thin blonde with bright orange fingernails. She spoke Perfect Southern.

"Sorry," I said. "Paperwork," I lied. I couldn't very well tell her the truth, which was getting supremely lost en route to buy a Taser gun. And then lost again on the way back.

Beth Dunn, like the other hosts I was introduced to, thought the place couldn't run without her. And my new casino job teetered on boring, so boring, in fact, that I began lulling myself into a safe place. It got safer by the minute. By my fourth day, I had moments of wondering if I'd cooked it all up. These people weren't out to get me! (Number one side effect of police work? Paranoia. Everyone's a felon. Everyone's after you. Everyone's got an agenda. Which was true, of course, about Eddie Crawford. That supreme ass.)

The casino host assistant assignment was like the housekeeping assignment in that I had to please my egomaniac bosses and coworkers behind door number one, plus the demanding casino patrons behind door number two. The most I could say was that this job smelled better, but I missed having Santiago to show me the way. Heather was very little help. "Sit here. Answer the phone. Take care of the hosts and the clients. I'll be right back." She didn't show up again until lunch.

I thought I would see a decidedly cleaner side of the clients from behind a desk instead of from behind a cleaning cart, but it was only an hour or two into my new position that I realized the players had dirty laundry both in the guest rooms and in the casino. Some of these gamblers were just nuts. They came busting through the double doors, scaring me to death, claiming the world was coming to an immediate end. Heather had told me, on her way out to run a quick errand (lasting two hours), that when this happened, to pull their In and Out. If they truly lost some monstrous sum (double their rating), I was to track down their host, who in turn would calm them down with surf and turf and straight shots of vodka. If that didn't work, they called them a cab. If that didn't work, they called security.

If I didn't have pirated Bellissimo software, I wouldn't even know what In and Out was, much less how to "pull" it, and Heather didn't bother to explain. In and Out is the electronic tracking of how much money the casino's making on a given player, gathered from the little identification cards the players carry around.

A woman from Atlanta, DeLonda Pierce, sat across from me my first morning, shell-shocked and mumbling the same words over and over, while I tried to find her host, Daniel Connolly. "He's gonna kill me. He's gonna kill me."

I covered the mouthpiece of the phone with my hand. "He won't!" I'd just met Mr. Connolly; he seemed like a pleasant enough fellow. "He won't be mad."

"I'm not talking about my *host*," she spat. "I'm talking about my *husbin'*."

I pulled up her In and Out. The woman had lost more than thirty thousand *dollars* playing slot machines that *morning*. I suppose a killing was in order.

"How can that even *happen*?" I asked Heather, who I found holding court with a jury of her equally deadbeat coworkers at the cappuccino machine.

"Well," Heather said, "a pro can get seven hundred plays an hour on a machine. She plays two ten-dollars at a time. That's," Heather looked up to the imaginary calculator on the ceiling, "that's twenty-eight thousand right there."

"Holy shit."

A half hour later, a sniffling DeLonda Pierce came out of Beth Dunn's office.

I turned to Heather, miraculously present. "I thought Daniel Connolly was her host."

"Yeah," Heather whispered, "Beth's really good with the people who've lost a truckload of money, and a whole lot of those get tossed to her."

I see. (I didn't see.) "And she doesn't mind?"

Heather shrugged. "Hey," she said. "I've got to zip to the bank. Cover for me? I won't be gone long."

I don't know how much steak and lobster Beth gave DeLonda Pierce, or what price DeLonda, in turn, sold them for, but by the end of the day (Heather still at the bank), when I pulled her In and Out, DeLonda had somehow managed to break even.

I'll be damned.

My second day on the job DeLonda stopped by our office again.

"I need to drop this off." It was a sealed envelope, Beth Dunn's name on the front, handwritten in block letters and underlined twice.

DeLonda looked like someone had taken her out back and beaten the tar out of her.

"So?" I asked. "Are things better?"

DeLonda chewed on the question. "Do you really want to know?"

I did.

"I came here to relax, have some fun." Her black eyes bore into mine. "And I'm leaving here hoping I can keep my husbin' and my house."

What? She'd won all the money back! "Seriously?"

"It's not as bad as it was yesterday," she said, "but trust me, it's still devastating."

I wanted to ask her a million questions, but instead I smiled at her and told her to hurry back to see us.

"Oh, it'll be awhile," she assured me. "A good, long while."

I checked her numbers again. For the trip, in the end, she'd actually won four thousand. Sure didn't sound devastating to me. I held the envelope up to the light.

* * *

Natalie, who dresses this puppet, most definitely didn't have me dolled up for this assignment. Not only did I have the mousy-blonde wig to contend with, I had oversized tortoise-shell glasses that slid down my nose seventeen times every single second. The clothes I had to choose from were either black or black turtlenecks and black or black long floppy skirts that didn't touch me anywhere and smelled like roses. The shoes were black flats, more like house slippers, and I had to sidestep old women carefully, because if they got a good look at them they'd whack me over the head with their walking sticks and yank them right off my feet. I could have easily been chosen for an ambush makeover. You! Mousy-blonde girl! Get out of those baggy black clothes! This isn't the library! All in all, I was as unmemorable a package as one could imagine. This came in handy when I inevitably screwed things up during my tenure as a Host Assistant. "Who told you that?" And the person would answer, "I don't remember."

The week passed with three more panicked players going behind closed doors with Beth Dunn, then later, the same three players dropped off mail for Beth. Just like DeLonda, the computer said they'd made up their huge losses, but just like DeLonda, you couldn't tell it from looking at them.

"What's in this, do you think?" I shook the most recent envelope. Always Bellissimo stationery and always sealed.

Heather's computer was glued to her Facebook page and Heather was glued to her computer. "Money," she said without a glance my way. "The hosts get tipped."

"Seriously?"

"Big time." Heather said. "And I'm next in line!" She updated her Facebook status. "*I'm next*!"

"Next for what?" I asked.

"To be a host!" She turned to me. "This assistant job," her hand passed back and forth between us, "is a stepping stone to being a casino host," she explained. "And they go by seniority. We just lost an assistant, and I took her spot. She was the only one who had more time than me."

"Oh, the girl, Heidi Dupree? I heard about that. What happened there?" I asked innocently.

Heather shrugged. "Some kind of family emergency." She picked up the small digital clock on her desk. "Didn't you say you had to leave early today?"

"I did say that." I had a date with Teeth. I was putting it off as long as possible. I'd stretched this assignment as long as I could, but it was time to move on to the next part of this gig. That meant sending Natalie an email telling her I needed a little assistance, and dammit, she sent it by way of Mr. Molars.

"Let me run to the little girl's room before you go."

"Sure."

"Give me ten minutes."

In Heather Math, that meant three to four hours. With her clear plastic crossover bag strapped on, she smiled at me and slipped out the door.

"Bye," I waggled my fingers at the door. I hated to leave the safety of this office, but I also hated these clothes. I slipped the envelope that was supposed to go to Beth Dunn's inbox into my purse and sent a text message to Teeth: BE THERE IN 30. I stuck my head in the back office and called out, "Can anyone watch the front until Heather gets back?" A young man raised a finger. Poor guy.

* * *

There were lots of reasons I'd rather not be alone in a room with Teeth. Among them: he didn't like me a bit, I didn't trust him a bit, his teeth scared me, and he had no sense of humor whatsoever. If that weren't enough, I felt certain Teeth and Eddie Crawford (that no-good excuse of a human) had a little Double Whammy Deuces Wild something going on, and as soon as I could squeeze out one free moment, I planned on nosing into it. Nonetheless, Teeth (Paul Bergman, but I couldn't bring myself to say it), and I enjoyed each other's company watching surveillance video from five-thirty on Friday until three o'clock the next Wednesday without a break.

Kidding, but it felt that long.

Teeth was dressed in what looked like all black, until the fabric of his suit (shirt, tie, and probably boxer shorts) caught light, at which point it took on a deep purple hue.

"Where do you buy your clothes?" I asked.

"None of your business."

I clasped my hands together to keep from going for my new Taser gun and rattling his big teeth out of his head.

It had been an incredibly long week for me. Being a nomad is taxing, and I'd climbed into ten different beds (all empty) in the past month. I didn't have roots; I was still living out of a suitcase. Starting a new job is stressful, and I'd started four in as many weeks. If I stayed here long enough, my resume would get me into the White House. "Is there anything you *haven't* done?" I'd answer, "Nope." Lurking, always present, in the back of my mind was the threat of the industrial vacuum cleaner, so I didn't want to complain too much about being tossed around lest I got tossed on it.

The thing is, I had other matters to attend to: I had developed a crush on my landlord, Bradley Cole, and wanted to keep nosing into his drawers and closets. Every day this week, after sitting behind a desk reimbursing high-rollers for the cost of the fuel their private jets gobbled to get them here (that they immediately gambled away), I'd returned to the condo to either try to find more photographs of Bradley Cole (good-looking guy, Mr. His High School type, great, normal teeth) or delve deeper into what happened to George/Morgan/my still-absent driver's son. And what Bianca Casimiro Sanders could possibly have to do with it to the point of George dropping off the grid and following her here, and, apparently, yon. And where, exactly, did Eddie the Ass fit in?

Just as soon as I placed the tiniest piece of what promised to be a very large puzzle, I'd look at the clock and realize I had to be at my Host Assistant desk in four hours. Let's put it this way: I'd been pulling doubles all week long, wearing a hot itchy wig for one of the shifts. If Natalie didn't stop with the wig stuff, I'd probably be walking into work with the wrong one on my head any day. And it would be spinning, because underneath it, my brain was so busy.

"You can't solve every crime, young lady." My father had warned me years ago. "Focus on one thing at a time."

"But what if they're all connected?"

"They probably aren't."

"But what if they *are*?"

* * *

Teeth had clearance for all things and he had the Big Brother program up and running on his laptop in the dungeon he and No Hair called home. By the way, they needed a very fragrant candle in there.

I'd supplied him with the dates and times of the visits, starting with the Atlanta woman, DeLonda Pierce, which had resulted in the Envelope.

"Speaking of which," I reached into my purse.

"I didn't say anything."

"What?"

"You said, 'speaking of which.' We weren't speaking."

"*What*?" I asked again.

He batted the air. "Never mind."

I plopped the envelope with Beth Dunn's name on it in front of the computer.

"Where you get that?" he asked.

"I took it."

He didn't know if he should pat me on the back or arrest me. "You've got some balls," he said.

"Open it," I said.

"I'm not opening it. You open it."

"I stole it. Surely you can open it."

He huffed. He reached for it. A sheet of stationery was folded in thirds, and nestled inside were four slot-machine cashout tickets in amounts ranging from eight hundred dollars up to twenty-two hundred, totaling almost five thousand. Teeth and I looked at each other, shrugged, and probably reached the same conclusion: In the privacy of her office, Beth Dunn was giving desperate players money to play with, then taking a cut on the back end. Here was the back end. Where was the front-end money coming from? Probably not her purse. I pushed them around with the eraser end of a pencil. Teeth deciphered.

"Let's see," he said. "This one's this morning; the other three are this afternoon."

"How do you know that?" I didn't see a time stamp.

"The Julian date is right here," he pointed, "and the time, military, is here."

Ah-ha.

"And here's the machine number."

I leaned in. Get this: Teeth's fingernails were professionally manicured.

"Let's watch." He was in charge of the mouse. He clicked.

I put my feet up on the desk and dug into the popcorn I'd microwaved. I slurped a Diet Coke.

"Do you mind?" Teeth asked.

"Sorry." I held the popcorn out to him.

"I meant hold down the noise," he said. "I don't eat popcorn. It gets stuck in my teeth."

Lord knows we wouldn't want *that*. This guy probably flossed with nylon rope, and no part of me wanted to be witness. "And what about those four-pound roasted turkey legs you wolf down?" I truly did not enjoy this man's company. "Do they get stuck in your teeth?"

He inhaled sharply. I cowered. "For your information," he said, "I'm on Jenny Craig. I don't eat between meals and if I did, it wouldn't be turkey legs." He sat back, crossing his huge arms over his purple chest. "How did you get this job?"

"Honestly?" I said through a mouthful of popcorn, "I don't know."

It took until midnight to watch the feed because to follow Beth we had to guess where she might go, and watch several feeds until we found her. If it were as simple as assigning surveillance to follow her, we could have finished in time to watch Funniest Home Videos at our separate residences, but me being me and this being this, we had to watch a whole lot of Funniest Davis Videos instead.

Because we were on Discretion Road, surveillance had not been following Beth Dunn's every step, so we had to track her down. The first camera angle we watched was the only surveillance camera that would pick her up leaving her office, and that camera was in the reception area outside her office, trained directly on ME.

I'd give anything to have anticipated that. I would have sat there still as a church mouse with my hands folded on top of the desk, before Teeth got to review my every single move, laughing his Jenny Craig ass off the entire time. When Heather was there with me, or a client was standing at the counter, it was boring. I sat there and worked. It was when Heather ran off for one of her seven-hour errands that I took two cat naps, head on desk, mouth wide open, took my bra off once, working the strap off my shoulder and out one sleeve, then the other, pulling it through, then dropping it in the garbage, and one time when I was alone I plucked my eyebrows, mouth wide open again. Teeth was about to wet his purple pants. The worst was Wednesday, when for some reason, I had my undies on backwards. Before I figured it out and threw them away in the ladies room, I stood at the copier, camera zeroing in on my rear end, and adjusted. Several times.

During Funny Davis, Beth Dunn would pass the desk on her way to the casino floor, and Teeth would thankfully switch camera feeds. It took repeated attempts to follow her, your classic needle-in-a-haystack scenario, which is why we had to sit there all night, but we nailed her every time. About a half hour after the four clients left her office, she'd go straight to the slot machine they were playing. How'd she know?

Teeth and I raised our eyebrows in silent question. And each time, Teeth would grab a pen and scribble something.

Finally, there was nothing left to watch. I turned to him.

He was rubbing his eyes the relieving way men who don't wear mascara do.

"What now?" I asked.

"We go back and do the same thing, only this time we follow the player. See how much money she's giving them to feed into the machines."

Oh, goody, goody. I couldn't wait.

"Then we'll do it again to see where the husband fits into the picture." He pushed back from the desk. "Get ready to do a whole lot more of what you just did."

"I wonder." I stretched. "If the machines she sends these players to are machines her husband has worked on right before."

Teeth's face scrunched up.

"And the money she's giving these clients isn't currency, it's tickets he's taken out of the machines when he's working on them."

Teeth's beady eyes narrowed to slits and he didn't seem to be breathing. I knew this because the man is a mouth breather. Who complains about chewing noises.

"And the player," I babbled on with my theory, "goes to that machine with the ticket, because it puts it back in the right place. And when they eventually win they have to give her a nice cut."

He stared at me as if I'd just said the Earth was flat.

"Get it?" I asked. "She's not giving them money, she's giving them tickets."

His nostrils flared.

"Or," I tried to backstroke quickly. Obviously I was way off.

"That's *exactly* it."

He slammed a fist.

I jumped a mile.

"The tickets Beth Dunn gives the players are lifted," Teeth said. "The tickets they give back to her," he shook the envelope containing the evidence, "are legit. She can go cash them out."

We enjoyed a stunned silence. I don't know who was more stunned, me or Teeth.

"That's exactly what they're doing." He stood. He walked a circle. He pulled a straight chair up and straddled it, interrogation style. He was in my face. "What team are you playing for?"

I stared into Teeth's eyes, and found nothing there.

He didn't intend to move until I gave him an answer.

"Are you asking me if I'm a lesbian?"

He jumped up and the chair went down. "I don't *care* if you're a lesbian."

He picked the chair up, holding it midair, and I thought he was about to throw it at me. Instead, he righted it and sat back down. In a lower voice he said, "I'm asking you if you're a *criminal*, because you think like one. All. The. Time."

* * *

I'd taken to wearing Bradley Cole's clothes. All. The. Time.

I climbed into his bed at two that morning wearing his green V-neck cotton sweater that came to my knees.

Did I think like a criminal? And was that a good thing, or a bad thing? Certainly, some (okay, all) of my post-divorce antics fell under the category of outside the letter of the law. But those were special circumstances, and let's not go there. The crazy thing was, and I couldn't possibly have known it then, my next assignment at the Bellissimo would be the one that would lead to a mug shot of my very own.

The question as to whether or not I had criminal tendencies, or just how far I was willing to go, would soon be answered.

TWELVE

Over the weekend, while I made myself more comfortable in Bradley Cole's condo, if that were even possible now that I was using his razor to shave my legs, Teeth and No Hair went to the movies, watching surveillance feed of Hank Dunn tinkering with slot machines.

Four out of five times the problem was a paper jam in the internal printer that produced the cashout tickets. He fiddled until the paper was free, printed a test ticket, sometimes two, sometimes ten. Next he'd scribble in a notebook housed inside the machine door, look at his watch, jot down the time, lock down the machine, then feed the test tickets back in. Teeth and No Hair backed up the tape, counted the test tickets he'd printed, then counted the test tickets he fed back into the machine. The count was off by one or two tickets almost every time.

We met in Mr. Sander's office on Monday. Teeth, No Hair, and I sat in chairs in front of his desk, Natalie in a chair beside and slightly behind Mr. Sanders. She had a pad of paper in her lap, a pen in one hand, and the coffee cup that went everywhere with her in the other. Teeth and No Hair just sat there taking up loads of space and sucking up all the oxygen. They both had such big feet it was hard not to stare. Did either of them fit in a normal bed? Car? Swimming pool?

"The test tickets are supposed to be zero value," Teeth said, "but he can override that and print them for any amount without altering the machine's count." Teeth was decked out in slate gray today.

"And the cash boxes are only audited on Tuesday and Friday," No Hair added. He was wearing a fruit salad tie: mandarin oranges, green apples, cherries, and kiwis. "If the test tickets are all back before the audit, no one's the wiser, because as we all know, it's an automated count. The audit's only going to flag a missing ticket, not a late one."

I kept my mouth shut, too busy staring at Richard Sanders to add to the conversation. In the short amount of time I'd spent in the same room with him, I'd decided his hair was his best feature, unlike Bradley Cole, who's each and every feature was his best.

Richard Sanders, however, had great man-hair. It was so much longer than you'd expect; it was the length of a sexy construction worker's hair. He could have pulled it into a ponytail. It was shiny, blond, and spilled over his collar in loose corkscrew curls.

"Davis?" Natalie asked. "Are you still with us?"

Everyone was looking at me.

"Sorry."

Great Hair cleared his throat. "How much money are we talking about?"

"He printed more than fifty for last week," Teeth said. "But we can only see where they disbursed sixteen of it."

They were talking dollars; I didn't have to ask. I was catching on to this casino business.

"Okay," Mr. Sanders said, "so we can't account for the balance?"

"We have no clue where all those tickets went," No Hair said.

"Maybe," the boss said, "they're feeding what they don't use back into the machines themselves."

I piped up, so everyone would know I was paying attention. "What are the chances she's selling them for cash, for less than their printed value?"

There was a dead silence while everyone else's jaws dropped open.

"What?" My hand flew to my chest. Had I said something stupid again?

"See?" Teeth asked the others. "You see what I'm saying?"

There was some coughing, some shifting in some seats, and some uncomfortable silence.

"We're going to need to catch them in the act," the boss said. "And let's make it section ten."

They all turned to me *again*. "What?" My heart was pounding. "Is this about the vacuum cleaner?"

Natalie pressed her lips together and looked away.

"Give us a minute," Mr. Sanders said.

We all stood.

"Not you, Davis. Keep your seat."

Oh, dear.

"Close the door, Natalie."

Oh, double dear.

* * *

We sat there smiling at each other for the next several hours, me, nervously, him, too cool for school. Between us, a dish full of cinnamon candy.

"How's it going, Davis?"

"Fine, Mr. Sanders."

"Is the new job working out for you?"

"Yes, sir. I really like it here."

"You're doing great. We're very pleased."

"I saw your wife." (A police trick. Deflect.)

In a blink, every muscle in his face did the opposite of what it had been doing. I'd seen the same expression on his face before, the day I met him, when he realized I looked like her. He was equally shocked today to learn that I knew. He rolled his wedding band around his finger at warp speed, then said, "Tit for tat. We need to talk about your ex-husband, Mr. Crawford."

I'm pretty sure I passed out, because I've never heard anyone refer to Eddie Crawford as *mister*.

Somewhere in the Bible, it says don't leave your money to your children; leave it to your grandchildren, which is what Papa Way did when I was four years old. It wasn't all that much money by today's standards—thirty-two thousand each—but after sitting in an investment trust through the dot-com bubble, Meredith and I had some buck on our hands when the estate attorney from Montgomery let us at it. It came in handy for her, because she had single-parenthood in her future; at the time, though, she used the bulk of her inheritance to open her shop, The Front Porch.

It came in handy for Eddie Crawford, too, because he stole almost every penny of mine.

The first thing I did after seven years of college and moving back home was to turn around and leave again for more education. My Basic Training was two hours away, and lasted from January until April, giving the residents of Pine Apple—namely my mother, along with Mel, Bea, and Eddie Crawford—plenty of time to get used to the idea of me being home.

I was twenty-three years old the first time I wore an officer's uniform, and the first time I ran into my ex-husband Eddie was my second day on the job, when I picked up him and his sidekick, Jug, for drinking and driving. While they were certainly drinking, they weren't driving so much as they were parked against the double doors of the Piggly Wiggly, our only grocery store, trapping four very angry people inside. They learned after the first twenty times they'd tried this trick that if they didn't block the back before blocking the front, the hostages were immediately free. By the time I was on the job, they'd honed it. I'd already been warned this was a bi-weekly occurrence, and that Daddy never actually booked them.

"They don't mean any harm," Daddy said. "It's Jug's way of flirting with Danielle."

Danielle Sparks was a girl I'd gone to school with all my life, and she was a cashier at the Pig. Jug had been after her since second grade. I'd butted heads with her since first.

I had the two idiots in the back of my patrol car and called my boss. "What do I do with them now, Daddy?"

"First move the car away from the door and let everyone out."

"I did that."

"Take them to the station, lock them up, and I'll be there in a minute."

"Do you want me to stay with them?"

"I'll come down, Sugar."

Was this really happening? "No, Daddy, go back to bed. I'll stay."

"They know where their pillows are. Call me if you need me."

It was Mayberry, and I was Barney Fife. They were Otis and Otis.

Jug had a lot of harsh words for me during the entire process, while Eddie didn't/wouldn't make eye contact, much less speak. I nodded off to Jug's drunken diatribe, me at the desk, them behind bars, and jolted awake to find Eddie Crawford's laser gawk locked on me. Oh, boy.

"Damn, you're pretty, Davis."

He was, too, but I wasn't about to say it.

"Who was that baby's daddy?"

It became a very boring routine, spending the night in my father's chair with them sleeping it off fifty yards away behind bars. The most I can say is that Eddie and I finally found some middle ground.

"Eddie," I told him one swelteringly hot night, "you're just bored. Why don't you find something to do with yourself?"

"I work."

"You go to the diner at eleven, slap out ten plates of meatloaf, and you're gone by noon," I said. "That's not work."

Eddie stared at me and sucked something out of his front teeth. "Easy for you to say, Miss Money Bags College."

"I will not have this fight with you, Eddie."

"You know, Davis." Jug had sobered. A little. "If you'll let me out of here for ten minutes, I'll fix the air."

Everyone knows that air conditioning compressors only break in July, and it was the tenth of. Daddy had put a call in to a repairman in Montgomery who said he'd try to get to us the next week. I was pretty sure I'd die of a heat stroke before then. I wasn't worried about my prisoners.

"You will not, Jug, and I'm not about to let you out until daylight. You'll just go wake up everyone at Danielle's. Her daddy's going to come after you with a shotgun if you don't leave them alone."

"Let him get the air on," Eddie said, fanning himself with the shirt he'd stripped out of. "He can fix anything."

"If that's true, then why don't you have a job, Jug?"

Just then, the oscillating fan on my desk popped, sparked, sizzled, then died. What would push the hot air around now? I did let Jug out. And I'll be damned if he didn't fix the air.

"Just needs rewiring," he said over his shoulder.

"Is that all?" I asked.

Six months later, I became the financial backer for their new business, E & J Electric. Eddie and Jug stopped drinking 40s for breakfast. They went to community college. They got licensed. They joined the IBEW. Jug bought a razor and learned to use it.

Things continued down a prolific path for the former troublemakers, with them staying clear of the back seat of my patrol car. The day the two local boys proved that they really could be productive was the day they finished laying underground lines throughout all four miles of Pine Apple, and we joined the twenty-first century with cable television and wireless Internet. It was the biggest thing that ever happened in Pine Apple, and it would seem the hometown boys had finished their metamorphosis from Neanderthal to civilized. By that time, I was settling into life in Pine Apple again.

One devastatingly lonely night, I settled into a bottle José Cuervo. A very large bottle. The next thing I knew, Eddie Crawford showed up and my Seven jeans went missing, at which point (have to give him this and *only* this) Eddie and I found some very common ground. For all he wasn't, there was one thing he was. And just that one. It took him awhile to convince me to marry him again, because I knew in my heart that he didn't want to be married to me any more than I wanted to be married to him. I had the nagging suspicion he simply wanted revenge for the first go-around. But you know what they say: Revenge is a dish best served by a really good looking man. So I married him again. We were twenty-five years old. Then a hurricane hit.

* * *

My landlord, Bradley Cole, for all he was, wasn't much of a cook. The kitchen was stocked with these things: salt, mustard, two cans of Little Nibbler dog food (hadn't seen a Little Nibbler around), and wine, wine, lots of wine. I was living on delivery pizza and wine, wine, lots of wine.

So after that lovely chat with Mr. Sanders, in which I was forced to say Eddie's name aloud several times, I was determined to go to the grocery store and buy some comfort food, but not until after I made my daily perimeter of the building looking for my driver, George.

I knew they knew. They knew I knew they knew. Knowing they knew, and them knowing I knew they knew, was quite another matter. At least I didn't have to worry about being fired if they found out, since they already knew.

I knew they knew. Dammit.

Note to self: Get in front of your scrubbed record when applying for a job because they already know.

Richard Sanders was neutral about the whole thing; he didn't pass judgment.

I didn't deny anything, apologize, or make excuses. I panicked, certainly, but held my own.

He actually gave me a compliment: "You're talented with a computer, Davis," he said, "and I wouldn't want to cross you."

"There's no love lost, Mr. Sanders, I need you to know that. I'm not here to win him back."

He rolled his wedding ring around, not saying anything.

"And I'm not here to settle a score on your time."

Roll, roll, roll, the wedding ring.

"The thing is, he's going to recognize me."

"No, he won't," Richard Sanders said. "He'll see my wife."

How did Eddie the Ass know what his wife looked like?

"I'm going to look at my calendar, Davis, and see when we might be able to talk about this more."

This what more? Hopefully his wife. I'd done all the talking about Eddie Crawford I cared to.

* * *

Natalie was pouring over a gargantuan stack of reports as if it were nine in the morning instead of nine in the evening. If his lights were on, hers were, too. I watched a look of relief cross her face as I staggered from Mr. Sanders' space to hers, probably because the door was the way she wanted it. Open.

"Got a minute?" I asked her.

"I always have a minute for you, Davis."

I found a chair and collapsed into it. "The cat's out of the bag."

She half smiled, half shrugged, the two halves making a whole expression of understanding my plight. "It's okay," she said. "We all have skeletons."

"It's hard to explain marrying the same idiot twice."

"You don't owe anyone an explanation."

"Tell that to my mother."

I looked to the open door that led to Mr. Sanders, who was on the phone. "Am I going to lose my job?" My ninety days weren't up. I hadn't made enough of a Visa dent. And now I had a big, fat condo lease.

"No!" *Silly!* "You've had plenty of opportunity to gun him down in the casino if that was your intent."

I hadn't even thought of that.

"Sometimes," she said, "you have to let things go."

"He stole a lot of money from me, Natalie."

"He's stolen a lot more here, Davis."

And there it went, another piece of the puzzle.

* * *

I could barely hold my head up. I left the vendor parking lot (where I hid my Bug) and drove around to the VIP entrance.

He looked up. We stared at each other for a long minute. I put it in reverse, swung a half circle, and drove off.

* * *

I was up and on the road at eight thirty Friday morning to be in New Orleans, a sixty-mile drive, by eleven. Having no idea where I was going, I allowed myself plenty of extra time. Natalie had warned me: "If you're even one minute late, just turn around and drive back."

My destination was the Salon du Beau Monde on St. Joseph's, for an appointment with someone named Seattle, the proprietor, and stylist to the stars.

"Are you sure about this?" I asked Natalie.

"You're the one who doesn't want to wear the wig." She pulled open a desk drawer and withdrew a crisp hundred-dollar bill.

"What's this for?"

"Seattle's tip. Be discreet."

"What does she charge for a haircut if her *tip* is a hundred dollars?"

"It's he. And he charges four hundred for a cut and color. And be discreet."

Four hundred dollars for a hair cut? My last hair cut had been fifteen dollars with a two-dollar tip. "If he's that special, how'd you get me an appointment?"

"I got people." She gave me an exaggerated wink. "And one more thing, Davis, before you get in there and get the shock of your life."

No, I'd already had that, when I'd been called on the carpet in Mr. Sander's office.

"He's Bianca Sanders' stylist. That subject might come up. Be discreet."

That was three times she'd told me to be discreet. Discretion, discreet, what was next? Dismember? This was a dangerous job.

"Theese color?" Seattle, who had the longest and most glorious hair I'd ever seen on a man, even putting Mr. Sanders' golden locks to shame, looked positively Hawaiian, spoke with an exaggerated French accent, and held the wig I'd worn for the photographs before I was hired as far away from his body as his arm would allow.

"Theese style? The cream blonde, yes?" He let the wig drop on a rolling table full of plug-in things and straight-edge razors, then circled me, tapping his chin. He twirled the chair so that I was facing the mirror, and pressed his cheek against mine, our eyes meeting in the reflection. "You already look just as her, no? The hair will be the finish, yes?"

This man had no whiskers. Smooth as a baby's butt.

"If you had the green eyes," Seattle's laugh was a nasally series of quick snorts, "I would find myself most frightened."

* * *

Morgan George, Jr. died on March 5, almost seven years ago. He was twenty-eight years old. His last known residence was Henderson, Nevada. I've never been to Vegas, but I'm pretty sure Henderson is right there.

The *Las Vegas Sun* offered so little that it screamed cover up: Henderson man found dead at his residence; police do not suspect foul play. What did they suspect? Parkinson's? Alzheimer's?

The obituary gave me more: Morgan George, Jr. was a magna cum laude graduate of UNLV's School of Math and Technology. He was there the same time the boss, Richard Sanders, was. He was employed by a software writer: Technology Systems Incorporated, in Henderson.

TSI's website listed, among its clients, Total Gaming Corporation, who manufactured slot machines, specifically video poker, their most popular game a familiar one even to me: Double Whammy Deuces Wild Progressives. A coincidence?

Total Gaming didn't brag about their clientele, because they claimed to have more than two-hundred thousand machines on casino floors worldwide; I guess that list would be too long. They did, however, show off their Board of Directors. The face that stood out in the crowd was the sandy-blond haired green-eyed one, Salito Casimiro.

Let's say it together: Conflict of interest.

Morgan George, Sr.'s obituary was a two-liner: Las Vegas Detective declared dead on Tuesday, June 16. Private memorial service; don't send anything. The only news I could match up with my driver's fake death was a single paragraph in the Metro section, the week after Jr. died, about an abandoned dingy floating in the middle of Lake Las Vegas. The police were searching for a body.

I could tell them where the body was. It was in a cab parked at the VIP entrance of the Bellissimo Resort and Casino in Biloxi, Mississippi.

I called my father. "Daddy, I need you to ship me my computer. All of it."

"Right away, Angel," he said. "I don't suppose you can do much damage with a computer."

I called Natalie. "Natalie, I need a slot machine here at my condo."

"You bought a condo?"

My head popped up and I tried to locate a clock. I'd woken her. "No, the one I'm leasing."

"Why do you need a slot machine?" she asked.

Because I smell a rat, I didn't answer.

"Never mind," she added quickly. "What kind?"

"The Double Whammy game. It's manufactured by Total Gaming with software written by Technology Systems, Inc."

"I've got three of those right here," she said.

"Really?"

She laughed. "Anything else?"

"That ought to do it."

I sat there a minute trying to decide if my next order of business could wait until tomorrow. No, it couldn't. I pulled on yoga pants to wear with Bradley Cole's Life Is Good sweatshirt, grabbed my keys, and locked the door behind me. I'd forgotten to wear shoes, and it was about thirty below and foggy. I danced across the frozen asphalt. I was ten minutes from the Bellissimo, but it was late, and there wasn't much traffic. I made it in six. The VIP entrance was deserted, yet there he was. I pulled alongside him facing the opposite direction, driver window to driver window.

"George, wake up." I beeped my horn.

He cut his black eyes my way. Finally, he lowered his window.

"I've got a question for you," and as I said it, I wished I were farther away. It occurred to me he might not like the question.

"What."

"Do you still have his textbooks? TSI operating manuals? Anything?"

George did the physical equivalent of collapsing, even though he was already sitting. He stared at his lap. He nodded yes without displacing one atom.

"Can you get them for me?"

He nodded again.

"What *happened*, George?"

He turned, dead on. "They slit his throat. My baby boy."

Evil almost knocked me down.

"Go away," George said.

* * *

"I love you being here with me, Davis," my father said, "it's a dream come true."

"Me too, Daddy."

"With one exception."

"What's that?" I couldn't move in my new uniform. I was wearing a *tie*. And a concrete *vest*. I had twenty extra pounds strapped around my middle—a piece, two extra mags, riot baton (as if), mace, cuffs, flashlight, knife, radio—and the pants were made of fabric so thick and coarse it felt like canvas. Very unflattering.

"Listen to me." Daddy held both my hands in his big strong ones. He spoke quietly. He looked me straight in the eye. "You're going to see evil. You're going to see hatred, violence, and injustice. You're going to see blood, Davis, more than you ever imagined a human body could hold. I can't even prepare you for things you're going to see, because as well as we try to do our jobs, we can't predict it. You're joining a clean-up crew, Angel. Part of your job is to help me clean up after evil's had his way. And from the moment you were born, all I've tried to do, all any parent tries to do, is keep you as far away from evil as possible."

"Here?" I asked. "In Pine Apple? Daddy! Nothing's going to happen."

"It will, Princess. It will."

It did.

Obviously, I got the fluff jobs. One was standing in the middle of our only true intersection between 7:45 and 8:15 in the morning, then again between 2:45 and 3:15 in the afternoon every single school day of the calendar year, ushering all sizes and shapes of children to and fro. In all those years, there were maybe ten days of nice weather.

There was a little boy, Tanner Pruett, who tugged on my heartstrings from day one, and it never occurred to me that my father would be anything but supportive. He never was.

"Sweet Pea?" I was off to the school crossing in pouring-down rain. "Where are you going with those groceries?"

"Oh." I was lost somewhere inside a rain poncho. Finally, I found the opening. "I like to slip a little something to the Pruetts for the weekend. You know," I found my arms, "so they can actually *eat* between now and Monday, when the school cafeteria opens again."

My father's chair scraped across the floor so fast it startled me. He grabbed the bag of peanut butter, lunch meat, bread, bananas, and Yoo-Hoos off my desk. "No," he said.

"Daddy!" I was shocked.

Tanner was the oldest child of Christine Pruett, an ongoing Pine Apple headache/heartache. She was a few years older than me, and I'd known her all my life. She'd been a cheerleader at Pine Apple High, rah-rah. Christine had exactly what the rest of us had—loving parents, a nice, warm home, a state-funded education, and all her faculties. Somehow, though, Christine had gone way off track. She'd gotten pregnant with Tanner sometime during eleventh grade. (Big whoop. Unplanned teen pregnancies were a rite of passage in Pine Apple.) Christine, though, seemed helpless to stop it, and she slipped up five more times with, those with eyeballs had to assume, five different men from five different ethnic origins. Between her third and fourth child, she met her true love, methamphetamine, at which point, she began cranking herself into oblivion.

Eventually, Christine didn't have a tooth in her head, and stopped leaving her trailer. We'd all done every single thing we could possibly do for Christine through the years. We locked her up. We cleaned her trailer. We had interventions. We scattered her children to foster homes. We held vigils. We did everything except cook her smack and shoot her up. She was, truly, a hopeless case.

But her firstborn Tanner wasn't. He was an old soul, and why wouldn't he be? He'd seen it all. He was a smart boy, a straight-A student. And he worked hard; he tried his best to take care of his mother. He mowed yards, he did odd jobs, he learned how to heat up ravioli and ration it out.

Daddy had a tight grip on the grocery bag. An uncommon and unnerving silence fell between us.

"Daddy," I whispered.

"Sit down, Davis."

I sounded like a plastic tarp going into the chair.

"You can't get involved. It's not your job. Don't get anywhere near those children without backup."

I couldn't believe the words coming out of my father's mouth. More than that, I couldn't believe the seriousness with which they were delivered. He wasn't giving me advice, there weren't options;

he was giving me a direct order. "You have no business with the Pruetts, and if I get wind of you around them, I'll fire you on the spot."

It was the first and last time I deliberately disobeyed my father. I continued to sneak things to Tanner: groceries, school supplies, and winter coats. When Christmas rolled around, I slipped him five twenty-dollar bills.

"Spend it wisely, Tanner," I said.

On Christmas Eve, both mine and Daddy's radios squawked the very second we started passing the potatoes. My mother said, "Whatever it is, Samuel, let Davis take care of it. I don't want you to miss Christmas Dinner."

"It's the Pruetts," my father said. "I'm sure it'll take both of us."

He killed his mother first, with a close shot between the eyes. He lined up his siblings, execution style, killing four of them instantly. The fifth bullet had unmercifully missed, but by the time we got there, he was in the middle of smothering that sister.

She died.

"Where did you get the gun, Tanner?" my father asked.

"I bought it."

"Where did you get the money to buy a gun?"

He pointed.

Evil was out there. I'd seen it up close and personal. You can't guess what form it might come in. There were times when it was impossible to know.

I leaned hard on José Cuervo for support. Unfortunately, he brought his friend Eddie along.

* * *

Tonight, I was leaning on Jack Daniels and Bradley Cole. Here's hoping these two were a better combination.

I'd taken to chatting with an eight-by-ten framed photograph of Bradley taken on a ski trip with his buddies. I kept it beside the bed, so that Bradley's face was the last thing I saw before dreaming, and the first thing I saw upon waking. In the privacy of my/his condo, I used it as a magic eight ball of sorts. (Maybe I should get a cat or a guinea pig. Or a magic eight ball.)

I asked him, before I turned out the light, if he thought there was enough good left in the world for us to bother. His answer: without a doubt. Did he like my new look? Definitely. I asked him if he minded me redecorating his dining room with a slot machine. He didn't. Even if I make a really big mess with it? No. I asked him if he thought my theory was right: there was some dirty, dirty business going on all around me that had somehow, someway, began with the murder of Morgan George, Jr. He said ask again later. And one last question: Did he think I could figure it out and avoid my ex-ex-husband at the same time? His sources said no.

THIRTEEN

One-tenth of the casino floor was devoted to the irresponsible gambler. It was called High Limits, where the table game minimums were weekly grocery-store budgets and the slot machines could eat an entire mortgage payment in fifteen minutes. It was elevated, smack-dab in the middle, cordoned off by brass rails, and all aisles led to it so that everyone eventually got a wistful glance and wished they had the mojo to play up there with the rich people. But off the main casino floor, in the northeast corner away from all other venues behind a backlit waterfall, there was a Ridiculously High Limit room. It was by invitation only. It was the most brutal gaming this side of Las Vegas. The draw was the anonymous geography; it was the reason so many private hangars were built for so many private jets fifteen miles away. In this room, school-teacher salaries were tips and the sticker price of luxury yachts was won and lost in seconds.

A different breed of gambler played in Private Gaming, the one they call a whale. Whales were one of these: famous, a professional athlete, a politician, or so inherently wealthy their portfolio had its own summer house in France. You might think you'd find self-made millionaires in every other seat, but Natalie told me not to bother looking for those, because people who earned their fortunes didn't give it to casinos.

"They gamble," she explained. "But you'll find them playing one hand at the five-dollar tables, not two hands at the five-thousand. The only other reason someone would play in Private

Gaming would be if they had something else entirely going on." She sat back and crossed her arms. "That'd be you, Davis."

"And you're telling me that Eddie Crawford plays in the private room? Seriously? How could that be?" I asked.

He wasn't famous, he wasn't athletic, probably couldn't tell you who the governor of Alabama was if you held a gun to his head, and his mailing address was Shady Acres Mobile Home Park, Slip 18, County Road 4, Pine Apple.

"I am," Natalie said, "and he does. He won big money a little more than four months ago."

"How big?"

"One point two," Natalie popped the words.

"One point two what?"

"Million." She said it in two syllables.

My hand slapped my own chest so hard I'm sure it left a mark. "*What?*" I shot up from the chair.

"Settle down, Davis."

Eventually, I stopped screaming and found the chair. That son of a bitch. And it wasn't just me; his mother drove a clunker minivan from the late eighties. What the hell was Eddie doing with that kind of money?

"Can we continue, Davis?"

I sat there quietly seething while she picked up where she left off: markers, tuxedos, women who were paid to hang out and look good. The Bellissimo Word of the Day—discretion—found its way in there several times.

"He's playing there," I said, "and you want me to play in there, too, right? Natalie, he'll see me and run."

"No, Davis. He won't."

"We met at the hospital when we were born, then I married him twice, Natalie. How is it you think he won't see me?"

Her voice lowered to a whisper. "He won't see Davis. He'll see Bianca."

"Mrs. *Sanders*? How does Eddie know what she even looks like?"

"Your ex-husband is Bianca Sanders' latest whim," Natalie said. "And he's her third."

"Her third what?" I was still having trouble breathing. "Whim? Her third *whim*?"

"Yes," she said. "The two before him are dead."

"How dead?"

"How many kinds of dead are there, Davis?"

"No. I meant how did they die?"

She inhaled sharply, her jaw clenched, and she didn't answer.

"Natalie," I started.

She waited.

"Natalie," I started again.

She waited.

"Natalie, is there something going on between Eddie and Bianca Sanders?"

"You could say that." She sniffed.

"What?"

"You could say there's something going on between them."

"*What*?"

She looked at me as if my last marble had just rolled out of my head, across the floor, and out of the building.

"What is going on between them?"

"That's what I want *you* to tell *me*, Davis."

"How do you suggest I go about doing that?"

Natalie closed the space between us. "You look just like her, Davis. *Be* her. Make him think you're her and find out how they're winning the money."

Well, there you go. And what a relief. They only wanted me to weasel the game secrets out of Eddie the Ass by pretending to be Bianca. I had been entertaining much more sinister scenarios, scenarios in which I was in way over my head, and this new perspective was very welcome, with the exception of the Eddie the Rotten Rat angle.

She let me connect the dots before she asked, "Anything else?"

I left her office with a lot on my mind, not the least of which was Eddie winning all that money four months ago, right about when I was dribbling hot chocolate on the classified ads back in Pine Apple, but the most of which was that I had to find a way to get the job done and leave him out of it at the same time.

I still had secrets to keep; otherwise, I'd end up behind bars.

* * *

Of the hours I'd logged on the job so far, very few had been in the casino. During my three weeks of toilet scrubbing, I'd forgotten it was even there. The casino-host office gig had been adjacent, but accessed from outside the casino. It all came flying back when I hit the red and gold carpet.

It was nine o'clock on Wednesday evening, just the right time for a cocktail. I was Marci Dunlow from San Antonio, Texas again, but with a Bianca Casimiro Sanders makeover. Before I left Bradley's place I did two things: I called my sister and described every detail of my outfit, and I checked the Bellissimo guest list and casino activity on the computer. No Eddie Crawford.

Marci was dressed in black capri pencil pants, an oversized pearly cashmere sweater on top of a white silk tank, and she was prancing around in four-inch Jimmy Choos of a dark metal color. My blonde hair, cut shoulder length, was pulled back loosely. My eyes were money green.

I wore Coco Chanel shades all the way through the casino.

When I reached the backlit waterfall that greeted the big fish, I took the sunglasses off and dropped them into my black Fendi hobo like they were a pack of Juicy Fruit. Natalie added jewelry to the mix this time, by way of two-carat princess-cut diamond solitaire earrings, a David Yurman turquoise and platinum cuff bracelet on my right arm, and a platinum and diamond Rolex on my left.

"It's all about the shoes and the watch, Davis," she told me. "If you're wondering if someone really has money, check their shoes and watch."

I was checking the fancy Rolex watch. I hoped it was waterproof, because I think I was drooling on it. "These are on loan from the jewelry store downstairs," she said. "Do not let anything happen to them."

I could feel all the luxury; my skin was hot beneath it. There'd never been a time in my life that I'd wanted for anything, but I had to admit that living the Fab Life gave me an entirely different attitude. Sixteen-hundred dollar shoes on my feet slowed my pace. What was the big hurry? I'd already arrived.

I felt no less than twenty sets of unblinking eyes on me, and I didn't know if that was simply because I'd stepped into the room or they thought I was Bianca. A young man on loan from Hollywood walked up and gave me a slight bow. "Welcome, Miss Dunlow."

I gave him a small sigh and an even smaller nod.

The whale room was more of the same and less of the same: more opulence, less people, more gaming, less noise. One thing was noticeably absent: the air of desperation. Either the waterfall sucked out the anxiety I'd seen on so many gambling faces, or these people had so much money it simply didn't matter.

The ratio of employee to gambler in the main casino was probably one to a hundred; in here it looked to be ten tuxedoed employees per gambler. Everything in this room was cranked up a notch, or ten, and at the same time, scaled down a notch, or twenty. The waterfall, in addition to the tranquility it lent, effectively blocked the noise behind it, and this was like being on a movie set. It was decadence at its finest.

Standing in the entrance I could see, to my right, an Asian man quietly playing blackjack, with his own entourage behind him and a Bellissimo dealer and pit boss in front of him, and I could hear someone playing a slot machine on my left. It would seem that I made three.

"This way." Hollywood held his arm out, and I felt him behind me as the Jimmy Choos sank into the thick carpet. Another tuxedoed man twenty yards away gave me a little bow and swept his right arm out like a ballroom dancer.

Half of the room was devoted to slot machines, the other half, tables. The two sides were separated by a bar and sunken seating area that fell in line behind the waterfall. I passed a short row of twenty-five dollar slot machines. They led to three rows of one-hundred dollar machines and the last two rows, five-hundred dollar machines.

"This way, Miss Dunlow," Tuxedo Two said.

I turned the corner and came face-to-face with four slot machines that ate five-thousand dollars per push of the button, and there they were, to the left of those: Double Whammy Deuces Wild video poker progressives. Nine of them, side by side, holding up a dark wall. A small LDC display above the three middle machines quietly announced the progressive total: $1,287,059, and climbing. These were one-hundred dollar machines. A full wager cost five hundred dollars. I saw the small logo: TGT. Total Gaming Technologies. It was the same game I had played weeks ago with the sisters, and it was exactly like the one in Bradley Cole's small dining alcove, except these weren't open and in a million pieces. And the stakes here were definitely higher.

"How much would you like to start with, Miss Dunlow?" Hollywood asked quietly as a cocktail waitress wearing shoes every bit as expensive as the ones I had on passed me a huge cut-crystal stemless globe full of white wine. I had to hold it with both hands. I tipped her twenty dollars, and she accepted the tip without taking her eyes off me and without saying a word. Nor did she move a muscle.

Hollywood cleared his throat.

The waitress snapped to and quietly left.

"Oh," I said to Hollywood, "ten?"

"Certainly." He backed away and returned with two tickets on a small silver tray valued at five-thousand each. "Your marker balance for the evening is forty thousand."

I blinked okay.

"Do you need anything else?"

I blinked no.

"Good luck, Miss Dunlow." And he stepped away leaving me alone to blow ten thousand dollars.

The wine was positively delicious, just like the shoes, and I made quick work of it. The waitress arrived with another without me asking. She leaned down to place it beside me and whispered, "Are you her sister?"

"Whose sister?" I asked innocently.

* * *

I didn't eat for four days beginning Sunday, August 28, 2005. I lived on coffee, whiskey, and very little sleep. One of those days, because my mother badgered me incessantly, I choked down three pretzels. I stayed glued to the television, then the police scanner and weather radio, then back to the television, as Hurricane Katrina sickeningly tore the holy shit out of my backyard. Eighteen hundred dead, more than one-hundred billion in destruction. Even in Pine Apple, almost two hundred miles inland, we were all but washed away, and spent more than twenty-four hours without power, wringing our hands by the glow of a lamp plugged into the generator at the station. Meredith and I slept in Eddie and Jug's cell, Mother and Daddy on cots between the desks. My husband of less than a year and his former partner-in-crime were in their truck doing electrical things most of that time, and when he wasn't working, Eddie was several miles away with his own parents. It was a horrifying, unimaginable, and helpless time. It got so much worse before it got any better.

"Listen, Davis," Eddie said on the Friday morning after the Storm, the television news in the background showing scene after scene of devastation and mayhem. "Me and Jug are going to head down there."

"Down where?"

"To New Orleans."

I turned down the volume on the television. "Is there a humanitarian hidden somewhere in you, Eddie? Do you want to save people? Do you want to pass out bottles of water?"

He actually scoffed at the idea. That's what a low-life he is.

"Why do you think?" He rose from his seat at our kitchen table and poured himself more coffee. "There's so much work there, I'll be able to retire off what I can make in the next six months."

"You can't even get on Interstate sixty-five," I said. "Much less fifty-nine. How do you plan to get down there? Sprout wings? And once you do, how do you plan on getting in? Land on the Super Dome?"

He never made it to New Orleans. He got as far as Biloxi, where he signed on with Coast Electrical Contractors to get the Bellissimo back up and running. After six months, I think we both forgot we were even married. He never really came home until the summons to appear in divorce court finally caught up with him years later, which was around when, some say, I began behaving badly.

Eddie was right about one thing: there was round-the-clock work in the beginning. The problem was he blew his paychecks at the casinos as they reopened. For the next three years he had everyone believing he was still hard at it, showing up in Pine Apple for the occasional Thanksgiving or Fourth of July, only he failed to mention he was hard at draining my investment fund of a hundred and fifty thousand dollars, not hard at anything that resembled work. For my part, I knew I didn't want him back in Pine Apple, so I left well enough alone. As far as the money went, I'd never kept an eye on it, because I'd never had a reason to. The statements were delivered quarterly, electronically, and they never had anything new to say so I didn't scroll through the seventy pages, just forwarded them to an accountant in Montgomery. I even missed it on the tax returns, with E & J Electric being set up as a C-corporation, there were three hundred pages of IRS forms to dig through, and it never occurred to me to look for the one-liner buried in there showing the taxes due on withdrawals from the investment account. After Eddie had been on the Gulf for almost three years, I accidentally downloaded and opened a statement. Out of boredom, I read it. By that time, the money was long gone.

I had an epic fit that ended with a horrible credit rating, a welcome divorce, and my father saying to me, "Turn in your badge and your gun before someone gets killed."

* * *

"Makers Mark. Make it a double. Neat."

I gambled in Private Gaming three nights in a row with one eye on the door and one on the game. I hadn't stopped looking for him, but I hadn't been listening. So on the fourth night, when I was very close to unclenching, I almost fell in the floor when I heard the biggest mistake of my life order a drink.

He turned the corner and was no more than ten feet away from me before I could even catch my breath. He sat down at the end of the row. There were four empty chairs between us, which weren't nearly enough. He tossed a pack of Marlboro Reds to the side of the video poker machine.

"Thanks, darlin'," he said to the waitress as she passed him the drink.

"Cheers," he finally turned my way, raised his glass, then froze mid-toast.

I suppose I reminded him of someone.

Here we were—Davis and Eddie—and he didn't even recognize me. Or her. What I'd dreaded for days was over. The whole thing was like having my eyebrows waxed: waiting for it was always the worst part. Eddie Crawford couldn't put two and two together on his best day jacked up on a massive dose of Adderall. Give him a whiff of whiskey, and he couldn't tell you his own name. It was borderline comical. He'd obviously had a few, so he couldn't decide if he was sitting across from his ex-wife, Bianca Sanders, or a perfect stranger.

I closed the space between us, took the glass of whiskey out of his hand, knocked it back in one swallow, took off my right Dolce & Gabbana lace platform pump, then drove the four-inch heel through his left eyeball.

(No, I didn't. I wouldn't do that to a shoe.)

I did, however, take the opportunity to look at Eddie from behind my green contacts, as he tried to get his bearings. *He* knocked back the whiskey in one swallow.

Eddie looks like the cover of a really trashy romance novel (*Rake in My Garden*) and—or—Zorro. That's the way it'd always been. He was a stray who didn't belong with the pack, or he could very well be the result of a hospital baby-swap. Mel Crawford was all gangly bones, stooped over and sunken, with a nose that took up most of his face. My former father-in-law always looked as if he'd just been dipped in a vat of boiling oil: the result of a lifetime of standing over a fryer and overserving himself Bombay Sapphire gin. His wife, Bea, who could eat no lean, had a little piggy head set atop a body that could only be replicated with jumbo beach balls, beady brown eyes set alarmingly far apart, and a mouth so small it was amazing all her trash talk escaped it. How they produced Eddie should be the Eighth Wonder of the World. And if it was a hospital faux pas, I'd sure hate to see the baby the Crawfords were *supposed* to take home.

Eddie Crawford was a gorgeous man—short messy black hair, black eyes, and a five o'clock shadow ten minutes after he shaved—easily the prettiest thing to ever hail from Pine Apple, and his good looks were his downfall. He'd leaned on them so hard he hadn't bothered to develop any other human characteristics.

Those who hadn't married him twice might say the good stuff came below his chiseled chin, with a dip that was almost a dimple, and while I'd love to disagree, I couldn't. Eddie Crawford was perfectly proportioned, had a knack for making any manner of clothing look good, carried himself so elegantly you'd think symphony music was playing in his head, and was unbelievably and inexplicably ripped.

With equal airtime, he was as dumb as a rock. It was all over the second he opened his mouth. Which he did.

"You look like two women I know," he said, "but that's not necessarily a bad thing." Then he smiled his let's-get-naked smile.

My heart pounding out of my chest, my face surely the color of a beet, I cut my green eyes at him, cashed out my machine, and got out of there as quickly as I could. If I acknowledged him in any way, I'd blow it all.

This job was supposed to be solving pesky internal problems. They'd really hired me to pretend like I was the boss's wife, get her boyfriend good and drunk, and find out how they kept filling their wallets. There had to be another way, because this way was never going to work.

* * *

I was still shaking when I climbed into the backseat.

"Rough night?" George asked.

I didn't know how to answer. He pulled out, and we made the commute to Bradley Cole's in silence. He parked the car, but left it running.

"I need more stuff, George." I passed him a slip of paper.

He muttered something under his breath, probably because I'd demanded he go to the grocery store for me the day before and I had tampons on the list. I was working day and night, either in my pajamas pulling a slot machine apart and trying like hell to make sense of his son's notes from years ago, or dressed up like a runway model playing a slot machine. I'd averaged three hours of sleep a night for the week. I couldn't do it without him, and he knew it. So he could mumble all he wanted. I'd just sat five feet away from my ex-husband, whom I loathed, and I didn't, at the moment, care.

He pulled reading glasses from his pocket and held the paper close to the glowing dash. "What is a Simonhex?"

"It's computer software," I told him. "No telling where you'll have to go to get it. Just ask around."

"Is it big?"

"It'll be a disk, George, or a slip of paper with numbers on it. You can put it in your pocket."

"What does it do?"

"It disassembles computer programs. It lets you read computer language backwards."

"Why do you need it?"

"I have a hunch."

"When?"

"When did I have the hunch?"

"No," George said. "When do you need the Simonhex?"

"Absolutely as soon as possible."

"What's your hunch?"

"My *what*?"

"Never mind."

The phone woke me at the ungodly hour of six the next morning. He didn't bother with hello. "They're telling me you buy it *on* the computer."

"I can't. I have to load it manually." I hung up, rolled over, and went right back to sleep.

I was too groggy to explain to George that downloading it onto my computer, with what I intended to do with it, would nail me if this thing went sour. But I might as well have downloaded it. I could have taken out a personal ad: DAVIS WAY, OF PINE APPLE, ALABAMA, IS USING THIS SOFTWARE TO CRACK THE CODE OF A SLOT MACHINE, WHICH IS TOTALLY AGAINST THE LAW, SO COME AND GET HER.

Because George using my debit card (that I'd forgotten I'd given him for Pop Tarts and peanut butter) was the equivalent of taking out an ad.

"Watch yourself," Mr. Sanders had said to me. "Because the Gaming Board won't care what your intent was."

"I get that." But did I? Did I really understand the significance of those words?

"Anything that happens on this property is within my jurisdiction," he said. "But I can't help you or anyone else if the Gaming Board gets involved. That's federal stuff, Davis."

Now I get it.

Boy, do I get it.

FOURTEEN

I hacked into every account Edward Meldrick Crawford ever dreamed of having. Next I hacked into the accounts of Mel and Bea Crawford, then the Mel's Diner accounts. I ran all three Social Security numbers forwards, backwards, up, down, and diagonally through every database known to man.

Between the three of them, a whopping $38,575 in income was reported to the IRS last year. I ran title searches, checked mortgage applications, and ran all of their credit cards. I looked at every single deposit, withdrawal, and processed check image for the last six months. Mel and Bea bought a new washer and dryer on their MasterCard last September, wrote one substantial check—$2,100 to Earl and Daughters Construction—and financed a new two-vehicle metal carport at Lowe's. (At 28% interest. Were they completely nuts?) (Yes.)

In the same six-month time period, Eddie made small cash advances and swiped his debit card at department stores, salons, and restaurants. There wasn't a single Bellissimo hotel charge, but there were multiple charges for the Lucky Tiger, a cheesy run-down excuse of a hotel-casino somewhere nearby. How cheesy? The room charges were $32.88 per night. He had one monthly direct debit: Good Body Gym in Biloxi. $49.99. (Welcome to your thirties, Eddie.) His income was intermittent, and cash, $3500 here, $3700 there, about once a month. It barely covered his living expenses. Where was homeboy getting his gambling bankroll for the Bellissimo?

The big money Eddie won in November was in mayonnaise jars buried somewhere in Mel's and Bea's backyard, stuffed in a mattress, or somebody had it wrong, and it wasn't there to begin with.

* * *

I didn't know who my friends were; I didn't know who my enemies were. It was hard to know where to turn, so I just turned around. And around. And around. When I was as dizzy as I could possibly be, I decided to take one step, one player, one question, at a time. First, I'd try to see what might be going on with Mr. and Mrs. Richard Sanders.

Natalie was out of the question. Not only did she guard the boss as if he was Fort Knox, the temperature in any room she occupied was a good ten degrees cooler than anywhere else. I wasn't going to her for Sanders' Marriage Dirt.

George, as much as he might have liked to help, wasn't close enough to either Sanders to be of any assistance. Even if he were, clearly, George thought there was a direct link between Bianca and his son's death, so any objectivity he might have had was out the window.

Teeth and No Hair scared me to death, just the bulk of them. But between the two, I felt like No Hair was the way to go. For reinforcement, or for procrastination, I called my father.

"Pine Apple Police."

"Daddy, it's me. Do you still have your notes on the two big guys I'm working with?"

"I do, Sweet Pea, right here."

I knew exactly what my father was doing two hundred miles away—tapping his right temple with one finger.

"If I needed to confide in one of them, who would you choose?"

"I'd go with Jeremy Coven."

I knew it. No Hair. (Lots of hair.) "Why?"

"Because Bergman's a retired football player, and he has priors that have been expunged."

"I wonder what."

"You have to assume," Daddy said, "if he tackled people for a living, then went into security, it would be assault related."

"Probably," I said.

Since he clearly wanted to choke me to death so often, it wasn't a big stretch to think he *had* choked someone to death.

"The other one," Daddy said, "Coven, is local. They found him at the Mississippi Bureau." (Of Investigation, he didn't say.) "And his record is clean as a whistle."

* * *

No Hair was off on Sundays. Teeth, Tuesdays. I waited until Tuesday, after lunch, when No Hair showed up for work, and dug the Bat phone out.

"It's Davis."

I heard No Hair suck in a breath like I'd said, "It's the Devil. Come on down."

"What do you want?"

"You know this slot machine you guys brought me?"

"What about it?"

"It fell over."

"It what?"

"It fell over on the floor."

"Slot machines don't fall over."

"This one did."

"So, you want sympathy? What?"

"No. I need you to help me get it back up."

"Are you pinned underneath it?"

"No."

"Then why are you calling me?"

I rolled my eyes. "I changed my mind. I am pinned underneath it."

No Hair, not one for pleasantries, didn't say goodbye, or hello either, when he pounded on Bradley Cole's door twenty minutes later, scaring the bejesus out of me. I practically had to have a step-ladder to look through the peephole, and not having one handy, I went ahead and jerked the door open, and there he was. All of him. Filling the doorway. A mouse couldn't have snuck past, not that it would have had the nerve to.

He surveyed. "A tornado run through here?"

"I resent that," I said. "I'll have you know I'm working around the clock." I turned and looked at Bradley's place through No Hair's beady little eyes, and had to admit that carrying out the garbage might not be a bad idea. Or at least corralling it. Considering I didn't really like Chinese food all that much, there were an inordinate number of take-out boxes on every available surface, and many unavailable surfaces, like the floor. And maybe just a few (hundred) discarded articles of clothing. I was having a little dust problem, too, because I'd doodled Bradley Cole's name in it on the entryway table, and No Hair was trying to read it. I kind of sat on it and scooted. Now I had dust all over my butt. Embarrassing.

"Does the landlord know you live like this?" He pushed past me and kicked the door closed with one of his dinosaur feet. "Good God." He recoiled. "Crack a window," he waved his hand in front of his face. "Didn't you just finish a housekeeping gig? Did you not learn anything?"

"Yeah," I was on his heels as he helped himself, poking his big bald head in every room. "I learned that I needed a break from cleaning."

He finished his tour at the upright slot machine. The door was ajar and most of the insides out. Wires were everywhere. He turned to me, paws on middle. Not having eyebrows didn't keep him from raising them.

I shrugged. "I lied."

His face contorted in a way that made me uncomfortable.

"I need to talk to you," I explained. In a place that's not bugged, I didn't explain.

He huffed, and turned toward the kitchen. I could imagine the light fixtures in the condo below Bradley's rattling in their sockets and clouds of dust and debris falling, tracing his footsteps.

No Hair helped himself to the deep cabinet beneath the sink. He banged around and came out with a roll of paper towels, a squirt bottle of something blue, a squirt bottle of something clear, and two garbage bags. He carefully loosened, slid out of, then neatly rolled his Snoopy and Woodstock necktie. He put it on top of the refrigerator. "We'll talk later." He passed me a garbage bag.

Who knew? Teeth was on Jenny Craig and No Hair was on Merry Maids.

* * *

I thought I'd been through every square inch of Bradley Cole's place, but I'd missed a storage closet off the kitchen. I knew it was there; I'd peeked in, but I hadn't turned on the light, so I hadn't seen the stacked washer and dryer. Or the broom and dustpan. Or the vacuum cleaner, the non-industrial type. It was a pleasant surprise, this bevy-of-cleanliness room, because not only were my clothes in need of a romp through the machines, so were most of Bradley Cole's.

No Hair asked for coffee as he was transferring a wet blob of bed sheets from the washer to the dryer, then loading mine and Bradley's underwear, separated by lights and darks, into the washer. He held up a pair of blue-striped boxer shorts by a stubby fingertip and waved them through the air like a flag. "Anything you'd like to say?"

I shook my head furiously. It was all extremely humiliating.

"What about that coffee?"

"There's no coffee here."

"I bet you a hundred bucks there's coffee here."

He won. There was a French press in one of the kitchen cabinets and coffee in the freezer. As warm coffee smells mingled with lavender-scented laundry smells—a definite improvement, I must say—I asked No Hair what was going on at work.

"Obviously nothing." He was folding towels. Perfect rectangles. "Or I wouldn't be here washing your clothes."

Touché.

"Natalie is out of the office, and Mr. Sanders is in New Hampshire," he said. "And that doesn't happen too often."

"I never go to New Hampshire either."

He gave me a look. "It doesn't happen often that they both are out of the office."

Right.

"What's going on in New Hampshire?"

"The Sanders' son, Thomas? Switching schools."

"It's a weird time of year to switch schools, don't you think? Why so far away? And why did Natalie go?"

He threw down a towel he was folding. "Lady. You make my head hurt. Why can't you ask one question at a time?"

Why do people ask me that? Is it so hard to follow simple conversation? How is it that my family talks this way and we all understand each other?

A clean condo later, we were sitting at the unearthed bistro table in the dining alcove, three computers up and running, and the dismantled slot machine that enveloped us the only mess left in the whole place. No Hair's bulk was torturing the chair; it cried out in pain.

"Tell me why you're doing this." No Hair was talking about the equipment that encircled us.

"Tell me about Mr. and Mrs. Sanders."

"Okay," No Hair said. "You first."

"No," I said, "you're my guest. You go first."

"Oh, no," No Hair said, "ladies first."

This went on awhile until No Hair got tired of it.

"Okay. Geesh," he said. "This is for you to know, not repeat." He looked at me like he'd kill me.

I held both hands up, surrendering, assuring him I wouldn't dare subject myself to death by him.

"How much do you know about hyenas?"

Fear gripped me. "Did you find one in here?" I jerked my feet off the floor.

He closed his eyes in a meditation sort of way. Without opening them he said, "They eat their young."

I made choking, gagging, ach noises.

"They're better mothers than Bianca Sanders," he said. "And what do you know about black widow spiders?"

I wasn't going to overreact. If he found some in here, I'm sure he vacuumed them up because he'd moved every piece of furniture away from the walls to vacuum behind, and even used the hose thing twice. Note to self: Put vacuum cleaner full of spiders outside with note: free to good home.

"They eat their mates," No Hair said about the spiders. "And they're better spouses than Bianca Sanders."

"Why would Mr. Sanders marry someone like that?"

"I'm his employee," No Hair said, "not his therapist. But my guess would be that she was a means to an end."

"People aren't that shallow," I said. "He wouldn't have married her unless he loved her."

"Funny," No Hair scoffed, "coming from you."

"You don't know a thing about me." I stuck my chin out. "Or why I got married."

"Whatever you say," he mocked me.

"You probably don't know a *thing* about being married, so don't judge me."

"I've been married to the same wonderful woman for twenty-two years, thank you. And if she kept house like you, it would have been twenty-two minutes."

Well, now, this changed things. I tapped my loose lips for a second and wondered how to weasel out. I gave him a sheepish apologetic smile, while also wondering what his wife's hair situation might be. He sat there daring me to say something else. So I did.

"What does any of this have to do with Natalie?"

"I don't know that it does have anything to do with Natalie. Why do you ask?"

"Didn't you say they were together?"

"No," No Hair said, "I said they were both out of the office. That doesn't necessarily mean they're together. What is it you're really asking here? If Natalie and Richard have something going on?"

The thought had never crossed my mind. Until just then.

"All I know," No Hair said, "is that it was Richard's decision to get his son out of town."

I looked to the four thousand pieces of slot machine. I was beginning to understand why Mr. Sanders might want his son far, far away.

No Hair poured himself more coffee. "Now. Your turn," he said. "What's all this?" His hands splayed open.

I sucked in a big breath. It was time to bring No Hair in on the big secret. "The big game? The one I'm playing in Private Gaming?"

He sniffed.

"Rigged."

No Hair shifted positions. "I got bad news for you."

"What?" I'm sure my eyes were saucers.

"Everybody knows that."

"Knows what?"

"That there's something going on with that game."

"You know she picks who wins?"

"Bianca?" No Hair asked.

I nodded. "The black widow hyena herself."

"Yes. We know that, too."

"Is there any special reason no one bothered to tell me?"

"Everything's a need-to-know, Davis. You didn't need to know. All you need to do is get dressed up like Bianca, wait until your ex-husband's got a few drinks in him, saddle up to him in Private Gaming, and say, 'Now, let's go over this again.'"

I opened my mouth to speak, closed it, opened it again.

"Why can't you do that?" he asked.

I fiddled, picked at things, hummed, and generally let the clock tick.

"Come on, motor mouth." No Hair tapped a big foot. "You could talk the paint off the wall. You can certainly talk about this."

"He doesn't know how to win the game," I said.

"How do you know that?"

"Because there's no money trail."

"Go on," No Hair said.

"Bianca's the brains behind it. She has the key, and she's keeping the money."

"How'd she get it?"

"Get what?"

"How!" No Hair raised both hands to the heavens like he was begging for mercy. "How did Bianca get the key?"

"It goes back years," I told him, "back to Vegas, and the programmer who wrote the software. Bianca must have gotten it from him, and the only other person who might know it is—" I clapped both of my hands over my mouth to keep the word *Teeth* in there. Something told me that if I tossed Teeth's name in the ring, No Hair would knock mine out, then ring my neck.

"Who?"

"Not Eddie."

"Who, then?"

"Who, when?"

"Oh, for God's sake!" No Hair shot up, reached the kitchen in one big step, retrieved his tie from the top of the refrigerator, then began flipping it around in a very practiced way. "What's it going to take for you to wind this up?"

"Figuring out the software." I did *ta-da!*

"What then?"

"What when?"

"After you figure out the software. What then?"

"I'll test it."

"How?"

"By winning the game."

No Hair half laughed. "That could be dangerous. Two of the three people who've won it are dead. Your ex is next in line."

And there it was, what I'd been gnawing on, and the reason I ordered Chinese food I couldn't choke down, and why I could only log two or three pillow hours in twenty-four: How far up my list should saving that rat bastard's life be? Should saving his sorry butt even be on my list?

"Man, you guys set me up." I let out a long frustrated puff of air.

"You were a perfect storm for the job." We sat in complete silence until he said, "And no one set you up. It's my understanding there's wording in the contract you signed that covers all this. Apparently you didn't bother to read it."

That damn phone book again. "If I'd known this had anything to do with my ex-husband," I said, "I wouldn't be here."

"Why?" he asked. "People get divorced every day of the week. No one's asking you to get back together with him."

I thought it best to push my cuticles back instead of respond.

"Does the guy bite?"

Which made me think of Teeth again.

"Your indignation is hard to understand, Davis," No Hair said. "You act as if you laid all your cards out on the table. You did *not*. You could have said, 'By the way, my ex-husband hangs out here and he doesn't like me much' but you didn't. Maybe if you had, some of this would have been explained to you."

"By whom?" I asked. "Who is running this show, No Hair?"

My hand flew to my mouth. Now we sat in dead silence. Oops.

"What did you call me?"

There is a God, and he called No Hair on the phone right then, keeping the oversized bully from squashing me like a bug. He listened, grunted, then stood. "I've got to get back." At the door, he turned to me. "Where does the old man fit in?"

"What old man?" I asked.

"The old guy you ride around with."

"I don't know what you're talking about."

"Give me a break," No Hair said. "You think the rest of us are idiots?"

My mouth dropped open. I thought the I-Spy-Davis program had pretty much ended. "Do you guys know when I shave my legs?"

"Nobody cares when you shave your legs."

Sadly enough, all too true, except Bradley Cole might care because it was his razor.

No Hair wasn't going to leave until I answered him, and I was ready, ready, ready for him to get going.

"I think his son went down first."

"The guy's a cab driver in south Mississippi. What could his son have to do with anything?"

"No," I said, lowering my voice. "The guy's a former Las Vegas detective. And his son is the one who wrote the glitch into the software."

"Where's the son?"

"Six. Feet. Under."

No Hair's eyes narrowed. "Do Natalie or Richard know any of this?"

"I don't know who knows what or what knows who."

His phone began ringing again. "Check those sheets," he said over his shoulder.

"What sheets?" I asked. Time sheets? Data sheets?

"The *bed* sheets."

FIFTEEN

No Hair's visit ate up the afternoon, most of it cleaning. I didn't go to the casino and play video poker that night, because Eddie Crawford was a registered guest at the Bellissimo, so I gave myself a pass. I'd drop-kicked Eddie out of my life twice already, both times of great personal loss, and figuring this out without having to clean up after his exit a third time was my goal.

Oddly enough, though, part of me wished I were going in to work tonight, certainly not to breathe the same air as Eddie the Ass, but because a shower, expensive clothes, makeup, and two lemon drop martinis would feel good. Who was I kidding? I wanted to play the video poker machines. I played with the equivalent of Monopoly money; no one, certainly not me personally, was losing real money when I discarded two cowboys (kings, remember?) and held the lone ace hoping for the miracle of three more on the second draw. I'd played the game long enough, including my first stint weeks ago with the retired-teacher-sisters, to be challenged by it. I knew what the cards were capable of, and wanted to be sitting there when they lined up. I wanted to hit a royal flush, and I hadn't even come close. The best I'd done on the Monster Machines in Private Gaming was hit a full house four different times. I was stunned by how intense the game was, to the point of losing track of the job, the luxury, and the green contacts. It was just me and the game.

Two long blasts from a car horn in the parking lot had me raising the mini blinds an inch, then all the way. George. The software. I beckoned him up with my hand.

He blinked his lights, like, *No, you come down here.*

So I pointed at the floor beneath me, like, *No, George, you get your lazy ass out of that cab.*

After the standoff, I won.

He backed the cab into an empty parking place.

"You want a cup of coffee, George?"

He was uncomfortable indoors, shifting his weight, holding his black knit cap with both hands and declining to have a seat, but I could see him admiring my spotlessly clean digs.

"I'm surprised you have coffee," he said.

"You and me both."

"You got anything stronger?" he asked.

* * *

George's eyes were as black as coal, his skin a deep caramel color, his hair gray in half-moon patterns behind his ears, with a white splotch the size and shape of a postage stamp above his right eye, along his receding hairline. George was roughly my father's age, but broken, where my father still had mischief and humor to spare.

"I lost Morgan's mother when he was four," George said. "It was just us all those years. I saved twenty percent of every paycheck from the day that boy was born to send him to college, and I shouldn't have bothered, because my boy was a genius, and the school paid him to go."

I refilled his short glass. I hoped George wouldn't end up sleeping on Bradley Cole's sofa. I knew all about loss, and if I were in his shoes, saying the words out loud, I'd end up on someone's sofa. Probably Dr. Someone's sofa.

"He was always smart. You know that Rubik's Cube game?"

I nodded.

"He could do that thing in three minutes flat."

I was impressed.

George stared at the floor. Not another word passed between us for the next five hours. It was just five minutes, but when you're sitting opposite a wound that raw, believe me, it feels like five years. Finally, he looked up.

"Tell me about the Casimiros, George."

He rubbed his stubbly chin. "That bunch is barely human. More like animals."

"So I've heard."

* * *

It was me who slept on the sofa. I woke up so disoriented, my first thought was Bradley Cole had come home, and he was in the bed.

"Bradley?" I listened. "Bradley Cole?"

The details of how the night before ended wouldn't come to me immediately. I ran to the window; George's car was gone. There were no signs of the dinner he'd cooked—George is a great cook—and he'd even carried out the garbage. I must have fallen asleep, and George let himself out.

I stretched, yawned, and logged into the Bellissimo system to find that my rotten ex-ex-husband had checked out.

Goody-goody! Let the games begin!

My inbox was full. There were emails from every website I'd ever visited, my sister, Websters-dot-com (Word of the Day), Joke-dot-com, (Joke of the Day), and Natalie.

> *Davis, head's up. We're going to need you in Bones for a few shifts starting tonight. I realize this will spread you thin, but it will only be for a couple of hours, and just two, maybe three, nights. Stop by and pick up your uniform around lunch and we'll talk. Thanks, Natalie*

What? Bones was an upscale fishery restaurant in the main lobby of the Bellissimo. I'd passed it several times, and had avoided passing it many more times than that. I don't like anything about fish. Things that swim make me nervous. There'd been an incident when I was very young—I barely remember it—but from that point forward, fish had never been served at my house. A few shifts? A uniform? Did I not have enough to do? And I wondered if she expected me to play video poker in the Richie Rich room, then ask Hollywood to watch my poker machine while I changed into a waitress uniform and served up lobster tempuras. I don't know the first thing about being a waitress. I couldn't pour myself a glass of water without sloshing most of it on the floor. This would be cute.

I was only half awake when I pulled the SimonHex software out of the thin jacket and popped it into my drive. It stumbled around, then gave me a prompt. Are you sure you want to load this? I'm sure. Do you want to register it now or later? There was no button for never.

It was barely seven in the morning. I'd sit here until ten, and then I'd go into work and try to talk Natalie out of making me serve dead floppy fish.

* * *

It is a travesty of the highest sort that an institute of higher learning would hand out a license to kill in the form of a diploma, when the recipient—me, in this case—has no more idea what they are doing than the average fourth-grader. I daresay, even unarmed with a degree in Computer Science, a fourth grader would've had an easier time than I was having, which is to say I was as far out of my element as I'd ever been in my life. To successfully manipulate any program or a system, it has to make sense. Most do. This didn't. I couldn't pinpoint the rhyme or reason. I spent more time staring at the three computer screens than anything else, and the knock on my door scared the living daylights out of me.

I jerked the door open. (I've got to stop doing that.) It was the dry-cleaning delivery guy. He'd picked up and delivered to me a handful of times since I'd moved in, and always late afternoon. He was an older guy, with a thick, ropey, protruding vein that separated one side of his forehead from the other.

The words out of my mouth were, "What the hell time is it?"

He stared at me, took a step back, shoved the plastic-covered clothes at me, and ran.

"If you're going to come early," I shouted after him, "you could give a person a little warning."

I decided to hang the clothes up, and unfortunately passed a mirror on the way. I was wearing Bradley Cole's bathrobe over his Milk: It Does a Body Good T-shirt. Hopefully I had underwear on, but I didn't check. My new-blonde hair was literally standing on end all over my head, and I'd accidentally smeared yesterday's mascara all over my face in the process of reading the backwards version of the binary forms of the slot machine's brains. I looked like scary hell. No wonder the guy had run. Honestly, it's a wonder he hadn't screamed.

There were three computer chips, all soldered to the motherboard inside the slot machine. Two contained the game data, and the third was a random number generator. It popped right off, and, as it turned out, wasn't so random a number generator. That made good sense to me, because if it was completely arbitrary, the casino wouldn't be able to guarantee that they would make money. Interesting, certainly, but I tossed that chip aside. I was more interested in the two that contained the game data written by Morgan George, Jr.

It took forever to get them off the motherboard. Their almost permanent adhesive was probably a security feature; otherwise savvy tech types would open slot machines, snap them off, and replace them with their own. It wasn't easy to remove the chips unscathed either, I'll tell you that. When I finally had them in my hand, I felt like I was holding kryptonite.

They were straightforward programs, both 110Gs, just like you'd find on any personal computer, and, as it turned out, simple code, just a lot of it. After I reversed the language with the SimonHex, I found a semblance of map: X = X. Every blue moon, X = Y, and that would be when the player wins a little. I was looking for X = Z, the jackpot, and I think I found it. I didn't stop to do the math, but my guess was the jackpot sequence occurred no more often than once every gazillion entries, because in all that, I only found it once.

What I eventually found were five incidents where X = B. B for Bingo. That's what I was looking for. I think. When decoded, the software was long strings of 1s and 0s. Thousands of long strings. Young Morgan George had, every bazillion bits of code, left half a space, five different times. I also stumbled upon five inverted Vs, each about the size of a gnat, in the 700-page binder he'd written that supported the software, supplied by the deceased's father that I had to have a magnifying glass to see. Bradley Cole didn't own a magnifying glass that I could find, so I used a clear drinking glass full of water, passing it back and forth along each page. On page 128 and then again on page 452, I accidentally dumped the glass of water all over the binder, thankfully missing everything else, but the fact remained, I shouldn't be trusted in a restaurant.

The problem was that the bleeps in the program language and the pencil marks in the damp binder didn't line up. Nothing said, "Here, Davis, these two go together." The code referenced hexadecimal numbers that, when triggered, located a specific combination of five of the fifty-two card values. And that was just the first time the player pushed the deal button. It happened all over again when the player decided which cards to discard and then pushed the deal button again, bringing the second computer chip into play.

And get this: it happened five different times on both chips. Five spaces, five inverted Vs, times two chips, that's ten total. I took a guess because there was only one thing I could think of that could happen five times in the game: the wager. Morgan George, Jr. had written something in the program that sent it on a different path based on the size of the bet: one, two, three, four, or five coins. It was all I could come up with short of tracking down a fourth grader to do the honors for me. My best guess was that between wagers, the program kicked into another gear. I honestly couldn't come up with anything else.

No wonder I looked like the crazy cat lady. My brain was fried. Had I even eaten? It had to be noon. It could, I glanced out the window to see the sun in a weird place, be even later. I looked for a clock. Five-thirty! In the afternoon! I raced to the bedroom and dug my cell phones out of my bag. I had seven missed calls from Natalie.

I took the world's fastest shower, pulled my wet hair back, and raced to the Bellissimo in my own car. If my day hadn't started on the sofa, maybe it would have ended differently.

SIXTEEN

Natalie hadn't quite known what to say. "Are you *afraid* of fish?"

"Well," I stumbled, "live fish, certainly. It would be safe to say I'm afraid of *live* fish. I don't even get in swimming pools."

She sat back and crossed her arms. "Davis, there aren't live fish in swimming pools."

"You never know."

I was trying to talk her into letting me be a waitress in one of the other restaurants. I wanted to talk her into letting me off the waitressing hook altogether, but seeing as how I'd stressed everyone out by being so MIA all day, I thought it best to shoot for a closer star. The No Fish star.

"We're not talking a permanent position, Davis," she said. "Salito Casimiro, Bianca's brother, is on his way to Biloxi. They always have dinner at Bones and I *need* you there. I need to know exactly what they say to each other. The easiest way to do that is for you to be on the staff. If you've had no waitressing experience whatsoever, you need to work a few shifts until you're comfortable."

"Again, Natalie, I'm not opposed to waitressing. I'm just opposed to fish." As anti-fish as I am, though, her interest level in "exactly what they say to each other" piqued my interest, too (why's she so concerned?), but not enough to hang out with things that swim. She had me on the fish fence.

I could see she didn't know which way to go, either. She tapped out a tune on her desk with her fingers. "Just try it tonight." She turned to her computer and her fingers flew across the keyboard. "They're barely booked," she said. "It will be, I promise you, a piece of cake."

Fish cake? Pass.

I rose reluctantly, and put my bravest smile on. With best foot forward, I entered her secret lounge and changed into the uniform, your basic black and white getup, pants this time, topped off with a narrow black necktie. Unfortunately, there was another wig involved, and this one looked closer to my actual hair than any of the others, just not as long. To mix things up, I guess, Natalie had supplied blue-tinted contact lenses for my waitressing gig.

"I love the transformation," she said.

I tried to smile.

"You can do this, Davis!"

I took a deep breath and tried harder to smile.

Ten minutes later, I entered the side door of the restaurant's kitchen, and two minutes after that, they called 911. I went into anaphylactic shock. It would seem I'm so highly allergic to shellfish, and there was such a large amount of it in such a small space, that my respiratory system shut down. I don't remember a bit of it, except seeing a long stainless-steel table covered with plates of upside-down orange-red creepy-crawlies when I pushed through the kitchen doors. The next thing I knew, I was in room 410 of Biloxi Memorial Hospital. I sat straight up in the bed and yelled, "Bradley?"

My mother, in a stiff plastic chair beside the bed asked, "Who is Bradley?"

* * *

"You know, Davis," my mother said, "I really thought you were on track for possibly the first time in your life. I just don't understand," she flipped through a magazine, her reading glasses perched on the tip of her nose, "why you'd dye your hair or tell your father that you were on a security staff if you were working in a restaurant."

"Mother," I tried again, "I'm not working in a restaurant." For some reason, I was slurring my words, like I'd had several chocolate martinis. And I needed sunglasses. My eyes felt like they had gravel in them.

"I know it wouldn't be easy, but you could wait tables at Mel's if that's what you want to do with your life, and be closer to your family." She let the magazine fall into her lap. "We could use your help with Riley, you know. And your father would surely, at some point, forgive you, and need your help at work." She picked up the magazine again. "You couldn't be making that much money working in a restaurant."

I pulled a pillow over my head. There were so many things wrong with what she'd said that there wasn't even a place to start.

"Is this about Eddie?" she demanded.

I moved the pillow an inch so I could see her. "Mother." She looked up. "Do you really want me to move back home?"

The answer was in her silence.

"Mother." She looked up again. "How is Daddy?"

The answer was in her smile.

I pulled the pillow over my head again.

"Knock, knock!" I heard a muffled voice. I peeked out and saw Natalie's feet. I knew they were her feet because I recognized the brown leather boots from my first day on the job. I stayed under the pillow. I listened to the boots cross the floor.

"You must be Mrs. Way." Natalie's muffled voice reached me, and so did my mother's cooing.

Here's where my mother turned on the charm to the point of me trying to tell anyone about how she really operates and them finding it hard to believe. Finally, my mother shut up, but not before working the conversation around to telling Natalie that she had an unused college degree because of me.

Natalie made the appropriate noises while Mother droned on, and when Mother finally took a breath, Natalie asked, "How's our patient?"

"Oh, goodness gracious," my mother gushed, "I'm not sure *what* Davis was thinking! She knows she's allergic to shellfish!"

I shot out from under the pillow. "Like hell, I knew it!"

Natalie's head jerked back and she clapped a hand over her mouth.

"If I'd *known*, Mother, I wouldn't be here!"

I saw my mother's sly smile. I looked to Natalie's shocked face. My mother—try to believe me—loved me getting caught with my pants down, and from the glint in her eye, I knew it was happening. I just didn't know how. Was I naked? I peeked. Almost, but no. Had I grown two heads? I'd better look. I jumped out of the bed and found the reflective box over the small sink. I almost passed out; the backs of my knees caved.

Two normal heads would have been a huge improvement over the one head I had. Enormous cherry-red welts covered the entire surface of my face, crept down my neck, and I could see them on my chest through the thin bed sheet someone had half tied on me. My lips were deep, blood red, almost black, swollen, and cracked. The area between my forehead and my nose was so blown up that my eyes appeared to be little recessed dots in the back of my head, and there was an ugly gash above the left one. For the second day in a row my blonde hair was standing on end, like it desperately wanted away from my scalp. I wasn't going to use the shampoo from the New Orleans stylist one more time. That stuff was toxic. It turned my hair into runaway straw during the night.

I whimpered into the mirror, drowning kitten sort of noises.

* * *

Wouldn't you know it? Bianca Sanders and her brother didn't even eat dinner at Bones. I could have died a fish death, and all for naught. Natalie casually dropped that bomb over the phone while I was snipping off my plastic hospital bracelet with a toenail clipper. To make it all better, she gave me some time off. (She didn't want me at work until I could be seen in public and said public not run and scream.)

"Will your mother stay with you until you're feeling better?" she asked.

"No," I said. "She's already halfway back to Pine Apple." Mother dropped me at the door after snapping a picture of me with her cell phone. We were at a red light between Patient Discharge and Bradley's Place. "Davis. Look here." I turned. Click. "Your father will want to see this." Now, as if I didn't have enough to do, I'd have to hack my own mother's phone.

The antihistamines the hospital sent me home with refused to let me sleep for more than ten minutes at a time. So while my system calmed down, I sat at my three computers and two slot machines in Bradley Cole's packed-out dining alcove. There were two slot machines now, because before I was released from the hospital, No Hair and Teeth had removed all seven thousand pieces of the first video poker machine and delivered two more that had, I assumed, yet an additional code to crack, because these were linked together. These were programmed to pay a progressive jackpot.

I wondered, not for the first time, what Bradley Cole's neighbors thought about his sublessee who, at the moment, looked like something out of a horror flick, and at most other moments, was entertaining all manner of men at all hours, testing a different shade and style of hair, dog-cussing dry-cleaning delivery guys, living on pizza and Moo Shu pork, or had slot machines running in and out the door.

* * *

The swelling in my face went down; the swelling in my brain went up. I went to work on the slot machines, wrestling six computer chips off two motherboards, tossing the random number generator chips again, then running the four containing the game data through the SimonHex software to look at them backwards. Forty hours, one nap, and three pizzas later, between the four game chips from the progressive machines and the two from the first video poker machine I'd demolished, I couldn't find a single digit reassigned. I knew there had to be a difference, other than the obvious, which was simple script at the end of the programs communicating to the machines left and right, and, truly, it turned out to be as simple as two plus two, so I spent an entire day and loads of Bellissimo money attempting to prove to myself there was no difference in the programming between stand-alone and progressive machines.

Because there *had* to be, unless an outside influence triggered the progressive win. I hoped to everything holy that it wasn't that, because if it were something outside the programming, I'd never find it. The possibilities were too infinite. It could be having seventeen rubber bands in one pocket, and three marbles in the other. It could have been a toothpick held between the teeth just right. Or maybe it was a lunar eclipse. Or a handheld trigger. Or singing the machine a Broadway tune in E-flat.

There was one thing left to try, then I'd have to do what they hired me to do: get it out of Eddie Crawford.

I couldn't decide which one I'd rather not deal with, Teeth or No Hair, so instead of calling their individual phones, I called their office. I got Teeth.

"You need a *what*?"

"A printer," I said. "A heavy-duty printer. And about six zillion sheets of transparent paper."

"See-through paper? There's no such thing," he said. "And what constitutes a heavy-duty printer anyway?"

Why did everyone argue with me? An hour and a half later, an Office Depot delivery truck blocked the main entrance into the builidng unloading two huge wooden crates followed by a rolling dolly stacked with smaller corrugated boxes.

I watched through the mini blinds, and raised the window an inch to listen when some unflattering chatter about me ensued.

"It's that subleaser on three." A man, who I'd seen in the elevator, was juggling grocery bags talking to a woman, who I'd seen in the lobby. They were shivering, trying to keep warm, awaiting entry to the building.

"You know, I thought we couldn't sublease," the woman said.

"I called him," the man said. "He's been transferred back to Las Vegas for six months."

What? He tattled to Bradley Cole about me?

"He said she was his cousin."

"Right," the woman said. "And I'm his mother."

"Were you here last week when someone delivered *slot* machines?"

"You have got to be kidding me," the woman said. "Like there aren't enough right down the street."

I slammed down the window. They both looked up, then shrugged at each other.

"Lady!"

I spun.

"Where in the world do you want to set this up?"

One of the Office Depot guys had uncrated the two parts of the printer. Good Lord. When I told Teeth I needed a heavy-duty printer, I hadn't exactly meant one that could print Christmas catalogs.

In the end, we shoved Bradley Cole's bed into the corner, and set the printer up in the bedroom. Getting the two parts through the doorway had taken its toll on both the door frame and the walls. Now I'd have to track down a carpenter and a painter.

"How am I supposed to get to the bed?" I asked.

"I guess you'll have to climb over the printer." The guy shoved a clipboard at me. "Sign here."

Here's one good thing that came from being married to Eddie Crawford: I knew a little, a very little, about things electrical, probably just enough to flash fry the whole building. (And my neighbors thought standing in the cold for ten teeny minutes was an inconvenience.) So instead of getting dressed and going to a store, pissing off Teeth a little more, or trying to get George to run my errands, the first thing I did was splice enough Ethernet cable to get the printer hooked up to my network. This required a steak knife, duct tape, squeezing my eyes shut and praying several times, and dragging one of the hard drives to the hall between the dining room and the bedroom. I surveyed my handiwork. This place was now officially an obstacle course.

I sat down at one of the keyboards and typed, DAVIS LOVES BRADLEY. I hit print, and heard the bedroom whir to life as the machine ejected a sheet of printed paper. Success. After loading the paper bin to the fill line with ream after ream of transparencies, I printed the encoded data for the long-gone slot machine. Loading the printer again, I queued up the readable code for the first of the two new machines, then the second. In the end, I had three stacks of transparencies on the kitchen counter that rose to the tip of my nose.

I turned from the massive stacks of work, opened a bottle of red wine (ignoring the dire warnings on the antihistamine prescription bottle), grabbed a Nelson DeMille paperback from Bradley Cole's shelf in the living room, made my way past the computers, climbed over the printer, and sat there staring at the bedroom walls, listening to the buzz still in my ears from the printer going non-stop for hours, sipping wine from the bottle. The printer had generated so much heat in such a small room that even though it was off, the room was still hotter than eight hells, so I fanned myself with the book instead of reading it. At some point, I passed out.

Twelve hours later, I woke up ready to call the pharmaceutical company that sold the antihistamines and tell them the way around the sleep deprivation the medicine induced was a bottle of red wine. I felt like a bear just up from hibernation.

I went straight to the shower, if you call crawling over a massive machine straight to, and stood under the hot water until it was gone. When the fog cleared, I saw in the mirror that I'd also slept off the last of the fish. I looked just like my old self, my old self in this case being a version of Bianca Casimiro Sanders. And I was starving.

* * *

The coast is different from mainland America in one decided way: the deep blue sea. Another difference was the language; the coast had extra words. I'd grown up two hundred miles from the spot upon which I stood, and we had a porch. Bradley Cole had a lanai, a porch that offered a view of the Gulf. After polishing off four frosted cherry Pop Tarts and three cups of coffee, I realized I had nowhere to work, because every single surface inside Bradley's condo was already designated workspace, so I bundled up in his Patagonia fleece jacket and transferred the stacks of transparencies to the lanai, then weighted the stacks against the wind with dinner plates.

I tugged out sheets one, one, and one from the three towers, tapped them together, and held them up to the winter sun in hopes of finding a variant between the three machines. I didn't. The three page ones were exact matches. So were pages 100. So were pages 1000.

I couldn't find anything in the software that triggered the massive wins. My best guess was something external in combination with the anomaly I found in the software was the ticket. The number five meant something, but I wasn't positive what. The pencil marks in the thick manual meant something, but again, I didn't know what. I wished I could pick up the phone and ask the guy who'd written it, but he was dead. Another solution would be to ask one of the three people who'd accomplished it, but only one of them was still alive, and I didn't want to talk to him. It was ten o'clock in the morning, and my brain hurt again. The walls were closing in on me; I wanted out.

I had two things on my to-do list. I needed an inside glimpse of the Casimiro family; I couldn't proceed on just George's word for it, and the Internet would only give me so much. That meant poking around in Richard Sanders' closet full of skeletons. While I didn't look forward to it, he certainly broke the ice when we cleaned out all my closets.

And I needed to find out what the three previous winners—the two dead ones and my rotten, rotten, rotten excuse for an ex-ex-husband—had in common. Eddie Crawford had one outstanding feature, one large attribute, and it wasn't in the intelligence department.

How in hell could it be *that*?

Richard Sanders probably earned an astronomical amount of money, like six figures a *week*. And rightly so, because he had a hellacious job, the details of which I didn't want to know. If I had his job I'd go in every day, close the door, put my head on the desk, then cry. I'd holler "Go away!" if anyone knocked.

In addition to his big job, he ran in powerhouse circles—financiers, tycoons, Democrats, celebrities. In spite of it all, I found him to be a very approachable guy, and as far as I could see, treated everyone, tennis pros and librarians, with the same level of interest and respect. (Last week a little-old-lady library assistant from Tupelo won a gigantic payday on a slot machine, the one with the wheel, and he took her out on the town to celebrate. It was all over the news.) So when he called and asked to see me, I didn't panic right away, because for one, he'd warned me this little chat was coming. For another, I'd almost choked to death right in front of him (how much worse could it get?), and for yet another, he already knew about my asinine ex-ex-husband, and for just one more, he was paying me a lot of money and if I wanted to keep spending it, I'd better make myself available.

"I need to work on my golf game, Davis, and I'd like you to join me."

Left field.

"Just nine," he said.

Nine what? Lives?

"There's a car waiting for you downstairs."

I peeked. It was a long, black hearse. Time to panic.

* * *

The driver, a large man dressed in black, whom I'd never laid eyes on, didn't say boo to me. He parked the car, then followed us from a distance the whole time.

"You've never played? Ever?" Mr. Sanders was studying his clubs. He chose a very largish one with a tasseled knit sweater/sock as opposed to one of the small silver naked ones.

"I've always liked the clothes," I said, "but no, I've never played. We don't have a golf course in Pine Apple. We don't even have Putt-Putt."

The sun was mercifully out, but so was an icy wind. I was about to freeze. Mr. Sanders moved so comfortably, it could have been eighty-five degrees in the middle of May. I was bundled up like a polar bear in everything Bradley Cole owned. Mr. Sanders was wearing a red v-neck sweater over a lemon-yellow golf shirt. And pants, of course.

"I enjoy it," he said, "it's relaxing. For the most part I only play business golf. I don't get very many opportunities to play for fun."

This was not my idea of fun. More chit chat: he wished his son could see the benefits of this "life sport," his short game had been oddly off for months, then finally Natalie's name came up ("...an instinctive, intuitive player"), which gave me my in.

"Did you hire Natalie?" I asked.

"No," he said. "She and Paul both came with the job."

Paul. That's Teeth.

"She's very good at what she does," I offered.

"Which is one of the reasons we're here," Mr. Sanders said. "She's almost too good."

This wasn't about me. This was about her. He had something to say he didn't want her to overhear.

"I need to make sure we're on the same page, Davis, and the easiest way to do that is to speak to you directly."

Natalie was on a different page? File away for later.

"It's Thomas."

Thomas—gamer/son.

"I'm interested in what's going on with the video poker," he said, "certainly. But there's a bigger goal, one I want to make sure you're working toward."

"Tell me what that goal is, Mr. Sanders," I said, "and I'll do everything I can." (I meant every word of that.)

"I just did," he said.

He did golf stuff while I drew designs in the dirt path with the toe of my right cowgirl boot and wished for hot chocolate. With whipped cream. Natalie was so adamant: the game, the game, the game. Find out how the game is won. Figure out the game. Mr. Sanders had me in the middle of nowhere, freezing, to point me in a different direction: his son. Which would be leave his son out of it. There was only one way to leave the son out, and that was to leave the mother out.

We traveled a bumpy pebble path to the next golf thing that looked just like first one. I had a feeling they all looked alike. And we were doing this nine different times? I'd have frostbite. Mr. Sanders put his golf stuff where he wanted it, shifted his weight around, tugged at his sleeves, but before he hit the ball, he looked at me from across the grass. "So?"

I took a deep, cold breath. "If you could answer a few personal questions," the words rushed out of me, "it would help."

I thought the driver shadowing us had taken a shot at me for the mere suggestion when Mr. Sanders smacked the ball across the wide expanse of crunchy brown grass.

"Shoot," he said.

I didn't know if he meant *ooops, you just got shot,* or, *ask away,* or, *rats, there goes my ball.*

"Sliced."

I grabbed for my neck. Maybe I'd been cut.

When I figured out I hadn't been (shot) (because you don't feel it at first), or had my throat slit (you don't feel that immediately either because with both, there's an interminable moment of disbelief, then you have to wait on your brain to send pain signals), I managed to get a question out. "Did you know what you were getting into?"

"Did I know what I was getting into with the marriage, or the gaming industry?"

"Both."

He filled his lungs with biting winter air, focused on something in the trees beyond, pulled another golf ball from his pocket, tossed it in the air, then caught it without looking. “Yes and no.”

Another shot rang out, but I recognized it this time, so I didn’t drop and roll.

Mr. Sanders tilted his head this way and that, craning off into the distance. After the longest he turned to me. “I learned the business from the ground up,” he said, “and studied it for years before that. So I was prepared for the work.” He bent over and picked up the little stick still in the ground, then put it between his teeth. He gestured toward the golf cart, and we turned in that direction. “For the record, no one in their mid-twenties can foresee the potential problems of marrying into an institution. It looks decidedly better from the outside.” We climbed into the cart. “And, yes, Davis, I knew I wasn’t marrying a nun, if that’s where you’re going with this.”

My temperature went up several degrees. “Not at all.”

“What I didn’t know was how the family worked.”

My head jerked back uncomfortably as we shot down the path. I accidentally screamed a little bit. He slowed down.

“For all practical purposes,” he said, “everything that happens in the Casimiro casinos is on the up-and-up, because the first rule of gaming is don’t cross the Gaming Commission. Without a gaming license, you’re out of business.”

The cart came to a sudden and unexpected stop, and I grabbed for the teeny dash. Note to self: don’t ever get in a car with the boss.

“But that’s not to say an audit of all other aspects of the corporation would pass the sniff test,” he said. “The Casimiros don’t keep forty attorneys and seventy accountants on the payroll for no reason. Now the family itself, that’s a different story.”

One I wanted to hear.

“Help me look for my ball,” he said, wandering off.

He told me that he’d worked his way through school, something I already knew, and that, truth be told, he’d married for the wrong reasons, something I’d already lived.

“Salvatore,” he said, “my father-in-law, raised four entitled, self-indulgent, spoiled brats, who never lifted a finger except to call for a maid. And when Bianca set her sights on me for a weekend, he pushed us both toward a more lasting arrangement, because he already knew I would roll up my sleeves and work where his jet-setting sons wouldn't. So the incentives were there for both of us."

He looked at me. "For taking his daughter off the streets and out of the headlines, I received a million tax-free dollars, a position in a Fortune 500 company that was otherwise decades out of my reach, and ten percent of the division he put me to work in. I'm not sure what Bianca's package included, but I have no doubt she was encouraged as well. Honestly, Davis, at the time there wasn't a good reason to *not* marry Bianca and millions of reasons to. I was working a ninety-hour week, and I have no idea what she was up to those early years; I barely saw her. Thomas, our son, surprised us both. If it hadn't been for him, I'm not sure what might have happened."

It was several minutes before either of us spoke.

"Yes, Davis, he is my son."

I could have died.

"And you need to know that if I divorce Bianca, I'll lose my job, and most likely, custody of my son."

"Is that in a prenup?" I asked.

"No," he said. "That's common sense."

A nice guy like Mr. Sanders spilling his guts to an almost total stranger suddenly made all sorts of sense, too. He needed some discretion. I was his discretion. Which meant the rest of his team, or somebody on it, wasn't his discretion. File away for later.

"There was a showdown several years ago," he picked up his own trail, "when Thomas was just a baby. I never saw it coming, because when I wasn't behind my desk or on the casino floor, I was with my son. I remember Bianca had been in Italy for months, and Salvatore called me to his office to inform me that not only had he fired all three of his sons, he'd changed his will to preclude them, and cut out their enormous allowances."

"Your wife's, too?"

"Yep," he said. "They handled it admirably, as you can well imagine."

"What did they do?"

"They turned to their mother," he said, "and that lasted a few years. But eventually, my three brothers-in-law went to work for different vendors that service the Casimiro casinos."

"Like Total Gaming Corporation?"

He turned to me. "Exactly."

I sucked in icy air. "When did you realize Bianca was supplementing her income in your casino?"

"I didn't," he said. "Nattie was the one who caught it."

We shared a long minute of listening to the wind whistle.

"Do you trust Natalie?"

"I couldn't do my job without her."

Not what I asked. "What's your goal, Mr. Sanders? How do you want this to end?"

He turned to me. "I want you to tell me my wife isn't responsible for anyone's death."

I might not be able to grant that wish. I wanted to ask him if he loved her, because I couldn't get a feel for where this was coming from—his heart, ego, or wallet—but I couldn't get the words out.

"I've known about the game for a while now," he said, "and I can honestly say that if it weren't for the dead bodies piling up, I'd be happy to look the other way."

He wasn't worried about the money.

"And Bianca's going to do exactly what she wants to do." He said this lightly, with a shrug and a grin, and every word on the edge of a laugh, like, *my goofy wife would sleep with the devil.*

Okay, not his ego.

"It's my son, Davis."

Ah. The heart.

"He can't have a murderess for a mother."

Was Mr. Sanders asking me to dig deeper or cover up?

I wandered to a sunny spot while he did more of the golf thing, and we didn't speak again until after we drove up and down even *more* brown hills. I needed a Dramamine.

"Do you know Morgan George, Mr. Sanders?"

"Morgan George." He tried it on. "Morgan George," he repeated. "I'm not sure if I recognize the name, or if it's so common that I feel like I should," he said. "Tell me who Morgan George is."

"It's Morgan George, Jr., actually. You were at UNLV at the same time he was."

Mr. Sanders shrugged one shoulder. "That doesn't mean a thing," he said. "Big place."

I twisted around in the seat. "He went on to work for Total Gaming, and he wrote the software for Double Whammy Deuces Wild."

Mr. Sanders looked off into the distance, a look of recognition playing across his face. "A black man," he said.

"Yes."

"I do know who he is," Mr. Sanders said. "Make that was."

"Did you meet him at school?"

Mr. Sanders shook his head.

"Work?"

"No."

I waited while Mr. Sanders did more golf: surveying, posturing, adjusting the visor he wore. He smacked the ball through the air, then watched, apparently pleased with where it plopped.

He looked over to me. "I walked in on him with my wife." He tossed the club he was holding into the air and caught it in the middle on the way down. "Six weeks later, the guy was dead."

I steeled myself, then asked, "Is your wife sleeping with my ex-husband?"

"I believe so."

SEVENTEEN

A day of golf, an afternoon of digging through archived news and obituaries on the Internet. A pleasant and productive phone call to the police department in Atlantic City pretending I was a reporter. Another call, this time playing the role of genealogist, with a nice woman at the *Las Vegas Sun*. The longest call to Total Gaming Technology's twenty-four-hour troubleshooting hotline, assuming the persona of a really stupid slot machine tech, and with the most patient human on Earth. A final phone exchange, this one impersonal and netting me exactly nothing, with my mother.

An evening with a peanut butter and banana sandwich, three almost-frozen Natural Lights, and a big box I exhumed from the back of Bradley Cole's closet. In it: handwritten letters dating back three decades, photographs, airline-ticket stubs, loose change, high school ring, buttons in teeny plastic bags, cuff links, more than twenty birthday cards from his mother, receipts for extended warranties on car things, and two old condoms. (I knew they were old because for one, they were crunchy. For two, I've never seen the brand behind the cashier in a checkout line.)

One last phone call to Natalie to weasel my way into yet another department of the Bellissimo I had no business being in. Two and a half hours of sleep.

The alarm screamed. I stumbled to the door to retrieve the package waiting on the welcome mat. It contained the most heinous outfit yet, much worse than the housekeeping uniform. I tugged it on in the bedroom, the copier blocking the only mirror, because I didn't care about seeing my reflection. Natalie sent a short, dark wig and wire-rimmed eyeglasses to complete the look. I didn't bother with makeup. I whined a lot during the process of getting dressed.

I'd arranged for George to shuttle me back and forth for this assignment, more to keep the lines of communication open between us than anything else, but when I climbed in the back seat of his cab at six in the dark morning and he started snickering at my latest costume, I decided I really didn't have a thing to say to him other than, "Shut up, George."

He turned around to face forward, but I could still see his shoulders rising and falling with mirth. "You're never going to catch a man dressed like that."

"Who says I'm trying to catch a man?"

He pulled out onto one of five empty lanes of Beach Boulevard, turning right toward the Bellissimo, several miles away, but more visible against the backdrop of the crystal night than I'd ever seen it during the day. I'd ridden away from the complex under the glow of the moon dozens of times, but never to. There had to be a million Bellissimo lights blinking against the black sky, and I was about to see the switch that turned them on. To get a glimpse of said switch, apparently you had to be head-to-toe in navy-blue canvas Dickies and wearing a boot that called itself Wolverine. I could barely move in this getup. The boots weighed about seven pounds each. The required head gear, which covered my lap, was a white hard hat.

"What time are you supposed to be there?" George asked.

"Seven."

"Where is it you need to go before?" He glanced at the clock on the dash. "You having your picture made?" He laughed at his own joke.

"Very funny." I set the hat aside so I could pick at the ugly pants. "I was thinking we'd get a donut."

"Come again?" He caught my eye in the rear view mirror.

"A donut, George. A cup of coffee and a donut."

After a long argument, which I won, I stayed in the car while George's lazy self went into the Krispy Kreme, doing a brisk business at this ungodly hour, where he stood in line to get me three chocolate-glazed and a bucket of coffee. A neon sign announcing hot donuts cast a blinking red glow on me.

When George returned, he drove a block east to a darkened fast-food restaurant, parked just left of a streetlight, then twisted in his seat so he could either watch me eat, or have another laugh at my expense. When I saw the set of his jaw, though, I knew the fun and games were over.

"You're not going to like it, George," I said through thick chocolate.

"I already hate it."

I explained my theory to him: Bianca Casimiro had made a deal with his son to write backdoor software for a video poker game, Double Whammy Deuces Wild Progressives.

"What kind of backdoor?" George asked.

"Where there'd be a key of sorts, George, where the game could be won at will."

"And he did this? My son rigged this game?"

"It looks like it."

I leaned heavily on the fact there was no evidence that led me to believe his son had out-and-out complied, or even profited in any way. It felt more like Morgan had been forced or coerced in some manner. I purposely left out the part about his son banging my boss's wife.

Afterward, it was so quiet in the car, I could hear the steam coming off my coffee. I had explained my theory as kindly, respectfully, and gently as I possibly could, and this in spite of how George had laughed his ass off at me not fifteen minutes earlier, but his heavy heart sucked all the air out of the car anyway, and I had to crack a window to breathe.

After several moments of silence, I wondered if George had fallen asleep.

Finally, he asked, "What else?"

"She knew how to win it," I said of Bianca, "but it's a two-man job, so she lined up pawns."

"Did she have sex with the pawns, too?" George asked.

So much for sparing him that piece of the story.

"It's safe to assume so," I answered. "But two of them are dead, George, so I can't very well ask."

"How did they die?"

"Their necks were snapped."

"Ah," George said. "Same killer. A large man with a martial arts background. And that means my son's death wasn't premeditated."

I agreed. Killers have their ticks, and this one went for the neck. Breaking a neck left very little in the way of evidence. Whoever did this hadn't thought out his first kill, or he wouldn't have made such a mess. He cleaned up his act before the next two victims met their maker. "I'm sure you're right, George." Unbelievably, the coffee still hadn't cooled enough to drink, but that didn't keep me from trying, and I got a scorched tongue for my efforts.

"I can think of two who might fit the bill," he said, "those big guys you work with. Got a pick between 'em?"

"I honestly don't know, George. I don't want to stick my foot out and trip the bald one, unlike the other one," I said, "the one with the big teeth. Every time I'm in the same room with him, I want to poke his eye out with a fork, but I've got nothing on either of them."

"Have you looked?"

"Briefly." Well, my father looked briefly. "I probably should nose around."

"Good idea," George said. "Rifle through their desks."

Their offices scared me. *They* scared me.

"George?"

"Hmm?"

"You know how sometimes you really don't know who has the hate?"

I beat down the evil that jumped in my throat, and I'm sure George was doing the same. In a very practiced process, I crawled up from the dark place so I could keep going, and I'm sure George was clawing his way back, too. We had a secret, me and George: the only way to keep going—left foot, right foot, inhale, exhale—was to know that you were here to stop it from happening to someone else. If you give up, you leave a hole. Then someone falls in it.

"They've got another shill in there now," I choked out, "who won, and yet he's still alive," I said. "At least so far. I don't know what's coming, George. I guess he's next if someone doesn't stop them."

"Your ex," George said.

My mouth dropped open. "Who? What?"

He started the car. "I wasn't born yesterday."

The new day finished dawning as we drove to the Bellissimo in silence, other than the music of me slurping coffee.

When we arrived, he turned to me. "Morgan fixed the machines so they'd pay out," he said. "What did the other guys do?"

"They were electricians."

"How do you know that?"

"It's right on the Internet, in their obituaries."

"What do you think that has to do with it? Surely it's not a coincidence."

"I think they knew how to cause the machines to lose power for a split second," I said, "long enough to reset. Somehow, they caused a power surge, which seems to be the trigger," I explained. "All three times the jackpot has hit, it's been within an hour of a power flash, and there's been an electrician there every time."

"How in the world," his black eyes bore into mine, "do you mess with the power in a casino?"

They didn't mess with all the power, just the one bank of machines, but now wasn't the time for details, or I'd be late for my meeting. I took a deep breath and let it out slowly. "I'm about to find out."

Fifteen minutes later, a very large man dressed just like me pushed through double doors to the reception room, where I waited alone. "Sandy?" he glanced between a clipboard and me.

I looked around for Sandy, too. Then I jumped up and shot out my hand. "That's me," I said. "Sandy McCormick."

"You're from accounting? Going to take a look around?"

"That's right."

"Well," he tipped his hard hat. "Welcome to Electrical Engineering. Follow me and I'll give you the ten-cent tour."

* * *

I trailed behind him into another world, a scary world. Every piece of equipment I could see was the size of a school bus. Half of them were on end, rising two stories into the air. Catwalks were built above everything, and scores of people dressed in the navy blue Dickies attire crawled all over the place. Wide walkways between the machines were marked by red-painted paths, and emergency cut-off switches were scattered along the walls. The noise alone would knock you down. My companion decided to add to it by screaming at me.

"On any given day, the Bellissimo load requirement is thirty-five megawatts, but we're built out to fifty-five. That's enough for a whole city. Hell," he laughed, "we *are* a whole city. Now over here, we've got thirteen-point-two kilovolt feeders coming in off three different substations. You see those?"

I followed his hand and nodded, but I had no idea what I was looking for, and he might as well have been speaking Russian.

"We've got six steel rooms here that are bolted together," he yelled. "This is just the first, the largest, and built on exterior walls for the head room. Follow me and we'll go downstairs and take a look at the conduit."

I trudged along, hoping a conduit wasn't a large animal. As promised, we took a look at the miles of conduit—not animal at all—and every navy blue Dickied electrician took a look at me. From there we walked a mile through a tunnel before climbing eerily silent steps. He swiped a card that hung on a chain from his neck, and glass doors slid open to allow us entry into the noise again.

"Do you know where you are?" he yelled.

"I don't have a clue," I yelled back.

"You're two levels below the casino. The vault is above us, over there." He pointed. "And the main banking center is over there." He swung his arm in the opposite direction, clearing my hard hat by a mile.

This room, as large as a theatre, without a splinter of natural light, had rectangular metal silver cabinets, each the size of a one-car garage, spaced along the walls with six huddled together in the middle of the concrete floor. I didn't count, but there had to be more than thirty altogether. Coming out of the cabinets were thousands of colorful ropes of wire that climbed up the walls and steel poles like rainbow vines, disappearing into the ceiling. The fronts of the metal boxes had blinking panels. I'd be afraid to even guess how many million lights were blinking in that room, just like I'd be afraid to guess how many million grains of sand were on a stretch of beach. If I really did work in accounting, I would go back and suggest this department's pay be doubled because of the sensory overload alone. As my eyes began to adjust, my guide started up with his electric mumbo-jumbo again.

"Every switch in here is on a single feeder with emergency generator backup. It all leads to a threesome."

Finally, a term I was familiar with.

"We're on thirteen breakers in this room, each on a twenty-five kilovolt automatic transfer. Every outgoing feeder ties straight into one of the main sources, and they're all connected to each other. So if we have an outage here," he pointed to one of the garages, "its neighbor," he pointed to another, "picks it up."

"How often does that happen?" I asked as I looked around the room. "An outage."

"We shoot for never," he said, "but you know the old saying, shit happens?"

"Sure."

"Well, shit happens here, too. Everything's color coded," he yelled. "If it's blue, it's a light fixture, and as you can see, we've got a ton of lights. It might be something as innocent as a light bulb blowing in one overhead that throws the switch."

We stepped over to a thick bundle of multi-colored cables coming out of a steel box that I couldn't have wrapped my arms around.

He picked out a blue cable with the tip of a finger. "If this guy blows," his finger inched over, "this guy picks him up. And the panel lets us know the fixture's on backup, then we repair the central. The only thing that happens upstairs is a blink. The backup system kicks in immediately."

"Does that work for slot machines, too?"

"Slot machines are the green cables," he said. "And they don't necessarily work like a light fixture, or say an oven in one of the restaurants. They're piggybacked," he looked at me, "backed up twice," he explained. "Because if they go down, it has to be reported to the Gaming Commission."

That pesky gaming board again.

"But it happens," he said. "We had an incident a couple of months ago where a lady somehow dropped a tiny earring, not any bigger than a minute, on the bill feeder, then sent a five-dollar bill through that caught the earring, and a whole bank of machines went black."

"Really?" I couldn't see Eddie Crawford wearing earrings.

"There was liquor involved."

"There would be," I said. "What happened?"

"Backup kicked in," he said. "The other slot machines tied in with the one that went down barely blinked, they didn't even stay down long enough to lose data. The players kept on playing while maintenance dug the fried earring out of the downed machine and the casino people did a week's worth of paperwork over a little gold hoop." He glanced at his wristwatch, then at the next door.

"Wait," I grabbed for his arm. "Can a player unplug a slot machine, then plug it back in?"

He looked at me like I'd lost my mind. "Hell, no. Ninety-eight percent of the machines have outlets underneath, through the cabinets and into the floor. I think someone would notice a player moving a machine and a cabinet to get to the outlet."

"What about the other two percent?"

He adjusted his hat. "Sometimes on the progressives, you've got an exposed floor switch tying the marquee to the bank of machines, but it's not like a light switch, clearly marked off and on. It's a recessed floor button no bigger than a pencil eraser. A player wouldn't know what to look for. There isn't *anyone* out there who'd know what to look for unless they were the one who'd installed it."

Oh, hallelujah.

"Now follow me through here," he said, "and I'll show you our babies."

"Babies?" I had to break into a run to keep up with him.

"We have our own fuel cells," he yelled over his shoulder. "They feed right into the central boiler room. Watch out," he swiped his card again, "it's hot in here."

* * *

"Same time tomorrow?" George asked me.

"No." I pulled off the hardhat and the black wig came with it. I used all ten digits to knead my head. George watched me in the mirror out of the corner of his eye, and he looked just this side of frightened. I looked, I'm sure, better than I felt.

The guided tour had lasted several more miles, then I had to sit in a glass-walled office and flip through hundreds of pages of overtime sheets as if I cared what was on them. Every once in a while, I'd jot a note. Mostly *Davis loves Bradley*. Nervous electrical engineers who didn't want to lose their overtime pay filed by regularly, smiling if they caught my eye. I went to the kitchenette twice for coffee, and got hit on by electricians both times. I wasn't going there again. No way.

My tour guide, whose name I finally caught after we reached the offices and everyone we walked past gave him a back-pat and a shout-out, Dale Boy, poked his head in the door at noon.

"I'm outta here, young lady."

"Thanks for your time, Dale Boy."

He looked offended. "It's just Dale."

"Dale."

And finally, at three, I closed up shop. I cut through the second level of the employee parking garage to get to the other side of the state of Mississippi where George was, and fell into the backseat. "Take me home, George." I leaned my head back and kept my eyes closed until the car stopped.

"What'd they do to you?" George asked. "Beat you up?"

"I walked ten miles in these concrete boots," I said, "and then sat under florescent lights for the next twenty hours."

"Girl, you need to toughen up."

"Says the man who naps in a car all day."

"I put my time in, thank you."

"Speaking of putting in your time, George, let me ask you something." I was talking to the floorboard, because I didn't intend to walk another step in these leather slabs. I fought with the hooks and laces, and noticed, while tugging on the tongue, that my boots were actually Wolverine *pups*. I was wearing little boy boots. No wonder my feet hurt.

"Say what?"

I raised my head. "Assuming you've had some time to think about this today, what's your theory on why they haven't been caught?"

His mouth twisted. "Time, for one thing."

"Time?"

"Yeah," he said. "So much time between events."

"Makes you wonder what they do with the rest of their time, huh?"

"Sure enough."

"I wonder what we're missing," I mused. "They're going through way more money than what these jackpots have paid out every other year, easy."

"No doubt."

"What else?" I asked.

"Geography," he said.

"Geography?"

"Yeah," George said. "It's a popular game. You can find it in most casinos, and they have. They've won it in Vegas, Atlantic City, and now Biloxi. No telling where else."

"No one's connecting the dots," I said.

George turned to look me in the eye. "Seems to me her husband's got her number."

And you, George. You have her number, too.

* * *

I passed out in the navy blue Dickies and sleep, glorious sleep, ruled my world for the next couple of hours. When I rolled over in Bradley's bed and looked at the clock, it was just after seven. Perfect. I stripped down to my skivvies, grabbed the Wolverine puppies, marched out the front door, down the hall to the garbage chute, and sent the uniform flying. The boots thudded down the metal tube. I turned, in a pink push-up and navy blue thong, to find Bradley's next-door neighbor in his open doorway holding Hefty bags in each hand. His mouth dropped so far open I could see his dental history. He began panting. Like a dog. I covered what I could, hugged the wall and scooted past him; he google-eyed me the whole way. I worked Bradley's front door well after I realized I'd locked myself out; I heard the neighbor's bags of garbage thud to the floor behind me.

An hour later, I removed the price tags off a platinum-colored silk top, $340, skinny white jeans, $480, and pulled Tory Burch wedges out of their raspberry and tangerine box, $570. I took a blow dryer to my $400 hair, applied about $200 of MAC makeup, armed a chocolate-brown leather Fendi hobo with a lipstick and the evening's identification, and closed the door behind me, this time, keys in hand.

I loved this part of my job.

Fifteen minutes later, I was unlocking Bradley's door. I'd forgotten the green contacts.

Twenty minutes after that, I walked past the waterfall, but taking a detour along the way to check in with my retired-schoolteacher friends Mary and Maxine at the $1 Double Whammys. I breezed by, not stopping, just slowing, and gave them a wink. No matter how Natalie dressed me, my old friends knew me, and in a million years, I knew they wouldn't breathe a word.

Mary elbowed Maxine, who clapped her hands at the sight of me. "Good luck, high roller!" Mary called after me.

A minute later, Hollywood, looking as delicious as the last time I'd been here, greeted me. "Welcome back, Miss Dunlow!"

I *love* this place!

* * *

I hate this place.

I blew through forty thousand dollars of casino credit without winning a penny in way under an hour. Almost eighty losing hands in a row at five-hundred dollars a pop. Trust me, it happens. It wasn't even my money, but time stood still, nothing mattered, and my world was reduced to me, *three* sweet-tea martinis with a floating curl of lemon zest in each, and one stupid machine.

Double Whammy Dammit.

I was so frustrated half an hour into it that I began sass-talking the slot machine when it dealt me garbage. "Are you kidding me? You're kidding me, right? Seriously?"

Hollywood, hovering around me in the background, looked nervous.

Note to self: Learn how to play this game.

Ten minutes, or I should say another ten thousand dollars later, I promise you, had I known how to trigger the win, I'd have done it then and there. On at least twenty hands, being dealt two face cards of the same suit, I went for the royal flush, holding the king and ace or the queen and jack, and when the machine dealt me the other three cards, I wasn't within a million miles of a royal, or even a pair. Not that I'd have known what to do if I hit it; the jackpot was up to $1,292,560 and some change. I could hear Natalie now: "You weren't supposed to *win* it."

The best hand I had was trip cowboys (three kings), but trying to get a few pennies back in the coffer, I accepted the machine's challenge to whammy, turning over yet another damn king on the whammy screen. (Where had he been thirty seconds ago when I could have really used him?) And that meant for me to win, the hidden card had to be an ace. Of course, I lost, turning over a worthless five of diamonds. I whammied, all right, the wrong way.

One thing's for sure: it's not nearly as much fun when you're not winning and it's miserable when you can't do *anything* but lose. I can only imagine how players who are stuffing their own hundred-dollar bills into the machines feel. If I'd truly lost this much money in this short a period of time, I'd fall in the floor, curl up in a ball, and cry. And maybe then, I'd be able to see the stupid switch I was looking for. If I didn't find the switch soon, I'd be forced to watch the video of my sorry ex-ex winning at this bank of machines. Way before my time at the Bellissimo, Teeth and No Hair had gone through the film repeatedly, frame by frame, and hadn't been able to pick out anything unusual, and that report had been good enough for me. But now that I halfway knew what to look for, where they hadn't had that advantage, I'd be forced to watch it myself if that asinine switch didn't show up soon.

In the end, I sat there in a daze, staring at the machine that had so thoroughly betrayed me.

"Would you like me to extend your marker, Miss Dunlow?" Hollywood kept his distance when he whispered the suggestion.

I turned to him. "Honestly, I don't know what to do." I surrendered with both hands. "I don't understand how I can play this hard and not win a damn thing."

He looked sympathetic, but he didn't say anything.

"What do people do when they lose everything?" I asked.

"They go home."

Right. Win or go home.

"Maybe you should play a different machine," he suggested.

"With what?"

"Casino Credit will up your marker by ten percent with just a phone call."

That would be another four thousand dollars. Eight hands. Natalie might have something to say about it, but, I could deal with her later. "Okay," I said. "Do it."

Hollywood took a step backwards. "I'll be right back," he said. "Why don't you pick out another machine?"

He was my best friend, my confidant, my advisor. We were in this together. "Should I? I mean, I have so much money in this one, don't you think it's about ready to give me a little of my money back?"

He gave me a gratuitous smile. "That's up to you, Miss Dunlow."

No, I was on my own. A place I knew well.

It took longer to get the four thousand than it did to lose it: ten minutes for Hollywood to return with a slip of paper for me to sign, five to give it back.

I went back to Bradley's place and slept for ten dreamless hours.

EIGHTEEN

It was Sunday, and I woke up with a gambling hangover, which isn't anything like waking up after losing a triple-elimination Jagermeister pong tournament, because that feels so much better than this. A gambling hangover is when you wake up with a lonely quarter in your purse, if that, wondering what in the world went wrong with your game. I snarled at the video poker machines on my way to the kitchen.

It was a glorious late-February morning. Signs of spring were everywhere this far south, and by my third cup of coffee, I'd convinced myself that *I* hadn't lost more than forty thousand dollars, Marci Dunlow had. *I* didn't have to figure out how to pay it back, *she* did. *I* didn't have the worst luck of anyone ever, that was her. As the gambling ire cleared, a sharp stab of loneliness took its place, a sentiment I don't entertain often, and I decided I'd better get to work on something before I wallowed so deep in self-pity that I did something stupid, like drive home.

Sunday was the one day when things were generally quiet within Corporate Bellissimo, which made it the best day of the week to snoop around and learn a little more about my coworkers. (The Internet would only give me so much. Natalie was making some *buck*. I thought they were paying me until I saw what they were paying her. What I wouldn't give to snoop around *her* office, but she'd hand me my head on a platter if I did. She'd know, too, because somehow she knew everything, and because there were ninety-seven security cameras in her office. Seriously. Every two inches.)

Mr. Sanders was in New Hampshire, returning on Monday, not that I wanted to snoop through his stuff. I had a good handle on him, and I already knew what was in his office. Cinnamon candy.

No Hair and/or Teeth's secrets would yield answers to a few of my questions, but I didn't have access. No Hair, I assumed, was enjoying the day being happily married. Teeth was on property, but I fully intended to avoid him.

I pulled the belt of Bradley Cole's robe tighter, and stepped onto the lanai with my Bat phone. I speed dialed No Hair.

"This had better be good."

"Hey. It's me, Davis."

"I know who it is."

"I need a little something-something," I said.

"It's my day off."

"What?"

"It's my day off. I've already had to go in once. Call Paul."

No Hair hung up on me, so I called him right back.

"*What?*" he demanded.

"Why'd you have to go in?"

"Who wants to know?"

"Me."

"None of your business. Call Paul."

"I did. I tried to call him." Which wasn't exactly true.

"I talked to him fifteen minutes ago," No Hair said. "You probably can't get him because he's on the thirtieth floor right now."

The thirtieth floor? My mind jumped back to my housekeeping days, and I located the thirtieth floor. "That's the Elvis floor," I said. "What's he doing there?"

I heard No Hair suck in a big breath and let it out slowly. "That's not the Elvis floor, Davis. That's the Sanders' residence. She's due in tonight, so he's sweeping the computer lines today. If you hurry, you can catch him."

"He's *sweeping*?" I laughed.

"He's *scanning*, Davis. Scanning, sweeping, debugging, call it what you like."

"Aren't you off on Sunday?"

"Yes, as a matter of fact, I am. We covered that ten seconds ago. And I'd like to get back to it."

"So he has to sweep by himself?"

He didn't answer my question. Instead, he said, "Cell phones are blocked on thirty, Davis. If you need him, you'll have to go up there."

"What if she's there?"

"If I thought she might be anywhere near, I wouldn't suggest you go."

"Exactly when will she be back?"

"Can we talk about this later?"

He told me how to get into his and Teeth's office (the very thing I wanted to do), and where, once in, to locate an elevator key that would allow me access to the thirtieth-floor elevator. "Don't touch a thing. Get the card and get out of my office. Stay out of my desk. Open that one drawer, get the passkey, then get out as fast as you can, and don't go into Paul's office at all."

Whatever.

"The elevator on thirty opens into a reception area," No Hair said, "where there'll be a security guard. Don't mess with him." He went on to tell me he'd call the guy and tell them I was headed his way. "You'll be a house-decorator person. Look like one."

"A what?"

"A curtain person. A sofa person. A knick-knack person," he said. "Take a tape measure with you."

"What am I supposed to do with it?"

"Measure a wall. Talk about countertops or something. You only need to get past that one desk. You can do it."

"You don't think Paul will want me to help him sweep, do you?"

"No, Davis," No Hair said. "I'm assuming you're not trained on the equipment."

"Who isn't trained on a *broom*?"

"We all know *you* are, but we're not talking about *flying*."

No Hair, after calling me a witch, hung up on me again. I opened the refrigerator door, and put the phone where there should have been eggs. I'd be dammed if I'd call him back and ask for *anything*.

* * *

At this juncture, I had a healthy collection of options to hide the blonde, all on hooks in the bathroom. I fingered through and chose the one that had come home with me from the hospital stuffed in a bag with the waitressing uniform. It was closest to my natural hair color, so at least when I caught my reflection in closing elevator doors, I wouldn't wonder who it was only to realize it was me. I had no intention of running into anyone, so I dressed in Lucky straight-leg jeans, a mint-green cashmere pullover, and short, caramel Ugg boots. Looking a little too much like myself, I went ahead and put contacts in, aiming for blue, but grabbing Bianca green.

Before I left, I jotted Bradley Cole a note: "B—had to run to work for a bit. Back soon. XXXOOO, Davis."

I drove the Bug to work, took note of George's absence, parked in the empty vendor lot, tiptoed past dark offices, took the stairs down two flights, walked four miles uphill in the snow, crossed a desert, and finally I was pressing the keypad outside Teeth and No Hair's cave. Catching my breath from the hike, I wondered again why their offices were so utterly removed from every other venue on this property, how far I was from any manner of natural light, and what in the world that smell was.

I couldn't locate a light switch to save my life, so using the penlight on my keychain, I batted my way to No Hair's door, stepped in his cubicle, and settled in behind his desk. The air was almost too thick to breathe. They needed potpourri, a very large fan, and lamps.

It took no time at all to hack his computer. He'd given me the codes to the door and his desk: four, five, six, seven, and five, six, seven, eight. Getting to the welcome screen of No Hair's computer was, naturally, six, seven, eight, nine. (He should know better. If I stumbled across an ATM card in his desk, I could drain his bank accounts.) The elevator pass was right where he'd said it would be.

Now that I had the glow of the computer monitor to work by, I snooped through the whole desk, finding nothing all that interesting, except for the fact that the lower right desk drawer was locked. That must be where the interesting stuff was. I dug around for the key, and it didn't immediately present itself. I'd have picked the lock, but didn't want to take the time.

It took forever to find the surveillance feed of Eddie the Ass winning the big money, and as soon as I did, I minimized it. I had other things to see first; I needed to know what had gone down before the win.

The facial-recognition software wasn't altogether user friendly, or I wasn't very good at it, because I couldn't find film of Eddie Crawford and Bianca Casimiro Sanders together. After three searches, I decided that was because there wasn't any. I gave him no credit for that, because they didn't pass out judiciousness in Pine Apple; had it been up to him, there would be a full-length movie, scene after scene of them exiting broom closets still panting, zipping, and tucking. I had to assume that either she was an expert adulteress who knew how to stay out of the camera's eye, or the evidence of the two of them together had been deleted from the system for the obvious reason: who wants a pissed-off boss? There was another possibility, but it was a stretch: maybe there was no footage of them together because The Affair was part of the scam. Maybe they were just business partners—not bed buddies. She was no saint, by her own husband's admission, and yes, random women did fall into Eddie's bed. Often. Likewise, Eddie was a smooth talker. And there was no denying Eddie looked good. Eddie would probably be a good-looking sixty-year-old, but I still couldn't see it. This woman was way too far out of Eddie Crawford's league. This woman was out of her own league.

I searched them separately, and retrieved enough of that to keep me glued to the screen for the next six weeks. For the fun of it, or to answer the nagging question of where Eddie got his gambling money, or to tie up loose ends, I minimized all the footage of Bianca and searched Beth Dunn, Eddie's casino host. I asked the computer to show me interaction between Beth and Eddie. It took less than five minutes to see who was footing his gambling bill, and the steam rising off the computer monitor left no doubt in my mind that he wasn't trading money for the rouge cashout tickets, he was trading favors of the more personal nature.

I didn't need or want to know another thing about Eddie, so I skipped to Bianca, fast-forwarding through miles of feed that dated back years.

The creepiest part was that looking at her was like looking in a mirror. There was, between us, almost a ten-year age difference, but for whatever reasons, probably Botoxish reasons, we didn't look a day apart.

Oh, for our bank balances to be twins.

She *never* smiled. She had a dead set to her jaw, and she wore oversized sunglasses indoors and out, rain or shine, so I wasn't treated to her steely stare but a few times. She didn't walk so much as she marched, and she was impatient, not pushing an elevator button once, but angrily trying to poke it through the panel. She slammed doors, she chewed food in a circular motion, she pressed against her bejeweled knuckles when forced to pretend she was listening to someone speak, and smoked long skinny cigarettes when she played the Double Whammy Deuces behind the waterfall. She shook her finger in people's faces—the spa staff, housekeepers, her son's nanny, and several times in the video histories, at her husband.

The woman dressed impeccably, and almost always in head-to-toe black. She could open a store with her jewelry. She could open a mall with her luggage and furs. I counted six different animal pelts on her just last month. She was in town four days, and managed to be seen in six different furs. Cruella.

The film had date and time stamps, and all told, it looked like Bianca spent an average of three to four weeks a year in Biloxi. Clips of her from June of last year (furless) were immediately followed by recordings from October (swathed in fur) with nothing in between. Where was this woman when she wasn't here? There wasn't one scrap of evidence she'd been within ten feet of her son in any venue on the property other than, assumedly, their private residence, which wasn't a viewing option.

Disturbingly enough, there was one constant: when she arrived or departed, which is about all she did, somewhere in the grainy background was my driver, George.

Zooming in on the bank of machines that had broken my heart last night, I queued them for sunrise on the day of Eddie's win, and almost fell asleep watching nothing. For the first three hours of tape, it was like staring at a still life, even though I had it running at warp speed. Between ten and eleven, a handful of people passed by the machines, mostly Bellissimo employees, one pushing a vacuum cleaner, and then nothing until three o'clock, when Hollywood strolled by. I rewound and watched an attendant wiping down the fronts of the machines at three-thirty that afternoon, but he didn't do anything but polish away fingerprints that most likely weren't there, because no one had touched them. Not one of the people who had been near the machines that day had taken the batteries out, pulled a plug, or whipped out a ray gun and zapped them. Then, at four twenty-seven in the afternoon, Bianca Casimiro Sanders waltzed in. I almost fell out of No Hair's chair. I knew she was in on it, but I never expected to see the elusive Mrs. Sanders at the scene of the crime.

She sat down at the fourth machine; I could see the small LCD display with the scrolling progressive total above the machine in the background. She tipped her chin Hollywood's way to grace him with a smile, and he appeared nervous on the small screen, stiff and fidgety without a clue as to what to do with his hands. She removed her dark glasses, hooking them in the already-plunging neckline of her black top, then looked straight into the camera. I jerked away from the screen and screamed out loud. The glint reflecting off her icy green eyes was trained directly at me, and it was a full-out threat: *Watch this and you'll be sorry.*

A waitress walked up with a tall drink, passing it to the Las Vegas princess, and when Bianca went to set it down, she missed. I watched the tape seven or eight times, slowing it to a crawl, and watched, frame by frame from every perspective offered, as she intentionally dumped the drink between video poker machines four and five.

Employees rushed to her aid from every camera angle. The screen was so full of attempts to keep her dry, with so many backs, rear ends, and arms flying in every direction possible, their collective life's missions redirected to sparing Bianca Casimiro Sanders any contact with moisture. Once the clean-up was complete, the waitress stepped back into the frame with a replacement drink, this one going straight to Bianca's dermal-filler-enhanced lips.

So much went on in such a short period of time that the first four times I watched it, I missed the LCD display and the slot machine lights blinking. When I finally caught it, the flash was so fast I couldn't even get a time on it. They went down, then powered back up in a split-second, just like Dale Boy said they would. If you didn't know exactly what you were looking for, there was no doubt you'd miss it. Just like my video-poker buddies, sisters Mary and Maxine, had told me. "The whole game goes black for a second," Maxine had said, "then it pulls right back up. It's real quick."

I will be damned. The lower-stakes version of this game, the one Mr. Sanders and Natalie sent me to my first day on the job, was rigged, too. The paydays were timed with the easily obtained Winner Winner Chicken Dinner advice, so no one suspected. It paid roughly $8000 every three weeks to a good-looking man named Eddie. But good-looking Eddie was only depositing half of the win into his checking account. What else did Mary and Maxine tell me? Who else was there every time it happened?

Say it ain't so.

I don't know how long I sat there before I pushed the play button and started the video feed again.

Bianca Casimiro Sanders stood. Six Bellissimo employees, including Hollywood, cleared a path for her. She walked away without ever playing. She'd been there eight minutes total, just long enough to dump a drink. Ten minutes later, Eddie Crawford walked up.

Showtime.

I split the screen into quads, and watched him win from four different vantage points. I was glad I'd skipped breakfast.

He chose a machine, ninth in the row of ten, fed it two thousand dollars in hundreds, and began playing, but only betting one credit. I wondered why he wasn't playing all five credits, because even I knew you didn't get a shot at the whammy feature unless you placed a full bet. No one seemed to pay a bit of attention to him, the staff, I bet, still reeling after the soggy encounter with the boss's wife.

On his sixth try, Eddie was dealt a straight, winning twenty-five credits, at which point he doubled his bet to two credits. Ten hands later he lined up eights, and the four of a kind paid him forty credits, then he began playing the maximum bet, five credits. After a dozen hands, he glanced at his watch. I zoomed in on it. A Cartier. With diamonds instead of numbers. That good-for-nothing bastard. After another three hands, he admired his diamonds again, at length, as if he were counting. I checked the time, since he seemed to be so interested in it. He'd been playing almost thirty minutes; it had been thirty-seven minutes since the game had reset itself after its cocktail.

Next, nothing I could see about the game prompting it, he dropped back down to a one-credit bet. He hit nothing: he won nothing. He ran his palms down the length of his thighs, and looked around. His shoulders rose as he took a deep breath, and he very deliberately placed a two-credit bet, poking the machine's button slowly, as if he didn't want to screw it up. Nothing. He collapsed against the chair back and his left hand rose to rub his forehead, a familiar (and unwelcome) Eddie tick that made me cringe a little. He rubbed his hands together, like *here we go,* and pushed the Bet One Credit button three times for his next hand. He was dealt two fours, he held them, but didn't manage another one on his second draw, losing that hand as well. I wasn't the least bit surprised when he placed a four-credit bet next, was dealt a soup hand (a little bit of everything), and lost again.

"And we have a winner," I announced to the dark empty room I occupied, as my ex-ex-husband placed a full-credit bet, but not with the Bet Max button. He pressed the Bet One Credit button five times in a row, hesitating on the last one, then pressed Deal.

Ding, ding, ding—Royal Flush.

I turned away from the computer and let Eddie celebrate from four video perspectives in private.

I didn't celebrate so much, even though I had good reason. X = B the first time for a one-credit bet, all the way to X = B the fifth time, for a five-credit bet. But only after you reset the jackpot by powering it down for a split second, and only when you rolled the credits up individually. And that's how it's done.

Now what? I scratched at the itchy wig.

I cleared the cache and hard drive of No Hair's computer for the time I'd been on it, then powered it down, plunging myself into total darkness. I batted for and found my purse when I thought I heard something beep. My head jerked up in the darkness.

I heard three more beeps. Someone was coding the exterior door.

I hit the deck, aiming for the space under No Hair's desk, just as the door to the reception area burst open. I banged my head on the edge of desk on the way down, saw stars, huddled into a tight ball, and stopped breathing altogether.

"Shhh! Be quiet! Did you hear something?"

It was my twin.

"No. Wait. Maybe. Why? What did you hear?"

It was my ex-ex.

Bianca: "I know I heard something."

Me: *You didn't hear anything. Don't come in here.*

Bianca: "Never mind. Hurry, Edward, and get it."

Me: *Edward*?

Eddie the Ass: "Which office?"

Me: *Not this one! Not this one! Not this one!*

A slice of bright cut across the carpeted floor of No Hair's office as they thankfully entered Teeth's. There was just enough ambient light under the desk for something to catch it, something shiny. I squinted, then quietly reached for it. It was a two-inch stretch of clear packing tape, and underneath it, a key. It could wait. I pressed myself farther into the recess under the desk, staring at the key, my chin on my knees, and my arms wrapped tightly around them.

The drawers of Teeth's desk were being opened and closed, and I couldn't make out the details of their conversation, other than they were irritated, in a hurry, and looking for something they couldn't find.

Just then, one of the cell phones in my bag began buzzing. I mistook it for an earthquake and almost had a stroke. Thank God I had it muted. It stopped vibrating for a half a second, then immediately began again.

Bianca: "It's not here. We need to go."

Me: *Yes, go.*

Eddie the Ass: "He said the key was here and it's not."

I stared at the key under the tape just inches from my nose.

Bianca: "Let me walk you through this, Edward."

Me: *Edward*?

Bianca: "The drawer isn't locked. If the drawer isn't locked, we don't need a key. Nothing's here."

Eddie the Genius, after a pause to process: "Oh."

Me: *Yeah, Bianca, get used to that.*

Everything went pitch black as the door to Teeth's office slammed shut. I jumped and hit my head *again*.

Bianca: "There it is again."

Edward the Ass: "What?"

Me: *Nothing. Get out of here.*

The exterior door opened, then closed, effectively plunging me back into total, and thankfully solitary, silent darkness.

For several hours, which might have actually been several minutes, I did nothing but sit there and pant, hand over heart to keep it in my chest. I was just about to calm down when the phone in my purse buzzed again sending shock waves back through me. I couldn't move, I couldn't breathe, and I wondered how many years of my life had been frightened away from me.

I reached up and pulled off the wig and let out the breath I'd been holding, still under the desk in the dark. I freed the key from beneath the tape, then crawled out, banging my head on the way up just like on the way down.

What now? I rubbed my head, and sank into No Hair's chair.

I placed the key on the desk. I dug in my purse and located my own keys, then used the penlight take a look at what all I'd managed to leave Bradley's place with. I had my Marci Dunlow a.k.a. Bianca Sanders twin identification, my super-secret cell phone, and nine dollars. The three calls I'd missed were from home: the station (my dad), home (my mother), and the Front Porch (Meredith). I knew what this was—a family feud—and it would have to wait.

I poked on the keypad that granted me entry into No Hair's desk again. With a stab of guilt, I tossed my cell phone in the middle drawer, knowing my mother would give me down-the-road for being out of reach, but I had bigger fish to fry just now. I tried to stuff the wig in with the phone—I couldn't even see past the damn thing—but it wouldn't fit. Now I had a good reason to open the mystery drawer, like I needed one. I slid the little key off the desk and stabbed at the small lock, hoping like hell the secret drawer wasn't full of porn, and thank goodness, it wasn't. It was full of Glock.

It was a beauty. A Glock 27 .40 caliber is only about six inches in length, it's a dead-eye, an automatic with a hair trigger, and looked like it was equipped with a standard nine mag. I wasn't about to touch it, but that was only until I caught a glimpse of what was underneath. I angled the penlight and sure enough, there they were, three bright blue Bellissimo casino chips. The casino chip I could see clearly was stamped 5000. Jackpot! A Glock .27 and $15,000.

What were Bianca and Eddie after? The gun or the money?

All of a sudden, I knew exactly what to do, and I'd have to touch the gun to do it. Emotion, or temporary insanity, rather than logic, took over. I love guns.

The next ten minutes of my life are a blur. I got a hold of the grip, only intent to scoot it out of the way, but honestly, I couldn't help myself. I hefted it up, groaned with pleasure at the cold, hard defense of it, immediately dropped into a Weaver stance, trained it on an imaginary bad guy across the dark room, and putting about as much pressure on the trigger as a cotton ball would, blew a new door into No Hair's otherwise solid wall.

The same scene could unfold a hundred more times in my life, and in ninety-nine of them, I would still assume that no one could possibly be a large enough idiot to lay down a loaded gun without the safety on.

I'm not sure what happened next.

When the ringing in my ears stopped I could hear myself panting and I was still seeing huge red blobs in the darkness from the flash. I would have happily tossed the gun through the nice big hole in the wall, like getting rid of a lit grenade, but knowing the safety wasn't on it occurred to me that if I threw it I'd probably shoot myself in the process, so I found enough wherewithal to gently lay it down on the desk, watching my own hand shake like a ninety-year-old's, and backed away until I bumped into a solid wall that I slid down. I sat there and waited in the dark for someone to come shoot *me*. I could smell gunfire.

I have no idea how much time passed before I began entertaining the idea that no one had heard the shot, no one was coming to get me, and my best move was to put as much distance between myself and this office as possible.

I pulled myself up from the floor. So the gun had misfired. It shouldn't have had a round in the chamber, and it certainly should have had the safety on. Even with all this justification, my legs were shaking so hard that covering the ten feet from the wall to No Hair's desk was still difficult.

I picked up the gun again, my hands still trembling, clicked the safety on and popped out the clip, well after the fact. I couldn't get it out of my hands fast enough, dropping the clip in the drawer, and placing the gun beside it. I felt around in the dark for the three casino chips, swiped them, then closed and locked the drawer. I swallowed the little key.

(No, I didn't.)

I ran, not bothering to lock up after myself with the new entrance and all, took the straightest path to the casino and once there, made my way to the closest bar.

"Whiskey." I white-knuckled the bar.

"Well?"

"Well, what?" I asked. "I need some whiskey. Please."

The guy rolled his eyes and poured me a shot.

I tossed it back.

Edward Crawford wouldn't win a million dollars today if Marci Dunlow was the early bird, worms and such. Then Bianca Sanders wouldn't kill him, which was only fair. She could get in line behind me. I was here first.

* * *

I got in line. Knowing the video poker machines wouldn't take the blue tokens, I made my way to the cashier cage, my throat and belly burning from the whiskey, and I was in good company. This was a popular spot.

There were five cashiers behind a tall marble counter with gold bars up to the ceiling. I guess that's why it's called a cage. Every line was four or five people deep, and no one seemed to be in any manner of hurry. The whiskey wasn't working yet, so I took deep measured yoga breaths, or maybe they were Lamaze, knowing that I had to calm down in order to finish this.

My wanderings hadn't put me in this particular queue before, and I noticed a kiosk of reading material cashier patrons could entertain themselves with while waiting. The racks were stuffed with pamphlets advising gamblers on how to go about saving themselves from the evil addiction. After picking one up and reading it in yet another attempt to distract myself from what I'd done, I'd summarize the message this way: If you can't be reasonable about how much you lose, you don't get to come back. So be reasonable. When I bored of reading, I took advantage of one of the standing antibacterial hand sanitizer dispensers planted at one-foot intervals. How can your hands be too clean when you've just fired a weapon?

It was at this point, when I was just about calm, that it occurred to me that I hadn't wiped down the gun.

Damn.

While I was trying to decide if I should go back and take care of the gun, imagining a crew of people examining the hole I'd blasted in the wall, the guy in front of me stepped away and it was my turn.

The counter rose almost to my shoulders, but the cashier on the other side was barely taller than me, so we did the short-girl smile. With a quick survey I saw the reason for the bars: stacks of banded currency and racks of casino chips were everywhere. I placed the three blue chips on the counter between us. "Can I get money for these?"

"Of course," she smiled. "Whoa! Congratulations!"

She spread out the three chips, displaying them for the seven hundred cameras that were trained on us, then scooped them up and tapped them twice against the counter. Her cash drawer popped open and bounced against her. She turned the chips over, pausing for the briefest of seconds, just long enough to catch my attention.

"I'll be right back." She backed away, smiling, and took the $15,000 in casino chips with her.

Before I could guess where she'd gone or why I was as nervous as a thirteen-year old at cheerleading tryouts, she returned with a man at her side. She smiled, he smiled, I smiled, we all smiled.

"Do you have a player's card?" he asked.

"Yes!" I dug it out.

"ID?" he asked.

I pulled that out, too. I was passing this test with flying colors.

A small plastic disk appeared. The cashier popped it open. "We need a thumbprint and index finger for anything over ten thousand," she said.

It sounded reasonable to me. And no risk, because my prints led exactly nowhere.

The man and woman exchanged a rapid-fire non-verbal communication of some sort, and I had a feeling they were about to tell me that for whatever reasons, they weren't cashing these chips for me, when he nodded, giving her the go-ahead.

She dropped a healthy stack of the green stuff into the top of a bill counter, depressed a button, and cash started flying on her side of the bars.

Before the man stepped away he asked, "Where will you be playing, Miss Dunlow?"

I pointed in the wrong direction, but these two, not to mention previous events, had me flustered. "Behind the waterfall," I said.

She placed the cash in front of me, and I grabbed it. The man smiled, the cashier smiled, I smiled. I backed away.

"Hey!" A lady I plowed into protested.

"Sorry."

I turned and quick-stepped to Private Gaming.

NINETEEN

It happened so fast.

A different young man was hosting the Big Bucks Room, Hollywood's weekend counterpart, I guessed, and this one more Broadway than Hollywood. He took one look at me, almost fell over, reached up and pressed his hidden earpiece, where apparently someone behind the curtain informed him that I was *not* Bianca Sanders, and then they probably told him to get it together.

"Good afternoon, Miss Dunlow," he said breathlessly, his face Christmas red.

"I'll need a bottle of water and a Bloody Mary," I breezed by him, "extra olives."

"Certainly."

Not for the first time, I wished this could wait until tomorrow, when I could run it all by Natalie and have some backup, but to quote Mr. Sanders, this iron was *hot*. I couldn't call her, because I'd left my phone in No Hair's desk. With Teeth now another notch up on my probably-a-bad-guy list since he was apparently hiding things for Bianca and Eddie, there was no one on property to assist me.

If I hadn't found the chips, I wouldn't be here at all, because I'd tapped out Marci Dunlow's line of credit the night before, and that couldn't be helped until, again, I could get with Natalie. Finding the chips was almost a sign, and if I didn't do this right now, backup or no backup, Miss Nevada and Mr. Alabama would be cashing in. Since one of the elements was obviously timing, with thirty-seven minutes passing between Bianca glitching the power and Cartier

Eddie winning, I had to get going. It was now or never. If I could win it, first of all, it'd be fun, and second of all, Eddie wouldn't.

I sat at the fourth machine and said, "Here goes nothing."

A waitress arrived with a tray. I took the drinks then shooed her away with a hundred-dollar bill. I knocked back half of the Bloody Mary, finally had something for breakfast that wasn't alcoholic (two olives), then reached for the water. I twisted off the lid, perched the bottle on the edge of the machine, then elbowed it.

"Uh-oh," I said aloud.

I let about half of the water loose before righting the bottle, hoping it would be enough to find the little button, and apparently it was, because almost immediately the video poker machines winked at me. I downed the rest of the Bloody Mary, hoping vodka and whiskey weren't a bad mix, and hoping no one in surveillance got winked at too. I noted the time, I tried to breathe, and the peppery tomato juice burned through me, causing me to hallucinate about Pine Apple. I missed home.

My arms felt like they weighed a hundred pounds each as I gathered my purse and Bloody Mary dregs, then traded the seat at the fourth machine for the ninth, the one Eddie won on. I pulled a half inch of hundreds from the nice stack, loaded the machine one by one, and let the music of the game calm me down. It had been eight minutes.

The next twenty minutes flew by. I had another drink, relaxed a little more, began winning back some of the money I'd lost the night before (whammy *this* you crazy game), and watched the clock.

Broadway was a squirmer. He left me alone for the first fifteen minutes I was there, thank goodness, because he might have taken issue with me dousing the carpet, but more and more, it felt like he was hovering.

"Where is everyone?" I asked him on one of his many trips by.

"What's that?" I swear the boy almost jumped out of his skin.

"Where did everyone go?" I asked.

He shrugged, his eyes dancing all over the room. "It's Sunday afternoon, you know. Not much going on."

"You must be expecting something," I poked at the screen, holding two tens.

"How's that?"

"The two men at the entrance," I tipped my head.

When I'd arrived, there was the usual one tuxedoed greeter. The next time I looked up there were two large suits, one dark gray, the other dark blue, flanking the waterfall. They looked almost menacing from behind, and they were most definitely packing, one a leftie, his shoulder-holster bulge on the wrong side. I assumed they were Bianca's Welcome Wagon, and what seeing them said to me was *hurry*.

"Oh," he said, "those guys." Broadway looked at everything but me, probably because my resemblance to you-know-who was too creepy for him to deal with. "We've got VIPs in the building."

I didn't tell him I'd just run into his VIP, right before I took out a wall.

Turning back to the machine, checking the time, I was almost too numb from earlier events to be the least bit excited when I began the sequence of play that would—God help me—hit the jackpot. I just wanted it over with and out of there.

With the one-credit and two-credit bets behind me, my stomach near the floor, I reached to place the three-credit bet as someone invaded my space from the left. A large hairy hand flew in front of my face and slapped the screen of the slot machine. With his other arm crooked, he pushed against my chest, separating me from the game. I didn't hear or see the two suits behind me, the ones who'd been at the entrance, until they unceremoniously jerked me out of my chair.

* * *

My world was reduced to three solid walls, one wall of dark window, a steel door, a long table, and four metal chairs. I'd been here before with the brother/sister safe-cracking team, the Duprees, but on the other side of the glass.

At first, the only thing I could come up with was I'd been yanked off the game so I wouldn't win it before Bianca and Eddie the Rat got the chance to, but as more and more time passed, I began imagining worse scenarios.

What worse, though? I hadn't *done* anything.

Except blow out a wall.

Which isn't worthy of all *this*.

I was left alone in the room with my hands cuffed behind my back to stew about it for long stretches. A woman who wouldn't speak to me carted me off to an adjacent restroom that smelled like sick at regular intervals, and four different times the guy who'd smacked my poker game with his furry paw came in and asked me my name.

"Marci Dunlow."

"How about any aliases? A middle name? Maiden name?"

"Discretion," I answered.

"Marci *Discretion* Dunlow?" He slapped the table with his open palm, and we both jumped, me and the table. "This will go so much easier for you," the man said, "if you'll cooperate, Marci *Discretion* Dunlow."

For the first three hours, I felt stronger about cooperating with the man who signed my paychecks than I did this idiot. It was the one directive I'd received from Richard Sanders, and it would take the fourth hour of leaving me in the room alone to decide that the only way out was to tell them my name. By that time, I'd convinced myself that Richard Sanders had never imagined *this* scenario when he'd insisted that I remain anonymous.

Or was he behind it all? Was this a test?

I might have been losing my marbles.

I devoted a small portion of my miserable time in the room coming to the decision that I absolutely had to start getting along better with my mother, and that distracted me a little. I was amazed at how caged-animal I felt by being bound. Things itched that I couldn't scratch—my ears, my nose, an ankle. At one point I was convinced that a stray eyelash was underneath one of the Bianca-green contacts, but there wasn't a thing I could do about it but try to blink it away.

My emotions flew between rage, stone-cold fear, and disbelief. Any second, I expected someone to rush in and apologize for this mix up, but the second didn't come. At the end of the fourth hour, my chin on my chest, having cried myself into a fog, Furry Paws was back, and he brought friends. Three suits filed in behind him, and one of them mercifully uncuffed me.

A new guy sat across from me. "I don't know what to call you," he said.

"Marci Dunlow."

He leaned in. "We both know you're not Marci Dunlow. We need your *name*, young lady."

We all waited an indeterminable amount of time for me to cave. There was no air in the room, and the only sound was the scrape of one chair. I got the words out in a whisper, but they all heard me.

"It's *Way*," I rubbed my wrists. "Davis Way. My name is Davis Way, and I work here."

The one closest to the door stepped out, and the other three and I listened to each other breathe for another long stretch until he returned.

"That's not anyone's name who works here," he announced, letting the door slam behind him. "I don't think that's anyone's name at all." He was the most menacing of the four, a gray-haired Fed-looking guy. He resumed his post against the closed door. "So this is how you want it to go, young lady?"

"I don't *want* any of this. You asked my name, I told you."

There was silent communication between the men, a throat clearing, a cough, a few long sighs, and some whimpering, but that was me.

"Okay," the one sitting in front of me said. "So be it." He introduced himself, saying he and gray-hair were with the Gaming Commission, which threw me, and the other two, including Furry Paws, were detectives with the Biloxi Police Department.

"What's your name?" Gaming Commission One, sitting directly across from me, asked.

"Davis Way," I said.

"Try again," Biloxi Detective One said.

"My name is Davis Way. Call Natalie Middleton, and she'll verify it. Call her," I begged. "I work in Security; I started six or seven weeks ago."

"Young lady," Gaming Commission One tapped his fingertips together. "Every employee on three shifts of the security staff has been brought in, along with every department head we could round up." He tipped his head toward the two-way mirror. "And not one of them could identify you. None has ever heard of Marci Dunlow. I can run this new alias by them, but I have a feeling they're not familiar with Davis Way either."

"Okay." I tried to breathe. "The only one here today is Teeth. And his real name is either Jeremy or Paul, Covey or—" I couldn't come up with it "—something else."

"Paul Bergman," Gaming Commission Two supplied, "and we brought him in first."

Son of a bitch. Terror grabbed me about the neck and strangled the very life out of me. I tried my best to process the information: Teeth threw me under the bus. No more wondering who he played for; he was on Team Teeth.

"Young lady," Gaming Commission One said, "I don't know how to phrase this delicately, so I'll just put it out there."

He waited until I looked directly at him.

"Your appearance has startled everyone." And he didn't mean it in a good way. "Are you possibly under psychiatric care?"

"Excuse me?"

A picture of Bianca Casimiro Sanders appeared on the table, and by all accounts, it was a shocking resemblance, even to me.

"Think about it," he said.

He was giving me the option of playing the Crazy Card, but instead, I played my Ace. "Call Richard Sanders," I said. "He'll explain it all to you."

"Well," Biloxi Detective Two laughed sarcastically, "it's not a very good time to call Mr. Sanders, now is it?"

"Right," I nodded for dear life. "He went to see his son, but he'll be here any minute. He's always here on Monday."

"He's in *surgery*," Detective Two got in my face, "and you'd better hope he makes it."

"*What*?" It came out on a huge woof of air.

They all stared at me.

"Is he okay?"

Gaming Commission One settled back in his chair. "Why don't you tell us? Is he okay? While you're at it, tell us your name."

"It's Way! Davis Way!" I insisted. "And how would I know if he's okay or not?" My jaw dropped as his implication hit home. I scanned the other accusatory faces. "Surely to God you don't think I shot Mr. Sanders! I was in the casino! You people dragged me out of the casino! I didn't *shoot* anybody!"

Gaming Commission One leaned in. "I never said he was shot."

My lungs collapsed.

"We'll get to that in a minute, young lady. For now, let's talk about the counterfeit chips."

It went downhill from there.

* * *

They left me alone for another hour, then burst back in. I don't know what I did during the hour, other than watch the clock tick and pray.

"Miss—"

"Way. It's Davis Way." I'd said it a million times.

Gaming Commission One reached up and scratched an ear, sighing deeply.

"One more time," he said. "We have Davis Way's prints, and they're not yours."

"There's a reason for that! Please! Contact my father, he'll explain everything!"

"We're trying. We've had to send agents to Pine Apple, because no one will answer a phone there."

That struck a fresh new terror in my heart.

"We did get through to the last number you gave us," he glanced at a slip of paper, "Mel and Bea Crawford, and when we asked if they knew a Davis Way, they disconnected, and the line has been unavailable since."

Oh, God, save me.

"And you're not Marci Dunlow, either," he said, "because she doesn't exist. Who are you? This is your last chance, and if you don't give me your name, I'm booking you as Jane Doe. With all you have ahead of you, trust me, you don't want to go in the system Jane Doe."

I had no idea what time it was, but I'd been in this room forever. I was cold, starving, and I'd cried so hard, I think I was dehydrated. At this point, I was truly willing to tell them anything—where and when I lost my virginity, where and when Bradley Cole lost his (I'd read the details in a letter from his high school sweetheart when she tried to start things up again after seeing him at their ten-year reunion), or even about the time I'd locked up my old nemesis Danielle Sparks for no good reason other than I couldn't stand her.

I'd spilled all the beans, told them everything, yet not one of them believed me and there was no one to back me up.

I took one last huge breath. "What is it, exactly, that you're going to charge me with?" I asked. "I've told you who I am, why I'm here, and where I got the casino chips. If someone who looks like me shot Mr. Sanders, you need to be looking at his wife. I work here, and I'm a former police officer."

I searched the faces for any traces of consideration, and found none.

The Gaming Commission representative who'd been manning the door the entire time crossed the room slowly, bent over, and put the tip of his nose almost up against mine. "One last chance," he said. "Why did you shoot Richard Sanders?"

"I didn't."

"Where did you get them?"

"Get *what*?"

"The counterfeit chips."

"Jeremy Covey's desk! Call him!"

"Jeremy Co*ven* is unavailable."

"Ask George Morgan."

"There is no George Morgan."

"Morgan George!" I shouted. "Morgan George!"

"Who's deceased!"

"What about Mary and Maxine? The little old ladies in the casino?"

"We've looked ten times. There are no little old ladies!"

Was it Sunday? The Lord's Day? Holy shit!

"Do you see a pattern here?" He stood, towering over me. "There is no Marci Dunlow, no Davis Way, no little old ladies, no George Morgan, no Morgan George! There is no cab! We finally heard back from Bradley Cole, and he said he thought his renter was a woman named Anna Merriweather, who, by the way, DOESN'T EXIST!"

Now a sudden-onset expert at crying, tears dropped off my chin that I didn't know were coming.

"You have the opportunity to help yourself here if you'll tell me who you are and where you got the counterfeit chips."

"From Jeremy Co*ven*'s desk."

"Before or after you shot Richard Sanders?"

"I. Didn't. Shoot. Richard. Sanders."

"Do you think we're idiots, Miss Doe?"

"At this point," I screamed, "I do! And stop calling me Jane Doe!"

The man shook his head in a tsk-tsk way, and motioned someone in at the same time. The door cracked open, and a female police officer entered.

"Stand up," my interrogator demanded.

I couldn't. There was no way my legs were going to hold me.

The female officer took two steps and helped me by jerking my shoulder out of its socket, wrenching me upright.

"Jane Doe, you're under arrest—" Jane's Miranda Rights followed.

I launched into a panicked screaming blubber. "My father! Why won't you call my father?"

Gaming Commission Two looked straight at me as I was being cuffed. "The chief of police in Pine Apple," he said, "who you claim is your father, has had a massive heart attack, and that, apparently, has made the whole town unavailable."

The room began spinning around me. I heard a woman's piercing scream, then everything went black.

TWENTY

It might have been hours, it could have been days later, when I woke up cuffed and shackled to a hospital bed. My left side was cuff-free, but connected to hospital apparatus. I was alone in the room, but saw an officer stationed outside of the door.

I turned, as best I could maneuver, toward the wall.

"Daddy." I said the word, but no sound came out.

There was no clock, the television screen was dark, and nothing was within my reach, not even a sip of water. My inclination was to scream, but I stifled that into the thin pillow. I stared at the wall, putting the pieces of the nightmare together, and I stayed that way, frozen, until a nurse, accompanied by a female police officer, entered the room.

"Oh," the nurse said and stopped short of the bed, the officer almost piling into her. "You're awake."

The officer turned away and spoke into her headset.

"Do you have any information about my father?" I begged her.

A look of confusion slid down her face, and she began flipping through the chart she was holding, as if the answer might be in there. "Your *father*?" she asked.

The officer's raspy voice filled the room. "No chitchat." She opened the door and stuck her head out to speak to the other officer, as the nurse began fiddling with the IV in my left arm, then strapped a blood pressure cuff around my bicep.

The nurse, probably in her late forties, had an ample midsection along with ample everything else, and she hugged my arm into her warm middle while she pumped the bulb of the blood-pressure gauge.

I looked up at her, and tears slid from my eyes. “Please find out if my father’s okay,” I whispered. “His name is Samuel Way, from Pine Apple, Alabama. He’s had a heart attack.”

“Hey!” the officer’s voice cut through the sanitized air. “Shut up, Doe.”

The nurse barely closed an eyelid, winking at me, and gave the quickest of nods. “You don’t look like you could hurt a flea.” Her lips didn’t move as she whispered it.

“How long have I been here?” I whispered. “What day is it?”

“It’s Sunday night,” she said, again without moving her lips. “You’ve been here several hours.”

I never saw her again.

Not much time passed before a different nurse accompanied by two female officers burst into the room. There was nothing warm and fuzzy about this nurse. She’d been in the room three seconds before she jerked the needle out of my arm, while the officer freed me from my cuffs and shackles from the other side of the bed. The second officer leaned against the wall looking bored. The words Mississippi Department of Corrections were embroidered on her uniform.

The first one said, “You have one minute in the bathroom.” She tossed me two orange squares of folded cotton. “Leave the door open.”

I was shackled to a wheelchair, but only as far as the front door. After that, I was jerked upright and dragged to the van that carted me off to the police station to be booked.

Bright lights were trained on me from every direction, and I ducked them as best I could. Fifty questions were shouted my way.

“Why’d you do it?” a particularly loud voice cut through the din. “Why’d you shoot Richard Sanders?”

* * *

An hour into the booking process I became numb and stopped fighting them. I was simply too stunned and too afraid. The fear factor had nothing to do with what was happening to me, I was afraid for my father. I stared at my cuffed hands in my lap without blinking. The clock on the wall struck midnight.

"Your name?"

"Davis Way."

The woman tapped a pencil against the desk. She quickly scanned the room—several other female officers were in various stages of booking several other female offenders—then leaned in. "This will go so much easier for you," she almost whispered, "if you'll tell me your name."

I felt a sliver of hope. She was a few years younger than me, probably fresh out of Officer's Training, and therefore not totally jaded. "Four-zero-seven. Six, one. Six, seven, eight, two," I said. "Look up my Social."

"I can't do that," she whispered.

"You can. It's right there on the screen."

"I'm not supposed to," she said, visually sweeping the room again.

Instead of grabbing for her pencil, which would have had her grabbing for her piece, I asked if I could write it down for her. "Look it up. You'll see I spent years on the job in Pine Apple, Alabama. Now I work undercover for the Bellissimo, and the list of reasons you can't find me in the system is ridiculously long."

She took the clipboard in front of her and pretended to write. With her head down she said, "Why won't anyone back you up?"

"Apparently they're busy." My head was bowed, too. "The president of the Bellissimo was shot." I covered my face with my hands, so anyone looking might think I was crying, and it being a room filled with all sorts of emotion, mostly rage, hopefully they'd be bored with me and instead watch the drunk twenty yards away who kept spilling out of her chair.

"I think my father had a heart attack," I said to my booking officer, "but they very well could be lying to me."

"Why would anyone lie to you about that?" the officer's eyes darted.

"To gauge my reaction," I said. "To see if I'm who I say I am. Would you please, *please* make a phone call for me?" I begged with my eyes.

She sniffed. She shuffled things around on her desk. "One," she whispered. "Only one." She reached for a yellow sticky note, just about when the drunk passed out cold, pitched into the lap of the officer trying to book her, then wet her pants. The officer screamed and spilled the drunk into the floor.

My officer ignored it. "And only if this is a real Social Security number."

This kind gesture was absolutely more than I could take, at which point I did begin bawling like a baby.

"Get a hold of yourself," she spoke through clenched teeth. "Let's go," she stood.

We had to step around the puddle of comatose drunk.

My booking officer, Raines, her badge read, took me through the fingerprinting process. "You want me to call a lawyer, right?" she whispered while rolling my left thumb. "If you're with the casino," she spoke without moving her lips, "call one of theirs."

"No," I whispered back. "I need you to call my sister. Find out about my father, and tell her I've been sent to—" my mind raced "—Dubai."

She looked at me as if I were crazy. "If I were you," she whispered, "I'd call a lawyer."

She didn't offer any additional advice while she completed another ten minutes of paperwork, then led me to yet another holding cell.

"What's this?" I asked, as bars clanked closed to separate us.

"We're going to need a gunpowder residue test."

A what? It took a second for her words to sink in, and when they did, I must have fallen into my own puddle on the floor because

I was only aware of hard, cold concrete. Voices broke through the fog. My officer. A man. "Get her on the cot," the man said. "You can still GSR her. Then cart her back to the hospital."

* * *

Having failed the gunpowder residue test, they carted me to the prison infirmary instead. The next day, I was dumped into General Population, better known as the Drunk Tank.

The words "bond hearing" weren't spoken to me, but the words "bang, bang Bianca" were, always in passing, always with snickers, and never directly to me. Apparently I was somewhat of a prison celebrity. I was pointed to, gawked at, and gossiped about relentlessly. I picked a spot to sit on a green metal bench, a spot on the wall to stare at, and sat there for two days and two nights while prostitutes and DUIs around me were either bonded out or processed.

Sometime during the third day, I was called to the desk.

"Doe!" the overweight and cranky officer in attendance yelled across the room. "Jane Doe!"

I picked up my heavy head and the room warbled around me.

"Jane Doe!"

I'd had so many names in the past two months that I no longer recognized any of them.

"Last call," the guard said, waving a piece of paper in the air. "Personal message for Jane Doe!"

I jumped up and almost fell down. "It's me," I called out, reaching for the wall. I made my way to the desk.

"You're Jane Doe?" I had seen this woman from across the room, but I had not yet been close enough to notice that she was balding. You could see every bit of her scalp through her thinning hair.

I stood there, holding the edge of her desk for support.

"You're the one who won't eat," she said.

"I guess."

"Don't blame you," she said. "You've got a message here from the officer who booked you," she said. "Maybe you'll know what it's about." She pushed her glasses up the wide bridge of her nose. "*Triple bypass.*"

* * *

From there, I spent two more days staring at the infirmary walls, then I was processed and assigned to B Block as Jane Doe, pretrial.

Pretrial status was prison purgatory, and there was no way out of it until someone within the system took an interest in the case. Being at the center of the biggest story since Hurricane Katrina, it was hard to guess if the momentum would speed things along or slow them to a crawl. I could be pretrial for a week; I could be pretrial for a decade.

My cellmates were both of Hispanic descent, and clearly didn't want a new roomie. They spoke nothing but Spanish above, below, and through me, but would speak choppy English to anyone else. Even though it was relayed to me in overdrive Spanish, I got the message the minute I was shoved into the cell: don't touch their things, don't breathe their air, don't make eye contact.

I crawled into the space they indicated was mine, my size coming in handy, because they didn't allot me much, a skinny top bunk and that was it. I curled into a ball, my back to the cold wall, and tried to cry, but I was too scared. I didn't know if my father was dead or alive, and no one from the Bellissimo had come to save me.

The charges against me were multiple fraudulent acts, felony theft, criminal conspiracy, computer trespassing, receiving stolen property, and criminal impersonation. The homicide charges were pending, and I could only guess that was because Richard Sanders was pending. I was told I'd be assigned an attorney as soon as I identified myself.

"Officer Butrum." I asked every guard every day. "When can I speak to an attorney?"

"You'll have to get with your counselor on that."

"I haven't been assigned a counselor!"

He sucked his teeth. "You will be."

Phone calls in prison were a joke. For one, you had to have money to use the phone, and I didn't have a dime. No one knew I was an inmate, so no one deposited money in my account. For another, the two pay phones in the prison cafeteria were under the jurisdiction of two gray-haired lifers, the female versions of Teeth and No Hair. They decided who used the phones, for how long, and in what order. I wasn't on the list. And lastly, who would I call? I had nothing to do but go over and over this in my mind, blindly and numbly walking the perimeter of the fenced-in prison yard where those of us who didn't have prison jobs were dumped for four-hour stretches twice a day, rain or shine.

If my father had survived the surgery, he was recovering. Not knowing where I was would certainly be less stress on him than knowing. I wouldn't call home. I couldn't contact anyone at the Bellissimo, because there wasn't a chance in hell the switchboard took prison calls, and I didn't know anyone's direct number; they'd all been programmed into my cell phones. If I could get through, Natalie would be the call I'd make, but according to a one-paragraph announcement in the business section of a three-day old *Biloxi Sun Herald* that had blown up against the fence in the yard, the Bellissimo was busy welcoming Evelyn Gardner, interim assistant to the interim President and CEO, Salito Casimiro. The quick announcement made no mention of Mr. Sanders, Jane Doe, the shooting, or his condition; I only knew Natalie and Mr. Sanders weren't at their desks. For all I knew, No Hair was gone, too. Teeth? I couldn't care less.

I was truly on my own.

* * *

Not soon enough, I was assigned a counselor. His name was Dick Crowder, and he was the most beautiful thing I'd seen in almost two weeks. He had a comb-over plastered onto the back half of his oversized freckled head, watery, buggy eyes, small, misshapen, brown teeth, and his polyester pants were hiked up so high, they were closing in on his man breasts. He had stick-thin twigs for legs and the smallest feet I'd ever seen on a man. He had a nasally, Jersey accent, and he wouldn't make eye contact when he was speaking; he looked off and up to the right.

"Miss Doe," he said to the calendar on the wall, "the wheels of justice are turning slowly for you, and for that I apologize." He shifted in his chair and switched focal points to something else lofty. "First," he said, "I'll ask how you're doing."

I nodded with my whole body, so grateful for his tone, his genuinely apologetic attitude, and to be sitting in a real chair away from my fellow inmates if only for a minute. Taking a deep breath, I measured my words, my desire being to have at least one decent relationship within these miles of razor wire.

"Mr. Crowder, my father has had a heart attack, and a subsequent triple bypass. If you could get me any information about his condition, I'd be forever grateful."

His eyes rolled along the squares of ceiling tiles, back and forth. "I'll see what I can do." He pushed a piece of paper and a pencil my way. "But under the circumstances, I will only be able to identify the inquiry as coming from incarcerated Jane Doe. Whoever you're writing down will most likely not be willing to release any information."

I scribbled down the name of the hospital I was born in and my family had frequented through the years. Stabler Memorial, in Greenville, Alabama, was a twenty-minute drive from Pine Apple if you needed a flu shot, but an eight-minute drive if you needed anything else and had a vehicle with sirens and a light bar. I slid the information to Mr. Crowder.

"What else?" he asked.

"I need to know Richard Sanders' status."

"That I can't help you with."

I didn't think so.

"You've got a lot of things up against you, Miss Doe," he said.

I cracked a bunch of knuckles and tried to get in his line of vision, which wasn't going to happen without wings.

"Pretrial drags on, as you're finding out first hand, not to mention what a high profile case yours is."

I felt like standing and waving. *Over here!*

He flipped through my file, then looked back to the calendar. "Let's start with the basics," he said. "What's your name?"

"Davis Way. D, A, V, I, S, W, A, Y."

He sniffed. "Have you come up with any way for us to verify it?"

"I've given out my personal information a million times, Mr. Crowder, and I'll be happy to do it again."

He stared at the calendar. "Unless you have something new, we can move on."

My shoulders slumped a little more. If that were possible.

"Okay, moving on. Is there anything you need that you don't have?"

That was a loaded question, but I knew what he meant. "I could use some things from the commissary, Mr. Crowder, and something that fits better." Three of me could have fit into my prison jumpsuit. "But what I need more than anything is a lawyer."

"Now there again, I can't help you with that."

And for some reason, he locked his gaze on the opposite wall, zeroing in on a framed eight-by-ten of the Governor. For the rest of our conversation he looked to his boss for reinforcement.

"We can assume," he said to the Governor, "that the District Attorney is dragging his feet on assigning someone until the formal charges are made on the homicide issue."

"*Homicide?*" I jumped up. "Has Mr. Sanders died?"

"I didn't say that," Mr. Crowder said to the Governor, "and have a seat."

I sat, using the chair arms to lower myself.

"What I was saying, like the rest of the justice system, there aren't enough people to go around." He proceeded to clear his lungs in a way that made me glad I hadn't eaten in weeks. Under normal circumstances, I'd have offered him a tissue, or a bucket, but these were anything but normal circumstances.

"Don't be in any hurry," he choked out. "As soon as they charge you on the homicide issue, you'll be moved down the hill."

The hill housed the petty criminals—Class C felonies and better. The ax murderers were below. I'd seen the small collection of maximum-security buildings while walking the yard, and never imagined myself there. How could things have gotten this far? And where would it go from here if Mr. Sanders had died? Chatter within the prison walls was just as ambiguous as my new counselor. Inmates continuously sneered and leered both "Bang, bang, Bianca! Shot him *dead*!" which would indicate Mr. Sanders hadn't survived the shooting, and with equal airtime, my fellow inmates hissed things like, "Boss man's coming after you, Bianca," which would indicate he had lived. I didn't acknowledge either; I kept to my corner.

"Miss Doe?"

I tried to breathe.

"I'll make a call on an attorney for you," he said, "because at least you can get started on this other business." He was apparently familiar with the long list of charges against me, although he was still talking to the Governor. He let out a whistle. "Until then," he pushed another piece of paper my way, "you can put up to three names on your visitor list and tell me what you need from the commissary. I'll see what I can do." He tore his gaze off the photo to look at his watch.

I'd already given at least fifty mental miles of pacing the perimeter of the yard to what names I would put on my visitor list. The other zillion miles of pacing, I tried to figure out why Bianca would want to kill her husband. I wrote down one name and pushed the paper toward him.

"That's it?"

I nodded.

"And what can I help you with from the commissary?"

"I need a bar of soap," I said. Why the prison passed out toothbrushes, toothpaste, and shampoo, but made you purchase a bar of soap was beyond me. "And some writing paper, envelopes, something to write with, and stamps."

He scratched his bald head, displacing the long strands plastered from ear to ear. Realizing this, he began patting. His fingernails were dirty.

"Have you not made any friends?" he asked. "It would seem some of the other women would help you with these things."

"I know better than to make friends in here, Mr. Crowder."

"So you've been incarcerated before?"

I slapped my head. "No! I'm a former police officer!"

Sure you are, his face said. "You know," he glanced at his watch again, "it would help so much if you'd give us your name. Really, Miss Doe, how much worse can it be? Are you concerned about extradition to another state?"

I pressed my lips together tightly and begged the sudden tears to stay in my head.

"Think about it, Miss Doe. Unless you're facing homicide charges somewhere else, you'd be so much better off just telling us."

"My name is Davis Way." I reeled off my Social. I opened my mouth to spout off more, but he held his hands up in a halt motion.

"Give me the name of an immediate family member who can verify your identity," he said, "in person. Show up with a birth certificate and baby pictures, and I'll call them in." After several minutes of complete silence, while silent tears made tracks down my face as he memorized the pattern on the Governor's tie, he tapped his pen and said, "I didn't think so."

He pushed back from his desk and pulled open the middle drawer. He passed me two pieces of paper and one stamped envelope. "This is all I can do. You'll have to purchase more, or get with a fellow inmate and work something out."

I reached for them, and found my voice. "Thank you, Mr. Crowder."

"Good luck, Doe. I'll see you next week."

I hoped not.

* * *

I had one shot. It took me until lights out, huddled in my corner, to write the letter. I wanted, more than anything, to use my resources to contact my sister, but that would do more harm than good. If I did not devote a good portion of my waking hours imagining my father's recovery—the crisp, pale sheets on my parent's bed, a Robert Parker thriller on the nightstand, the afternoon sun streaming through the plantation shutters and cutting lines across the foot of the bed—I would no longer be able to breathe. I would not divert attention from his healing by turning the spotlight on myself. Besides, I could just hear my mother now: "Of course she's in jail. Where else would she be when he really needs her? No, Meredith, don't you lift a finger. She got herself in there, let her get herself out."

Of my small Bellissimo crew, I felt certain at least one of them knew exactly where I was and exactly why, and they wanted things this way. Contacting the wrong one could spell conviction for me. And George. How do you address a letter to a man using an alias who lived in a nameless cab? I didn't have an attorney to contact, so that left me with one rotten option.

Eddie, Mel, and Bea,

I swear to you, all three, on all that is holy and unholy, if you do not respond to this letter immediately I will make the rest of your lives a living, breathing hell. I need out of this prison, and I need out NOW, and if one of you doesn't get to Biloxi and get me out, your chicken-fried chicken-liver Thursdays are OVER. I will burn that place to the ground with the three of you chained to the fryer. Breathe a word of this to my family, and you'll be so sorry.

I'll see you tomorrow.

Bring a lawyer,

Davis

I had no way to erase it, and less than a quarter of an inch of ink showing through the rubbery prison pen casing, so I used the rest of that sheet of paper to draft the letter that I sealed and turned in at mail call.

Eddie,

You only know the second half of how to win the money. I know the first.

Another thing I know is that you only received a cut, and if you'll help me, not only will I forgive and forget about the money from the past, I will let you walk away with every penny of what you win. There's about a one-week window on this, so you'd better not spend a whole lot of time thinking about it. To get the money, Eddie, you're going to have to get me out of jail. I'm in prison, in Biloxi, and I need an attorney who can get me bonded out. Call that guy in Montgomery who gets you out of your DUIs and get him to give you the name of the best criminal defense attorney in the state of Mississippi.

I desperately need to know about my father, Eddie.

And for God's sake, put a twenty in my prison account. They've got me in as Jane Doe, Block B, Harrison County Women's Correction. Get a lawyer who can get me bonded, get a bondsman, and do it NOW.

You've been waiting on your big break all your life, Eddie, and this is it. A million dollars to do with what you want. All you have to do is get me out of here.

Don't write me back about any of this. They can't read what I write to you, but if you write me back, the prison system will read it first. Don't write, just show up. Don't mention any of this to anyone in my family or the deal is OFF, and bring food, anything, four loaded cheeseburgers, whatever, when you show up.

You'll no longer owe me, Eddie. Instead, I'll owe you.

Davis

I sat back and waited. To pass the time, I played video poker in my head. On the third morning after sending it, I held my breath every time a guard's footstep fell outside my cell, thinking they were coming to tell me I'd been bonded out.

On day seven, my increasing panic turned to despair. I'd mailed the letter to his parents' house, knowing Eddie was here in Biloxi, but also knowing his nosy mother would get in touch with him to tell him he had a letter from a prison in Mississippi to be opened by him only, and as nosy as he was, he'd hustle home and read it. Enough time had passed for all of that to happen, yet it hadn't. In the seven days since I'd mailed the letter, I'd had one slice of stale bread, and no more than two ounces of murky water that had floaties.

On day eleven, my worst fears were realized. "Jane Doe" was one of the first names announced at mail call. Eddie wrote me back to tell me to kiss his ass, but in fact, it was even worse than that. The letter was from his mother, and it wasn't the original. It was a copy.

> *To whom it may concern, because I don't really believe it's you, Davis, but if it is, I couldn't care less about whatever kind of mess you've gotten yourself into, and for the life of me, I can't figure out why you'd try to drag my son into it. Haven't you done enough? I would think, with all your family is going through, that you'd be thinking about something else other than the money you SAY Eddie owes you. You were <u>married</u>. It was his money too. Get over it. If you think getting him to steal for you is the right way to get yourself out of trouble, then you have bigger problems than we ever imagined.*
>
> *Not that it's any of your business, but we haven't heard a word from our son in months. One more thing, whoever you are, don't write me back. You know what they say—you make your bed, you lie in it.*
>
> *Bea Crawford*

I should have sent the first letter.

The people in charge read the letter a hundred times before I did, and the District Attorney read between the lines and decided "financial gain" was the motive he'd been seeking, and what a stretch, with Bea's letter his only evidence.

Well, that, and they knew I'd fired a weapon on the night in question.

I knew the system well enough to know that bringing formal charges against me meant my future held a lot more of the same. I would sit here and rot in pretrial status while the steam built up on their airtight case of greed, a smoking gun, and an obsession with Richard Sanders that led to me impersonating his wife, then shooting him. They'd assign me the sorriest lawyer they could find, someone who couldn't get his own mother out of a speeding ticket, and in a year when this thing finally went to trial, I wouldn't have a chance in hell against a jury of my peers.

Three days after receiving Bea's letter, I was charged with the attempted homicide of Richard Sanders, plus a laundry list of other charges. The worst was Bea's snipe about what my family was going through. The only ray of light was that Richard Sanders must be alive.

* * *

Interestingly enough, Mississippi doesn't require your physical presence to accuse you of taking a kill shot at an unarmed pillar of the community. I was heavily escorted to a room on the second floor of the prison's administrative building and shoved into a metal chair with a video camera and television in front of me. The camera was on a tripod and the television was on a rolly cart. Attempted homicide charges against Jane Doe were handed down via video conferencing.

I kept one eye on the television, watching the pre-hearing activities inside the courtroom, while one of my captors barked instructions and threats. I made cooperating gestures and noises. From what I could see inside the courtroom, the judge, already on the bench, along with the bailiff, suits, and court clerks, looked bored. They were having coffee, private conversations, and passing around yawns. Someone must have been interested, though, because intermittent strobes of light bounced around the room and off their faces. Soon enough, there was order in the court, and my director gave the three-finger countdown.

"My name is Davis Way!" I shouted. "Help me, Judge!"

The video camera light went from green to red, and the guard with his finger on the trigger looked at me in disgust. "Did we not just go over this? No bullshit."

I squeezed my eyes shut and rocked back and forth.

"Do you think you can keep it together?" he asked.

I nodded with my whole body. At least I had my name out there. Surely it would be repeated a thousand times today. Surely someone somewhere would start digging.

The camera guard gave me a threatening look, and three others pulled out stun guns. The electronics whirred to life again, the judge's long face filling the screen.

"No more outbursts," he warned.

I shook my head vigorously, agreeing. I was stunned enough.

"You're in a lot of trouble, young lady."

Again, I agreed.

"Answer yes or no only to the following question," he warned. "Do you have an attorney?"

"No."

The judge complained to his audience at length about chicken-shit corporate crackpots who would never know a career-making pro bono if it walked up and bit them, he then turned his attention back to me. "You will be assigned a public defender forthwith," he said.

The charges against me were read. I was given the option of postponing my response until some poor soul was roped into representing me. I declined.

"Not guilty."

"Held without bail."

The screen went dead.

* * *

The next day they transported me down the hill to live with the ax murderers. I was processed and shoved into a two-bunk cell with a convicted felon.

As it turned out, my new roommate liked me even less than my old roommates. She eyed me for two seconds, then yelled, "You!" Her steel gaze turned to the guards. "No way! Get her out!" She came at me swinging, and she must have connected, because I woke up in the infirmary again, completely confused, with a needle in my arm.

I'd immediately recognized the face of the girl who'd put me here, as it had happened, but couldn't place her before I saw stars. Sometime during my infirmary respite, my subconscious put a name to the irate face. Heidi Dupree, the Casino Marketing assistant who, along with her brother, had been cleaning out room safes. And she could've been my ticket out of there, because she could verify my identity enough to make someone listen, except for the fact that I never saw her again. That and she hated my guts.

Rising on an elbow, I counted eight empty beds in the room I was becoming increasingly familiar with.

"Morning." The only other patient, a tremendously pregnant prisoner, greeted me.

"Do you know what day it is?"

"Nope," she said. She was peeling an orange, the citrus scent bursting through the small room. It was the first edible thing I'd been close to in weeks, and had one of my ankles not been shackled to the metal frame of the bed, I'd have pounced on the pregnant woman and confiscated it.

"Doe! Nice of you to join us." A jolly prison physician suddenly filled the room, interrupting my plans to drag the bed with me to hijack the fruit. "I was coming in to give you some wake up juice, and you saved me the trouble. And the state a thousand dollars." He chuckled at this, and dropped the syringe he'd been holding into the pocket of his white coat. He appeared to be well past retirement age, grossly overweight, sweating profusely, and looked like he helped himself to treats from the prison pharmacy cabinet about every ten minutes.

"I've got some advice for you, Doe." He licked his pale, cracked lips. "Your fasting program is going to kill you. You might like it better here in the infirmary, but you're going to end up in a body bag if you don't start eating."

I thought of the mound of colorless mush prisoners were served twice a day, accompanied by a paper cup of a transparent purple liquid, and knew I'd stick with the fasting no matter how many times I ended up in here.

"Big day for you, Doe, you're moving," he announced. "So up and at 'em. Your infirmary vacation is over. You're headed to solitary."

"What? Why?" I tried to sit all the way up, but the room spun around me. "I haven't done anything!"

"You're in here because of a fight, right?"

"I'd hardly call it a fight!"

"Whatever," the doctor said. "The State doesn't consult with me on the rules or the room assignments."

A female guard appeared at the end of the narrow bed and began separating me from it.

"You have fifteen minutes to clean yourself up." The doctor nodded toward the adjacent infirmary facilities as he none-too-gently yanked the needle out of my arm. "You have a visitor downstairs. Your counselor's going to let you have fifteen minutes of visitation before the transfer."

I almost passed out again at the thought of a visitor. No one could show up and ask to see you in prison; they had to be on your list unless they were clergy. I had a list—a short, short list that was a long, long shot. Chances were a Bible thumper was waiting patiently in the visitation room to save my degenerate soul. Well, I could work with that. And if he believed me, he might save my incarcerated butt.

The shower was wonderful, private (if your definition of private is no curtain or door and a guard watching), and the infirmary toiletries almost up to EconoLodge standards. The female guard passed me what would be my new uniform: granny panties, a sports bra laundered within an inch of its life, hospital-type scrubs in a pale blue color, and slip-on plastic shoes. After the shower and the merciful time with a real toothbrush and a real squeeze of Crest, I fingered my wet hair, dressed, and honestly felt as good as I had the first time I'd donned a Natalie outfit. Thank God someone finally knew I was here.

* * *

I spotted him right away, alone at a cafeteria-style table in a corner. Wasting a full one-fifteenth of my time, I found a wall to hold me up and drank him in. I made my way across the room on wobbly legs and fell into the chair opposite him. We stared at each other for another precious minute, him scanning my face, looking for anything familiar.

"Bradley Cole." I could hardly breathe. "Thank you for coming."

"I got your note," he said, his cautious eyes smiling.

What note?

"The one you left on the fridge. That you had to go to work, and you'd be right back."

I closed my eyes to squeeze in the humiliation. I opened them one at a time, and he looked, more than anything else, amused.

"I would have called," he said, "but my phone was in the refrigerator."

I crawled under the table.

(No, I didn't.)

"How did you find me?" I asked.

"You left a lot of clues," he pushed the sleeves of my favorite green sweater of his up an inch. "To tell you the truth, I can hardly move around the clues. I hope you don't mind, but I put your copy machine in a storage unit."

In spite of everything, and for the first time in weeks, I smiled. Then laughed. "My lease said no pets. It didn't say anything about office equipment."

He nodded slowly, smiled, then he shrugged. "I guess you're right."

"So the copier led you straight to me?"

"Not exactly."

Bradley Cole laced his fingers, and his clasped hands were dangerously close to mine on the table between us.

"I found more than a few sets of identification, a hundred wigs, several Bellissimo uniforms, and two destroyed slot machines. I pieced it together with the six-o'clock news, and," he surrendered, "here I am."

"Here you are." I whispered the words.

My joy, my gratitude, and my thankfulness overwhelmed me. It didn't help that he was such a perfectly gorgeous man, more so in person than any photograph had ever thought of capturing.

"And you've gotten messages," he said.

"Messages?"

He nodded. "There was an envelope under the door when I got home, and someone threw a rock with a note through the window."

"Did you bring them?"

"I didn't bring the rock."

That did it. If I wasn't completely in love with Bradley Cole before, I certainly was now.

"The guards wouldn't let me through with the notes."

"Tell me you read them," I said.

"I did," he answered, "not being nosy, more like seriously trying to figure out who you were and where you'd run off to."

I nodded.

"You must really like Pop Tarts."

For the second time since my incarceration, I laughed. Glorious laughter. Maybe I would try prison food; this man made me want to stay alive long enough to get out.

There was so much commotion in the large room—kids everywhere—that no one kept a clock on me, and I spent twenty-eight minutes with Bradley Cole, who was decidedly more impressive in person than in spirit. Too soon, though, a guard shouted, "Doe. Time's up."

If Bradley Cole and I marry and have a posse of children, this story will be repeated as often as my mother likes to tell the one about me ruining her life: "Daddy came to see Mommy at the prison. And that's where we met. There was a big table. And nine months later, you were born."

He was Robin Hood. He was Officer John McClane. Bradley Cole was Dudley Do-Right, and I was Nell, tied to the tracks.

The first thing we talked about was my father. Bradley promised me he'd know my father's status an hour from right now, and he'd get news to me as quickly as the prison system would allow.

I was without words. I kept my lips pressed tightly together, and gripped the seat of the chair I sat in with both hands to keep myself from tackling Bradley Cole and smothering him with my unwavering love and eternal gratitude.

"That being said, let's try to talk about your situation."

My father's health was my situation.

"Richard Sanders," he said.

And there was that.

"Is he going to make it?" I held my breath.

"Absolutely," Bradley Cole said.

I exhaled and patted my chest.

"He took the shot above the ear, through and through," Bradley said, "and it hit his optical nerves and a retinal artery."

I covered my eyes with my hands. "Owww!"

"It looked," he said, "being a head-shot, a lot worse than it really was, which led to a ridiculous amount of sensationalized media, and he was taken by helicopter to the Shreveport Cranial Trauma Center for a seven-hour surgery, which in turn made the story even bigger. The media had him fighting for his life, when he was in fact," Bradley said, "fighting for his *eye*."

"The surgery, was it successful? Did they save his eye? And what about his hair?"

"His what?" Bradley asked.

"Never mind." I waved. "Can he see?"

Bradley shook his head. "No word on that yet, but it's only the one eye. Worst-case, he's lost vision in one eye."

"Are you reading all this in the paper?"

"No." Bradley shifted in his seat, and I got a whiff of his sandalwood soap that I loved to shower with. Make that used to love to shower with. I wondered, for a split-second, if the prison would let him bring me some. Then I thought of razor blades and bars of soap, and decided they wouldn't.

"I'm getting it at work," he said.

"The soap?" I asked.

Bradley blinked several times.

"The messages," I switched gears quickly. "What did they say?" The weeks of famine must have brought out my inner idiot. I forced myself to ignore how shockingly handsome Bradley Cole was in person, and to snap back into the here (prison), now (attempted homicide charges), and why (would he be here to help me?).

"Right," Handsome said, "the messages."

"I don't understand," I said, "why anyone would've come to the condo to leave me a message. They *have* to know I'm here." I held my hands out like a Price Is Right model, displaying the magnificence of the Mississippi prison system. "Yet no one has made any attempt to help me."

"From what I understand," he said, "mine is the only name on your visitor list. How do you know they haven't tried?"

"Until I can figure out how I ended up here," I said, "the wrong person coming to see me would do more harm than good."

"Do you know who the wrong person is?" he asked.

"I have a guess," I said, "but it's a frightening one. Other than that, I'm pretty sure Mr. Sanders' wife is in it up to her eyeballs."

He processed the information, then he closed what little space there was between us. His green eyes had a gold tint, which played perfectly off his five-o'clock shadow, golden as well. "What *is* your name?"

"It's Davis," I said. "Davis Way."

"I like it," Bradley Cole sat back. "Davis Way," he tried it on. "Nice." And then he smiled, honestly, a first-date smile. I felt it, I swear, all the way from my dyed-blonde hair to my new slip-on plastic shoes.

"Why are you back in Biloxi, Bradley? I thought you were out of town until June."

"I had a long weekend," he said, "so I came back to evict you."

"*What*?"

"Davis." He threw his hands in the air. "My phone rings off the hook about you. I've taken calls from neighbors," he ticked the list off on his fingers, "from the building super, and then a few weeks ago about forty calls asking me about Marci somebody, and none of the calls were particularly nice."

"Well, your neighbors aren't exactly nice either, Bradley. And neither is your dry-cleaning guy."

With a wide smile across his handsome face, he came across the table again, making my heart pound again. "Did you send my mother a hundred tulips for her birthday and sign the card from me?"

I could feel myself turning several shades of red.

"How in the world did you know it was my mother's birthday?"

Oh, dear.

In the twenty-eight minutes we spent together, he never asked me if I shot Richard Sanders.

* * *

One thing I found in Solitary that I hadn't found anywhere else in this entire institution was a human.

Her name was Fantasy Erb: five-foot-ten, thirty-one-years old, mother of three boys, and she should have been a runway model in New York, not a prison guard, or CO as they were called, Corrections Officer, in Mississippi. She worked the day shift, and the only way I knew that in my timeless world was because she delivered the first of my two food trays, the one that had the boiled egg (green yolk) beside the mound of gruel instead of the later-in-the-day side of gray mushy stuff, which might have been mutated cauliflower or potato, beside the mound of gruel.

Fantasy was the one who told me why I had been placed in solitary.

"They didn't have anywhere else to put you, honey. We're built out for twelve hundred guests, and we're busting at the seams with twice that."

"That's a relief."

"Depends on how you look at it," she said. "Mississippi's not so relieved."

"It's most likely all the casinos around," I offered in a friendly tone. "Cash brings out the criminal in otherwise law-abiding citizens."

Fantasy's eyes narrowed.

"I didn't mean me!"

She took a retreating step, as if to separate herself from her new homicidal ward. She turned to walk away, her keys clanging, then stopped, spun, and took two long strides back to my cell. She looked left and right. "I will say this," she kept her voice soft, "if you listen to local chatter, there's a whole lot of confusion as to what happened on this Bellissimo thing."

"I didn't shoot him."

"Of course not, honey."

Right. Everyone in prison was innocent.

"No, seriously," Fantasy said, "you seem harmless, and I'm not just saying that because you're two feet tall. Believe me, honey, I know the difference."

She looked like she was about to stroll away, and I had to keep her here, if for nothing else, just civil conversation. "How long have you worked here?"

"Too long," she said. "I've climbed up the pay ladder to the point of being stuck. I can't go anywhere else and make this money," she said. "And I've got a kid with bone-plate problems that would be a pre-existing anywhere else. So here I am," she said. "Stuck."

I knew exactly how she felt.

She locked a laser beam on me. "And I won't do anything that might get me unstuck."

I got it—boundaries. Or in this case, bars. So instead of asking her to pass me her Sig Sauer P238, I asked about my father. I'd see her again before Bradley Cole would cut through the solitary-confinement red tape.

I couldn't sleep that night, waiting for Fantasy's shift to start.

"I'm so sorry, honey," she said. "My boys had homework coming out their ears last night, and the only thing I can tell you is that there isn't anything bad on the Internet. The only story I could find says what you already know: He had a heart attack and a triple bypass."

* * *

Thanks to Fantasy, I began eating again.

"Girl, tell them you're diabetic."

"But I'm not," I said.

"So? Everyone in here lies out their ass. Tell them you are, and until your next physical when they find out you aren't, which could be when pigs fly, you'll get fresh fruits and vegetables," she explained, "instead of Mystery Casserole."

From that day on, I had a banana, a small container of fat-free peanut butter, and a slice of wheat toast for breakfast. My second meal was almost always tomato soup, five stale crackers, and an apple or an orange. Starvation problem solved, and more than that, she snuck me food.

"Up and at 'em, Doe. Inspection."

She came in, flipped my mattress, pretended to frisk me, shined a light down the sink drain and in every corner, and when she left I had a glorious cornbread muffin, warm, swimming in butter, and a Dr. Pepper over crushed ice. I almost cried.

She snuck me to the shower, too, and even allowed me a small slice of privacy, in the room with me, but with her back turned. I was allowed two showers a week; she got me out of there every day. "What are you doing scratching that head, Doe? Get up. We're going to the showers."

She brought me a second set of prison digs, and a between the cotton top and drawstring pants was a zipped plastic bag, sandwich size, with a tablespoon of thick liquid green stuff in it. "Wash the one you're wearing in the sink," she said, "then spread it out under your mattress to dry."

When I wasn't eating, showering, worrying about my father, or planning my jailbreak, I was thinking about Bradley Cole.

My history with men was pathetic. The stuff of nightmares. Four years passed between my life-altering encounter with Mr. World Cultures Teacher and the next time I worked up the nerve. When I did it was a three-night stand, and as everyone knows, those don't even count. Then another year passed before I dated a biology major, Geoff, for six boring months, immediately followed by a two-night stand (again, doesn't count) with the coxswain on the UAB rowing team (he smelled funny), then the long, tumultuous decade of debauchery with (do I have to say it aloud?) Eddie the Ass. That's it. Sum total. None of which had prepared me for Bradley Cole. Just like all the photographs hadn't prepared me for the 3-D version.

For example, his hair wasn't dark blond, like in the pictures. Bradley Cole's hair was gold. Fourteen subtle shades of gold, including sunshine, candlelight, and honey. It was neat, short, very lawyerly, and looked soft. His green eyes weren't just green; they were green flecked with gold, and they like the rest of Bradley Cole: warm, engaging, and brilliant. The man glowed. (Maybe that was me glowing.) Past all the glow, he was five-foot ten, maybe eleven, with an athletic body, the tapering kind, that said baseball. (Bradley Cole's body said Varsity Pitcher Throws Perfect Game No-Hitter Shutout in State Championship.)

I couldn't stop thinking about his hands.

Sadly, my only true point of reference was Eddie the Ass. He was the physical man-bar in my life, and, admittedly, he was pretty. Bradley Cole wasn't pretty—he was all the way *handsome.* It took days for me to figure out what was missing in Bradley Cole. Eddie the Ass had *something* Bradley Cole didn't. I finally put my finger on it: the Sleaze Factor.

* * *

Day six of solitary confinement dawned to the music of Fantasy rolling a cart down the hall. I sat up, feeling the metal supports beneath the wafer-thin pad pretending it was a mattress, to see, first thing in the morning, the not-Fantasy guard, Jerry. "You got a package from your attorney, Doe."

My bare feet hit the cold floor.

I have an attorney?

A shock of blonde hair fell into my face, while it all registered. I *am* a blonde, I am in prison, and this guy is in charge of me. And more than that, the glowing Bradley Cole *is* an attorney.

Jerry used a handheld device, trained a beam, and the opening in the gate that made up the fourth wall of my cell slid open, at the same time a rubber support protruded, the exact shape of the food trays, but this time instead of a bowl of soup, Jerry tossed in books. One slid into the floor, and seeing what I could attach to as a personal possession, I dove for it.

One afternoon I'd stretched out on the bed and taken mental inventory of all my stuff, both in Biloxi and at home. It was a crazy long list of things I owned, everything from an antique typewriter I'd swiped from Meredith's shop, a Dutch Doll quilt Grandmother Way had hand-stitched, to Burberry rain boots I'd only worn once. In here, I was cut off from it all, both things that mattered and things that didn't, and the three books being *mine*, I certainly didn't want anything to happen to them.

From my knees, clutching the fallen book to my chest, I looked up for Jerry to thank him, but he'd closed the opening in the door and was gone, back to the desk chair he used as a La-Z-Boy.

I spread them out and sat on the cold floor with them. I picked them up, one by one, hugging them, inhaling them, then running my fingers over all the surfaces. I turned each one over, gently shook them, and of course nothing fell out. I lined them up by size.

The smallest was *Sit Still and Wait for It*, by Sasha Jones. I could have fit it in my back pocket had I had one. The next was a previously well-loved paperback romance, *The Missing Secretary*, by Lilly Jasmine. Lastly, largest, and the bestseller as far as I was concerned, *A Bypass Surgery Survivor's Guide to a Long and Healthy Life*, by P. Derrick Ameston.

I didn't wake up screaming that night.

TWENTY-ONE

Bradley Cole had warned me that he wouldn't be back until he had news, but he'd failed to warn me that with hope, which he'd given me, it would be a long wait.

Receiving the best news ever, that my father was recovering, didn't provide the relief I thought it would. Initially, of course, it did; I cried, danced, laughed, and relived every moment of my childhood. I fell to my knees and assured God I'd keep all the prison promises I'd made, and after an entire day of that, I collapsed in relief. The biggest relief? No more endless hours of imaging my father without life or my life without my father.

But I had to fill the hours with something, and as they dragged on, his healing actually served to make my situation worse: I had to get out of here and get to Daddy before someone else did. I had to get out of here before Daddy put two and two together and came up with trouble. I had to dig myself out before Daddy was forced to. If my father learned of my predicament, he'd have a heart attack.

I got that Bradley Cole wanted me to *Sit Still and Wait for It*. Regardless, after another day, I began pacing my four-by-six cell, and read *The Missing Secretary* twice, the good parts more times than that.

I replayed the twenty-eight minutes with Bradley a million times, picking it to pieces, and tried to make sense of the book titles. Where in the world was Natalie? I used Fantasy as a sounding board when she had time, but she was more interested in the Bradley Cole angle than anything else. "Girl," Fantasy said. "You've got it bad for him."

"He is pretty wonderful." I looked at her. "And I miss his clothes."

The rock through the window had to have been George, and the accompanying message asked more questions than it answered. The note around the rock had three words, written in block letters, and underlined twice: IT WASN'T HER.

It wasn't her? Her who? Bianca?

"Why would he throw a rock through my window?" Bradley had asked.

"So he wouldn't be recorded by the condo's security cameras," I answered. "George's story is a long one, and he operates completely under the radar."

"He's the cab driver who parks at the VIP entrance, right?" Bradley asked. "Where the shooting took place?"

I nodded.

"Then he saw the whole thing. All we have to do is track him down."

"No," I shook my head. "He only knows who it wasn't. If he knew who it was, he'd have said."

"I'll find him." Bradley promised.

"That will never happen," I said. "George is so long gone it's as if he was never even here."

The note under the door had been from No Hair. Bradley paraphrased it for me: No Hair said this was my own fault for snooping around in his desk. While he knew of my predicament, there wasn't a lot he could do about it, seeing as how I'd left a trail.

"The note said you left your *hair* in his office and that she walked right to it. He doesn't say who 'she' is or what 'it' is. Do you know, Davis," Bradley asked, "who 'she' is, what it means by 'you left your hair,' or how you left a trail?"

I couldn't answer because my life was flashing before my eyes.

"The note said he was with Richard Sanders." Bradley's voice was far away. "But it didn't say where."

I couldn't respond because the world's worst news was sinking in.

"Davis?" Bradley waved a hand in my face. "Can you fill me in?"

"Sorry," I shook the cobwebs out. "George is saying Bianca didn't shoot her husband, and No Hair's saying I forgot my wig, and my prints are on the gun."

Bradley Cole could not have been more confused. "No *what*?" he asked. "No *hair*, did you say? I'm very confused on the *hair* issue."

I couldn't explain because I was too busy thinking about lethal injections.

"What gun, Davis? You shot a gun that day? Your prints are on *what* gun?"

"Doe!" A guard interrupted. "Time's up."

Bradley Cole reached out and placed his strong, warm hands on top of my cold shaky ones. The room spun around me at his touch.

"Don't worry," he'd said. "I'll dig into this. Don't worry, Davis."

Seven ridiculously long days and nights had passed since that meeting, with no word from him other than the books. There were times I wondered if I'd dreamed it.

"Stop fretting," Fantasy advised. "He'll be back."

She'd no sooner finished repeating the comforting words to me on my eighth day of solitary confinement when the intercom in my room squealed. "Doe. Your lawyer's here. Transport in ten."

"See?" Fantasy asked. "I told you."

* * *

Now that he was my attorney of record, I could meet with him anytime, and we didn't have to do it in the crowded visitation room, although honestly, I'd have done it with him anywhere: crowd, no crowd, judges, videographers, zoo animals, I didn't care.

We were allowed thirty minutes in a private room: all glass walls, guards on every corner, and speakers that could be turned on should the penal system think I was spouting off geographical coordinates to all the bodies I'd buried.

Bradley could bring his brief case, any documents related to my defense, and his cell phone, although no signals got in or out of the bunker. He had to leave his keys, weapons, and any street drugs for resale he was sneaking to me at the door.

Today he was wearing a white button-down oxford shirt under a navy blue knit sweater and khaki pants. His shoes were the Italian loafers that at last sighting were on his closet floor tucked between my (Meredith's) Tory Burch peep-toes and Michael Kors black clogs.

I was wearing blue prison scrubs.

Honestly, we gooed at each other for the first little bit like he was there to pick me up for the prom. I wondered if I might be imagining it. Maybe it was just me doing all the gooing.

"How are you holding up, Davis?"

I nodded, smiling. "I'm better," I said. "Better."

"You got the books," he said.

"I did. I love them all. Although there's not much to *Sit Still and Wait for It*," I said. "Dull stuff."

He laughed. "I didn't read it. But if you'll write me a little review, I'll post it on the Internet for you."

Things got real serious real quick. "So he's okay?"

Bradley's voice was soft. "He's fine, Davis. He's doing fine. He's making a great recovery."

I squeezed my eyes closed, swallowed hard, and tried not to blubber.

"I picked up the phone to call a dozen times," he said, "and couldn't figure out what to say. So I got in the car and drove to scenic Pine Apple, Alabama."

He reached for his cell phone, pushed buttons, and passed it to me. Our hands touched, and a guard banged on the window with his baton.

I scrolled through the underwater photos, underwater because I began crying as soon as I saw the first image of my father, dressed in gray wool pants and a pale yellow V-neck sweater that hung on him like he was a wire hanger, strolling the rows of Mother's winter garden beside my parents' house, my mother and sister at his elbows, my niece apparently running circles around them.

"Sorry I couldn't get closer."

"Oh, God, Bradley, please don't apologize," I rearranged the tears so they were all over my face instead of two boring rivers. There were more than twenty images, and in all of them Daddy looked so thin, and so scary pale, but he was alive, smiling in several shots, and seemingly not too much less of himself after the heart attack and surgery. I fell against the chair back, exhaling the breath I'd been holding for so long with the proof in my hands. I clutched the evidence against my chest, and Bradley looked a little nervous for his phone, or maybe jealous, because most days, today being one of them, I skipped the threadbare sports bras. They were itchy.

I could live the rest of my life with Fantasy as my only friend, Bradley as my only link to the outside world, these prison scrubs my entire wardrobe, the prison walls my only view, as long as my father was okay.

Finally, I passed the phone back to him, our hands meeting again, and mouthed two words I'd uttered a million times, but never before from the rock bottom of my heart. "Thank you."

He waited patiently until I indicated that I was ready for more, and when he saw that I was, he landed an envelope on the table between us. Meredith's handwriting jumped off the white paper.

"Oh, crap." I stared at it.

Bradley Cole didn't move a muscle.

Davis,

What the hell. You've pulled some stunts in your day, but this one takes the cake.

Daddy's going to be fine.

I got a crazy phone call telling me you were in Asia, or Africa, I can't even remember it was all so scary-horrible-chaos those first days, but I do remember this—I didn't believe a word of it. Once we got Daddy home and I turned on a television, I knew exactly where you were. I left poor Mother alone with our very ill father, buckled Riley up, and drove to the prison only to sit there—with my CHILD—for TEN HOURS, DAVIS, to be told over and over again that you weren't there, and that I couldn't see the Jane Doe they were holding on the casino shooting. What the hell, Davis?

No, Mother and Daddy don't know, although Daddy's on the right track, and he'll know soon. You had a little grace period as your father was TOO SICK to even worry about you, but that's over, and he's snooping around. Yes, as always, I'm trying to cover for you, making up phantom phone calls and even sending Get Well cards.

Seriously, Davis.

Meredith

After reading it several times, I turned the letter over so Meredith would stop screaming at me. "When did you get this?" I assumed my sister had just slipped it underneath the door at the condo.

"I'd been in Pine Apple ten minutes when she walked right up to me and said we needed to talk."

"No!" This felt no different than the time Meredith caught me smoking pot and I had to wash the dinner dishes on her nights for months on end. No telling what this would cost me.

Bradley nodded. "I thought I was being sneaky."

"Yeah," I looked away and sighed. "She was raised by a police chief."

"Your hometown's really small, isn't it?"

"It is," I agreed.

"I liked her store," he said.

It didn't seem to me that Bradley Cole would be wasting time making small talk about the Front Porch if there wasn't something else about his meeting Meredith that he didn't want to tell me.

"What else?"

"Nothing."

I crossed my arms and waited.

"She said for me to tell you that she wasn't an idiot," he said, "and that your ex-husband is nowhere to be found."

"And?" I asked.

He took his time. "She said the whole town thinks you've run off with him."

We sat quietly for a beat.

"So?" Bradley took a tread-lightly breath. "You and your ex?"

I wondered if he was asking regarding my current state of affairs, or life in general. It didn't matter; the answer was the same.

"Honestly, Bradley," I said. "I'd rather be *here* than anywhere with my ex-husband."

"Okay, Davis." He shifted in his seat. "Time to tell me the whole story."

I did the best I could.

"You realize," he said at the end, "I'm not a criminal lawyer."

"Bradley," I replied, "I don't care if you're a Tootsie Roll lawyer."

I didn't leave anything out.

He listened intently, made notes but asked no questions, and made only one comment at the end: "It's eerie how much you *do* look like her."

TWENTY-TWO

On my fifty-sixth day in prison, Teeth washed up in the St. Bernard Bay, ninety miles west of the Bellissimo. His dentist identified the body over the phone. It didn't take long to find the cause of death, as the bullet was wedged so tightly in the base of his skull that even the ocean residents hadn't managed to free it. It came from the gun with my prints on it. For the moment, it was Metairie, Louisiana's problem, but it was only a matter of paperwork before it would be mine.

The object of my dreams—and truly, I mean it, I'd been dreaming about him since the first time I'd climbed into his bed—had said he had good news and bad news.

"Which do you want first?"

Thinking there might be bad news about my father, I demanded it.

He told me about Teeth.

"Oh my God." I was incredulous. "This isn't *bad* news," I cried. "This is the straw that will nail my broke-back camel's coffin!"

"No," Bradley Cole was calm, "it's not."

"I'm going to be charged with it! This is devastating!" I was pacing, crying, and panicked. "I didn't really like Teeth all that much, and there's no doubt he had something to do with all this, but I sure wouldn't have wished the guy dead!"

"Please sit down, Davis." He patted the chair beside him.

He reached for and found my hand underneath the table, which gave me all manner of new sensations to add to the electric-chair sensations I was already entertaining.

With his free hand, he pushed paper in front of me. It was the ballistics report from the Richard Sanders' unpleasantness. I used my teeth to turn the pages to avoid letting go of Bradley's hand.

(No, I didn't.)

After looking at the report from every possible angle, I turned to him. "Am I reading this right?"

Bradley Cole nodded. "You are."

According to the ballistics report, the bullet that hit Richard Sanders had whizzed above his ear back to front. Shreveport Cranial Trauma Center agreed: entry posterior, exit anterior. He and Bianca had been face-to-face, and Bellissimo surveillance backed it up with forty-four zillion stills. The shot that hit him had come from the bushes behind him, not the wife in front of him. Bianca had squeezed off a round, and they had recovered the casing, but the estimated trajectory indicated she had been aiming for someone in Hot Springs, Arkansas—not her husband. Taking a hard look at what had really happened, it was amazing the shot that did hit Richard Sanders didn't go through him, then into Bianca.

So, who shot J.R.?

"How did you get this?"

"I've got people." Bradley Cole's eyes danced, and I reached up and ran a hand through my blonde hair, because his words made me think of Natalie getting me an appointment with the hair person Shreveport, Sacramento, whatever his name was. Bradley had people. Natalie had people. Why didn't I have people?

I suppose I had a strange look on my face, because Bradley studied me intently, then asked, "Where in the world are you going with this, Davis?"

I looked at him. "I was thinking about my hair."

Bradley nodded slowly. "Of course."

Things got very quiet, and very personal.

"You are amazing, Davis," he whispered, our heads close.

"So are you, Bradley," I whispered back.

Honestly, I couldn't feel my nose. Or my toes. Or much in between. It took forever to get back on track, because, as my Granny

Dee used to say, love is a many splendored thing, and I was completely splendored by this man. Eventually, though, the prison clock ticking, the subject of Teeth's big dead body landed between us, shoving all the would-be romance aside.

"They'll still charge me with it," I said, my heart rate having finally returned to normal range. "They have my prints."

"Even if, Davis, it's in another state, so there's a small window of opportunity before Louisiana comes knocking."

"Opportunity for *what*, Bradley?"

"Ah!" He had the most dazzling smile. "That's the best news! I think I can get you released before a charge is made on the Louisiana murder."

It made no sense. "How?"

"I file a motion to dismiss the attempted homicide charges in Mississippi based on the ballistics report." He tapped the papers on the table.

We stared at the ballistics report that clearly exonerated Bianca, which is to say the ballistics report that clearly exonerated *me*.

"That will never happen," I said. "It will take six weeks of court proceedings to dig through the report. By then, I'll be knee-deep in the Teeth deal."

"Well, we're asking for the moon," he said, "but we're shooting for a star."

"The bail star."

"Right," Bradley Cole said. "Then we'll prove it was Bianca holding the gun, and let *her* worry about having the charges dismissed."

I had stars in my eyes.

"What if we don't find her before I'm knee-deep in the Teeth deal?" I asked.

"We'll worry about that when it happens. Let's concentrate on getting you out of here so you can go home."

"Home?" I popped out of the chair. "Bradley! I don't even *have* a home! Even if they release me, they're not going to let me cross a state line!"

"Let's take this one step at a time," he said. "First step, bail."

It would be nice to on the outside. I needed to get to San Antonio again, and fast, because my red hair was peeking out.

* * *

Six days later, Bradley squeezed my hand under the table. "Are you ready for this, Davis?" he whispered.

I said yes with my eyes, which were burning from all the sunshine pouring in through the windows of the courtroom.

"I need you to be really ready," he whispered, "for anything."

"What are you talking about?" I whispered back. Something about the way he said it set off a few dozen of my alarms, but they could barely be distinguished from the hundreds of other earsplitting alarms going off inside me.

Just then, the bailiff started his speech, the judge took his seat, and the packed room of gawkers, media, and who knows who else grew quiet.

I raised my right hand and agreed that I'd be truthful.

I sat down; Bradley stood up.

He asked that the court grant me bail. The whole time he was doing the legal mumbo jumbo I was tugging on his jacket; he kept smacking my hand away. This was supposed to be about dropping the attempted homicide charges, *then* bail.

"We need to know who your client is, Mr. Cole," the judge said. "I'm not releasing someone whose name I don't even know. Not even with this." The judge waved what had to be the ballistics report through the air. "Not even for an hour. Not even in your custody."

Bradley cleared his throat. "The defense calls Chief Samuel Way to the stand, your honor."

My head spun around like a demon woman's. "Daddy!" I screamed it a million times as my father made his way down the aisle.

The judge banged his gavel.

The cameras clicked unmercifully.

"Hello, Punkin'." His smile was wide. He reached for me as he passed and our fingertips touched. Meredith was beside him. She hissed at me.

After much ado, I was released until the trial, which was to begin in only three weeks, but under house arrest at the address listed on my last paycheck: Bradley's. And even better, in Bradley's custody. At that moment, and, well, lots of other moments if I was being truthful, which I'd sworn on a Bible I'd do, there was no custody I'd've rather been in.

"You'd better not put a toe out the door, young lady."

"Yes, sir."

They had to keep me close, because they were waiting on Louisiana to finish crossing their Ts and dotting their Is, then charge me with real-live murder instead of this attempted bullshit.

The same long-faced judge had the same parting words for me. "You're in a lot of trouble, young lady."

* * *

We put the ankle monitor on Meredith, and she was none too happy about it. We did it at Bradley's, over steaming bowls of gumbo from Mary Mahoney's, crusty French bread, and, before it was over, three bottles of red wine.

"You can't tamper with it." Meredith initially laughed it off. "The alarm will go off the minute you touch it."

My father reached behind Meredith's ear and pulled out an ankle-monitor key.

I clapped my hand over my mouth and laughed at Daddy's magic.

Meredith did not.

"If you can unlock it," she argued, "just leave it on the table! Why do I have to wear it?"

"Because it tracks movement, for one thing," Bradley said, "and it will expect a little more than lying perfectly still around the clock. Too, you have to answer the check-in calls every two hours." He gave a nod to the newest intrusion to his home, the speaker unit near the front door. "You have to be Davis when they call."

Meredith tossed a crust of bread in her empty bowl, then grabbed the wine bottle. "I have a child, you know." She glared at me.

"Riley's fine with Mother," our father patted her hand. "You need to help your sister out on this one, Mer, or she'll end up in the pokey for something she didn't do."

"How do you know she didn't do it, Daddy?"

"Meredith!" I yelled.

I came out of the shower, which I'd taken behind closed doors for a nice change, wearing my own red hair—thank you, Miss Clairol—and ran smack dab into Bradley Cole.

He stared at me for a long moment, getting his first good look at the real me, and then said, "My robe's a little big on you, Red."

Thirty minutes later, I was stretched out on the carpet alarmingly close to Bradley, who was in a nearby chair. I had a real pillow under my head, a real blanket covering me, my real-live father just a hug away, and all that after having a real meal. To top it off, I had a real good wine buzz going.

We let Daddy have the bed. Even though it was barely eight o'clock, the strain of his first big outing since the surgery had taken its toll, and he'd need to get a good night's sleep before the drive back to Pine Apple.

"I get the sofa," Meredith smirked at me.

"I don't care if I sleep on the bathroom floor," I said, so relieved to not be tucking myself into a cold cot behind steel bars.

We all looked to Bradley. It was, after all, his home. "I'll go to work and get a room."

"Are you sure?" I asked him as my head found the pillow again.

I don't remember a thing after that, a snatch of conversation, or even saying goodnight to my father. I did nothing but sleep dreamlessly until the fire alarm went off.

I jolted upright, not having any idea where I was, what the noise was, or what the flashing red light in the darkness meant until I heard a strange voice repeating my name from the intercom by the door. "Last call, Way."

"Get up, Davis." Meredith was somewhere near in the dark, and she was in no better mood than she'd been in earlier. "Answer the damn box."

"You do it! You're the one with the ankle bracelet on."

A throw pillow caught me in the side of the head.

I raced across the room for my Harrison County Penal System courtesy call.

Afterward, Meredith already fast asleep again, I drank in my free, dark, and quiet surroundings, which made me want a drink of water. I tiptoed to the kitchen, still hugging my blanket, so grateful for the luxury of drinking water close by. Bathrooms with doors. Socks. Food. Bradley's clothes to sleep in again. At the sink, I slipped the window up an inch to breathe the uncarcerated air.

It was a bright, clear, beautiful night. I could see fourteen billion stars. I turned, wrapping the blanket tighter, and quietly stepped out onto the lanai, because I wanted a whole lot more of the free air, and I wanted to see the moon's promise twinkling across the water.

"It's beautiful, isn't it?" the dark wicker lanai sofa asked.

I barely heard him.

I turned slowly. "Are you not *freezing*?"

"I could use another blanket," he said.

"I just happen to have one."

I heard him scoot, making room for me.

"I thought you were going to the hotel."

"Changed my mind."

"My father's two feet away."

"Then be quiet," Bradley Cole said.

TWENTY-THREE

The trail I found led to Las Vegas, so we headed there the next morning on a Gulfstream V with the words "Grand Palace Casino" splashed across both sides, nose to tail.

"Let me get this straight." Meredith was fit to be tied. "I sit here and answer the prison box while you go to Vegas on his private plane."

"It's not his, it's his company's. And it's not *that* private, Meredith. There are two pilots and a chick who serves cocktails. Right, Bradley?"

Bradley agreed. "But we get the cabin to ourselves."

My father's eyebrows shot up.

"Lovely." Meredith's mouth was one thin line. Her eyes were slits. When her hands balled up into fists, I took a giant step back. "You kids have fun while I just sit here." Meredith, tapping a foot, gave me the stink eye, then turned it on Bradley, then Daddy, and then me again.

"Keep the blonde wig close by in case they show up to arrest me," I said.

"And what do I do then, Davis? Go to prison for you? A foot too tall and in a blonde wig?"

"If it gets to that," I suggested, "make sure they put you in solitary. There's a really nice girl there."

"Oh. For. God's. Sake."

"Mother and Riley will be here soon, Meredith!" I called out to my retreating sister.

"Yeah, Davis?" She spun. "Well, you'd better scoot."

I turned to Bradley. "Do you have a brother?"

"I think if I did, you'd already know. Why?"

"She needs a boyfriend."

Meredith, it would seem, had something else to say, because she was only in the kitchen for thirty seconds before she stomped back in to the living room. "You know what, Davis? This is about Eddie."

"Now, Meredith," our father interrupted.

"It's always about Eddie," Meredith stabbed a finger my way. "You and Eddie."

I took a deep breath. "Meredith," I said calmly. "It's not. If I don't find Bianca Sanders, I go back to jail. It has nothing to do with him."

Meredith hmmmph'd.

She stomped out again, and I mouthed *boyfriend* to Bradley.

Bradley's eyes smiled.

"Sweet Pea?"

Daddy was in the middle of the sofa, my research in mountains everywhere: on the coffee table in front of him, on the cushions to his left and right, and in the floor at his feet. He looked so good, so whole. If I could ignore the pharmaceutical sampler platter he inhaled every few hours, or the way he favored his left leg, or that his right hand absentmindedly explored what had to be the raging scar beneath his cardigan sweater, I wouldn't know what he'd been through.

"What's the connection between the secretary, Natalie, and the deceased, Paul Bergman?"

"The connection?" I scratched at the long, brunette wig I was sporting. "None that I know of. Other than she's missing. And he *was* missing. Why?"

Daddy looked up. "They have a lot of history," he said. "Too much."

Bradley and I looked at each other. I'm sure we were thinking the same thing: Any minute, poor Natalie's body was going to turn up and poor me would be the number one suspect. Who in hell was *shooting* everyone?

"We'd better hurry," Bradley hefted our bags.

* * *

"Gorgeous plane," I said.

"Yeah," he replied, "gamblers, you know? Only the best for the whales."

"Right." I fidgeted. I let two long seconds elapse. "Do you fly in it often?"

"Not often enough."

We admired the roomy cabin, outfitted like a luxury den with sofas, mahogany side tables, and swiveling leather recliners.

"So just every once in a while?" I asked.

"A lot here lately."

I bobbed my head. Smiled.

"And this same run, too," he added. "Biloxi, Vegas."

I smiled.

"Vegas, Biloxi." His voice trailed off.

I smiled.

"How about something to drink, Davis?"

"I'm good." I looked out the window at retreating Biloxi. "Thanks, though."

"You're welcome."

"Nice weather, huh?" I asked.

"Really mild for this time of year."

Three seconds crawled by.

"Your sister," he said. "She's a little irritated."

"Boy, I'll say." I tried to laugh, but it came out sideways.

We were naked over all of Louisiana and Texas.

We woke as the landing gear ground from below the leather recliner we were asleep in.

* * *

"This can't be right." We were in a Grand Palace limo.

Bradley was zipping. "Davis, there's not one single thing right about this."

"I wasn't speaking to issues of attorneys and clients and privileges," I said. "I meant this far from town. Why would they be here?" I asked, eyeing the wig stuffed in my purse that I would soon have to don. "Why wouldn't they be in Vegas at one of the Casimiro's casinos?"

"We don't know that Bianca and Eddie are here," Bradley said. "We only know that a Bellissimo credit card was swiped here."

We'd asked the driver to take us to Wild Bill's, a place neither of us had even heard of, closed the privacy screen, and I'm not sure what all happened next. Now we were forty miles west of Las Vegas proper near the California line, in Primm, Nevada.

Bradley picked up a phone to talk to the driver half a block away. This thing was the size of a school bus, and we'd covered every inch of it.

"We're going to need to find a restaurant or a strip mall to park behind." He looked out the window as he talked to the driver. "We're a little too conspicuous."

Bradley listened.

"Right. Wild Bill's. But don't pull up to the door."

We hiked through tall weeds across an empty lot, zigzagged across four lanes of traffic, then traded natural light and breathable air for casino clamor, stale smoke, and plus-sized waitresses, all on the elderly side, all wearing very skimpy uniforms.

"Wow," I said. "This place needs an image consultant."

Our hands were still hooked by pinkie fingers.

"Let's look around," Bradley suggested. "See what brought them here."

The casino floor wasn't all that big, and the appeal of this particular destination didn't take long to find.

"I'll be damned," I said.

"What?"

"Look." My arm shot out to point to the bank of Double Whammy Deuces Wild hundred-dollar progressives.

There were nine video poker machines in a recessed hall that led straight to the restrooms, exactly where everyone wants to gamble. The tops of the machines were littered with diluted drinks, balled-up napkins, and empty glasses-slash-ashtrays. The second machine from the left was dark and had yellow out-of-order tape in an X across the screen.

Just then, a heavily bearded man exited the men's room, tugging on the dark blue jumpsuit he wore. His Wild Bill's identification hung from around his neck. He was cut through the middle by a tool belt so heavy with hardware that he sounded like Christmas. Bradley stopped him.

"Excuse me."

The guy turned. His eyes were so bloodshot they made mine hurt.

"When will this machine be repaired?" Bradley threw a thumb.

The guy snorted. "I just answered that same question." He smoothed his moustache with a greasy thumb and index finger. "These things don't get played twice a year," he said, "and now two people asking." A two-way radio hidden somewhere between the jackhammers on his belt squawked. "There's a guy coming tomorrow. Says he is, anyway." Without another word, he jangled off.

Bradley and I looked at each other.

"Let's go snoop at the front desk," I said.

"Good idea."

Bradley slowly pushed a one-hundred dollar bill toward the desk clerk. "No," he said, "I don't need a room, but I could use your help."

The woman smiled as she tucked the Ben in her vest pocket. "Whatcha need?"

"Just a little information about one of your guests."

She perched her fingers over the keyboard in front of her.

"Bianca Sanders," Bradley said.

Tap, tap, tap.

"I have a B. Sanders. Checked in Tuesday," the woman said.

Three days ago, and it took a little mental computation on my part to get there. In the past forty-eight hours I'd been in jail, in court, a blonde, a redhead, reunited with my father, and my year-long dry spell had ended multiple times. If anyone asked me what time zone we were in, I'd probably say July.

After a long pause, Bradley asked, "And?"

"That's all I know." The clerk crossed her arms atop her flat chest and smiled.

Bradley pulled another hundred out of his wallet.

"And nothing," the woman said, without looking at the screen again. "No room service, no restaurant charges, no mini bar, no movies, no phone fees, no casino play."

"What room number?" Bradley asked.

The woman seemed to be weighing the pros and cons of violating such a universal rule of hotelery, and Bradley cracking leather again turned out to be in the pro column.

"Sixteen-sixty," she said.

The housekeeper on the sixteenth floor, naturally, didn't speak a word of English, but lucky for us, Bradley had a seemingly endless supply of hundred-dollar bills, and he spoke Spanish.

"Mandarin Chinese, too," he smiled.

"Wow." I was impressed. Of course I was impressed with Bradley Cole before I knew he spoke Swahili and Spanish. Hell, I was impressed with Bradley Cole before I met him. I was so impressed with him at the moment, I could barely walk.

He and the housekeeper had a little chat: enchilada, burrito, Si Senor, Feliz Navidad. The translation was that the room hadn't been touched. Another hundred from Bradley's wallet and then it was touched. By us.

"They're not here."

"How do you know?" Bradley asked.

"I just do," I said. "No one's been here."

His head was in the closet. "Someone's been here."

I walked from the bathroom to the closet and looked in.

"I know that bag," I said.

It was a teal-blue canvas duffel with caramel leather trim.

I used a tissue from the box in the bathroom to unzip it, revealing a neatly folded stack of women's clothes, the perfume of which sent me staggering backwards. The bed caught me. It all fell so neatly into place it would have knocked me down had I not been there already.

"I see boots," Bradley was poking through the bag.

"Brown leather boots."

Bradley turned to me. "Yes."

"Size six."

"I don't know," he said. "Do you want me to look?"

"You don't need to."

* * *

Bradley had a huge corporation behind him, and that meant a residential suite at the Grand Palace overlooking the Las Vegas Strip (pretty from afar, nasty up close).

"Nice." I fell backwards into the middle of the bed for a second time in as many hours. "A far cry from Wild Bill's."

Bradley's gaze went from me, stretched across the bed, to the phone, blinking red on the desk. Then back to me. Then back to the phone. "Those calls are probably from Biloxi," he said, "and they're probably about you."

He was right. There were two, both from my sister.

Message One:

> *Davis, the people you worked with before you were a jailbird are looking for you. A man named Jeremy has called and said it was urgent, and a woman named Natalie called and said the same thing. They both want to know where you are.*

Oh, God! Did she tell?

Message Two:

I'm taking this phone off the hook. The man won't stop calling.

Just then, the phone rang. I screamed.

"Okay," Bradley was trying to calm me, log on his laptop, and hold the phone between his ear and shoulder at the same time. "Got it. Thanks."

Every casino in town had Double Whammy Deuces Wild, but only three had banks of hundred-dollar progressives: Bellagio, Mandalay Bay, and Wynn. Very upper crust. Just her style.

* * *

Mandalay Bay was our last stop, and that was where she breezed by us, never batting an eye, because she certainly wasn't looking for Bradley, and she was the very reason I didn't look like myself.

It was almost four in the morning; we hadn't slept since we'd napped on the airplane. We were about half, if not whole, drunk from hanging around the video poker machines at the first two casinos.

At Bellagio, it was a slot attendant we got chummy with, who told us that no one had touched the machines in days.

"To tell you the truth," he said, "no one ever plays these."

At Wynn, it was a waitress. "I've been in these mothers eight hours." She showed us her gold shoes. "And no one's played these. In a few minutes, Candy will be here, thank God, and she can tell you if anyone played on her shift last night."

Another round of drinks, then Candy showed. Same gold heels.

Nope.

We weren't surprised, but look under every rock, you know?

There were two things wrong at both casinos: Bellagio had five machines hooked to the progressive, Wynn had eight, and both had totals inching toward the two-and-a-half million mark, so no one had come anywhere near winning them in months, if not years.

"It has to be the right set-up," I explained to Bradley. "Nine machines. Like at Wild Bill's."

"One last stop."

Mandalay Bay was at one end of the Strip, and even in a city that's famous for not distinguishing between night and day, the Mandalay Bay seemed to know what time it was, because it was deserted. We couldn't even find a waitress for (one thing) coffee or for (another thing) information. What we did find were the Double Whammy Deuces Wild, in the right configuration. They were even spaced far enough apart to see the magic button between machines four and five.

"I can't see a thing," Bradley said, peering between the machines. "Must be the tequila."

We took off in search of buckets of coffee, so that we might be able to hold our heads up until we at least found a warm body and got some kind of information out of it. Both of us were exhausted beyond all reason.

"If I'd known all this was going to happen, I'd have gotten more sleep in prison."

"If we don't hurry," Bradley said, "you'll get to go back and get a nice, long nap."

"Only if you go with me."

He smiled. "Don't tempt me."

The only coffee to be had at that ungodly hour was an escalator ride below the casino at a twenty-four hour bistro. The sound of our footsteps bounced off the domed ceiling until we reached the end of an empty corridor full of dark, locked retail shops. The bistro was ghostly quiet, with one machine hissing steam, one employee asleep behind the pastry counter, and the rest of the room divided into sections of unoccupied seating areas of upholstered chairs, sofas, and circular ottomans.

"Let's take ten." Bradley held two smoking cups of coffee.

"You betcha."

We sank into an armless sofa with a view of the corridor, both of us groaning.

"What does this tunnel lead to?" I asked.

"The Four Seasons," he said.

"And they don't have the poker machines, right?"

"They don't have *any* machines."

"Is it like your casino?" I blew across the top of the coffee. "Mostly table games?"

"The Four Seasons doesn't have a casino at all," he said.

"Wait," I said. "Are we not still on the Strip?"

"We are," Bradley said. "Can you believe there's a hotel here without a casino?"

"I can't. Who stays there?"

"Celebrities," Bradley said, "high rollers who have markers all over town, and anyone else with a ton of money who wants to hide."

I let my head fall back. My view reduced to a thin line of the empty corridor.

"Davis," Bradley whispered, "don't fall asleep."

I shook myself awake, then had to fix the damn wig again.

"We should have gotten espresso instead of coffee," he said, "so we could get hyped up in a hurry."

If I hadn't been so tired, I'd have laughed, because it was so Natalie. Espresso. And at that exact moment, she appeared.

Natalie Middleton, wheeling a Louis Vuitton, was a smoky-glass storefront away, on her way to the Four Seasons.

I thought I might be hallucinating until she stopped right in front of us, glanced at the bistro, took a quick peek at her watch, then changed her mind about coffee and kept going.

It was Nattie, all right.

Without taking my eyes off her, I grabbed at Bradley, aiming for his thigh.

His head was against the sofa back, his eyes closed. "Honestly, Davis, I'm not sure if I can."

* * *

I ran into the passageway, my love interest/lawyer/landlord on my heels, but no Natalie. She had disappeared into thin air.

"Davis," Bradley said, "you're so tired. Maybe you just thought you saw her."

"It was her."

There was nothing between the bistro and two huge gold doors that led to the Four Seasons except a fire escape, and it was heavy on the dire warnings side.

"Don't do it, Davis. There's an alarm on that door that will wake people up in Dallas. She didn't go in there."

I slid down the cold wall to the floor and rested my head on my knees.

"Come on," Bradley held a hand out. "Let's see if we can find her at the hotel."

Bradley Cole could have had enough hundred-dollar bills in his wallet to wallpaper the front lobby, and there was still no getting any information out of the Four Season's Customer Service Associate behind the desk. Or his boss. They passed me a house phone. It was Security, who strongly suggested we might want to speak to the Las Vegas Police, and he had them on speed dial, at which point we decided to call it a night. We took a cab back the four blocks back to the Grand Palace, because neither of us could walk.

* * *

We'd been asleep no more than three minutes when I sensed something wrong, a presence of some sort. I sat straight up in the bed to find No Hair twenty feet away in a chair, staring at me. He was wearing a tie that was, I kid you not, an eye-exam chart. The big E was under the knot.

"Morning," he said. "Or noon, rather."

I was down to the sixth line of the eye exam when I had to squint to read it. R, D, F, C, Z, P. Without taking my eyes off the chart, I reached over and batted at Bradley to wake him up.

"Okay, Davis," he said to the pillow. "This I can do."

No Hair stood. "I ordered us coffee. I'll be in the next room."

"No Hair." My first words of the day. "It's Natalie."

"I know."

TWENTY-FOUR

"When did you know?" I tied the belt of the Grand Palace robe tighter and settled in a chair across from No Hair.

"A few days ago," he said, "or a few years ago. I can't decide which. You?"

"A long time ago," I said, "or yesterday. I can't decide which."

We locked brains.

"So, Natalie. Miss Follow the Rules, and—" it was on the tip of my brain.

"Paul."

"Paul," the word tasted funny, "have been behind all this."

No Hair nodded slowly.

"And Bianca hasn't killed anyone or had anyone killed."

"Bianca is a lot of things," No Hair said, "but to the best of my knowledge, she's not a killer."

"Was I set up to go to jail from the beginning?"

"You stumbled into jail on your own, Davis."

"Yeah," I added thick sarcasm, "that was all me."

"The only goal in bringing you in was for you to figure out how to win the game. You going to jail was just gravy."

No Hair gave me a quiet moment.

"Listen," he said. "What's done is done. From here on out, it's damage control."

"Okay." I placed my coffee cup in the saucer. "Let's establish a timeline. At what point did you suspect Bianca had gone around knocking off electricians?"

"Natalie started in on that a while back," No Hair said, "maybe a year ago. We knew Bianca was skimming from the poker game; it was already the elephant in the room. Then one day Natalie began hinting that maybe there was more to it than money."

"Like what?" I asked.

"Like homicide."

"Brave of her to toss that out there, considering."

"She's as cold as they come."

As hard as I was listening, the picture wouldn't come into complete focus. "When did you realize it was a setup?"

"In a way?" No Hair squirmed. "From the beginning." His facial features caved in on one another as he frowned in concentration. He opened his mouth to explain, then changed his mind. Finally, he leaned way in. "You know how they say if it walks like a duck, looks like a duck, and quacks like a duck, it must be a duck?"

"Yeah?" I had no idea where he was going with this. As far as my memory would stretch, I couldn't remember any ducks. "Who's the duck here? Natalie or Bianca?"

"Both," No Hair said. "There's way too much money around Bianca for her to kill for it. It was just a game for her, like her boyfriends. Natalie, on the other hand, was dead serious. I knew when she brought you in that she would stop at nothing."

"Quack," I said.

"Exactly."

"Natalie's a murderer."

"Yes and no," No Hair said. "Paul was the actual triggerman."

"Why?" I asked. "Why would Paul go around killing electricians? They didn't know how to win the money. Their role, and even their payday, was small."

"I'm pretty sure Natalie gets that now. I think it just got away from them, you know? Here Natalie is, making Bianca's toe polish appointments, and all the while Bianca, who's never worked a day in her life and wears those damn furs all the time, walks into the casino and leaves with a million dollars anytime she wants. Natalie wanted in on the action, but she couldn't figure out how to do it. So she goes to the software guy, can't get anything out of him. She starts thinking he'll rat her out, and the next thing you know, the software guy's dead."

I thought of poor George.

"Now she's locked in," No Hair said, "but doesn't know how to win the money. A few months down the road, Bianca lands another windfall. Natalie and Paul figure out there's an electrician in the picture, try to get it out of him, and next thing you know, they've got a second dead body on their hands."

"So Bianca's off the hook?"

"Well," No Hair struggled with the answer, "she's broken all kinds of laws in the casino, for sure," he said, "but even at that she's had some poor dumb bastard pushing the buttons every time, so proving it would be tough. And would her family, in the end, really bother? Other than that," he shrugged, "she's only guilty of being a first-class bitch. Bianca thinks she's above the law, which made her an easy mark."

"That's two easy marks for Natalie," I said, "Bianca and me."

"You were a means to an end, Davis," Bradley Cole, wrapped in a robe that matched mine but fit him better, his hair wet from the shower, stood in the doorway between the two rooms. "I doubt you were her target."

"Okay," I threw my hands in the air, "I won't take this personally."

The two men formally introduced themselves, handshakes and such.

"I like your tie, man."

"Thanks," No Hair said.

Bradley poured himself a cup of coffee, patted me on the head, then sat in a chair beside me. He asked, "How did she find Davis to begin with, Jeremy?"

Who?

"We were looking at Bianca's new boyfriend," No Hair said, "when we ran across you." He gave me a bald-headed nod. "Natalie jumped all over the look-alike thing, convinced us you knew him well enough and looked enough like Bianca to get in there and figure out what was going on, but she didn't define 'going on.'"

"She wanted Davis to show her how to win the game," Bradley said.

"Correct," No Hair agreed, then turned to me. "I told you, you were a perfect storm for the job. You had the background, you had the know-how, you looked just like Bianca, and it was your ex-husband, for Pete's sake."

I've never understood the for-Pete's-sake thing. Wouldn't it be "for St. Peter's sake"?

"So her only motive was money?" Bradley asked. "You don't think she wanted to kill Richard Sanders?"

"That's certainly a possibility," No Hair said, "heat-of-the-moment, or maybe he touched her coffeepot one too many times. For all we know she was aiming for Bianca but hit Richard instead."

Totally conceivable.

"The only thing we know for certain," No Hair went on, "is that Natalie wanted Davis to go down for her crimes. Past and present. Her time was running short; she realized that it's not so easy to set up someone with Bianca Sanders' resources, but having *two* Biancas gave her the out, because you, Davis," his head whipped my way again, "turned out to be an excellent candidate for jail, and she knew it before the rest of us heard your name. If she could get you in the door, pin everything on you, get *you* in jail, she could walk away."

I was speechless.

"And you handed it to her on a platter."

I couldn't breathe.

"First and foremost," No Hair went on, "she knew you'd figure out how Bianca was winning the money, something she couldn't do herself, and couldn't get out of the electricians."

"I'll tell you one thing." I looked at both men. "I wasn't being paid nearly enough for all this."

No Hair snorted.

"What happened that night?" I asked. "Walk me through it."

No Hair shifted in his seat. Poor seat. "It was my day off," he said, "but I had to go in because we were having a little counterfeit chip problem."

At this point, I tiptoed out.

(No, I didn't.)

"Why'd you have to go in?" Bradley asked. "Why didn't they just call Metro?"

"Because it was Salito Casimiro."

Ah.

"I was on my way to lock up the chips in my desk, and I smelled Natalie's perfume. I flattened myself against the wall and watched her put a gun in Paul's desk."

How in the world No Hair flattened himself against a wall was beyond me.

"I should've taken the gun with me," No Hair said, "But I locked everything up in my own desk, and we all know what happened next." He turned on me and thumped me on the head with his eyeballs. "When I told you to stay out of my desk, I meant it."

No Hair went on to fill in the blanks that he could. Natalie, with her eyes and ears everywhere, knew I'd gone to No Hair's office, knew I'd had the small gun accident, and watched me cash in the counterfeit chips. She saw her opportunity and sprang into action. She got the Sanders' ball rolling by telling Richard his wife was getting ready to kill another boyfriend, then told Bianca that Richard was onto her. At the same time, she had Teeth pounding the nails in my coffin—erasing my alibi from the hard drive and calling in the casino dogs.

Several questions remained: When did the woman sleep? (I might have been the only one wondering that.) When did Teeth bite the big one? And the most important question—where was she now?

I looked away and whistled a little tune, "Taps," I think. Natalie Middleton covered all her bases. Tag, Davis, you're it. "Do we have *any* evidence against Natalie?"

"Not an ounce," No Hair said. "Every scrap of film is erased, so we don't have her planting the gun. And there's only one camera that caught the shooting directly, but Natalie's not in it for even a split second. All you see is who everyone believes to be Davis aiming, firing, and running."

"We're going to have to catch her," I said.

"If she isn't already long gone," No Hair said. "She's hit the game twice this week, stockpiling to make a run for it, because she has a brand new fly in her ointment."

"What would that be?" I asked.

"You." Bradley and No Hair said it at the same time.

I bent over double again.

"She didn't count on anyone coming to your rescue, Davis." No Hair's voice was softer.

"Happy to help." Bradley reached over and gently pushed my hair out of my face. He smiled at me.

* * *

We ordered food while discussing where to go from here, because No Hair was ranting about famine and hypoglycemia. I couldn't have swallowed a bite of food if Natalie walked in, put a gun to my head, and demanded I eat. Bradley asked, "Not even a Pop Tart, Davis?"

When I'd been staring out the window at the Las Vegas Boulevard traffic long enough for Bradley and No Hair to think I might be contemplating jumping, No Hair spoke up.

"You're not going to jail, Davis. We'll find her."

Her who? I needed both of them. I had to have Bianca to be cleared on the first charge, and I had to have Natalie or I'd go to jail for Teeth's murder.

Before room service knocked on the door with food, Bradley's cell phone rang in the bedroom with news.

A minute later, No Hair asked, "Is he speaking Spanish?"

"Yeah," I said. "Go figure."

"We'd better get moving." Bradley appeared in the doorway, phone in hand. "She's at Wild Bill's."

No Hair rose from his seat. The seat looked so relieved. “She’s there to get herself another payday.”

Just then Bradley’s phone rang again. He looked at the caller ID, then at me. “It’s Harrison County Department of Corrections.”

TWENTY-FIVE

Another line on my resume: fugitive from the law.

Meredith slept through a check-in, and that was strike three. Her first strike was stepping over the threshold to reach the newspaper at the elevator.

("I swear it was not even two seconds.")

She missed yet another hello-prison call when she was in the shower.

("No one ever said, 'Don't take a shower.'")

Then the nap.

("I heard it, but I thought it was one of Riley's toys.")

They hauled her in only to find out she wasn't me.

("Jail people don't *listen*. I told them I wasn't you a million times.")

Bradley was also in a bit of trouble, but he lied to give us more time. "Look," he said. "My place has windows. She climbed out one while I was asleep."

Someone on the other end yelled at him.

"Have you seen her?" Bradley demanded. "She could get out of the peephole of my front door if she wanted to."

The person on the other end yelled at him a little more. He winked at me.

"That's exactly what I'm doing. Give me forty-eight hours."

I was listening and pulling on clothes at the same time. I eyed the wig.

Not a chance.

The limo ride to Wild Bill's wasn't nearly as much fun with No Hair along.

"Did it take this long to get there yesterday?" I asked Bradley.

For the most part, we rode in silence, each of us examining our own personal worst-case-scenarios. Bradley, I'm sure, was in fear of being stripped of his license to practice law, I knew I was in more trouble in Harrison County, Mississippi than ever, and No Hair loudly lamented our leaving before room service arrived, thus putting him in grave danger of missing two meals in a row for the first time in his life and subsequently starving to death in a limo.

We were all concerned about how it would go down when we were face-to-face with Natalie Middleton. There were three of us, one of her, and No Hair was packing.

Still.

When we weren't riding quietly with our individual demons, we were on cell phones: I talked to Daddy and an enraged Meredith, Bradley to his boss and then one of the other attorneys he worked with, and No Hair caught Mr. Sanders up, who sent me greetings, apologies for my troubles, and assurances that my job was safe (big whoop at the moment), and then No Hair called Mrs. No Hair, which was borderline nauseating. He actually blew smacky kisses to the woman over the phone. Then he whispered sweet nothings, and I do mean nothings: "No, I love *you* more. No, you don't, I love *you* more. I don't want to hang up first. *You* hang up first. No, *you*." I rolled my eyes so far back in my head, I almost fell out of the limo. Bradley found it, as was his peaceful and accepting nature, quietly entertaining.

Soon enough, we were there. The driver stopped a block away this time.

"I'm not hiking through the woods," No Hair said.

"There are no woods in Nevada, No Hair."

"You really better watch yourself." His finger was in my face.

"Hey, kids," Bradley said, "be nice. Let's stay focused here."

The three of us looked at each other as we approached the entrance.

No Hair zeroed in on Bradley. "You're the only one she doesn't know," he said. "You go to the game. That'll get her, because she doesn't want anyone to accidentally win it before she does."

"No!" I grabbed Bradley's arm.

"What's she going to do?" No Hair asked. "Shoot him in the middle of the casino?"

"He's right," Bradley said. "She isn't going to do anything."

I was a nervous wreck.

"We'll hold back," No Hair said to me, "so she won't see us."

"You think?"

He actually growled at me.

During this tête-à-tête, we'd crossed most of the casino floor.

"No worries, guys," I said. "She's not going to see us." I took another step. "We're too late."

As we approached the bank of machines, Bradley and No Hair could see there wasn't anyone on the game, every seat empty.

"Maybe she's not down from her hotel room yet," No Hair scanned the area, "we'd better pull back so we don't run her off."

"She's gone," I said.

They both looked at me.

"Look at the total." I pointed to the LCD display above the nine machines.

The progressive jackpot was $500,403. Make that $500,408.

"It resets at half a million. She already won it."

* * *

"No way."

"Davis," Bradley said, "come on."

"I'm not sitting in the same room with him, Bradley. Period."

"You married him twice. You can't sit in the same room with him once?"

We were in a large conference room at the Grand Palace. Most of the chairs were occupied, and most of the occupants were on their phones.

No Hair was devouring several pounds of raw cow, two heads of lettuce drowning in fragrant lumpy white stuff with a pound of yellow cheese grated on top, and a baked potato the size of my foot, another pound of cheese on it. He was washing it down with a gallon of milk.

"Milk?" I asked.

No Hair swallowed. "Calcium, Davis, vitamin D. You should try it."

"When's the last time you had that cholesterol checked, No Hair?"

"Excuse me, guys." Bradley scooted my chair down the table with me in it, then put his, with him in it, between me and No Hair.

The General Manager of Las Vegas Grand Palace was there, accompanied by two note-taking staffers. Representatives from the Four Seasons, and the Casino Manager from Mandalay Bay were there. Four of Las Vegas' boys in blue were there, huddled in a corner, waiting to take me into custody for extradition to Mississippi. Three representatives from the Nevada Gaming Control Board had arrived. Bianca Sanders and Eddie Crawford were on their way from the Casimiro's Mother Ship, the Glitz Resort and Casino, half a mile away.

"The second he walks in and sees me, he'll make a run for it anyway," I said. "So," I waved a *whatever*. "It doesn't matter."

A nosy policeman spoke up. "Don't worry, ma'am. We won't let him get away."

After being told for two hours that Bianca Sanders was unavailable, then a tad under the weather, she was given a choice: come in and talk of your own free will or we'll come get you, and you'll be wearing handcuffs while we talk. Word was returned that she'd finally agreed, yet she didn't arrive for almost three additional hours.

When her limo finally pulled in and the entourage escorted up, the sun had set, and all the details had been worked out, which was fine, because Bianca hadn't been invited to work out details anyway. She was there to have discharging a firearm in public, fleeing the scene, withholding information, and hindering an investigation explained to her. According to Mississippi, charges against me wouldn't be dropped until charges against her were filed. Eddie Crawford was just a wart on her ass—we had to look at him until she decided to cut him off.

State Gaming Boards shut down Double Whammy Deuces Wild progressives across the map starting in the northeast: Atlantic City, Detroit, and Philly, then Tunica, Biloxi, New Orleans, and Baton Rouge. There were two banks in California; they'd been unplugged, along with the Wild Bill's machines, just for good measure. Bellagio's were roped off, just like Wynn's.

The only game in town, coast-to-coast, was Mandalay Bay's.

Four plainclothesmen were in place.

One of the Four Seasons' representatives closed his phone and addressed the assembly. "There's still no sign of her. The last time her hotel door opened was nine o'clock this morning when she rode in one of our limos to Wild Bill's in Primm."

We all knew the rest of the story. She'd instructed the driver to wait for her, that she'd be no more than an hour, but she never returned to the limo.

Wild Bill's reviewed every inch of surveillance footage. One of the last images of Natalie Middleton was of her stepping into the main cage office to be paid her jackpot of more than $1.2 million dollars. She requested the payment in $50,000 cash and the balance in electronic transfer, which cost her a $5,000 cash tip, but would cost Wild Bill's a fortune when the Gaming Board finished with them over the no-no. She'd presented—get this—Marci Dunlow's identification, but with her likeness, not mine, on the Arizona driver's license. (Note to self: find out if there really is a Marci Dunlow somewhere.)

There was no footage of her leaving the main cage office, but the cashier, two witnesses, and the casino manager all told the same story: Natalie/Marci asked for directions and was shown out a side door to the adjacent restrooms, where a camera clearly caught her pushing into the ladies' room, and from there, she disappeared. She never exited the restroom.

They continued pouring over the footage, but it looked as if Natalie Middleton had simply evaporated.

Everyone turned to the three of us.

Well? Twenty faces asked.

Before we could issue any possible explanations or suggest any options, Bianca Casimiro Sanders burst in. While I was in the process of picking myself up off the floor, she was in the process of scanning the room. She found me.

"You only wish you looked like me."

No, I most certainly did not.

Then she said, "Your ex-husband is an idiot."

Now that, I couldn't argue with.

TWENTY-SIX

Bianca Sanders was traveling to Las Vegas for her father's 70th birthday. The male passenger on the flight manifest (I'd hacked) was not Eddie Crawford, it was her and Richard Sanders' thirteen-year-old son, Thomas. The Casimiro family was gathering from all over to celebrate.

Or so she said.

She hadn't come to Vegas for a family reunion, she'd come to Vegas for a makeover party.

The Bianca Sanders who burst through the double doors had Steven Tyler's mouth on her. I swear, it was as if someone had taken a bicycle-tire pump to the woman's smackers. Her engorged lips were snarled so far away from everything else on her face, we could see all of her gums. Her lips entered the room a full minute before she did, and as she began her tirade, spitting venom with every word, it soon became obvious that in addition to the lips (as if that weren't enough) her facial features were completely frozen. She kept the same icy mask on her face for every word, be they "fluffy baby bunnies" or "I will slit your throat in your sleep."

Under the weather? The woman looked like she'd been tossed under a train.

"I've seen her this way before," No Hair said from behind his hand. "She'll go back to normal in a week or so."

In the end, Bianca very reluctantly agreed to return to Biloxi within twenty-four hours to face trumped-up felony charges that would be dismissed as soon as they were read, but the formalities were necessary for my release. No one doubted how little she thought of the program.

The room fell completely silent in her wake: jaws were slack, heads shook, liquor flowed freely.

One of the Grand Palace Vegas attorneys turned to Bradley. "I wonder if that's where your girl is," he said. "At a doctor's office, having her facial features rearranged."

It wasn't a bad idea, and we were out of good ideas, so police details woke plastic surgeons all around town with Natalie's photograph, but the next morning as I was boarding the plane to return to prison in Mississippi, they hadn't scared her up.

Natalie Middleton was gone.

* * *

There are worse ways to travel, but still, five hours in the Casimiro jet with two U.S. Marshals—one mine and one Bianca's—was unsettling for me and the end of the world for her.

Salvatore Casimiro offered me the ride, not giving his science-experiment of a daughter a choice. I certainly had another choice—Con Air—but I'd have to wait in a Vegas jail cell for days, if not weeks, to catch one of those chartered flights, then zigzag across the country in an air bus with felons being assigned and reassigned. Mississippi was adamant: Go to jail. Go directly to jail. Do not pass GO. Do not collect $200. And, no, you aren't in the custody of your attorney any longer, in fact, we have a few choice words for him, too.

Bianca washed down two Xanex with vodka, then retreated to the in-flight bedroom for the duration of the trip, her escort dozing at the door. I slept most of the way, too. When I woke, I panicked about going back to jail and I missed Bradley Cole.

It took more than thirty hours to process me at the prison. If Bianca Sanders had been the least bit cooperative it might have only taken three. As it turns out, Bianca was supposed to spend most of her first forty-eight post-op hours on her back, so the fresh toxins in her face wouldn't run amok. So every hour, on the hour, proceedings came to a complete stop while Bianca stretched out and a masseuse shuttled over from the Bellissimo manipulated her face. She whined, to everyone within earshot, she had no intention of ever shooting a gun again, because the aftermath of red tape was unbearable, the locale deplorable.

By the time I was finally released, Bradley had returned to Biloxi. He was waiting for me in the lobby. He stood, he put an arm around me, then led me out of a correctional institution for the second time since we'd met.

"Did you drive by, Bradley?"

"He's not there, Davis."

"Can you take me there?"

"Davis, honey," Bradley stopped me in the dark parking lot. "He's not there. I asked the limo drivers if they'd seen him, and they haven't. In more than two weeks."

My heart hurt. I looked up and memorized every line of sweet Bradley's face. "Could you take me there anyway?"

"Why, Davis?"

"I need some sleep!"

"Then let's take you home," he said.

"I can't go to Pine Apple, Bradley. I can't cross a state line until this mess if over."

"Davis," he said. "Your lease isn't up for another two months."

* * *

Richard Sanders returned to the Bellissimo with much fanfare. It was a new day. On his arm, his wife. Neither No Hair nor I said a word. A large part of our job was to look the other way. Bianca Casimiro Sanders summoned me her first morning back in Biloxi. She picked a really bad time to call.

"Don't answer it!"

"I have to, Bradley. It's the Bat phone!"

I stepped off the elevator onto the Elvis floor, and I was escorted to Mrs. Sanders. She wore full makeup, perfect hair, a purple silk robe, and matching purple stiletto heels at eight in the morning. At her feet were two furry rats. They may have been dogs, because I don't think rats yip like that, and they both had purple silk bows on their heads that matched Bianca's getup. The urgent matter she so rudely interrupted my morning for went like this: "You'll need to stand in for me at events. Ribbon-cuttings and such. That'll be all."

Mr. Sanders hired a new secretary who was just that—a secretary. She answered the phone, made appointments and coffee, and ushered people in and out. When five o'clock rolled around, she punched out. She didn't know what blood type Richard Sanders was and she never would.

I got a raise and an office. No Hair was promoted; he was my new boss, and we were looking for a third, and possibly fourth, addition to the team. I tracked down Fantasy Erb from my behind-bars days—not that many days ago, actually—and No Hair agreed to interview her. She was savvy, strong, she knew how to follow rules and when to show mercy. I wanted her in quickly because there was something fishy going on at Club Meridian, Bellissimo's ridiculously popular (and ridiculously loud) nightclub, that involved the almost-naked dancers and I wanted no part of almost-naked dancing. In public, anyway.

Meanwhile, No Hair and I spent long days digging, pouring, and searching for clues as to Natalie's whereabouts, but there were none to be found. It had been six days since she'd disappeared from the restroom in Primm, Nevada, and with each tick of the clock, the possibility of finding her diminished.

"She's in Jamaica," No Hair suggested. "Or St. Bart's. We'll never catch her."

A bench warrant had been issued for the contents of Natalie's condo in New Orleans, and we were digging through the whole bunch of nothing retrieved from there. No other warrants had been issued, because the last thing we wanted to do was scare her away. All of us held out the hope she'd stumble and we'd nail her.

I was hard at work when I felt No Hair staring at me, and not for the first time since we'd returned.

"What's eating at you, Davis?" he asked.

I had nothing to lose by saying it out loud. "It's George."

"The cab driver?"

PMS, or PMDD, or INSANITY took over, because it turned out I did have something to lose by saying it aloud—hydration. I started crying and I couldn't stop.

"Good Lord." No Hair jumped up and began looking for something—a baseball bat, a tranquilizer gun, a box of Kleenex. "Get a grip, Davis." He stood two feet away from me and awkwardly patted my back. "There, there, now. Come on and stop leaking. What's the problem?" No Hair scanned the room, looking for backup, I imagine. "Has something happened to the old guy?"

"That's just it, No Hair." I used my sleeve. And then I used my other sleeve. "I think Natalie got to him. He's *nowhere*! He's disappeared!"

"I didn't realize you two were so close." Beads of sweat had popped out all over No Hair. He tugged on Albert Einstein, who was on his tie. You'd think after twenty-two years of marriage, the guy would have witnessed a female having a smallish meltdown. He stumbled around, then found a seat a comfortable distance from me. "He's probably right outside, sleeping in his cab."

"He is not," I barely said it aloud. "I kept an eye out for him the entire time we were in Vegas, and I've checked the VIP entrance a dozen times a day since we've been back." I launched into that kind of crying where it's hard to catch your breath. "The only one as smart as her is him, No Hair! George probably figured it out days before we did and she *killed* him." I took a deep shaky breath. "And that's it for George! There'll never be justice for his son's death, and now there'll never be justice for *his*!"

"You don't know that," No Hair said. "I'll tell you what, Davis. I'll help you look into it just as soon as this court stuff is over."

I sniffed. "You promise?"

No Hair tried to crack a smile, and I recognized it as such because I'd seen him do it before, but the first few times I mistook it for food poisoning.

"So, how's it going with you and the lawyer?" he cautiously changed the subject.

I mopped my tears, sat back, and sighed/smiled.

"See?" No Hair asked. "I told you."

"You didn't tell me shit, No Hair."

"I wish you'd watch your language, Davis. Do you talk like that in front of him?"

* * *

The first of what would be many hearings was set for Monday morning, eight sharp, all parties be present or be in contempt. The proceedings were closed so that the media might get as little information as possible, because wherever Natalie Middleton was, she was staying on top of things, of that we had no doubt. If just one reporter got a hold of her name, it'd be over.

The State would drop all charges against me after I proved myself innocent in a court of law. That meant Bianca Sanders on the stand, testifying on my behalf.

The media was starving for any crumb of news. To compensate for what they didn't know, they filled the airways and information outlets with what they did know, which was amazingly little. The evening before, Bradley and I, having taken a break from watching the Wild Bill surveillance footage for the umpteenth time, were channel surfing, and breezed by a still of a high school yearbook photograph of me in my retro majorette finery. I grabbed for the remote to make it go away.

"No!" Bradley held it a mile out of my reach. "Let me see this!"

Agents from several government agencies had several things to discuss with Eddie Crawford, so naturally, he'd disappeared.

Fine by me.

Bianca Sanders told the authorities Edward was dead to her, and don't bring up his name again in her presence, which forced the rest of us to do all the Eddie explaining, including what we knew of the Sanders' Open Marriage policy.

"Do you have any idea where he might be?" a state gaming agent asked me.

"Pine Apple, Alabama," I said.

He scribbled it down.

"No," I said. "Two words. Pine. Apple."

"You're kidding, right? That's hilarious. And what did you say your name was?"

* * *

We knew there'd be media coverage, but we had absolutely no idea there'd be a convention. Halfway down the courthouse steps and bunched in a semi-circle around the doors, reporters and cameras were twenty-deep.

"What the hell?" Bradley asked.

"I wish I had a hat," I said.

"Bianca must be up there holding her own court."

We couldn't find an empty parking space for several blocks.

"Should we go in the back way?"

"No," Bradley said. "Let's see what's going on."

Bradley took two steps, then turned around to see me rooted to the sidewalk.

"Come on, Davis. You've got to do this." He held his hand out. "Whatever they ask, just say no comment."

I was afraid that as soon as one of them saw me we'd be trampled. A few at the back of the pack seemed to recognize me, but only glanced. No microphones were shoved my way.

Bradley and I shrugged.

"Maybe this will go easier than we thought," he said.

"What in the world are they all looking at?"

Natalie Middleton, wearing the same clothes she'd been in eleven days ago, looked like she'd crawled to Biloxi on her hands and knees from Wild Bill's Casino in Primm, Nevada. She was chained to the massive courthouse doors. She was so thoroughly chained that upon being discovered, a welding crew had been called.

That idea was scrapped after they all but fried her leg, so a second crew had been called in, this one with chainsaws. It would seem that chainsaw crews didn't move with anywhere near the efficiency that news crews did, because the only tools present were cameras.

The crowd, recognizing me, parted. Bradley and I stopped a few feet away.

Her left leg was tucked beneath her, propping her up. Her right arm, twisted behind her head, was chained to the bent leg pulley fashion, so if she moved one she risked injury to the other. She looked mighty uncomfortable. Her left arm was stretched above her head, chained to the brass handles of the massive courthouse doors, the opposite leg, the one that had a big red welding welt across her bare ankle, to a stone pillar.

She wasn't going anywhere.

"Good God," Bradley said.

Natalie and I shared a long, cold look.

There were so many things I wanted to say to her. I'd been rehearsing for days: while brushing my teeth, to the steering wheel of my Volkswagen, at three in the morning with Bradley. Yet I found I couldn't. My mouth was wide open, but nothing would come out. The pathetic position she was in took my speech away.

They say every path has its puddle. Natalie Middleton had landed in hers face-first and she would drown in it. She knew it. She didn't need to hear it from me.

I stepped away, shielded my eyes against the sun, and began searching the street.

He was standing at parade rest beside his cab.

My hands flew to my heart.

He saluted me, got in, and drove away.

Photo by Garrett Nudd

Gretchen Archer

Gretchen Archer is a Tennessee housewife who began writing when her daughters, seeking higher educations, ran off and left her. She lives on Lookout Mountain with her husband, son, and a Yorkie named Bently. *Double Whammy* is her first Davis Way crime caper. You can visit her at www.gretchenarcher.com.

Don't Miss the 2nd Book in the Series

DOUBLE DIP

Gretchen Archer

A Davis Way Crime Caper (#2)

Davis Way's beginner's luck may have run out. Her professional life is dicey and she's on a losing streak at home. She can't find her gun, her evil twin's personal assistant has disappeared, Bellissimo's Master of Ceremonies won't leave her alone, and her boyfriend Bradley Cole thinks three's a crowd.

Meanwhile, she's following a slot tournament trail that leads to Beehive, Alabama, where the So Help Me God Pentecostal Church is swallowing up Bellissimo's high rollers. The worst? Davis doesn't feel so hot. It could be the banana pudding, but it might be the pending pitter patter of little feet.

DOUBLE DIP is a reckless ride in the fast lane, and Davis Way can't find the brakes.

Don't Miss the 2nd Book in the Series

DOUBLE STRIKE

Gretchen Archer

A Davis Way Crime Caper (#3)

Bellissimo Resort and Casino Super Spy Davis Way knows three things: Cooking isn't a prerequisite for a happy marriage, don't trust men who look like David Hasselhoff, and money doesn't grow on Christmas trees. None of which help when a storm hits the Gulf a week before the Bellissimo's Strike It Rich Sweepstakes. Securing the guests, staff, and property might take a stray bullet. Or two.

Bellissimo Resort and Casino Super Spy Davis Way has three problems: She's desperate to change her marital status, her new boss who speaks in hashtags, and Bianca Sanders has confiscated her clothes. All of which bring on a headache hot enough to spark a fire. Solving her problems means stealing a car. From a dingbat lawyer.

Bellissimo Resort and Casino Super Spy Davis Way has three goals: Keep the Sanders family out of prison, regain her footing in her relationship, and find the genius who wrote the software for futureGaming. One of which, the manhunt one, is iffy. Because when Alabama hides someone, they hide them good.

DOUBLE STRIKE. A VIP invitation to an extraordinary high-stakes gaming event, as thieves, feds, dance instructors, shady bankers, kidnappers, and gold waiters go all in. #Don'tMissIt.

Henery Press Mystery Books

And finally, before you go...
Here are a few other mysteries
you might enjoy:

BOARD STIFF

Kendel Lynn

An Elliott Lisbon Mystery (#1)

As director of the Ballantyne Foundation on Sea Pine Island, SC, Elliott Lisbon scratches her detective itch by performing discreet inquiries for Foundation donors. Usually nothing more serious than retrieving a pilfered Pomeranian. Until Jane Hatting, Ballantyne board chair, is accused of murder. The Ballantyne's reputation tanks, Jane's headed to a jail cell, and Elliott's sexy ex is the new lieutenant in town.

Armed with moxie and her Mini Coop, Elliott uncovers a trail of blackmail schemes, gambling debts, illicit affairs, and investment scams. But the deeper she digs to clear Jane's name, the guiltier Jane looks. The closer she gets to the truth, the more treacherous her investigation becomes. With victims piling up faster than shells at a clambake, Elliott realizes she's next on the killer's list.

PILLOW STALK

Diane Vallere

A Mad for Mod Mystery (#1)

Interior Decorator Madison Night has modeled her life after a character in a Doris Day movie, but when a killer targets women dressed like the bubbly actress, Madison's signature sixties style places her in the middle of a homicide investigation.

The local detective connects the new crimes to a twenty-year old cold case, and Madison's long-trusted contractor emerges as the leading suspect. As the body count piles up like a stack of plush pillows, Madison uncovers a Soviet spy, a campaign to destroy all Doris Day movies, and six minutes of film that will change her life forever.

From the Henery Press Chick Lit Collection

THE BREAKUP DOCTOR

Phoebe Fox

The Breakup Doctor Series (#1)

Call Brook Ogden a matchmaker-in-reverse. Let others bring people together; Brook, licensed mental health counselor, picks up the pieces after things come apart. When her own therapy practice collapses, she maintains perfect control: landing on her feet with a weekly advice-to-the-lovelorn column and a successful consulting service as the Breakup Doctor: on call to help you shape up after you breakup.

Then her relationship suddenly crumbles and Brook finds herself engaging in almost every bad-breakup behavior she preaches against. And worse, she starts a rebound relationship with the most inappropriate of men: a dangerously sexy bartender with anger-management issues—who also happens to be a former patient.

As her increasingly out-of-control behavior lands her at rock-bottom, Brook realizes you can't always handle a messy breakup neatly—and that sometimes you can't pull yourself together until you let yourself fall apart.

FINDING SKY

Susan O'Brien

A Nicki Valentine Mystery

Suburban widow and P.I. in training Nicki Valentine can barely keep track of her two kids, never mind anyone else. But when her best friend's adoption plan is jeopardized by the young birth mother's disappearance, Nicki is persuaded to help. Nearly everyone else believes the teenager ran away, but Nicki trusts her BFF's judgment, and the feeling is mutual.

The case leads where few moms go (teen parties, gang shootings) and places they can't avoid (preschool parties, OB-GYNs' offices). Nicki has everything to lose and much to gain – including the attention of her unnervingly hot P.I. instructor. Thankfully, Nicki is armed with her pesky conscience, occasional babysitters, a fully stocked minivan, and nature's best defense system: women's intuition.

From the Henery Press Chick Lit Collection

BET YOUR BOTTOM DOLLAR

Karin Gillespie

The Bottom Dollar Series (#1)

Welcome to the Bottom Dollar Emporium in Cayboo Creek, South Carolina, where everything from coconut mallow cookies to Clabber Girl Baking Powder costs a dollar but the coffee and gossip are free. For the Bottom Dollar gals, work time is sisterhood time.

When news gets out that a corporate dollar store is coming to town, the women are thrown into a tizzy, hoping to save their beloved store as well their friendships. Meanwhile the manager is canoodling with the town's wealthiest bachelor and their romance unearths some startling family secrets.

The first in a series, *Bet Your Bottom Dollar* serves up a heaping portion of small town Southern life and introduces readers to a cast of eccentric characters. Pull up a wicker chair, set out a tall glass of Cheer Wine, and immerse yourself in the adventures of a group of women who the *Atlanta Journal Constitution* calls, "... the kind of steel magnolias who would make Scarlett O'Hara envious."

MACDEATH

Cindy Brown

An Ivy Meadows Mystery (#1)

Like every actor, Ivy Meadows knows that *Macbeth* is cursed. But she's finally scored her big break, cast as an acrobatic witch in a circus-themed production of *Macbeth* in Phoenix, Arizona. And though it may not be Broadway, nothing can dampen her enthusiasm—not her flying caldron, too-tight leotard, or carrot-wielding dictator of a director.

But when one of the cast dies on opening night, Ivy is sure the seeming accident is "murder most foul" and that she's the perfect person to solve the crime (after all, she does work part-time in her uncle's detective agency). Undeterred by a poisoned Big Gulp, the threat of being blackballed, and the suddenly too-real curse, Ivy pursues the truth at the risk of her hard-won career—and her life.

CPSIA information can be obtained at www.ICGtesting.com
Printed in the USA
BVOW08s2159310516

450256BV00001B/15/P